Mine Till Midnight

Mine Till Midnight

LISA KLEYPAS

St. Martin's Paperbacks

This is a work of fiction. All of the characters, organizations, and events portrayed in this novel are either products of the author's imagination or are used fictitiously.

MINE TILL MIDNIGHT

Copyright © 2007 by Lisa Kleypas.
Excerpt from *Sugar Daddy* copyright © 2007 by Lisa Kleypas.

All rights reserved.

For information address St. Martin's Press, 175 Fifth Avenue, New York, NY 10010.

ISBN: 978-1-250-13066-2

Our books may be purchased in bulk for promotional, educational, or business use. Please contact your local bookseller or the Macmillan Corporate and Premium Sales Department at 1-800-221-7945, ext. 5442, or by e-mail at MacmillanSpecialMarkets@macmillan.com.

Printed in the United States of America

St. Martin's Paperbacks edition / October 2007

St. Martin's Paperbacks are published by St. Martin's Press, 175 Fifth Avenue, New York, NY 10010.

20 19 18 17 16 15 14 13 12 11 10

*To Cindy Blewett,
a wonderful Web designer,
not to mention a wise, witty,
and much appreciated friend.*

Chapter One

LONDON 1848

AUTUMN

Finding one person in a city of nearly two million was a formidable task. It helped if that person's behavior was predictable and he could usually be found in a tavern or gin shop. Still, it wouldn't be easy.

Leo, where are you? Miss Amelia Hathaway thought desperately as the carriage wheels rattled along the cobbled street. Poor, wild, troubled Leo. Some people, when faced with intolerable circumstances, simply . . . broke. Such was the case with her formerly dashing and dependable brother. At this point he was probably beyond all hope of repair.

"We'll find him," Amelia said with an assurance she didn't feel. She glanced at the Gypsy who sat opposite her. As usual, Merripen showed no expression.

One could be forgiven for assuming Merripen was a man of limited emotions. He was so guarded, in fact, that even after living with the Hathaway family for fifteen years, he still hadn't told anyone his first name. They had known him simply as Merripen ever since he had been found, battered and unconscious, beside a creek that ran through their property.

When Merripen had awakened to discover himself surrounded by curious Hathaways, he had reacted violently. It had taken their combined efforts to keep him in bed, all of them exclaiming that he would make his injuries worse, he must lie still. Amelia's father had deduced the boy was the survivor of a Gypsy hunt, a brutal practice in which local landowners rode out on horseback with guns and clubs to rid their properties of Romany encampments.

"The lad was probably left for dead," Mr. Hathaway had remarked gravely. As a scholarly and forward-thinking gentleman, he had disapproved of violence in any form. "I'm afraid it will be difficult to communicate with his tribe. They are probably long gone by now."

"May we keep him, Papa?" Amelia's younger sister Poppy had cried eagerly, no doubt envisioning the wild boy (who had bared his teeth at her like a trapped wolverine) as an entertaining new pet.

Mr. Hathaway had smiled at her. "He may stay as long as he chooses. But I doubt he will remain here longer than a week or so. Romany Gypsies—the Rom, they call themselves—are a nomadic people. They dislike staying under one roof too long. It makes them feel imprisoned."

However, Merripen had stayed. He had started out as a small and rather slight lad. But with proper care and regular meals, he had grown at a near-alarming rate into a man of robust and powerful proportions. It was difficult to say exactly what Merripen was: not quite a family member, not a servant. Although he worked in various capacities for the Hathaways, acting as a driver and jack-of-all-trades, he also ate at the family table whenever he chose, and occupied a bedroom in the main part of the cottage.

Now that Leo had gone missing and was possibly in

danger, there was no question that Merripen would help find him.

It was hardly proper for Amelia to go unaccompanied in the presence of a man like Merripen. But at the age of twenty-six, she considered herself beyond any need of chaperonage.

"We shall begin by eliminating the places Leo would not go," she said. "Churches, museums, places of higher learning, and polite neighborhoods are naturally out of the question."

"That still leaves most of the city," Merripen grumbled.

Merripen was not fond of London. In his view, the workings of so-called civilized society were infinitely more barbaric than anything that could be found in nature. Given a choice between spending an hour in a pen of wild boars or a drawing room of elegant company, he would have chosen the boars without hesitation.

"We should probably start with taverns," Amelia continued.

Merripen gave her a dark glance. "Do you know how many taverns there are in London?"

"No, but I'm certain I will by the time the night is out."

"We're not going to start with taverns. We'll go where Leo is likely to find the most trouble."

"And that would be?"

"Jenner's."

Jenner's was an infamous gaming club where gentlemen went to behave in ungentlemanly ways. Originally founded by an ex-boxer named Ivo Jenner, the club had changed hands upon his death, and was now owned by his son-in-law, Lord St. Vincent. The less-than-sterling reputation of St. Vincent had only enhanced the club's allure.

A membership at Jenner's cost a fortune. Naturally Leo had insisted on joining immediately upon inheriting his title three months ago.

"If you intend to drink yourself to death," Amelia had told Leo calmly, "I wish you would do it at a more affordable place."

"But I'm a viscount now," Leo had replied nonchalantly. "I have to do it with style, or what will people say?"

"That you were a wastrel and a fool, and the title might just as well have gone to a monkey?"

That had elicited a grin from her handsome brother. "I'm sure that comparison is quite unfair to the monkey."

Turning cold with increasing worry, Amelia pressed her gloved fingers to the aching surface of her forehead. This wasn't the first time Leo had disappeared, but it was definitely of the longest duration. "I've never been inside a gaming club before. It will be a novel experience."

"They won't let you inside. You're a lady. And even if they did allow it, I wouldn't."

Lowering her hand, Amelia glanced at him in surprise. It was rare that Merripen forbade her to do anything. In fact, this may have been the first time. She found it annoying. Considering that her brother's life might be at stake, she was hardly going to quibble over social niceties. Besides, she was curious to see what was inside the privileged masculine retreat. As long as she was doomed to remain a spinster, she might as well enjoy the small freedoms that came with it.

"Neither will they let *you* inside," she pointed out. "You're a Roma."

"As it happens, the manager of the club is also a Roma."

That was unusual. Extraordinary, even. Gypsies were

known as thieves and tricksters. For one of the Rom to be entrusted with the accounting of cash and credit, not to mention arbitrating controversies at the gambling tables, was nothing short of amazing. "He must be a rather re-markable individual to have assumed such a position," Amelia said. "Very well, I will allow you to accompany me inside Jenner's. It's possible your presence will induce him to be more forthcoming."

"Thank you." Merripen's voice was so dry one could have struck a match off it.

Amelia remained strategically silent as he drove the covered brougham through the highest concentration of at-tractions, shops, and theaters in the city. The poorly sprung carriage bounced with abandon along the wide thorough-fares, passing handsome squares lined with columned houses and tidily fenced greens, and Georgian-fronted buildings. As the streets became more lavish, the brick walls gave way to stucco, which soon gave way to stone.

The West End scenery was unfamiliar to Amelia. De-spite the proximity of their village, the Hathaways didn't often venture into town, certainly not to this area. Even now with their recent inheritance, there was little they could afford here.

Glancing at Merripen, Amelia wondered why he seemed to know exactly where they were going, when he was no more acquainted with town than she. But Merripen had an instinct for finding his way anywhere.

They turned onto King Street, which was ablaze with light shed from gas lamps. It was noisy and busy, con-gested with vehicles and groups of pedestrians setting out for the evening's entertainment. The sky glowed dull red as the remaining light percolated through the haze of coal smoke. Crowns of lofty buildings broke the horizon, rows of dark shapes protruding like witches' teeth.

Merripen guided the horse to a narrow alley of mews behind a great stone-fronted building. Jenner's. Amelia's stomach tightened. It was probably too much to ask that her brother would be found safely here, in the first place they looked.

"Merripen?" Her voice was strained.

"Yes?"

"You should probably know that if my brother hasn't already managed to kill himself, I plan to shoot him when we find him."

"I'll hand you the pistol."

Amelia smiled and straightened her bonnet. "Let's go inside. And remember—*I'll* do the talking."

An objectionable odor filled the alley, a city-smell of animals and refuse and coal dust. In the absence of a good rain, filth accumulated quickly in the streets and tributaries. Descending to the soiled ground, Amelia hopped out of the path of squeaking rats that ran alongside the wall of the building.

As Merripen gave the ribbons to a stableman at the mews, Amelia glanced toward the end of the alley.

A pair of street youths crouched near a tiny fire, roasting something on sticks. Amelia did not want to speculate on the nature of the objects being heated. Her attention moved to a group—three men and a woman—illuminated in the uncertain blaze. It appeared two of the men were engaged in fisticuffs. However, they were so inebriated that their contest looked like a performance of dancing bears.

The woman's gown was made of gaudily colored fabric, the bodice gaping to reveal the plump hills of her breasts.

She seemed amused by the spectacle of two men battling over her, while a third attempted to break up the fracas.

"'Ere now, my fine jacks," the woman called out in a Cockney accent, "I said I'd take ye both on—no need for a cockfight!"

"Stay back," Merripen murmured.

Pretending not to hear, Amelia drew closer for a better view. It wasn't the sight of the brawl that was so interesting—even their village, peaceful little Primrose Place, had its share of fistfights. All men, no matter what their situation, occasionally succumbed to their lower natures. What attracted Amelia's notice was the third man, the would-be peacemaker, as he darted between the drunken fools and attempted to reason with them.

He was every bit as well dressed as the gentlemen on either side . . . but it was obvious this man was no gentleman. He was black-haired and swarthy and exotic. And he moved with the swift grace of a cat, easily avoiding the swipes and lunges of his opponents.

"My lords," he was saying in a reasonable tone, sounding relaxed even as he blocked a heavy fist with his forearm. "I'm afraid you'll both have to stop this now, or I'll be forced to—" He broke off and dodged to the side just as the man behind him leaped.

The prostitute cackled at the sight. "They got you on the 'op tonight, Rohan," she exclaimed.

Dodging back into the fray, Rohan attempted to break it up once more. "My lords, surely you must know"—he ducked beneath the swift arc of a fist—"that violence"—he blocked a right hook—"never solves anything."

"Bugger you!" one of the men said, and butted forward like a deranged goat.

Rohan stepped aside and allowed him to charge straight into the side of the building. The attacker collapsed with a groan and lay gasping on the ground.

His opponent's reaction was singularly ungrateful. Instead of thanking the dark-haired man for putting a stop to the fight, he growled, "Curse you for interfering, Rohan! I would've knocked the stuffing from him!" He charged forth with his fists churning like windmill blades.

Rohan evaded a left cross and deftly flipped him to the ground. He stood over the prone figure, blotting his forehead with his sleeve. "Had enough?" he asked pleasantly. "Yes? Good. Please allow me to help you to your feet, my lord." As Rohan pulled the man upward, he glanced toward the threshold of a door that led into the club, where a club employee waited. "Dawson, escort Lord Latimer to his carriage out front. I'll take Lord Selway."

"No need," said the aristocrat who had just struggled to his feet, sounding winded. "I can walk to my own bloody carriage." Tugging his clothes back into place over his bulky form, he threw the dark-haired man an anxious glance. "Rohan, I will have your word on something."

"Yes, my lord?"

"If word of this gets out—if Lady Selway should discover that I was fighting over the favors of a fallen woman—my life won't be worth a farthing."

Rohan replied with reassuring calm. "She'll never know, my lord."

"She knows everything," Selway said. "She's in league with the devil. If you are ever questioned about this minor altercation . . ."

"It was caused by a particularly vicious game of whist," came the bland reply.

"Yes. Yes. Good man." Selway patted the younger man on the shoulder. "And to put a seal on your silence—" He reached a beefy hand inside his waistcoat and extracted a small bag.

"No, my lord." Rohan stepped back with a firm shake of his head, his shiny black hair flying with the movement and settling back into place. "There's no price for my silence."

"Take it," the aristocrat insisted.

"I can't, my lord."

"It's yours." The bag of coins was tossed to the ground, landing at Rohan's feet with a metallic thud. "There. Whether you choose to leave it lying on the street or not is entirely your choice."

As the gentleman left, Rohan stared at the bag as if it were a dead rodent. "I don't want it," he muttered to no one in particular.

"I'll take it," the prostitute said, sauntering over to him. She scooped up the bag and tested its heft in her palm. A taunting grin split her face. "Gor', I've never seen a Gypsy what's afraid o' blunt."

"I'm not afraid of it," Rohan said sourly. "I just don't need it." Sighing, he rubbed the back of his neck with one hand.

She laughed at him and slid an openly appreciative glance over his lean form. "I 'ates to take something for noffing. Care for a little knock in the alley before I goes back to Bradshaw's?"

"I appreciate the offer," he said politely, "but no."

She hitched a shoulder in a playful half shrug. "Less work for me, then. Good evenin'."

Rohan responded with a short nod, seeming to contemplate a spot on the ground with undue concentration. He

was very still, seeming to listen for some nearly imperceptible sound. Lifting a hand to the back of his neck again,
he rubbed it as if to soothe a warning prickle. Slowly he
turned and looked directly at Amelia.

A little shock went through her as their gazes met. Although they were standing several yards apart, she felt the
full force of his notice. His expression was not tempered
by warmth or kindness. In fact, he looked pitiless, as if he
had long ago found the world to be an uncaring place and
had decided to accept it on its own terms.

As his detached gaze swept over her, Amelia knew
exactly what he was seeing: a woman dressed in serviceable clothes and practical shoes. She was fair skinned
and dark haired, of medium height, with the rosy-cheeked
wholesomeness common to the Hathaways. Her figure
was sturdy and voluptuous, when the fashion was to be
reed-slim and wan and fragile.

Without vanity, Amelia knew that although she wasn't a
great beauty, she was sufficiently attractive to have caught
a husband. But she had risked her heart once, with disastrous consequences. She had no desire to try it again. And
God knew she was busy enough trying to manage the rest
of the Hathaways.

Rohan looked away from her. Without a word or a nod
of acknowledgment, he walked to the back entrance of the
club. His pace was unhurried, as if he were giving himself
time to think about something. There was a distinctive
ease in his movements. His strides didn't measure out distance so much as flow over it like water.

Amelia reached the doorstep at the same time he did.
"Sir—Mr. Rohan—I presume you are the manager of the
club."

Rohan stopped and turned to face her. They were standing close enough for Amelia to detect the scents of male exertion and warm skin. His unfastened waistcoat, made of luxurious gray brocade, hung open at the sides to reveal a thin white linen shirt beneath. As Rohan moved to button the waistcoat, Amelia saw a quantity of gold rings on his fingers. A ripple of nervousness went through her, leaving an unfamiliar heat in its wake. Her corset felt too tight, her high-necked collar constricting.

Flushing, she brought herself to stare at him directly. He was a young man, not yet thirty, with the countenance of an exotic angel. This face had definitely been created for sin . . . the brooding mouth, the angular jaw, the golden-hazel eyes shaded by long straight lashes. His hair needed cutting, the heavy black locks curling slightly over the back of his collar. Amelia's throat cinched around a quick breath as she saw the glitter of a diamond in his ear.

He accorded her a precise bow. "At your service, Miss . . ."

"Hathaway," she said precisely. She turned to indicate her companion, who had come to stand at her left. "And this is my companion, Merripen."

Rohan glanced at him alertly. "The Romany word for 'life' and also 'death.' "

Was that what Merripen's name meant? Surprised, Amelia looked up at him. Merripen gave a slight shrug to indicate it was of no importance. She turned back to Rohan. "Sir, we've come to ask you a question or two regarding—"

"I don't like questions."

"I am looking for my brother, Lord Ramsay," she continued doggedly, "and I desperately need any information you may possess as to his whereabouts."

"I wouldn't tell you even if I knew." His accent was a subtle mixture of foreignness and Cockney, and even a hint of upper class. It was the voice of a man who kept company with an unusual assortment of people.

"I assure you, sir, I wouldn't put myself or anyone else to the trouble, were it not absolutely necessary. But this is the third day since my brother has gone missing—"

"Not my problem." Rohan turned toward the door.

"He tends to fall in with bad company—"

"That's unfortunate."

"He could be dead by now."

"I can't help you. I wish you luck in your search." Rohan pushed open the door and made to enter the club.

He stopped as Merripen spoke in Romany.

Since Merripen had first come to the Hathaways, there had been only a handful of occasions on which Amelia had heard him speak the secret language known to the Rom. It was heathen-sounding, thick with consonants and drawn-out vowels, but there was a primitive music in the way the words fit together.

Staring at Merripen intently, Rohan leaned his shoulder against the door frame. "The old language," he said. "It's been years since I've heard it. Who is the father of your tribe?"

"I have no tribe."

A long moment passed, while Merripen remained inscrutable in the face of Rohan's regard.

The hazel eyes narrowed. "Come in. I'll see what I can find out."

They were brought into the club without ceremony, Rohan directing an employee to show them to a private receiving room upstairs. Amelia heard the hum of voices, and music coming from somewhere, and footsteps going to and fro. It was a busy masculine hive forbidden to someone like herself.

The employee, a young man with an East London accent and careful manners, took them into a well-appointed room and bid them wait there until Rohan returned. Merripen went to a window overlooking King Street.

Amelia was surprised by the quiet luxury of her surroundings: the hand-knotted carpet done in shades of blue and cream, the wood-paneled walls and velvet-upholstered furniture. "Quite tasteful," she commented, removing her bonnet and setting it on a small claw-footed mahogany table. "For some reason I had expected something a bit . . . well, tawdry."

"Jenner's is a cut above the typical establishment. It masquerades as a gentlemen's club, when its real purpose is to provide the largest hazard bank in London."

Amelia went to a built-in bookshelf and inspected the volumes as she asked idly, "Why is it, do you think, that Mr. Rohan was reluctant to take money from Lord Selway?"

Merripen cast a sardonic glance over his shoulder. "You know how the Rom feel about material possessions."

"Yes, I know your people don't like to be encumbered. But from what I've seen, Romas are hardly reluctant to accept a few coins in return for a service."

"It's more than not wanting to be encumbered. For a *chal* to be in this position—"

"What's a *chal*?"

"A son of the Rom. For a *chal* to wear such fine clothes,

to stay under one roof so long, to reap such financial bounty . . . it's shameful. Embarrassing. Contrary to his nature."

He was so stern and certain of himself, Amelia couldn't resist teasing him a little. "And what's your excuse, Merripen? You've stayed under the Hathaway roof for an awfully long time."

"That's different. For one thing, there's no profit in living with you."

Amelia laughed.

"For another . . ." Merripen's voice softened. "I owe my life to your family."

Amelia felt a surge of affection as she stared at his unyielding profile. "What a spoilsport," she said gently. "I try to mock you, and you ruin the moment with sincerity. You know you're not obligated to stay, dear friend. You've repaid your debt to us a thousand times over."

Merripen shook his head immediately. "It would be like leaving a nest of plover chicks with a fox nearby."

"We're not as helpless as all that," she protested. "I'm perfectly capable of taking care of the family . . . and so is Leo. When he's sober."

"When would that be?" His bland tone made the question all the more sarcastic.

Amelia opened her mouth to argue the point, but was forced to close it. Merripen was right—Leo had wandered through the past six months in a state of perpetual inebriation. She put a hand to her midriff, where worry had accumulated like a sack of lead shot. Poor wretched Leo—she was terrified nothing could be done for him. Impossible to save a man who didn't want to be saved.

That wouldn't stop her from trying, however.

She paced around the room, too agitated to sit and wait calmly. Leo was out there somewhere, needing to be rescued. And there was no telling how long Rohan would have them bide their time here.

"I'm going to have a look around," she said, heading to the door. "I won't go far. Stay here, Merripen, in case Mr. Rohan should come."

She heard him mutter something beneath his breath. Ignoring her request, he followed at her heels as she went out into the hallway.

"This isn't proper," he said behind her.

Amelia didn't pause. Propriety had no power over her now. "This is my one chance to see inside a gaming club—I'm not going to miss it." Following the sound of voices, she ventured toward a gallery that wrapped around the second story of a huge, splendid room.

Crowds of elegantly dressed men gathered around three large hazard tables, watching the play, while croupiers used rakes to gather dice and money. There was a great deal of talking and calling out, the air crackling with excitement. Employees moved through the hazard room, some bearing trays of food and wine, others carrying trays of chips and fresh cards.

Remaining half-hidden behind a column, Amelia surveyed the crowd from the upper gallery. Her gaze alighted on Mr. Rohan, who had donned a black coat and cravat. Even though he was attired similarly to the club members, he stood out from the others like a fox among pigeons.

Rohan half sat, half leaned against the bulky mahogany manager's desk in the corner of the room, where the hazard bank was managed. He appeared to be giving directions to an employee. He used a minimum of gestures, but even so, there was a suggestion of showmanship in his movements, an easy physicality that drew the eye.

And then . . . somehow . . . the intensity of Amelia's interest seemed to reach him. He reached up to the back of his neck, and then he looked directly at her. Just as he had done in the alley. Amelia felt her heartbeat awaken everywhere, in her limbs and hands and feet and even in her knees. A tide of uncomfortable color washed over her. She stood immersed in guilt and heat and surprise, red-faced as a child, before she could finally gather her wits sufficiently to dart behind the column.

"What is it?" she heard Merripen ask.

"I think Mr. Rohan saw me." A shaky laugh escaped her. "Oh, dear. I hope I haven't annoyed him. Let's go back to the receiving room."

And risking one quick glance from the concealment of the column, she saw that Rohan was gone.

Chapter Two

Cam pushed away from the mahogany desk and left the hazard room. As usual, he couldn't leave without being stopped once or twice . . . there was an usher, whispering that Lord so-and-so wished to have his credit limit raised . . . an underbutler asking if he should replenish the sideboard of refreshments in one of the card rooms. He answered their questions absently, his mind occupied with the woman awaiting him upstairs.

An evening that had promised to be routine was turning out to be rather peculiar.

It had been a long time since a woman had aroused his interest as Amelia Hathaway had. The moment he had seen her standing in the alley, wholesome and pink-cheeked, her voluptuous figure contained in a modest gown, he had wanted her. He had no idea why, when she was the embodiment of everything that annoyed him about English-women.

It was obvious Miss Hathaway had a relentless certainty in her own ability to organize and manage everything around her. Cam's usual reaction to that sort of female was to flee in the opposite direction. But as he had stared into her pretty blue eyes, and seen the tiny determined frown hitched between them, he had felt an unholy urge to snatch her up and carry her away somewhere and do something uncivilized. Barbaric, even.

Of course, uncivilized urges had always lurked a bit too close to his surface. And in the past year Cam had begun to find it more difficult than usual to control them. He had become uncharacteristically short-tempered, impatient, easily provoked. The things that had once given him pleasure were no longer satisfying. Worst of all, he'd found himself attending to his sexual urges with the same lack of enthusiasm he was doing everything else these days.

Finding female companionship was never a problem— Cam had found release in the arms of many a willing woman, and had repaid the favor until they had purred with satisfaction. There was no real thrill in it, however. No excitement, no fire, no sense of anything other than having taken care of a bodily function as ordinary as sleeping or eating. Cam had been so troubled that he'd actually brought himself to discuss it with his employer, Lord St. Vincent.

Once a renowned skirt-chaser, now an exceptionally devoted husband, St. Vincent knew as much about these matters as any man alive. When Cam had asked glumly if a decrease in physical urges was something that naturally occurred as a man approached his thirties, St. Vincent had choked on his drink.

"Good God, no," the viscount had said, coughing slightly as a swallow of brandy seared his throat. They had been in the manager's office of the club, going over account books in the early hours of the morning.

St. Vincent was a handsome man with wheat-colored hair and pale blue eyes. Some claimed he had the most perfect form and features of any man alive. The looks of a saint, the soul of a scoundrel. "If I may ask, what kind of women have you been taking to bed?"

"What do you mean, what kind?" Cam had asked warily.

"Beautiful or plain?"

"Beautiful, I suppose."

"Well, there's your problem," St. Vincent said in a matter-of-fact tone. "Plain women are far more enjoyable. There's no better aphrodisiac than gratitude."

"Yet you married a beautiful woman."

A slow smile had curved St. Vincent's lips. "Wives are a different case altogether. They require a great deal of effort, but the rewards are substantial. I highly recommend wives. Especially one's own."

Cam had stared at his employer with annoyance, reflecting that serious conversation with St. Vincent was often hampered by the viscount's fondness for turning it into an exercise of wit. "If I understand you, my lord," he said curtly, "your recommendation for a lack of desire is to start seducing unattractive women?"

Picking up a silver pen holder, St. Vincent deftly fitted a nib into the end and made a project of dipping it precisely into an ink bottle. "Rohan, I'm doing my best to understand your problem. However, a lack of desire is something I've never experienced. I'd have to be on my deathbed before I stopped wanting—no, never mind, I was on my deathbed in the not-too-distant past, and even then I had the devil's own itch for my wife."

"Congratulations," Cam muttered, abandoning any hope

of prying an earnest answer out of the man. "Let's attend to the account books. There are more important matters to discuss than sexual habits."

St. Vincent scratched out a figure and set the pen back on its stand. "No, I insist on discussing sexual habits. It's so much more entertaining than work." He relaxed in his chair with a deceptive air of laziness. "Discreet as you are, Rohan, one can't help but notice how ardently you are pursued. It seems you hold quite an appeal for the ladies of London. And from all appearances, you've taken full advantage of what's been offered."

Cam stared at him without expression. "Pardon, but are you leading to an actual point, my lord?"

Leaning back in his chair, St. Vincent made a temple of his elegant hands and regarded Cam steadily. "Since you've had no problem with lack of desire in the past, I can only assume that, as happens with other appetites, yours has been sated with an overabundance of sameness. A bit of novelty may be just the thing."

Considering the statement, which actually made sense, Cam wondered if the notorious former rake had ever been tempted to stray.

Having known Evie since childhood, when she had come to visit her widowed father at the club from time to time, Cam felt as protective of her as if she'd been his younger sister. No one would have paired the gentle-natured Evie with such a libertine. And perhaps no one had been as surprised as St. Vincent himself to discover their marriage of convenience had turned into a passionate love match.

"What of married life?" Cam asked softly. "Does it eventually become an overabundance of sameness?"

St. Vincent's expression changed, the light blue eyes warming at the thought of his wife. "It has become clear to me that with the right woman, one can never have enough. I would welcome an overabundance of such bliss—but I doubt such a thing is mortally possible." Closing the account book with a decisive thud, he stood from the desk. "If you'll excuse me, Rohan, I'll bid you good night."

"What about finishing the accounting?"

"I'll leave the rest in your capable hands." At Cam's scowl, St. Vincent shrugged innocently. "Rohan, one of us is an unmarried man with superior mathematical abilities and no prospects for the evening. The other is a confirmed lecher in an amorous mood, with a willing and nubile young wife waiting at home. Who do *you* think should do the damned account books?" And, with a nonchalant wave, St. Vincent had left the office.

"Novelty" had been St. Vincent's recommendation— well, that word certainly applied to Miss Hathaway. Cam had always preferred experienced women who regarded seduction as a game and knew better than to confuse pleasure with emotion. He had never cast himself in the role of tutor to an innocent. In fact, the prospect of initiating a virgin was distinctly off-putting. Nothing but pain for her, and the appalling possibility of tears and regrets afterward. He recoiled from the idea. No, there would be no pursuit of novelty with Miss Hathaway.

Hastening his pace, Cam went up the stairs to the room where the woman waited with the dark-faced *chal*. Merripen was a common Romany name. Yet the man was in a most uncommon position. It appeared he was acting as the woman's servant, a bizarre and repugnant situation for a freedom-loving Roma.

So the two of them, Cam and Merripen, had something in common. Both of them worked for *gadjos* instead of roaming the earth freely as God intended.

A Roma didn't belong indoors, enclosed by walls. Living in boxes, as all rooms and houses were, shut away from the sky and wind and sun and stars. Breathing in stale air scented with food and floor polish. For the first time in years Cam felt a surge of mild panic. He fought it back and focused on the task at hand—getting rid of the peculiar pair in the receiving room.

Tugging at his collar to loosen it, he pushed at the half-open door and entered the room.

Miss Hathaway stood near the doorway, waiting with tightly leashed impatience, while Merripen remained a dark presence in the corner. As Cam approached and looked into her upturned face, the panic dissolved in a curious rush of heat. Her blue eyes were smudged with faint lavender shadows, and her soft-looking lips were pressed into a tight seam. Her hair had been pulled back and pinned, dark and shining against her head.

That scraped-back hair, the modest restrictive clothing, advertised her as a woman of inhibitions. A proper spinster. But nothing could have concealed her radiant will. She was . . . delicious. He wanted to unwrap her like a long-awaited gift. He wanted her vulnerable and naked beneath him, that soft mouth swollen from hard, deep kisses, her pale body flushed with desire. Startled by her effect on him, Cam made his expression blank as he studied her.

"Well?" Amelia demanded, clearly unaware of the turn of his thoughts. Which was a good thing, as they likely would have sent her screaming from the room. "Have you discovered anything about my brother's whereabouts?"

"I have."

"And?"

"Lord Ramsay visited earlier this evening, lost some money at the hazard table—"

"Thank God he's alive," Amelia exclaimed.

"—and apparently decided to console himself by visiting a nearby brothel."

"Brothel?" She shot Merripen an exasperated glance. "I swear it, Merripen, he'll die at my hands tonight." She looked back at Cam. "How much did he lose at the hazard table?"

"Approximately five hundred pounds."

The pretty blue eyes widened in outrage. "He'll die *slowly* at my hands. Which brothel?"

"Bradshaw's."

Amelia reached for her bonnet. "Come, Merripen. We're going there to collect him."

Both Merripen and Cam replied at the same time. *"No."*

"I want to see for myself if he's all right," she said calmly. "I very much doubt he is." She gave Merripen a frosty stare. "I'm not returning home without Leo."

Half amused, half alarmed by her force of will, Cam asked Merripen, "Am I dealing with stubbornness, idiocy, or some combination of the two?"

Amelia replied before Merripen had the opportunity. "Stubbornness, on my part. The idiocy may be attributed entirely to my brother." She settled the bonnet on her head and tied its ribbons beneath her chin.

Cherry-red ribbons, Cam saw in bemusement. That frivolous splash of red amid her otherwise sober attire was an incongruous note. Becoming more and more fascinated, Cam heard himself say, "You can't go to Bradshaw's. Reasons of morality and safety aside, you don't even know where the hell it is."

Amelia didn't flinch at the profanity. "I assume a great deal of business is sent back and forth between your establishment and Bradshaw's. You say the place is nearby, which means all I have to do is follow the foot traffic from here to there. Goodbye, Mr. Rohan. I appreciate your help."

Cam moved to block her path. "All you'll accomplish is making a fool of yourself, Miss Hathaway. You won't get past the front door. A brothel like Bradshaw's doesn't take strangers off the street."

"How I manage to retrieve my brother, sir, is no concern of yours."

She was correct. It wasn't. But Cam hadn't been this entertained in a long time. No sensual depravities, no skilled courtesan, not even a room full of unclothed women, could have interested him half as much as Miss Amelia Hathaway and her red ribbons.

"I'm going with you," he said.

She frowned. "No, thank you."

"I insist."

"I don't need your services, Mr. Rohan."

Cam could think of a number of services she was clearly in need of, most of which would be a pleasure for him to provide. "Obviously it will be to everyone's benefit for you to retrieve Ramsay and leave London as quickly as possible. I consider it my civic duty to hasten your departure."

Chapter Three

Although they could have reached the brothel on foot, Amelia, Merripen, and Rohan went to Bradshaw's in the ancient barouche. They stopped before a plain Georgian-style building. For Amelia, whose imaginings of such a place were framed with lurid extravagance, the brothel's façade was disappointingly discreet.

"Stay inside the carriage," Rohan said. "I'll go inside and inquire as to Ramsay's whereabouts." He gave Merripen a hard look. "Don't leave Miss Hathaway unattended even for a second. It's dangerous at this time of night."

"It's early evening," Amelia protested. "And we're in the West End, amid crowds of well-dressed gentlemen. How dangerous could it be?"

"I've seen those well-dressed gentlemen do things that would make you faint to hear of them."

"I never faint," Amelia said indignantly.

Rohan's smile was a flash of white in the shadowed interior of the carriage. He left the vehicle and dissolved into the night as if he were part of it, blending seamlessly except for the ebony glimmer of his hair and the sparkle of the diamond at his ear.

Amelia stared after him in wonder. What category did one put such a man in? He was not a gentleman, nor a lord, nor a common workingman, nor even fully a Gypsy. A shiver chased beneath her corset stays as she recalled the moment he had helped her up into the carriage. Her hand had been gloved, but his had been bare, and she had felt the heat and strength of his fingers. And there had been the gleam of a thick gold band on his thumb. She had never seen such a thing before.

"Merripen, what does it mean when a man wears a thumb ring? Is it a Gypsy custom?"

Seeming uncomfortable with the question, Merripen looked through the window into the damp night. A group of young men passed the vehicle, wearing fine coats and tall hats, laughing among themselves. A pair of them stopped to speak with a gaudily dressed woman. Still frowning, Merripen replied to Amelia's question. "It signifies independence and freedom of thought. Also a certain separateness. In wearing it, he reminds himself he doesn't belong where he is."

"Why would Mr. Rohan want to remind himself of something like that?"

"Because the ways of your kind are seductive," Merripen said darkly. "It's difficult to resist them."

"Why must you resist them? I fail to see what is so terrible about living in a proper house and securing a steady income, and enjoying things like nice dishes and upholstered chairs."

"Gadji," he murmured in resignation, making Amelia grin briefly. It was the word for a non-Gypsy woman.

She relaxed back against the worn upholstered seat. "I never thought I would be hoping so desperately to find my brother inside a house of ill repute. But between a brothel or floating facedown in the Thames—" She broke off and pressed the knuckles of her clenched fist against her lips.

"He's not dead." Merripen's voice was low and gentle.

Amelia was trying very hard to believe that. "We must get Leo away from London. He'll be safer out in the country . . . won't he?"

Merripen gave a noncommittal shrug, his dark eyes revealing nothing of his thoughts.

"There's far less to do in the country," Amelia pointed out. "And definitely less trouble for Leo to get into."

"A man who wants trouble can find it anywhere."

After minutes of unbearable waiting, Rohan returned to the brougham and tugged the door open.

"Where is he?" Amelia demanded as the Gypsy climbed inside.

"Not here. After Lord Ramsay went upstairs with one of the girls and, er . . . conducted the transaction . . . he left the brothel."

"Where did he go? Did you ask—"

"He told them he was going to a tavern called the Hell and Bucket."

"Lovely," Amelia said shortly. "Do you know the way?"

Seating himself beside her, Rohan glanced at Merripen. "Follow St. James eastward, turn left after the third crossing."

Merripen flicked the ribbons, and the carriage rolled past a trio of prostitutes.

Amelia watched the women with undisguised interest. "How young some of them are," she said. "If only some charitable institution would help them find respectable employment."

"Most so-called respectable employment is just as bad," Rohan replied.

She looked at him indignantly. "You think a woman would be better off to work as a prostitute than to take an honest job that would allow her to live with dignity?"

"I didn't say that. My point is that some employers are far more brutal than pimps or brothel bawds. Servants have to endure all manner of abuse from their masters— female servants in particular. And if you think there is dignity in working at a mill or factory, you've never seen a girl who's lost a few fingers from cutting broom straw. Or someone whose lungs are so congested from breathing in fluff and dust at a carding mill, she won't live past the age of thirty."

Amelia opened her mouth to reply, then snapped it shut. No matter how much she wanted to continue the debate, proper women—even if they were spinsters—did not discuss prostitution.

She adopted an expression of cool indifference and looked out the window. Although she didn't spare a glance for Rohan, she sensed he was watching her. She was unbearably aware of him. He wore no cologne or pomade, but there was something alluring about his smell, something smoky and fresh, like green cloves.

"Your brother inherited the title quite recently," Rohan said.

"Yes."

"With all respect, Lord Ramsay doesn't seem entirely prepared for his new role."

Amelia couldn't restrain a rueful smile. "None of us are.

It was a surprising turn of events for the Hathaways. There were at least three men in line for the title before Leo. But they all died in rapid succession, of varying causes. It seems that becoming Lord Ramsay causes one to become short-lived. And at this rate, my brother probably won't last any longer than his predecessors."

"One never knows what fate has in store."

Turning toward Rohan, Amelia discovered he was glancing over her in a slow inventory that spurred her heart into a faster beat. "I don't believe in fate," she said. "People are in control of their own destinies."

Rohan smiled. "Everyone, even the gods, are helpless in the hands of fate."

Amelia regarded him skeptically. "Surely you, being employed at a gaming club, know all about probability and odds. Which means you can't rationally give credence to luck or fate or anything of the sort."

"I know all about probability and odds," Rohan agreed. "Nevertheless, I believe in luck." He smiled with a quiet smolder in his eyes that caused her breath to catch. "I believe in magic and mystery, and dreams that reveal the future. And I believe some things are written in the stars . . . or even in the palm of your hand."

Mesmerized, Amelia was unable to look away from him. He was an extraordinarily beautiful man, his skin as dark as clover honey, his black hair falling over his forehead in a way that made her fingers twitch with the urge to push it back.

"Do you believe in fate too?" she asked Merripen.

A long hesitation. "I'm a Roma," he said.

Which meant yes. "Good Lord, Merripen. I've always thought of you as a sensible man."

Rohan laughed. "It's only sensible to allow for the possibility, Miss Hathaway. Just because you can't see or feel something doesn't mean it can't exist."

"There is no such thing as fate," Amelia insisted. "There is only action and consequence."

The carriage came to a halt, this time in a much shabbier place than St. James or King Street. There was a beer shop and three-penny lodging house on one side, and a large tavern on the other. The pedestrians on this street had the appearance of sham gentility, rubbing elbows with costers, pickpockets, and more prostitutes.

A brawl was in progress near the threshold of the tavern, a writhing mixture of arms, legs, flying hats, and bottles and canes. Anytime there was a fight, the greatest likelihood was that her brother had started it.

"Merripen," she said anxiously, "you know how Leo is when he's foxed. He's probably in the middle of the fray. If you would be so kind—"

Before she had even finished, Merripen made to leave the carriage.

"Wait," Rohan said. "You'd better let me handle it."

Merripen gave him a cold glance. "You doubt my ability to fight?"

"This is a London rookery. I'm used to the kind of tricks they employ. If you—" Rohan broke off as Merripen ignored him and left the carriage with a surly grunt. "So be it," Rohan said, exiting the carriage and standing beside it to watch. "They'll slice him open like a mackerel at a Covent Garden fish stand."

Amelia came out of the vehicle as well. "Merripen can handle himself quite well in a fight, I assure you."

Rohan looked down at her, his eyes shadowed and cat-like. "You'll be safer inside the vehicle."

"I have you for protection, do I not?" she pointed out.

"Sweetheart," he said with a softness that undercut the noise of the crowd, "I may be the one you most need protection from."

She felt her heart miss a beat. He met her wide-eyed glance with a steady interest that caused her toes to curl inside her practical leather shoes. Fighting for composure, Amelia looked away from him. But she remained sharply aware of him, the relaxed alertness of his posture, the unknown pulse secreted beneath the elegant layers of his clothing.

They watched as Merripen waded into the chaos of brawling men, sorted through a few of them. Before a half minute had passed, he unceremoniously hauled someone out, easily deflecting blows with his free arm.

"He's good," Rohan said in mild surprise.

Amelia was overwhelmed with relief as she recognized Leo's disheveled form. "Oh, thank God."

Her eyes flew open, however, as she felt a gentle touch at the edge of her jaw. Rohan's fingers were nudging her face upward, his thumb brushing the tip of her chin. The unexpected intimacy sent a little shock through her. His flame-bright gaze had seized hers again.

"Don't you think you're being a bit overprotective, chasing your grown brother across London? He's not doing anything all that unusual. Most young lords in his position would behave the same."

"You don't know him," Amelia said, sounding shaken to her own ears. She knew she should pull away from his warm fingers, but her body remained perversely still, absorbing the pleasure of his touch. "It's far from usual behavior for him. He's in trouble. He—" She broke off.

Rohan let a gentle fingertip follow the shining trail of her bonnet ribbon to the place where it tied beneath her chin. "What kind of trouble?"

She jerked away from his touch and turned as Merripen and Leo approached the carriage. A rush of love and agonized worry filled her at the sight of her brother. He was filthy, battered, and grinning unrepentantly. Anyone who didn't know Leo would assume he hadn't a care in the world. But his eyes, once so warm, were dull and wintry. His formerly fit body was paunchy, and the visible portion of his neck was bloated. There was still a long way to go before Leo was in total ruins, but he seemed determined to hasten the process.

"How remarkable," Amelia said casually. "There's still something left of you." Plucking a handkerchief from her sleeve, she strode forward and tenderly wiped sweat and a smear of blood from his cheeks. Noticing his unfocused gaze, she said, "I'm the one in the middle, dear."

"Ah. There you are." Leo's head bobbed up and down like a string puppet's. He glanced at Merripen, who was providing far more support than Leo's own legs were. "My sister," he said. "Terrifying girl."

"Before Merripen puts you in the carriage," Amelia said, "are you going to cast up your accounts, Leo?"

"Certainly not," came the unhesitating reply. "Hathaways always hold their liquor."

Amelia stroked aside the dirty brown locks that dangled like strands of yarn over his eyes. "It would be nice if you would try to hold a bit less of it in the future, dear."

"Ah, but sis . . ." As Leo looked down at her, she saw a flash of his old self, a spark in the vacant eyes, and then it was gone. "I have such a powerful thirst."

Amelia felt the smart of tears at the corners of her eyes, tasted salt at the back of her throat. Swallowing it back, she said in a steady voice, "For the next few days, Leo, your thirst will be slaked exclusively by water or tea. Into the carriage with him, Merripen."

Leo twisted to glance at the man who held him steady. "For God's sake, you're not going to put me in her custody, are you?"

"Would you rather dry out in the care of a Bow Street gaolkeeper?" Merripen asked politely.

"He would be a damn sight more merciful." Grumbling, Leo lurched toward the carriage with Merripen's assistance.

Amelia turned to Cam Rohan, whose face was inscrutable. "May we take you back to Jenner's, sir? It will be tight quarters in the carriage, but I think we can manage."

"No, thank you." Rohan walked slowly around the carriage with her. "It isn't far. I'll go on foot."

"I can't leave you stranded in a London rookery."

Rohan stopped with her at the back of the carriage, where they were partially sheltered from view. "I'll be fine. The city holds no fears for me. Hold still."

Rohan turned her face up again, one hand cradling her jaw while the other descended to her cheek. His thumb brushed gently beneath her left eye, and with surprise she felt a smudge of wetness there.

"The wind makes my eyes water," she heard herself say unsteadily.

"There's no wind tonight." His hand remained at her

jaw, the smooth band of the thumb ring pressing lightly against her skin. Her heart had begun to thump until she could hardly hear through the blood rush in her ears. The clamor of the tavern was muted, the darkness thickening around them. His fingers slid over her throat with stunning delicacy, finding secreted nerves and stroking gently.

His eyes were above hers, and she saw that the golden-hazel irises were rimmed with black. "Miss Hathaway . . . you're quite certain fate had no hand in our meeting tonight?"

She couldn't seem to breathe properly. "Qu-quite certain."

His head bent low. "And in all likelihood we'll never meet again?"

"Never." He was too large, too close. Nervously Amelia tried to marshal her thoughts, but they scattered like spilled matchsticks . . . and then he set fire to them as his breath touched her cheek.

"I hope you're right. God help me if I should ever have to face the consequences."

"Of what?" Her voice was faint.

"This." His hand slid to the back of her neck and his mouth covered hers.

Amelia had been kissed before. Not all that long ago, as a matter of fact, by a man she had been in love with. The pain of his betrayal had cut so deep, she had sworn never to allow any man close to her again. But Cam Rohan hadn't asked her consent or given her any chance to protest. She stiffened and brought her hands to his chest, exerting pressure against the hard surface. He seemed not to notice her objection, his mouth subtle and insistent. One of his arms slid around her, lifting slightly as he pulled her against the solid contours of his body.

With each breath she drew in a deeper scent of him, the sweetness of beeswax soap, the hint of salt of his skin. The supple power of his body was all around her, and she couldn't stop herself from relaxing into it, letting him support her. More kisses, one beginning before another had quite finished, moist and intimate caresses, secret strokes of pleasure and promise.

With a soft murmur—foreign words that fell pleasantly on her ears—Rohan took his mouth from hers. His lips wandered along the flushed curve of her neck, lingering on the most vulnerable spots. Her body felt swollen inside her clothes, the corset cinching around the desperate pitch of her lungs.

She quivered as he reached a place of exquisite sensation and touched it with the tip of his tongue. As if the taste of her were some exotic spice. A pulse awakened in her breasts and stomach and between her thighs. She was filled with a dreadful urge to press against him, she wanted to fight free of the layers and layers of smothering fabric that made up her skirts. He was so careful, so gentle—

The crash of a bottle on the pavement jolted her from the haze.

"No," she gasped, now struggling.

Rohan released her, his hands steadying her as she fought for equilibrium. Amelia turned blindly and staggered toward the open door of the carriage. Everywhere he had touched, her nerves stung with the desire for more. She kept her head low, grateful for the concealment of her bonnet.

Desperate for escape, Amelia ascended to the carriage

step. Before she could climb in, however, she felt Rohan's hands at her waist. He held her from behind, trapping her long enough to whisper near her ear, *"Latcho drom."*

The Romany farewell. Amelia recognized it from the handful of words Merripen had taught the Hathaways. An intimate shock went through her as the heat of his breath collected in her ear. She didn't, couldn't, reply, only climbed into the carriage and awkwardly pulled the mass of her skirts away from the open doorway.

The door was closed firmly, and the vehicle started forward as the horse obeyed Merripen's guidance. The two Hathaways occupied their respective corners of the seat, one of them drunk, the other dazed. After a moment Amelia reached to untie her bonnet with trembling hands, and discovered the ribbons were hanging loose.

One ribbon, actually. The other . . .

Removing her bonnet, Amelia regarded it with a perplexed frown. One of the red silk ribbons was gone except for the tiny remnant at the inside edge.

It had been neatly cut.

He had taken it.

Chapter Four

One week later, all five Hathaway siblings and their belongings had removed from London to their new home in Hampshire. Despite the challenges that awaited them, Amelia was strongly hopeful their new situation would benefit them all.

The house in Primrose Place held too many memories. Things had never been the same since both Hathaway parents had died, her father of a heart ailment, her mother of grief a few months afterward. It seemed the walls had absorbed the family's sorrow until it had become part of the paint and paper and wood. Amelia couldn't look at the hearth of the main room without remembering her mother sitting there with her sewing basket, or visit the garden without thinking of her father pruning his prized Apothecary's Roses.

Amelia had recently sold the house without compunction, not for lack of sentimentality but rather an excess. Too much feeling, too much sadness. And it was impossible to look forward when one was constantly being reminded of painful loss.

Her siblings hadn't offered a word of objection to selling their home. Nothing mattered to Leo—one could tell him the family intended to live in the streets, and he would have greeted the news with an indifferent shrug. Win, the next oldest sister, was too weak from prolonged illness to protest any of Amelia's decisions. And Poppy and Beatrix, both still in their teens, were eager for change.

As far as Amelia was concerned, the inheritance couldn't have come at a better time. Although she had to admit, there was some question as to how long the Hathaways would manage to retain the title.

The fact was, no one wanted to be Lord Ramsay. For the previous three Lord Ramsays, the title had been accompanied by a streak of singular ill fortune capped by untimely death. Which explained, in part, why the Hathaways' distant relatives had been quite happy to see the viscountcy go to Leo.

"Do I get any money?" had been Leo's first question upon being informed of his ascendancy to the peerage.

The answer had been a qualified yes. Leo would inherit a Hampshire estate of limited acreage and a modest annual sum that wouldn't begin to account for the cost of refurbishing it.

"We're still poor," Amelia had told her brother after poring over the solicitor's letter describing the estate and its affairs. "The estate is small, the servants and most of the tenants have left, the house is shabby, and the title is apparently cursed. Which makes the inheritance a white elephant, to say the least. However, we have a distant cousin who may arguably be in line before you—we can try to throw it all off on him. There is a possibility that our great-great-great-grandfather may not have been legitimate issue, which would allow us to apply for forfeiture of the title on the grounds of—"

"I'll take the title," Leo had said decisively.

"Because you don't believe in curses any more than I do?"

"Because I'm already so damned cursed, another one won't matter."

Having never been to the southern county of Hampshire before, all the Hathaway siblings—with the exception of Leo—craned their necks to view the scenery.

Amelia smiled at her sisters' excitement. Poppy and Beatrix, both dark-haired and blue-eyed like herself, were filled with high spirits. Her gaze alighted on Win and stayed for a moment, taking careful measure of her condition.

Win was different from the rest of the Hathaway brood, the only one who had inherited their father's pale blond hair and introspective nature. She was shy and quiet, enduring every hardship without complaint. When scarlet fever had swept through the village a year earlier, Leo and Win had fallen gravely ill. Leo had made a complete recovery, but Win had been frail and colorless ever since. The doctor had diagnosed her with a weakness of the lungs, caused by the fever, that he said might never improve.

Amelia refused to accept that Win would be an invalid forever. No matter what it took, she would make Win well again.

It was difficult to imagine a better place for Win and the rest of the Hathaways than Hampshire. It was one of the most beautiful counties in England, with intersecting rivers, great forests, meadows, and wet heath lands. The Ramsay estate was situated close to Stony Cross, one of the largest market towns in the county. Stony Cross exported cattle, sheep, timber, corn, a plenitude of local cheeses, and wild-flower honey . . . rich territory, indeed.

"I wonder why the Ramsay estate is so unproductive?" Amelia mused as the carriage traveled alongside lush pastures. "The land in Hampshire is so fertile, one almost has to try *not* to grow something here."

"But our land is cursed, isn't it?" Poppy asked with mild concern.

"No," Amelia replied, "not the estate itself. Just the titleholder. Which would be Leo."

"Oh." Poppy relaxed. "That's fine, then."

Leo didn't bother responding, only huddled in the seat corner looking surly. Although a week of enforced sobriety had left him clear-eyed and clear-headed, it had done nothing to improve his temper. With Merripen and the Hathaways watching over him like hawks, he'd had no opportunity to drink anything other than water or tea.

For the first few days Leo had been given to uncontrollable shaking, agitation, and profuse sweating. Now that the worst of it was over, he looked more like his old self. But few people would believe Leo was a man of eight and twenty. The past year had aged him immeasurably.

The closer they came to Stony Cross, the lovelier the scenery was until it seemed nearly every view was worth painting. The carriage road passed tidy black-and-white cottages with thatched roofs, millhouses and ponds shrouded with weeping willows, old stone churches dating back to the Middle Ages. Thrushes busily stripped ripe berries from hedgerows, while stonechats perched on blossoming hawthorns. Meadows were dense with autumn crocus and meadow saffron, and the trees were dressed in gold and red. Plump white sheep grazed in the fields.

Poppy took a deep, appreciative breath. "How bracing," she said. "I wonder what makes the country air smell so different?"

"It could be the pig farm we just passed," Leo muttered.

Beatrix, who had been reading from a pamphlet describing the south of England, said cheerfully, "Hampshire is known for its exceptional pigs. They're fed on acorns and beechnut mast from the forest, and it makes the bacon quite lovely. And there's an annual sausage competition!"

He gave her a sour look. "Splendid. I certainly hope we haven't missed it."

Win, who had been reading from a thick tome about Hampshire and its environs, volunteered, "The history of Ramsay House is impressive."

"Our house is in a history book?" Beatrix asked in delight.

"It's only a small paragraph," Win said from behind the book, "but yes, Ramsay House is mentioned. Of course, it's nothing compared to our neighbor, the Earl of Westcliff, whose estate features one of the finest country homes in England. It dwarfs ours by comparison. And the earl's family has been in residence for nearly five hundred years."

"He must be awfully old, then," Poppy commented, straight-faced.

Beatrix snickered. "Go on, Win."

" 'Ramsay House,' " Win read aloud, " 'stands in a small park populated with stately oaks and beeches, coverts of bracken, and surrounds of deer-cropped turf. Originally an Elizabethan manor house completed in 1594, the building boasts of many long galleries representative of the period. Alterations and additions to the house have resulted in the grafting of a Jacobean ballroom and a Georgian wing.' "

"We have a ballroom!" Poppy exclaimed.

"We have deer!" Beatrix said gleefully.

Leo settled deeper into his corner. "God, I hope we have a privy."

It was early evening by the time the hired driver turned the carriage onto the private beech-lined drive that led to Ramsay House. Weary from the long journey, the Hathaways exclaimed in relief at the sight of the house, with its high roofline and brick chimney stacks.

"I wonder how Merripen is faring," Win said, her blue eyes soft with concern. Merripen, the cook-maid, and the footman had gone to the house two days earlier to prepare for the Hathaways' arrival.

"No doubt he's been working ceaselessly day and night," Amelia replied, "taking inventory, rearranging everything in sight, and issuing commands to people who don't dare disobey him. I'm sure he's quite happy."

Win smiled. Even pale and drained as she was, her beauty was incandescent, her silvery-gold hair shining in the waning light, her complexion like porcelain. The line of her profile would have sent poets and painters into raptures. One was almost tempted to touch her to make certain she was a living, breathing being instead of a sculpture.

The carriage stopped at a much larger house than Amelia had expected. It was bordered by overgrown hedges and weed-clotted flower beds. With some gardening and considerable pruning, she thought, it would be lovely. The building was charmingly asymmetrical with a brick and stone exterior, a slate roof, and abundant leaded-glass windows.

The hired driver came to set out a movable step and assist the passengers from the vehicle.

Descending to the crushed-rock surface of the drive, Amelia watched as her siblings emerged from the carriage. "The house and grounds are a bit unkempt," she warned. "No one has lived here in a very long time."

"I can't imagine why," Leo said.

"It's very picturesque," Win commented brightly. The journey from London had exhausted her. Judging from the slump of her narrow shoulders and the way her skin seemed stretched too tightly over her cheekbones, Win had little strength left.

As her sister reached for a small valise that had been set by the carriage step, Amelia rushed forward and picked it up. "I'll carry this," she said. "You are not to lift a finger. Let's go inside, and we'll find a place for you to rest."

"I'm perfectly well," Win protested as they all went up the front stairs into the house.

The entrance hall was lined with paneling that had once been painted white but now was brown with age. The floor was scarred and filthy. A magnificent curved stone staircase occupied the back of the hall, its wrought-iron balustrade clotted with dust and spiderwebs. Amelia noticed that an attempt had already been made to clean a section of the balustrade, but it was obvious the process would be painstaking.

Merripen emerged from a hallway leading away from the entrance room. He was in his shirtsleeves with no collar or cravat, the neck of the garment hanging open to reveal tanned skin gleaming with perspiration. With his black hair falling over his forehead, and his dark eyes smiling at the sight of them, Merripen cut a dashing figure. "You're three hours behind schedule," he said.

Laughing, Amelia pulled a handkerchief from her

sleeve and gave it to him. "In a family of four sisters, there is no schedule."

Wiping at the dust and sweat on his face, Merripen glanced at all the Hathaways. His gaze lingered on Win for an extra moment.

Returning his attention to Amelia, Merripen gave her a concise report. He had found two women and a boy at the village to help clean the house. Three bedrooms had been made habitable so far. They had spent a great deal of time scrubbing the kitchen and stove, and the cook-maid was preparing a meal—

Merripen broke off as he glanced over Amelia's shoulder. Unceremoniously he brushed by her and reached Win in three strides.

Amelia saw Win's slight form swaying, her lashes lowering as she half collapsed against Merripen. He caught her easily and lifted her in his arms, murmuring for her to put her head on his shoulder. Although his manner was as calm and unemotional as ever, Amelia was struck by the possessive way he held her sister.

"The journey was too much for her," Amelia said in concern. "She needs rest."

Merripen's face was expressionless. "I'll take her upstairs."

Win stirred and blinked. "Bother," she said breathlessly. "I was standing still, feeling fine, and then the floor seemed to rush up toward me. I'm sorry. I *despise* swooning."

"It's all right." Amelia gave her a reassuring smile. "Merripen will take you to bed. That is—" She paused uncomfortably. "He will convey you to your bedroom."

"I can manage by myself," Win said. "I was just dizzy for a moment. Merripen, do put me down."

"You wouldn't make it past the first step," he said, ignoring her protests as he carried her to the stone staircase. And as he walked with her, Win's pale hand lifted slowly around his neck.

"Beatrix, will you go with them?" Amelia asked briskly, handing her the valise. "Win's nightgown is in here—you can help her change clothes."

"Yes, of course." Beatrix scampered toward the stairs.

Left in the entrance hall with Leo and Poppy, Amelia turned in a slow circle to view all of it. "The solicitor said the estate was in disrepair," she said. "I think a more accurate word would have been 'shambles.' Can it be restored, Leo?"

Not long ago—though it seemed a lifetime—Leo had spent two years studying art and architecture at the Grand Ecole des Beaux-Arts in Paris. He had also worked as a draftsman and painter for the renowned London architect Rowland Temple. Leo had been regarded as an exceptionally promising student, and had even considered setting up a practice. Now all that ambition had been extinguished.

Leo glanced around the hall without interest. "Barring any structural repairs, we would need about twenty-five to thirty thousand pounds, at least."

The figure caused Amelia to blanch. She lowered her gaze to the pockmarked floor at her feet and rubbed her temples. "Well, one thing is obvious. We need the advantage of wealthy in-laws. Which means you should start looking for available heiresses, Leo." She flicked a playful glance at her sister. "And you, Poppy—you'll have to catch a viscount, or at the very least a baron."

Her brother rolled his eyes. "Why not you? I don't see why you should be exempt from having to marry for the family's benefit."

Poppy gave her sister a sly glance. "At Amelia's age, women are far beyond thoughts of romance and passion."

"One never knows," Leo told Poppy. "She may catch an elderly gentleman who needs a nurse."

Amelia was tempted to skewer them both with the tart observation that she had already been in love once, and she would not care to repeat the experience. She had been pursued and courted by Leo's best friend, a charming young architect named Christopher Frost, who, like Leo, had been articled to Rowland Temple. But on the day he had led her to believe a proposal was forthcoming, Frost had ended the relationship with brutal abruptness. He said he had developed feelings for another woman, who conveniently happened to be Rowland Temple's daughter.

It was only to be expected of an architect, Leo had told her with grim remorse, outraged on behalf of his sister, sorrowful at the loss of a friend. Architects inhabited a world of masters and disciples and the endless pursuit of patrons. Everything, even love, was sacrificed on the altar of ambition. To be otherwise was to miss the few precious opportunities one might have to practice the art of design. Marrying Temple's daughter would give Christopher Frost a place at the table. Amelia could never have done that for him.

All she had been able to do was love him.

Swallowing back her bitterness, Amelia glanced up at her brother and managed a rueful smile. "Thank you, but at this advanced stage of life, I have no ambitions to marry."

Leo surprised her by bending to brush a light kiss on her forehead. His voice was soft and kind. "Be that as it may, I think someday you'll meet a man worth giving up your independence for." He grinned before adding, "Despite your encroaching old age."

For a moment Amelia's mind chased back to the memory of the kiss in the shadows, the mouth slowly consuming hers, the gentle masculine hands, the whisper at her ear. *Latcho drom* . . .

As her brother turned to walk away, she asked with mild exasperation, "Where are you going? Leo, you can't leave when there's so much to be done."

He stopped and glanced back at her with a raised brow. "You've been pouring unsweetened tea down my throat for days. If you have no objection, I'd like to go out for a piss."

She narrowed her eyes. "I can think of at least a dozen polite euphemisms you could have used."

Leo continued on his way. "I don't use euphemisms."

"Or politeness," she said, making him chuckle.

As Leo left the room, Amelia folded her arms and sighed. "He's so much more pleasant when he's sober. A pity it doesn't happen more often. Come, Poppy, let's find the kitchen."

With the house so stale and dust-riddled, the atmosphere was hard on poor Win's lungs, causing her to cough incessantly through the night. Having awakened countless times to administer water to her sister, to open the windows, to prop her up until the coughing spasms had eased, Amelia was bleary-eyed when morning came.

"It's like sleeping in a dust box," she told Merripen. "She's better off sitting outside today, until we can manage to clean her room properly. The carpets must be beaten. And the windows are filthy."

The rest of the family was still abed, but Merripen, like Amelia, was an early riser. Dressed in rough clothes and

an open-necked shirt, he stood frowning as Amelia reported on Win's condition.

"She's exhausted from coughing all night, and her throat
is so sore, she can barely speak. I've tried to make her take
some tea and toast, but she won't have it."

"I'll make her take it."

Amelia looked at him blankly. She supposed she
shouldn't be surprised by his assertion. After all, Merripen
had helped nurse both Win and Leo through the scarlet
fever. Without him, Amelia was certain neither of them
would have survived.

"In the meanwhile," Merripen continued, "make a list of
supplies you want from the village. I'll go this morning."

Amelia nodded, grateful for his solid, reliable presence. "Shall I wake Leo? Perhaps he could help—"

"No."

She smiled wryly, well aware that her brother would be
more of a hindrance than a help.

Going downstairs, Amelia sought the help of Freddie,
the boy from the village, to move an ancient chaise out to
the back of the house. They set the furniture on a brick-
paved terrace that opened onto a weed-choked garden bordered by beech hedges. The garden needed resodding and
replanting, and the crumbling low walls would have to be
repaired.

"There's work to be done, mum," Freddie commented,
bending to pluck a tall weed from between two paving
bricks.

"Freddie, you are a master of understatement." Amelia
contemplated the boy, who looked to be about thirteen. He
was robust and ruddy-faced, with a ruff of hair that stood

up like a robin's feathers. "Do you like gardening?" she asked. "Do you know much about it?"

"I keeps a kitchen plot for my ma."

"Would you like to be Lord Ramsay's gardener?"

"How much does it pay, miss?"

"Would two shillings a week suffice?"

Freddie looked at her thoughtfully and scratched his wind-chapped nose. "Sounds good. But you'll have to ask my ma."

"Tell me where you live, and I'll visit her this very morning."

"All right. It's not far—we're at the closest side of the village."

They shook hands on the deal, talked a moment more, and Freddie went to investigate the gardener's shed.

Turning at the sound of voices, Amelia saw Merripen carrying her sister outside. Win was dressed in a nightgown and robe and swathed in a shawl, her slim arms looped around Merripen's neck. With her white garments and blond hair and fair skin, Win was nearly colorless except for the flags of soft pink across her cheekbones and the vivid blue of her eyes.

". . . that was the most terrible medicine," she was saying cheerfully.

"It worked," Merripen pointed out, bending to settle her carefully on the chaise.

"That doesn't mean I forgive you for bullying me into taking it."

"It was for your own good."

"You're a bully," Win repeated, smiling into his dark face.

"Yes, I know," Merripen murmured, tucking the lap blankets around her with extreme care.

Delighted by the improvement in her sister's condition, Amelia smiled. "He really is dreadful. But if he manages to persuade more villagers to help clean the house, you will have to forgive him, Win."

Win's blue eyes twinkled. She spoke to Amelia, while her gaze remained on Merripen. "I have every faith in his powers of persuasion."

Coming from anyone else, the words might have been construed as a piece of flirtation. But Amelia was fairly certain that Win had no awareness of Merripen as a man. To her he was a kindly older brother, nothing more.

The feelings on Merripen's side, however, were more ambiguous.

An inquisitive gray jackdaw flapped to the ground with a few *tchacks,* and made a tentative hop in Win's direction. "I'm sorry," she told the bird, "there's no food to share."

A new voice entered the conversation. "Yes there is!" It was Beatrix, carrying a breakfast tray containing a plate of toast and a mug of tea. Her curly dark hair had been pulled back into an untidy bunch, and she wore a white pinafore over her berry-colored dress.

The pinafore was too young a style for a girl of fifteen, Amelia thought. Beatrix was now at an age when she should be wearing her skirts to the floor. And a corset, heaven help her. But in the past year of turmoil, Amelia hadn't given much thought to her youngest sister's attire. She needed to take Beatrix and Poppy to a dressmaker, and have some new frocks made for them. Adding that to the long list of expenditures in her head, Amelia frowned.

"Here's your breakfast, Win," Beatrix said, settling the tray on her lap. "Are you feeling well enough to butter the toast yourself, or shall I?"

"I will, thank you." Win moved her feet and gestured for Beatrix to sit at the other end of the chaise.

Beatrix obeyed promptly. "I'm going to read to you while you sit out here," she informed Win, reaching into one of the huge pockets of her pinafore. She withdrew a little book and dangled it tantalizingly. "This book was given to me by Philomena Parsons, my best friend in the entire world. She says it's a terrifying story filled with crimes and horrors and vengeful phantoms. Doesn't it sound lovely?"

"I thought your best friend in the world was Edwina Huddersfield," Win said with a questioning lilt.

"Oh, no, that was *weeks* ago. Edwina and I don't even speak now." Snuggling comfortably in her corner, Beatrix gave her older sister a perplexed glance. "Win? You have the oddest look on your face. Is something the matter?"

Win had frozen in the act of lifting a teacup to her lips, her blue eyes round with alarm.

Following her sister's gaze, Amelia saw a small reptilian creature slithering up Beatrix's shoulder. A sharp cry escaped her lips, and she moved forward with her hands raised.

Beatrix glanced at her shoulder. "Oh, drat. You're supposed to stay in my pocket." She plucked the wriggling object from her shoulder and stroked him gently. "A spotted sand lizard," she said. "Isn't he adorable? I found him in my room last night."

Amelia lowered her hands and stared dumbly at her youngest sister.

"You've made a pet of him?" Win asked weakly. "Beatrix, dear, don't you think he would be happier in the forest where he belongs?"

Beatrix looked indignant. "With all those predators? Spot wouldn't last a minute."

Amelia found her voice. "He won't last a minute with me, either. Get rid of him, Bea, or I'm going to flatten him with the nearest heavy object I can find."

"You would murder my pet?"

"One doesn't murder lizards, Bea. One exterminates them." Exasperated, Amelia turned to Merripen. "Find some cleaning women in the village, Merripen. God knows how many other unwanted creatures are lurking in the house. Not counting Leo."

Merripen disappeared at once.

"Spot is the perfect pet," Beatrix argued. "He doesn't bite, and he's already house-trained."

"I draw the line at pets with scales."

Beatrix stared at her mutinously. "The sand lizard is a native species of Hampshire—which means Spot has more right to be here than we do."

"Nevertheless, we will not be cohabiting." Walking away before she said something she would regret later, Amelia wondered why, when there was so much to be done, Beatrix would be so troublesome. But a smile rose to her lips as she reflected that fifteen-year-old girls didn't choose to be troublesome. They simply were.

Lifting handfuls of her skirts to pull them away from her legs, Amelia bounded up the grand central staircase. Since they would not be receiving guests or paying calls, she had decided not to wear a corset that day. It was a wonderful feeling to breathe as deeply as she wished and move freely about the house.

Filled with determination, she pounded on Leo's door. "Wake up, slugabed!"

A string of foul words filtered through the heavy oak panels.

Grinning, Amelia went into Poppy's room. She pulled the curtains open, releasing clouds of dust that caused her to sneeze. "Poppy, it's . . . *achoo!* . . . time to get out of bed."

The covers had been drawn completely over Poppy's head. "Not yet," came her muffled protest.

Sitting on the edge of the mattress, Amelia eased the covers away from her nineteen-year-old sister. Poppy was groggy and sleep-flushed, her cheek imprinted with a line left by a fold of the bedclothes. Her brown hair, a warmer, ruddier tint than Amelia's, was a wild mass of tangles.

"I hate morning," Poppy mumbled. "And I'm sure I don't like being awakened by someone who looks so bloody pleased about it."

"I'm sorry." Continuing to smile, Amelia stroked her sister's hair away from her face repeatedly.

"Mmmn." Poppy kept her eyes closed. "Mama used to do that. Feels nice."

"Does it?" Amelia laid her hand gently over the curve of Poppy's skull. "Dear, I'm going to walk to the village to ask Freddie's mother if we can hire him as our gardener."

"Isn't he a bit young?"

"Not in comparison to the other candidates for the position."

"We have no other candidates."

"Precisely." She went to Poppy's valise in the corner,

and picked up the bonnet poised atop it. "May I borrow this? Mine still hasn't been repaired."

"Of course, but . . . you're going right now?"

"I won't be long. I'll cover the territory quickly."

"Would you like me to go with you?"

"Thank you, dear, but no. Dress yourself and have some breakfast—and keep a close watch on Win. She's in Beatrix's care at the moment."

"Oh." Poppy's eyes widened. "I'll hurry."

Chapter Five

It was a pleasantly cool, nearly cloudless day, the southern climate far milder than London. Amelia walked briskly through a fruit orchard beyond the garden. The tree branches were weighted with large green apples. Fallen fruit had been half eaten by deer and other animals, and left to ferment and spoil.

Pausing to tug an apple from a low-hanging branch, Amelia polished it on her sleeve and took a bite. The flavor was intensely acidic.

A honeybee buzzed close by, and Amelia jerked back in alarm. She had always been terrified of bees. Although she had tried to reason herself out of her fear, she couldn't seem to control the panic that overcame her whenever one of the dratted beasts was in the vicinity.

Hurrying from the orchard, Amelia followed a sunken lane that led past a wet meadow. Despite the lateness of the season, heavy beds of watercress flourished everywhere. Known as "poor man's bread," the delicate pepper-flavored leaves were eaten in bunches by local villagers, and made into everything from soup to goose stuffing. She would gather some on her way back, she decided.

The shortest route to the village crossed through a corner of Lord Westcliff's estate. As Amelia passed the invisible boundary between the Ramsay estate and Stony Cross Park, she could almost feel a change in the atmosphere. She walked on the outskirts of a rustling forest, too dense for daylight to penetrate the canopy. The land was luxurious, secretive, the ancient trees anchored deeply into dark and fertile ground. Removing her bonnet, Amelia held it by the brim and enjoyed the breeze against her face.

This had been Westcliff's land for generations. She wondered what kind of people the earl and his family were. Terribly proper and traditional, she guessed. It would not be welcome news that Ramsay House was now occupied by an ill-mannered, red-blooded lot like the Hathaways.

Finding a well-worn footpath that cut through the forest, she disrupted a pair of wheatears, who flapped away with indignant chirps. Life abounded everywhere, including butterflies of almost unnatural color and beetles as bright as sparks. Taking care to stay on the footpath, Amelia picked up her skirts to keep them from dragging through the leaf litter of the forest floor.

She emerged from a copse of hazel and oak into a broad dry field. It was empty. And ominously quiet. No voices, no cheep of finches, no drone of bees or rattle of grasshoppers. Something about it filled her with the instinctive tension that warned of an unknown threat. Cautiously she proceeded up the gentle rise of the meadow.

Reaching the brow of a stunted hill, Amelia paused in bewilderment at the sight of a towering contraption made of metal. It appeared to be a chute propped up on legs, tilted at a steep angle.

Her attention was caught by a minor commotion farther afield . . . two men emerging from behind a small wooden shelter . . . they were shouting and waving their arms at her.

Amelia instantly realized she had stumbled into danger, even before she saw the smoldering trail of sparks move, snakelike, along the ground toward the metal chute.

A *fuse*?

Although she didn't know much about explosive devices, she was aware that once a fuse had been lit, nothing could be done to stop it. Dropping to the sun-warmed grass, Amelia covered her head with her arms, having every expectation of being blown to bits. A few heartbeats passed, and she let out a startled cry as she felt a large, heavy body fall on hers . . . no, not fall, *pounce.* He covered her completely, his knees digging into the ground on either side of her as he made a shelter of his body.

At the same moment, a deafening explosion pierced the air, and there was a violent *whoosh* over their heads, and a shock went through the ground beneath them. Too stunned to move, Amelia tried to gather her wits. Her ears were filled with a high-pitched buzz.

Her companion remained motionless over her, breathing heavily in her hair. The air was sharp with smoke, but even so, Amelia was aware of a pleasant masculine scent, skin-salt and soap and an intimate spice she couldn't quite identify. The noise in her ears faded. Raising up on her elbows, feeling the solid wall of his chest against her back, she saw shirtsleeves rolled up over forearms cabled with muscle . . . and there was something else . . .

Her eyes widened at the sight of a small, stylized design inked on his arm. A tattoo of a black winged horse with eyes the color of brimstone. It was an Irish design, of a nightmare horse called a pooka: a malevolent mythical creature that spoke in a human voice and carried people away at midnight.

Her heart stopped as she saw the heavy rounded band of a thumb ring.

Wriggling beneath him, Amelia tried to turn over.

The strong hand curved around her shoulder, helping her. His voice was low and familiar. "Are you hurt? I'm sorry. You were in the way of—"

He stopped as Amelia rolled to her back. The front of her hair had come loose, pulled free of a strategically anchored pin. The lock fanned over her face, obscuring her vision. Before she could reach up to push it away, he did it for her, and the brush of his fingertips sent ripples of liquid fire along intimate pathways of her body.

"You," he said softly.

Cam Rohan.

It can't be, she thought dazedly. Here, in Hampshire? But there were the unmistakable eyes, gold and hazel and heavy lashed, the midnight hair, the wicked mouth. And the pagan glitter of a diamond at his ear.

His expression was perturbed, as if he'd been reminded of something he had wanted to forget. But as his gaze slid over her bewildered face, his mouth curved a little, and he settled into the cradle of her body with an insolent familiarity that temporarily robbed her of breath.

"Mr. Rohan . . . how . . . why . . . what are you doing here?"

He replied without moving, as if he were planning to lie

there and converse all day. His infinitely polite tone was an unsettling contrast to the intimacy of their position. "Miss Hathaway. What a pleasant surprise. As it happens, I'm visiting friends. And you?"

"I live here."

"I don't think so. This is Lord Westcliff's estate."

Her heart thundered in her breast as her body absorbed the details of him. "I didn't mean *precisely* here, I meant over there, on the other side of the woods. The Ramsay estate. We've just taken up residence." She couldn't seem to stop herself from chattering in the aftermath of nerves and fright. "What was that noise? What were you doing? Why do you have that tattoo on your arm? It's a pooka—an Irish creature—isn't it?"

That last question earned her an arrested stare. Before Rohan could reply, the other two men approached. From her prone position, Amelia had an upside-down view of them. Like Rohan, they were in their shirtsleeves, with waistcoats left unbuttoned.

One of them was a portly old gentleman with a shock of silver hair. He held a small wood-and-metal sextant, which had been strung around his neck on a lanyard. The other, black-haired man looked to be in his late thirties. He wasn't as tall as Rohan, but he had an air of authority tempered with aristocratic arrogance.

Amelia made a helpless movement, and Rohan lifted away from her with fluid ease. He helped her stand, his arm steadying her. "How far did it go?" he asked the men.

"Devil take the rocket," came a gravelly reply. "What is the woman's condition?"

"Unharmed."

The silver-haired gentleman remarked, "Impressive,

Rohan. You covered a distance of fifty yards in no more than five or six seconds."

"I would hardly miss a chance to leap on a beautiful woman," Rohan said, causing the older man to chuckle.

Rohan's hand remained at the small of Amelia's back, the light pressure causing her blood to simmer.

Easing away from his distracting touch, Amelia raised her hands to the dangling front locks of her hair, tucking them behind her ears. "Why are you shooting rockets? And more to the point, why are you shooting them at my property?"

The stranger nearby gave her a sharp, assessing glance. "*Your* property?"

Rohan interceded. "Lord Westcliff, this is Miss Amelia Hathaway. Lord Ramsay's sister."

Frowning, Westcliff executed a precise bow. "Miss Hathaway. I was not informed about your arrival. Had I been aware of your presence, I would have notified you about our rocketry experiments, as I have everyone else in the vicinity."

It was clear that Westcliff was a man who expected to be informed about everything. He looked annoyed that the new neighbors had dared to move into their own residence without telling him first.

"We arrived only yesterday, my lord," Amelia replied. "I had intended to call on you after we settled in." Under ordinary circumstances, she would have left it at that. But she was still off balance, and there was no stopping the flow of comments from her own mouth. "Well. I must say the guidebook didn't warn adequately about the occurrence of rocket fire amid the peaceful Hampshire scenery." She reached down and whacked at the dust and bits of leaf that clung to her skirts. "I'm sure you don't know the Hathaways well enough to shoot at us. Yet. When we become better acquainted, however, I have no doubt you'll find ample reason to bring out the artillery."

Over her head, she heard Rohan laugh. "Considering our issues with aim and accuracy, you have nothing to fear, Miss Hathaway."

The silver-haired gentleman spoke then. "Rohan, if you wouldn't mind finding out where that rocket landed—"

"Of course." Rohan took off at an easy lope.

"Agile fellow," the older man said approvingly. "Fast as a leopard. Not to mention steady of hands and nerves. What a sapper he'd make."

Introducing himself as Captain Swansea, formerly of the Royal Engineers, the elderly gentleman explained to Amelia that he was a rocketry enthusiast who was continuing his scientific work in a civil capacity. As a friend of Lord Westcliff, who shared his interest in engineering science, Swansea had come to experiment with a new rocket design in the country, where there was sufficient land to do so. Lord Westcliff had enlisted Cam Rohan to help with the flight equations and other mathematical calculations necessary to evaluate the performances of the rockets. "Quite extraordinary, really, his facility with numbers," Swansea said. "You'd never expect it to look at him."

Amelia couldn't help but agree. In her experience scholarly men such as her father were pale from spending much of their time indoors, and they had paunches and spectacles and rumpled, tweedy appearances. They were not exotic young men who looked like pagan princes and had gold rings and tattoos.

"Miss Hathaway," Lord Westcliff said, "to my knowledge, there hasn't been a Ramsay in residence in nearly a decade. I find it difficult to believe the house is habitable."

"Oh, it's in fine condition," Amelia lied brightly, her pride rising to the fore. "Of course, some dusting is needed—and a few minor repairs—but we are quite comfortable."

She thought she had spoken convincingly, but Westcliff looked skeptical. "We are having a large supper at Stony Cross Manor this evening," he said. "You will bring your family. It will be an excellent opportunity for you to meet some local residents, including the vicar."

A supper with Lord and Lady Westcliff. Heaven help her.

Had the Hathaway family been well-rested, had Leo been a bit further along on the path of sobriety, had they all possessed suitable formal attire, had they been given enough time to study etiquette . . . Amelia might have considered accepting the invitation. But as things were, it was impossible. "You are very kind, my lord, but I must decline. We've only just arrived in Hampshire, and most of our clothes are still packed away—"

"The occasion is informal."

Amelia doubted his definition of "informal" matched hers. "It's not merely a matter of attire, my lord. One of my sisters is somewhat frail, and it would be too taxing for her. She needs a great deal of rest after the long journey from London."

"Tomorrow night, then. It will be a much smaller affair, and not at all taxing."

In light of his insistence, there was no way to refuse. Cursing herself for not staying at Ramsay House that morning, Amelia forced a smile to her lips. "Very well, my lord. Your hospitality is much appreciated."

Rohan returned, his breath quickened from exertion. A mist of sweat had accumulated on his skin until it gleamed like bronze. "Right on course," he said to Westcliff and Swansea. "The stabilizing fins worked. It landed at a distance of approximately two thousand yards."

"Excellent!" Swansea exclaimed. "But where is the rocket?"

Rohan's white teeth flashed in a grin. "Buried in a deep, smoking hole. I'll go back to dig it up later."

"Yes, we'll want to see the condition of the casing and the inner core." Swansea was red-faced with satisfaction. He used a handkerchief to blot his steaming, wrinkled countenance. "It's been an exciting morning, eh?"

"Perhaps it's time to return to the manor, Captain," Westcliff suggested.

"Yes, quite." Swansea bowed to Amelia. "A pleasure, Miss Hathaway. And may I say, you took it rather well, being the target of a surprise attack."

"The next time I visit, Captain," she said, "I'll remember to bring my white flag."

He chuckled and bid her farewell.

Before turning to join the captain, Lord Westcliff glanced at Cam Rohan. "I'll take Swansea back to the manor, if you'll see to it that Miss Hathaway is delivered home safely."

"Of course," came the unhesitating reply.

"Thank you," Amelia said, "but there's no need. I know the way, and it isn't far."

Her protest was ignored. She was left to stare uneasily at Cam Rohan, while the other two men departed.

"I'm hardly some helpless female," she said. "I don't need to be delivered anywhere. Besides, in light of your past behavior, I'd be safer going alone."

A brief silence. Rohan tilted his head and regarded her curiously. "Past behavior?"

"You know what I—" She broke off, flushing at the memory of the kiss in the darkness. "I'm referring to what happened in London."

He gave her a look of polite perplexity. "I'm afraid I don't follow."

"You're not going to pretend you don't remember," she exclaimed. Perhaps he had kissed so many legions of women, he couldn't possibly recollect them all. "Are you also going to deny that you stole one of my bonnet ribbons?"

"You have a vivid imagination, Miss Hathaway." His tone was bland. But there was a flare of provoking laughter in his eyes.

"I have no such thing. The rest of my family is *steeped* in imagination—I'm the one who clings desperately to reality." She turned and began to walk at a brisk pace. "I'm going home. There's no need for you to accompany me."

Ignoring her statement, Rohan fell easily into step beside her, his relaxed stride accounting for every two of hers. He let her set their pace. In the openness of their surroundings, he seemed even larger than she had remembered. "When you saw my arm," he murmured, "the tattoo . . . how did you know it was a pooka?"

Amelia took her time about replying. As they walked, the shadows of nearby branches crossed their faces. A red-tailed hawk glided across the sky and disappeared into the heavy wood. "I've read some Irish folklore," she finally said. "A wicked, dangerous creature, the pooka. Invented to give people nightmares. Why would you adorn yourself with such a design?"

"It was given to me as a child. I don't remember when it was done."

"For what purpose? What significance does it have?"

"My family would never explain." Rohan shrugged. "Perhaps they might now. But it's been years since I've seen them."

"Could you ever find them again, if you wished?"

"Given enough time." Casually he fastened his waist-coat and rolled down his sleeves, concealing the heathen symbol. "I remember my grandmother telling me about the pooka. She encouraged me to believe it was real—I think she half believed it herself. She practiced the old magic."

"What is that? Do you mean fortune-telling?"

Rohan shook his head and slid his hands into the pockets of his trousers. "No," he said, looking amused, "although she did tell fortunes to *gadjos* at times. The old magic is a belief that all of nature is connected and equal. Everything is alive. Even the trees have souls."

Amelia was fascinated. It had always been impossible to coax Merripen to say anything about his past or his Romany beliefs, and here was a man who seemed willing to discuss anything. "Do you believe in the old magic?"

"No. But I like the idea of it." Rohan reached for her elbow to guide her around a rough patch of ground. Before she could object to the gentle touch, it was gone. "The pooka isn't always wicked," he said. "Sometimes it acts out of mischief. Playfulness."

She gave him a skeptical glance. "You call it playful for

a creature to toss you on its back, fly up to the sky, and drop you into a ditch or bog?"

"That's one of the stories," Rohan admitted with a grin. "But in other accounts, the pooka only wants to take you on an adventure . . . fly you to places you can only see in dreams. And then he returns you home."

"But the legends say that after the horse takes you on his midnight travels, you're never the same."

"No," he said softly. "How could you be?"

Without realizing it, Amelia had slowed their pace to a relaxed amble. It seemed impossible to walk with brisk efficiency on a day like this, with so much sun and soft air. And with this unusual man beside her, dark and dangerous and charming.

"Of all the places to see you again," she said, "I would never have expected Lord Westcliff's estate. How did you come to be acquainted? He's a member of the gaming club, I suppose."

"Yes. And friends with the owner."

"Are Lord Westcliff's other guests accepting of your presence at Stony Cross Manor?"

"You mean because I'm a Roma?" A sly smile touched his lips. "I'm afraid they have no choice but to be polite. First, out of respect for the earl. And then there's the fact that most of them are obliged to come to me for credit at the club—which means I have access to their private financial information."

"Not to mention private scandals," Amelia said, remembering the alley fight.

His smile lingered. "A few of those, too."

"Nevertheless, you must feel like an outsider at times."

"Always," he said in a matter-of-fact tone. "I'm an

outsider to my people, as well. You see, I'm a half-breed—
poshram, they call it—born of a Gypsy mother and an Irish
gadjo father. And since the family's lineage goes through
the father, I'm not even considered Roma. It's the worst vi-
olation of the code for one of our women to marry a *gadjo*."

"Is that why you don't live with your tribe?"

"One of the reasons."

Amelia wondered what it must be like for him, caught
between two cultures, belonging to neither. No hope of
ever being fully accepted. And yet there was no trace of
self-pity in his tone.

"The Hathaways are outsiders, as well," she said. "It's
obvious we're not suited to a position in polite society.
None of us have the education or breeding to carry it off.
Supper at Stony Cross Manor should be a spectacle—I'm
sure it will end with us being tossed out on our ears."

"You may be surprised. Lord and Lady Westcliff don't
usually stand on formality. And their table includes a great
variety of guests."

Amelia was not reassured. To her, upper society resembled the ornamental tanks used for exotic fish-keeping in
fashionable parlors, filled with glittering creatures who
darted and circled in patterns she had no hope of understanding. The Hathaways might as well attempt to live underwater as to belong in such elevated company. And yet
they had no choice but to try.

Spying a heavy growth of watercress on the bank of
a wet meadow, Amelia went to examine it. Grasping a
bunch, she pulled until the delicate stems snapped. "Watercress is plentiful here, isn't it? I've heard it can be made
into a fine salad or sauce."

"It's also a medicinal herb. The Rom call it *panishok*.

My grandmother used to put it in poultices for sprains or injuries. And it's a powerful love tonic. For women, especially."

"A what?" The delicate greenery fell from her nerveless fingers.

"If a man wishes to reawaken his lover's interest, he feeds her watercress. It's a stimulant of the—"

"Don't tell me! Don't!"

Rohan laughed, a mocking gleam in his eyes.

Giving him a warning glance, Amelia brushed a few stray watercress leaves from her palms and continued on her way.

Her companion followed readily. "Tell me about your family," he coaxed. "How many of you are there?"

"Five in all. Leo—that is, Lord Ramsay—is the oldest, and I am the next, followed by Winnifred, Poppy, and Beatrix."

"Which sister is the frail one?"

"Winnifred."

"Has she always been that way?"

"No, Win was quite healthy until a year ago, when she nearly died from scarlet fever." A long hesitation, while her throat tightened a little. "She survived, thank God, but her lungs are weak. She has little strength, and she tires easily. The doctor says Win may never improve, and in all likelihood she won't be able to marry or have children." Amelia's jaw hardened. "We will prove him wrong, of course. Win will be completely well again."

"God help anyone who stands in your way. You do like to manage other people's lives, don't you?"

"Only when it's obvious I can do a better job of it than they can. What are you smiling at?"

Rohan stopped, obliging her to turn to face him. "You. You make me want to—" He stopped as if thinking better of what he'd been about to say. But the trace of amusement lingered on his lips.

She didn't like the way he looked at her, the way he made her feel hot and nervous and giddy. All her senses informed her that he was a thoroughly untrustworthy man. One who abided by no one's rules but his own.

"Tell me, Miss Hathaway . . . what would you do if you were invited on a midnight ride across the earth and ocean? Would you choose the adventure, or stay safely at home?"

She couldn't seem to tear her gaze from his. The topaz eyes were lit by a glint of playfulness, not the innocent mischief of a boy, but something far more dangerous. She could almost believe he might actually change form and appear beneath her window one night, and carry her away on midnight wings . . .

"Home, of course," she managed in a sensible tone. "I don't want adventure."

"I think you do. I think in a moment of weakness, you might surprise yourself."

"I don't have moments of weakness. Not that kind, at any rate."

His laughter curled around her like a drift of smoke. "You will."

Amelia didn't dare ask why he was so certain of that. Perplexed, she lowered her gaze to the top button of his waistcoat. Was he flirting with her? No, it must be that he was mocking her, trying to make her look foolish. And if there was one thing she feared in life more than bees, it was appearing foolish.

Gathering her dignity, which had scattered like bits of dandelion fluff in a high wind, she frowned up at him. "We're nearly at Ramsay House." She indicated the outline of a roof rising from the forest. "I would prefer to go the last part of the distance alone. You may tell the earl that I was safely delivered. Good day, Mr. Rohan."

He gave a nod, took her in with one of those bright, disarming glances, and stayed to watch her progress as she walked away. With each step Amelia put between them, she should have felt safer, but the sense of disquiet remained. And then, she heard him murmur something, his voice shadowed with amusement, and it sounded as if he had said, "Some midnight . . ."

Chapter Six

The news that they were to have supper at the home of Lord and Lady Westcliff was received with a variety of reactions from the Hathaways. Poppy and Beatrix were pleased and excited, whereas Win, who was still trying to regain her strength after the journey to Hampshire, was merely resigned. Leo was looking forward to a lengthy repast accompanied by fine wine.

Merripen, on the other hand, flatly refused to go.

"You are part of the family," Amelia told him, watching as he secured loose paneling boards in one of the common rooms. Merripen's grip on a carpenter's hammer was deft and sure as he expertly sank a handmade nail into the edge of a board. "No matter how you may try to deny all connection to the Hathaways—and one could hardly blame you for that—the fact is, you're one of us and you should attend."

Merripen methodically pounded a few more nails into the wall. "My presence won't be necessary."

"Well, of course it won't be necessary. But you might enjoy yourself."

"No I wouldn't," he replied with grim certainty, and continued his hammering.

"Why must you be so stubborn? If you're afraid of being treated badly, you should recall that Lord Westcliff is already acting as host to a Roma, and he seems to have no prejudice—"

"I don't like *gadjos*."

"My entire family—*your* family—are *gadjos*. Does that mean you don't like us?"

Merripen didn't reply, only continued to work. Noisily.

Amelia let out a taut sigh. "Merripen, you're a dreadful snob. And if the evening turns out to be terrible, it's your obligation to endure it with us."

Merripen reached for another handful of nails. "That was a good try," he said. "But I'm not going."

The primitive plumbing at Ramsay House, its poor lighting, and the dinginess of the few available looking glasses made it difficult to prepare for the visit to Stony Cross Manor. After laboriously heating water in the kitchen, the Hathaways hauled buckets up and down the stairs for their own baths. Everyone except Win, of course, who was resting in her room to preserve her strength.

Amelia sat with unusual submissiveness as Poppy styled her hair, pulling it back, making thick braids and pinning them into a heavy chignon that covered the back of her head. "There," Poppy said with pleasure. "At least you're fashionable from the ears upward."

Like the other Hathaway sisters, Amelia was dressed in a serviceable bombazine gown of twilled blue silk and worsted. Its design was plain with a moderately full skirt, the sleeves long and tightly fitted.

Poppy's gown was a similar style, only in red. She was an uncommonly pretty girl, her fine features lit with vivacity and intelligence. If a girl's social popularity were based on merit rather than fortune, Poppy would have been the toast of London. Instead she was living in the country in a rattle-trap house, wearing old clothes, hauling water and coal like a maidservant. And she had never once complained.

"We'll have some new dresses made very soon," Amelia said earnestly, feeling her heart twist with remorse. "Things will improve, Poppy. I promise."

"I hope so," her sister said lightly. "I'll need a ball gown if I'm to catch a rich benefactor for the family."

"You know I only said that in jest. You don't have to look for a rich suitor. Only one who will be kind to you."

Poppy grinned. "Well, we can hope that wealth and kindness are not mutually exclusive . . . can't we?"

Amelia smiled back at her. "Indeed."

As the siblings assembled in the entrance hall, Amelia felt even more remorseful as she saw Beatrix turned out in a green dress with ankle-length skirts and a starched white pinafore, an ensemble far more appropriate for a girl of twelve instead of fifteen.

Making her way to Leo's side, Amelia muttered to him, "No more gambling, Leo. The money you lost at Jenner's would have been far better spent on proper clothes for your younger sisters."

"There is more than enough money for you to have taken them to the dressmaker," Leo said coolly. "Don't make me the villain when it's your responsibility to clothe them."

Amelia gritted her teeth. As much as she adored Leo, no one could make her as angry as he, and so quickly. She longed to administer some heavy clout on the head that might restore his wits. "At the rate you've been going through the family coffers, I didn't think it would be wise of me to go on a spending spree."

The other Hathaways watched, wide-eyed, as the conversation exploded into a full-on argument.

"You may choose to live like a miser," Leo said, "but I'll be damned if I have to. You're incapable of enjoying the moment because you're always intent on tomorrow. Well, for some people, tomorrow never comes."

Her temper flared. "*Someone* has to think of tomorrow, you selfish spendthrift!"

"Coming from an overbearing shrew—"

Win stepped between them, resting a gentle hand on Amelia's shoulder. "Hush, both of you. It serves no purpose to make yourselves cross just before we are to leave." She gave Amelia a sweet quirk of a smile that no one on earth could have resisted. "Don't frown like that, dear. What if your face stayed that way?"

"With prolonged exposure to Leo," Amelia replied, "it undoubtedly would."

Her brother snorted. "I'm a convenient scapegoat, aren't I? If you were honest with yourself, Amelia—"

"Merripen," Win called out, "is the carriage ready now?"

Merripen came through the front door, looking rumpled and surly. It had been agreed that he would drive the Hathaways to the Westcliffs' residence and return for them later. "It's ready." As he glanced at Win's pale golden beauty, it seemed his expression turned even surlier, if such a thing were possible.

Like a word puzzle that had just solved itself in her brain, that stolen glance made a few things clear to Amelia. Merripen wasn't attending the dinner that evening because he was trying to avoid being in a social situation with Win. He was trying to keep a distance between them, while at the same time he was desperately worried about her health.

It troubled Amelia, the notion that Merripen, who never displayed strong feelings about anything, might be entertaining a secret and powerful longing for her sister. Win was too delicate, too refined, too much his opposite in every way. And Merripen knew that.

Feeling sympathetic and maudlin, and rather worried herself, Amelia climbed into the carriage after her sisters.

The occupants of the vehicle were silent as they proceeded along the oak-lined drive to Stony Cross Manor. None of them had ever seen grounds so richly tended or imposing. Every leaf on every tree seemed to have been affixed with careful forethought. Surrounded by gardens and orchards that flowed into dense woods, the house sprawled over the land like a drowsing giant. Four lofty corner towers denoted the original dimensions of the European-styled fortress, but many additions had given it a pleasing asymmetry. With time and weathering, the house's honey-colored stone had mellowed gracefully, its outlines dressed with tall, perfectly trimmed hedges.

The residence was fronted by a massive courtyard—a distinctive feature—and sided by stables and a residential wing. Instead of the usual understated design of stables, these were fronted by wide stone arches. Stony Cross Manor was a place fit for royalty—and from what they knew of Lord Westcliff, his bloodlines were even more distinguished than the Queen's.

As the carriage stopped before the porticoed entrance, Amelia wished the evening were already over. In these stately surroundings, the Hathaways' faults would be magnified. They would appear no better than a group of vagabonds. She glanced over her siblings. Win had donned her usual mask of irreproachable serenity, and Leo looked calm and slightly bored—an expression he must have learned from his recent acquaintances at Jenner's. The younger girls were filled with a bright exuberance that drew a smile from Amelia. They, at least, would have a good time, and heaven knew they deserved it.

Merripen helped the sisters from the carriage, and Leo emerged last. As he stepped to the ground, Merripen checked him with a brief murmur, an admonition to keep a close watch on Win. Leo shot him a vehement glance. Enduring Amelia's criticism was bad enough—he wouldn't tolerate it from Merripen. "If you're so bloody concerned about her," Leo muttered, "then you go inside and play nanny."

Merripen's eyes narrowed, but he didn't reply.

The relationship between the two men had never been what one could describe as brotherly, but they had always maintained a cool cordiality.

Merripen had never tried to assume the role of second son, in spite of the Hathaway parents' obvious fondness for him. And in any situation which might have lent itself to a competition between the two boys, Merripen had always drawn back. Leo, for his part, had been reasonably pleasant to Merripen, and had even deferred to Merripen's opinions when he had judged them better than his own.

When Leo had fallen ill with scarlet fever, Merripen had helped care for him with a mixture of patience and kindness that had surpassed even Amelia's. Later she had told Leo that he owed Merripen his life. Instead of being grateful, however, Leo seemed to hold it against Merripen.

Please, please don't be an ass, Leo, Amelia longed to beg, but she held her tongue and went with her sisters to the brightly lit entrance of Stony Cross Manor.

A pair of massive double doors opened into a cavernous hall hung with priceless tapestries. A grand stone and marble staircase curved up to the lofty second-floor gallery. Even the most distant corners of the hall, and the entrances of several passages leading away from the great room, were lit by a massive crystal chandelier.

If the outside grounds had been well tended, the interior of the manor was nothing short of immaculate, everything swept and sparkling and polished. There was nothing of newness in their surroundings, no sharp edges or modern touches to disrupt the atmosphere of easeful splendor.

It was, Amelia thought bleakly, exactly the way Ramsay House should look.

Servants came to take hats and gloves, while an elderly housekeeper welcomed the new arrivals. Amelia's attention was immediately drawn to the sight of Lord and Lady Westcliff, who were crossing the hall toward them.

Clad in precisely tailored evening clothes, Lord Westcliff moved with the physical confidence of a seasoned sportsman. His expression was reserved, his austere features striking rather than handsome. Everything about his appearance indicated he was a man who demanded a great deal of others and even more of himself.

There was no doubt that someone as powerful as Westcliff should have chosen the perfect English bride, a woman whose icy sophistication had been instilled in her since birth. It was with surprise, then, that Amelia heard Lady Westcliff speak in a distinctly American voice, the words tumbling out as if she couldn't be bothered to think everything over before speaking.

"You can't know how often I've wished for new neighbors. Things can get a bit dull in Hampshire. You Hathaways will do nicely." She surprised Leo by reaching out and shaking hands in the way men did. "Lord Ramsay, a pleasure."

"Your servant, my lady." Leo didn't seem to know quite what to make of this singular woman.

Amelia reacted automatically as she was accorded a similar handshake. Returning the firm pressure of Lady Westcliff's hand, she stared into tip-tilted eyes the color of gingerbread.

Lillian, Lady Westcliff, was a tall, slender young woman with gleaming sable hair, fine features, and a raffish grin. Unlike her husband, she radiated a casual friendliness that instantly put one at ease. "You are Amelia, the one they fired upon yesterday?"

"Yes, my lady."

"I'm so glad the earl didn't murder you. His aim is hardly ever off, you know."

The earl received his wife's impudence with a slight smile, as if he were well accustomed to it. "I wasn't aiming at Miss Hathaway," he said calmly.

"You might consider a less dangerous hobby," Lady Westcliff suggested. "Bird-watching. Butterfly-collecting. Something a bit more dignified than setting off explosions."

Amelia expected the earl to frown at this irreverence, but he only looked amused. And as his wife's attention moved to the rest of the Hathaways, he stared at her with warm fascination. Clearly there was a powerful attraction between the two.

Amelia introduced her sisters to the unconventional countess. Thankfully they all remembered to curtsy, and they managed polite responses to her forthright questions, such as did they like to ride, did they enjoy dancing, had they tried any of the local cheeses yet, and did they share her dislike of slimy English fare such as eels and jellied hog loaf?

Laughing at the droll face the countess had made, the Hathaway sisters went with her to the receiving room, where approximately two dozen guests had gathered in anticipation of going in to supper. "I like her," she heard Poppy whisper to Beatrix as the two of them walked behind her. "Do you think all American women are so dashing?"

Dashing . . . yes, that was an appropriate word for Lady Westcliff.

"Miss Hathaway," the countess said to Amelia in a tone of friendly concern, "the earl says Ramsay House has been unoccupied for so long, it must be a shambles."

Mildly startled by the woman's directness, Amelia shook her heard firmly. "Oh no, 'shambles' is too strong a word. All the place wants is a good thorough cleaning, and a few small repairs, and . . ." She paused uncomfortably.

Lady Westcliff's gaze was frank and sympathetic. "That bad, is it?"

Amelia hitched her shoulders in a slight shrug. "There's a great deal of work to be done at Ramsay House," she admitted. "But I'm not afraid of work."

"If you need assistance or advice, Westcliff has infinite resources at his disposal. He can tell you where to find—"

"You are very kind, my lady," Amelia said hastily, "but

there is no need for your involvement in our domestic affairs." The last thing she wanted was for the Hathaways to appear to be a family of cheapjacks and beggars.

"You may not be able to avoid our involvement," Lady Westcliff said with a grin. "You're in Westcliff's sphere now, which means you'll get advice whether or not you asked for it. And the worst part is, he's almost always right." She sent a fond glance in her husband's direction. Westcliff was standing in a group at the side of the room.

Becoming aware of his wife's gaze, Westcliff's head turned. Some voiceless message was delivered between them . . . and he responded with a quick, almost indiscernible wink.

A chuckle rustled in Lady Westcliff's throat. She turned to Amelia. "We'll have been married four years, come September," she said rather sheepishly. "I had supposed I would have stopped mooning over him by now, but I haven't." Mischief danced in her dark eyes. "Now, I'll introduce you to some of the other guests. Tell me whom you wish to meet first."

Amelia's gaze had moved from the earl to the group of men around him. A ripple of awareness went down her spine as her attention was caught by Cam Rohan. He was dressed in black and white, identical to the other gentlemen's attire, but the civilized scheme only served to make him more exotic. With the dark silk of his hair curling over the starched white collar, the swarthiness of his complexion, the tiger eyes, he seemed completely out of place in these decorous surroundings. Catching sight of her, Rohan bowed, which she acknowledged with a stiff bow of her own.

"You've already met Mr. Rohan, of course," Lady

Westcliff commented, observing the exchange. "An interesting fellow, don't you think? Mr. Rohan is charming and very nice, and only half civilized, which I rather like."

"I . . ." Amelia tore her gaze from Rohan with effort, her heart thrumming erratically. "Half civilized?"

"Oh, you know all the rules the upper class has devised for so-called polite behavior. Mr. Rohan can't be bothered with most of them." Lady Westcliff grinned. "Neither can I, actually."

"How long have you known Mr. Rohan?"

"Only since Lord St. Vincent took possession of the gambling club. Since then, Mr. Rohan has become a sort of protégé, of both Westcliff's and St. Vincent's." She gave a quick laugh. "Rather like having an angel on one shoulder and a devil on the other. Rohan seems to manage them both quite well."

"Why have they taken such an interest in him?"

"He's an unusual man. I'm not certain anyone knows what to make of him. According to Westcliff, Rohan has an exceptional mind. But at the same time, he is superstitious and unpredictable. Have you heard about his good-luck curse?"

"His what?"

"It seems no matter what Rohan does, he can't help making money. A lot of money. Even when he tries to lose it. He claims it's wrong for one person to own so much."

"It's the Romany way," Amelia murmured. "They don't believe in owning things."

"Yes. Well, being from New York, I don't altogether understand the concept, but there you have it. Against his will, Mr. Rohan has been given a percentage of the profits at the club, and no matter how many charitable donations or unsound investments he makes, he keeps getting massive windfalls. First he bought an old racehorse with short legs—Little Dandy—who won the Grand National last April. Then there was the rubber debacle, and—"

"The what?"

"It was a small, failing rubber manufactory on the east side of London. Just as the company was about to go under, Mr. Rohan made a large investment in it. Everyone, including Lord Westcliff, told him not to, that he was a fool and he would lose every cent—"

"Which was his intention," Amelia said.

"Exactly. But to Rohan's dismay, the whole thing turned around. The company's director used his investment to acquire the patent rights for the vulcanization process, and they invented these little stretchy scraps of tubing called rubber bands. And now the company is a blazing success. I could tell you more, but it's all variations on the same theme—Mr. Rohan throws the money away and it comes back to him tenfold."

"I wouldn't call that a curse," Amelia said.

"Neither would I." Lady Westcliff laughed softly. "But Mr. Rohan does. That's what makes it so amusing. You should have seen him sulking earlier in the day when he received the latest report from one of his stockjobbers in London. All good news. He was gnashing his teeth over it."

Taking Amelia's arm, Lady Westcliff led her across the room. "Although we have a sad lack of eligible gentlemen tonight, I promise we'll have quite an array visiting later in the season. They all come to hunt and fish—and there's usually a high proportion of men to women."

"That is good news," Amelia replied. "I have high hopes that my sisters will find suitable gentlemen to marry."

Not missing the implication, Lady Westcliff asked, "But you have no such hopes for yourself?"

"No, I don't expect ever to marry."

"Why?"

"I have a responsibility to my family. They need me." After a brief pause, Amelia added frankly, "And the truth is, I should hate to submit to a husband's dictates."

"I used to feel the same way. But I must warn you, Miss Hathaway . . . life has a way of fouling up our plans. I speak from experience."

Amelia smiled, unconvinced. It was a simple matter of priorities. She would devote all her time and energies to creating a home for her siblings, and seeing them all healthy and happily married. There would be nieces and nephews aplenty, and Ramsay House would be filled with the people she loved.

No husband could offer her more.

Catching sight of her brother, Amelia noticed there was a peculiar expression on his face, or rather a lack of expression that indicated he was concealing some strong or private emotion. He came to her at once, exchanged a few pleasantries with Lady Westcliff, and nodded politely as she asked leave to attend to an elderly guest who had just arrived.

"What is it?" Amelia whispered, looking up as Leo cupped her elbow in his hand. "You look as though you'd just gotten a mouthful of rotten cork."

"Don't let's trade insults just now." He gave her a glance that was more concerned than any he'd given her in recent memory. His tone was low and urgent. "Bear up, sis—there's someone here you don't want to see. And he's coming this way."

She rolled her eyes. "If you mean Mr. Rohan, I assure you, I'm perfectly—"

"No. Not Rohan." His hand went to her waist as if anticipating the need to steady her.

And she understood.

Before she even turned to see the man who approached them, Amelia knew the reason for Leo's strange reaction, and she went cold and hot and unsteady. But somewhere in the internal havoc, a certain resignation lurked.

She had always known she would see Christopher Frost again someday.

He was alone as he approached them—a small mercy, as one would have expected him to have his new wife in tow. And Amelia was fairly certain she couldn't have tolerated being introduced to the woman Christopher had abandoned her for. As it was, she stood stiffly with her brother and tried desperately to resemble an independent woman who was greeting her former love with polite indifference. But she knew there was no disguising the whiteness of her face—she could feel the blood shooting straight to her overstimulated heart.

If life were fair, Frost would have appeared smaller, less handsome, less desirable than she had remembered. But life, as usual, wasn't fair. He was as lean and graceful and urbane as ever, with alert blue eyes and thick, close-trimmed hair, too dark to be blond, too light to be brown. That shining hair contained every shade from champagne to fawn.

"My old acquaintance," Leo said. Although his tone held no rancor, neither did it evince any pleasure. Their friendship had been shattered the moment Frost had left Amelia. Leo had his faults, certainly, but he was nothing if not loyal.

"My lord," Frost said quietly, bowing to them both. "And Miss Hathaway." It seemed to cost him something to meet her gaze. Heaven knew it cost her to return it. "It has been far too long."

"Not for some of us," Leo returned, not flinching as Amelia surreptitiously stepped on his foot. "Are you staying at the manor?"

"No, I'm visiting some old family friends—they own the village tavern."

"How long will you hang about?"

"I have no firm plans. I'm mulling over a few commissions while enjoying the calm and quiet of the countryside." His gaze strayed briefly to Amelia and returned to Leo. "I sent a letter when I learned of your ascendancy to the peerage, my lord."

"I received it," Leo said idly. "Although for the life of me, I can't remember its contents."

"Something to the effect that while I was pleased for your sake, I was disappointed to have lost a worthy rival. You always drove me to reach beyond the limits of my abilities."

"Yes," Leo said sardonically, "I was a great loss to the architectural firmament."

"You were," Frost agreed without irony. His gaze remained on Amelia. "May I remark on how well you look, Miss Hathaway?"

How odd it was, she thought dazedly, that she had once been in love with him, and now they were speaking to each other so formally. She no longer loved him, and yet the memory of being held by him, kissed, caressed . . . it tinted every thought and emotion, like tea-dyed lace. One could never fully remove the stain. She remembered a bouquet of roses he had once given her . . . he had taken one and stroked the petals over her cheeks and parted lips, and had smiled at her fierce blush. *My little love,* he had whispered—

"Thank you," she said. "In turn, may I offer my congratulations on your marriage?"

"I'm afraid no felicitations are in order," Frost replied carefully. "The wedding didn't take place."

Amelia felt Leo's hand tighten at her waist. She leaned against him imperceptibly and looked away from Christopher Frost, unable to speak. *He isn't married.* Her thoughts were in anarchy.

"Did she come to her senses," she heard Leo ask casually, "or did you?"

"It became obvious we didn't suit as well as one would have hoped. She was gracious enough to release me from the obligation."

"So you got the boot," Leo said. "Are you still working for her father?"

"Leo," Amelia protested in a half-whisper. She looked up in time to see Frost's wry, brief grin, and her heart twisted at the painful familiarity of it.

"You were never one to mince words, were you? Yes, I'm still employed by Temple." Frost's gaze moved slowly over Amelia, taking measure of her brittle guardedness. "A pleasure to see you again, Miss Hathaway."

She sagged a little as he left them, turning blindly toward her brother. Her voice was tattered at the edges. "Leo, I would *very* much appreciate it if you could cultivate just a little delicacy of manner."

"We can't all be as suave as your Mr. Frost."

"He's not my Mr. Frost." A pause, and she added dully, "He never was."

"You deserve a hell of a lot better. Just remember that if he comes sniffing around your heels again."

"He won't," Amelia said, hating the way her heart leaped behind her well-manufactured defenses.

Chapter Seven

Just before the Hathaways had arrived, Captain Swansea, who had spent four years serving in India, had been regaling some of the guests with an account of a tiger hunt in Vishnupur. The tiger had stalked the spotted deer, brought it down with a pounce, and clamped the back of its neck in its jaws. Women and even a few men had grimaced and exclaimed in horror as Swansea described how the tiger had proceeded to eat the chital while it was still alive. "The vicious beast!" one of the women had gasped.

But as soon as Amelia Hathaway entered the room, Cam had found himself entirely in sympathy with the tiger. There was nothing he wanted more than to bite the tender back of her neck and drag her to some private place where he could feast on her for hours. In a crowd of elaborately dressed women, Amelia stood out in her simple gown and unadorned throat and ears. She looked clean and winsome and appetizing. He wanted to be alone with her, outside in the open air, his hands free upon her body. But he knew better than to entertain such thoughts about a respectable young woman.

He watched the tense little scene involving Amelia, her

brother, Lord Ramsay, and the architect, Mr. Christopher Frost. Although he couldn't hear their conversation, he read their postures, the subtle way Amelia leaned into her brother's support. It was clear some kind of history was shared between Amelia and Frost . . . not a happy one. A love affair that had ended badly, he guessed. He imagined them together, Amelia and Frost. It provoked him far more than he would have liked. Tamping down the surge of inappropriate curiosity, he dragged his attention away from them.

As he anticipated the long, bland supper to come, the interminable courses, the mannered conversation, Cam sighed heavily. He had learned the social choreography of these situations, the rigid boundaries of propriety. At first he had even regarded it as a game, learning the ways of these privileged strangers. But he had grown tired of hovering at the edge of the *gadjo* world. Most of them didn't want him there any more than he did. But there seemed no other place for him except at the periphery.

It had all started approximately two years earlier, when St. Vincent had thrown a bank passbook at him in the casual manner he might have used to toss a rounders ball.

"I've established an account for you at the London Banking House and Investment Society," St. Vincent had told him. "It's on Fleet Street. Your percentage of Jenner's profits will be deposited monthly. Manage them if you wish, or they'll be managed for you."

"I don't want a percentage of the profits," Cam had said, thumbing through the passbook without interest. "My salary is fine."

"Your salary wouldn't cover the annual cost of my bootblacking."

"It's more than enough. And I wouldn't know what to do with this." Cam had been appalled by the figures listed on the balance page. Scowling, he tossed the book to a nearby table. "Take it back."

St. Vincent had looked amused and vaguely exasperated. "Damnation, man, now that I own the place, I can't have it said that you're paid pauper's wages. Do you think I'll tolerate being called a skinflint?"

"You've been called worse," Cam had pointed out.

"I don't mind being called worse when I deserve it. Which is often, I'm sure." St. Vincent had stared at him in a considering way. And, with one of those damnable flashes of intuition you would never expect from the former profligate, he murmured, "It means nothing, you know. It doesn't make you any less of a Roma whether I pay you in pounds, whales' teeth, or wampum."

"I've compromised too much already. Since I first came to London, I've stayed under one roof, I've worn *gadjo* clothes, I've worked for a salary. But I draw the line at this."

"I've just given you an investment account, Rohan," St. Vincent had said acidly, "not a pile of manure."

"I would have preferred the manure. At least it would be good for something."

"I'm afraid to ask. But curiosity compels me . . . what in God's name is manure good for?"

"Fertilizer."

"Ah. Well, then, let's approach it this way: money is just another variety of fertilizer." St. Vincent had gestured to the discarded bank passbook. "Do something with it. Whatever pleases you. Although I would advise something other than composting it in sod."

Cam had resolved to get rid of every cent, by scattering

it in a series of lunatic investments. That was when the good-luck curse had befallen him. His growing fortune had begun to open doors that should never have been open to him, especially now that upper society was being raided by men of industry. And, having walked through those doors, Cam was behaving in ways, thinking in ways, that weren't usual for him. St. Vincent had been wrong—the money did make him less of a Roma.

He had forgotten things; words, stories, the songs that had lulled him to sleep as a child. He could barely remember the taste of dumplings flavored with almonds and boiled in milk, or boranija stew spiced with vinegar and dandelion leaves. The faces of his family were a distant blur. He wasn't certain he would know them if he met them now. And that made him fear he was no longer Roma.

When was the last time he had slept out under the sky?

The company proceeded as a whole into the dining hall. The informal nature of the gathering meant they would not have to be arranged in order of precedence. A line of footmen clad in black, blue, and mustard moved forward to attend the guests, pulling out chairs, pouring wine and water. The long table was covered by an acre of pristine white linen. Each place setting, bristling with silverware, was surmounted with a hierarchy of crystal glasses in assorted sizes.

Cam wiped all expression from his face as he discovered he had been seated next to the vicar's wife, whom he had met on previous visits to Stony Cross Park. The woman was terrified of him. Whenever he looked at her, tried to talk to her, she cleared her throat incessantly. Her sputtery noises brought to mind a tea kettle with an ill-fitting lid.

No doubt the vicar's wife had heard one too many stories of Gypsies stealing children, placing curses on people, and attacking helpless females in a frenzy of uncontrolled lust. Cam was tempted to inform the woman that, as a rule, he never kidnapped or pillaged before the second course. But he kept silent and tried to look as unthreatening as possible, while she shrank in her chair and made desperate conversation with the man at her left.

Turning to his right, Cam found himself staring into Amelia Hathaway's blue eyes. They had been seated next to each other. Pleasure unfolded inside him. Her hair shone like satin, and her eyes were bright, and her skin looked like it would taste of some dessert made with milk and sugar. The sight of her reminded him of an old-fashioned *gadjo* word that had amused him when he had first heard it. Toothsome. The word was used for something appetizing, conveying the pleasure of taste, but also sexual allure. He found Amelia's naturalness a thousand times more appealing than the powdered and bejeweled sophistication of other women present.

"If you're trying to look meek and civilized," Amelia said, "it's not working."

"I assure you, I'm harmless."

Amelia smiled at that. "No doubt it would suit you for everyone to think so."

He relished her light, clean scent, the charming pitch of her voice. He wanted to touch the fine skin of her cheeks and throat. Instead he held still and watched as she adjusted a linen napkin over her lap.

A footman came to fill their wine glasses. Cam noticed that Amelia kept stealing glances at her siblings like a mother hen with chicks gone astray. Even her brother, seated only two places away from the head of the table, was subjected to the same relentless concern. She stiffened as she caught sight of Christopher Frost, who was seated near the far end of the table. Their gazes locked, while the ripple of a swallow chased down Amelia's throat. She seemed mesmerized by the *gadjo*. It was obvious an attraction still existed between the two. And judging from Frost's expression, he was more than willing to rekindle their acquaintance.

It required a great deal of Cam's willpower—and he had a considerable supply—not to skewer Christopher Frost with a dining utensil. He wanted her attention. All of it.

"At the first formal supper I attended in London," he told Amelia, "I expected to come away hungry."

To his immediate satisfaction, Amelia turned to him, her interest refocusing. "Why?"

"Because I thought the little side plates were what the *gadjos* used for their main course. Which meant I wasn't going to get much to eat."

Amelia laughed. "You must have been relieved when the large plates were brought out."

He shook his head. "I was too busy learning the rules of the table."

"Such as?"

"Sit where they tell you, don't speak of politics or bodily functions, drink soup from the side of the spoon, don't use the nut pick as a fork, and never offer someone food from your plate."

"The Rom share food from each other's plates?"

He stared at her steadily. "If we were eating Gypsy-style,

sitting before a fire, I would offer you the choicest bites of meat. The soft inside of the bread. The sweetest sections of fruit."

The color heightened in her cheeks, and she reached for her wine glass. After a careful sip, she said without looking at him, "Merripen rarely talks about such things. I believe I've learned more from you than I have after twelve years of knowing him."

Merripen . . . the taciturn *chal* who had accompanied her in London. There had been no mistaking the easy familiarity between the two, betraying that Merripen was more than a mere servant to her.

Before Cam could pursue the matter, however, the soup course was brought out. Footmen and underbutlers worked in harmony to present huge steaming tureens of salmon soup with lime and dill, nettle soup with cheese and caraway floats, watercress soup garnished with slivers of pheasant, and mushroom soup laced with sour cream and brandy.

After Cam chose the nettle soup and it was ladled into a shallow china bowl in front of him, he turned to speak to Amelia again. To his disgruntlement, she was now being monopolized by the man on her other side, who was enthusiastically describing his collection of Far East porcelain.

Cam took a quick inventory of the other conversations around him, all featuring mundane subjects. He waited patiently until the vicar's wife had bent her attention to the soup bowl in front of her. As she raised a spoon to her papery lips, she became aware that Cam was looking at her. Another throat-clearing noise, while the spoon quivered in her hand.

He tried to think of something that would interest her. "Horehound," he said to her in a matter-of-fact manner.

Her eyes bulged with alarm, and a pulse throbbed visibly in her neck. "H-h-h . . ." she whispered.

"Horehound, licorice root, and honey. It's good for getting rid of phlegm in the throat. My grandmother was a healer—she taught me many of her remedies."

The word "phlegm" nearly caused her eyes to roll back in her head.

"Horehound is also good for coughs and snake bites," Cam continued helpfully.

Her face drained of color, and she set her spoon on her plate. Turning away from him desperately, she gave her attention to the diners on her left.

His attempt at polite discussion having been rebuffed, Cam sat back as the soup was removed and the second course was brought out. Sweetbreads in béchamel sauce, partridges nestled in herb beds, pigeon pies, roast snipe, and vegetable soufflé laced the air with a cacophony of rich scents. The guests exclaimed appreciatively, watching in anticipation as their plates were filled.

But Amelia Hathaway barely seemed aware of the sumptuous dishes. Her attention was focused on a conversation at the end of the table, between Lord Westcliff and her brother Leo. Her face was calm, but her fingers clenched around a fork handle.

". . . obvious you possess a large acreage of good land that has gone unused . . ." Westcliff was saying, while Leo listened without apparent interest. "I will make my own estate agent available to you, to apprise you of the standard terms of tenancy here in Hampshire. Usually these arrangements are unwritten, which means it is an obligation of honor on both sides to uphold the agreements—"

"Thank you," Leo said after downing half his wine in

an expedient gulp, "but I'll deal with my tenants in my own time, my lord."

"I'm afraid time has run out for some of them," Westcliff replied. "Many of the tenant houses on your land have run to ruins. The people who now depend on you have been neglected for far too long."

"Then it's time they learn my one great consistency is neglecting the people who depend on me." Leo flicked a laughing glance at Amelia, his eyes hard. "Isn't that right, sis?"

With visible effort, Amelia forced her fingers to unclench from the fork. "I'm certain Lord Ramsay will lend his close attention to the needs of his tenants," she said carefully. "Pray don't be misled by his attempt to be amusing. In fact, he has mentioned future plans to improve the tenant leaseholds and study modern agricultural methods—"

"If I study anything," Leo drawled, "it will be the bottom of a good bottle of port. The Ramsay tenants have proven their ability to thrive on benign neglect—they clearly don't need my involvement."

A few guests tensed apprehensively at Leo's insouciant speech, while others gave a few forced chuckles. Tension thickened the air.

If Leo was deliberately trying to make an enemy of Westcliff, he couldn't have chosen a better way of doing it. Westcliff had a deep concern for those less fortunate than himself, and an active dislike for self-indulgent noblemen who failed to live up to their responsibilities.

"Drat," Cam heard Lillian mutter beneath her breath, as her husband's brows lowered over cold dark eyes.

But just as Westcliff parted his lips to deliver a withering speech to the insolent young viscount, one of the female guests gave an earsplitting shriek. Two other ladies jumped up from their chairs, along with several of the gentlemen, all of them staring in white-eyed horror at the center of the table.

All conversation had stopped. Following the guests' collective gazes, Cam saw something—a lizard?—wriggling and slithering its way past sauceboats and salt cellars. Without hesitation he reached out and captured the small creature, cupping it in closed hands. The lizard squirmed furiously in the space between his closed palms.

"I've got it," he said mildly.

The vicar's wife half fainted, slumping back in her chair with a low moan.

"Don't hurt him!" Beatrix Hathaway called out anxiously. "He's a family pet!"

The assembled guests glanced from Cam's closed hands to the Hathaway girl's apologetic face.

"A pet? . . . What a relief," Lady Westcliff said calmly, staring down the length of the table at her husband's blank countenance. "I thought it was some new English delicacy we were serving."

A swift wash of color darkened Westcliff's face, and he looked away from her with fierce concentration. To anyone who knew him well, it was obvious he was struggling not to laugh.

"You brought Spot to supper?" Amelia asked her youngest sister in disbelief. "Bea, I told you to get rid of him yesterday!"

"I tried to," came Beatrix's contrite reply, "but after I left him in the woods, he followed me home."

"Bea," Amelia said sternly, "reptiles do not follow people home."

"Spot is no ordinary lizard. He—"

"We'll discuss it outside." Amelia rose from her chair, obliging the gentlemen to hoist themselves out of their seats. She threw Westcliff an apologetic glance. "I beg your pardon, my lord. If you will excuse us . . ."

The earl gave a composed nod.

Another man . . . Christopher Frost . . . stared at Amelia with an intensity that raised Cam's hackles. "May I help?" Frost asked. His voice was carefully devoid of urgency, but there was no doubt in Cam's mind about how much the man wanted to go outside with her.

"No need," Cam said smoothly. "As you can see, I have everything in hand. At your service, Miss Hathaway." And, still holding the squirming reptile, he accompanied the sisters from the room.

Chapter Eight

Cam led them away from the dining hall, through a pair of French doors that opened to a conservatory. The outdoor room was sparsely furnished with cane-back chairs and a settee. White columns around the edge of the conservatory were interspersed with lush hanging plants. Clouds sulked across the humid sky, while torchlight sent a brisk dance of light across the ground.

As soon as the doors were closed, Amelia went to her sister with her hands raised. At first Cam thought she intended to shake her, but instead Amelia pulled Beatrix close, her shoulders trembling. She could barely breathe for laughing.

"Bea . . . you did it on purpose, didn't you? . . . I couldn't believe my eyes . . . that blasted lizard running along the table . . ."

"I had to do something," the girl explained in a muffled voice. "Leo was behaving badly—I didn't understand what he was saying, but I saw Lord Westcliff's face—"

"Oh . . . oh . . ." Amelia choked with giggles. "Poor Westcliff . . . one moment he's def-fending the local population from Leo's tyranny, and then Spot comes s-slithering past the bread plates . . ."

"Where is Spot?" Twisting away from her sister, Beatrix approached Cam, who deposited the lizard in her outstretched palms. "Thank you, Mr. Rohan. You have very quick hands."

"So I've been told." He smiled at her. "The lizard is a lucky animal. Some people say it promotes prophetic dreaming."

"Really?" Beatrix stared at him in fascination. "Come to think of it, I *have* been dreaming more often lately—"

"My sister needs no encouragement in that regard," Amelia said. She gave Beatrix a meaningful look. "It's time to say farewell to Spot, dear."

"Yes, I know." Beatrix heaved a sigh and peered inside the loose cage of her fingers at her erstwhile pet. "I'll let him go now. I think Spot would rather live here than at the Ramsay estate."

"Who wouldn't? Go find a nice place for him, Bea. I'll wait for you here."

As her sister scampered off, Amelia turned and gazed at the dim verge of the house, its outline melding into an ironstone wall set along the bluff overlooking the river.

"What are you doing?" Cam asked, approaching her.

"I'm taking a good last look at Stony Cross Manor, since this is the last time I'll ever see it."

He grinned. "I doubt that. The Westcliffs have welcomed back guests who have done far worse."

"Worse than setting wild creatures loose at the supper table? Dear heaven, they must be desperate for company."

"They have a great tolerance for eccentricity." He paused before adding, "What they don't take well, I'm afraid, is callousness."

The reference to her brother caused a delicate play of emotions on her face, humor fading to chagrin. "Leo was never callous before." She wrapped her arms tightly across her chest, as if she wanted to tie herself into a self-protective bundle. "It's only been in the past year that he's become so intolerable. He's not himself."

"Because he inherited the title?"

"No, that has nothing to do with it. It's because—" Looking away from him, she swallowed hard. He heard a nervous tapping from a foot half concealed beneath her skirts. "Leo lost someone," she finally said. "The fever struck many people in the village, including a girl he . . . well, he was betrothed to her. Laura." The name seemed to stick in her throat. "She was my best friend, and Win's, too. A beautiful girl. She liked to draw and paint. She had a laugh that would make you laugh, too, just to hear it."

Amelia was silent for a moment, lost in her memories. "Laura was one of the first to fall ill," she said. "Leo stayed with her every possible moment. No one expected her to die . . . but it happened so quickly. After three days she was so feverish and weak you could barely feel her pulse. Finally she lost consciousness and died a few hours later in Leo's arms. He came home and collapsed, and we realized he had caught the fever. And then Win had it, too."

"But the rest of you didn't?"

Amelia shook her head. "I had already sent Beatrix and Poppy away. And for some reason, neither I nor Merripen were susceptible. He helped me nurse them both through it. Without his help, they would both have died. Merripen made a syrup with some kind of toxic plant—"

"Deadly nightshade," Cam said. "Not easy to find."

"Yes." She gave him a curious glance. "How did you

know? You learned it from your grandmother, I suppose."

He nodded. "The trick is to administer enough to counteract the poison in the blood, but not enough to kill the patient."

"Well, both of them came through it, thank God. But Win is quite fragile, as you can probably see, and Leo . . . now he cares for nothing and no one. Not even himself." Her foot resumed its nervous tapping. "I don't know how to help him. I understand how it feels to lose someone, but . . ." She shook her head helplessly.

"You're referring to Mr. Frost," he said.

Amelia gave him a sharp glance and flushed deeply. "How did you know? Did he say something? Was there gossip, or—"

"No, nothing like that. I saw it when you talked to him earlier."

Shaking her head, Amelia raised her hand to her heat-infused cheeks. "Dear heaven. Am I that easy to read?"

"Perhaps I'm one of the *Phuri Dae,*" he said, smiling at her. "A mystical Gypsy. Were you in love with him?"

"That's none of your concern," she said, a bit too quickly.

He watched her closely. "Why did he leave you?"

"How did you—" She broke off and scowled as she understood what he was doing, throwing out provocative questions and gleaning the truth from her reactions. "Bother. All right, I'll tell you. He left me for another woman. A prettier, younger woman who happened to be his employer's daughter. It would have been a very advantageous marriage for him."

"You're wrong."

Amelia gave him a perplexed glance. "I assure you, it would have been an *enormously* advantageous—"

"She couldn't possibly have been prettier than you."

Her eyes widened at the compliment. "Oh," she whispered.

Approaching her, Cam touched her vibrating foot with his own. The tapping stopped.

"A bad habit," Amelia said abashedly. "I can't seem to rid myself of it."

"A hummingbird will do that in spring. She hangs on the side of the nest and uses her other foot to tamp down the floor."

Her gaze chased around as if she couldn't decide where to look.

"Miss Hathaway." Cam spoke gently, while she fidgeted before him. He wanted to take her in his arms and hold her until she quieted. "Do I make you nervous?"

She brought herself to look up at him, her eyes harboring the blue-black glitter of a moonlit lake. "No," she said immediately. "No, of course you . . . *yes.* Yes, you do."

The vehement honesty of her answer surprised both of them. The night deepened—one of the torches had burned out—and the conversation devolved into something halting and broken and delicious, like pieces of barley sugar melting on the tongue.

"I would never hurt you," Cam said in a low voice.

"I know. It's not that—"

"It's because I kissed you, isn't it?"

"You . . . you said you didn't remember."

"I remember."

"Why did you do it?" she asked in a half-whisper.

"Impulse. Opportunity." Aroused by her nearness, Cam tried to ignore the coursing readiness of his own body. "Surely you would have expected no less of a Roma. We take what we want. If a Roma desires a woman, he steals her for himself. Sometimes right out of her bed." Even in the darkness he could see the rich renewal of her blush.

"You just said you would never hurt me."

"If I carried you away with me . . ." The idea of it, her soft, struggling weight in his arms, sent his blood surging. He was caught by the primitive appeal of it, all reason crushed beneath the thumping heat of desire. "The last thing on my mind would be hurting you."

"You would never do such a thing." She was trying very hard to sound matter-of-fact. "We both know you're too civilized."

"Do we? Believe me, the issue of my civility is entirely open to question."

"Mr. Rohan," she asked unsteadily, "are you *trying* to make me nervous?"

"No." As if the word required emphasis, he repeated softly, "No."

Hell and damnation, he thought, wondering what he was doing. He was at a loss to comprehend why this woman, in her intelligent prickly innocence, should have captivated him so thoroughly. All he knew was a fierce longing to reach something in her, to strip away all the artificial trappings of stays and laces and shoes, the curtain of her gown, the little hooks of her hairpins.

Amelia took a deep breath. "What you didn't mention, Mr. Rohan, was that if a Roma steals a woman from her bed according to tradition, it is with the purpose of marriage in mind. And the so-called stealing is prearranged and encouraged by the bride-to-be."

Cam gave her a charming smile, deliberately dispelling the tension. "It lacks subtlety, but it hastens the proceedings considerably, doesn't it? No asking for the father's permission, no banns, no prolonged betrothal. Very efficient, a Romany courtship."

Their conversation was checked by the reappearance of Beatrix. "Spot's gone," she reported. "He seemed quite happy to take up residence at Stony Cross Park."

Seeming relieved by her sister's return, Amelia went to her, brushed at the crumbs of soil on her sleeve, and straightened her hair bow. "Good luck to Spot. Are you ready to go back in to supper, dear?"

"No."

"Oh, everything will be fine. Just remember to look chastened while I grimace in an authoritative manner, and I'm certain they'll allow us to stay through dessert."

"I don't want to go back," Beatrix moaned. "It's so dreadfully dull, and I don't like all that rich food, and I've been sitting beside the vicar who only wants to talk about his own religious writings. It's so redundant to quote oneself, don't you think?"

"It does bear a certain odor of immodesty," Amelia agreed with a grin, smoothing her sister's dark hair. "Poor Bea. You don't have to go back, if you don't wish it. I'm sure one of the servants can recommend a nice place for you to wait until supper is done. The library, perhaps."

"Oh, thank you." Beatrix heaved a sigh of relief. "But who will create another distraction if Leo starts being disagreeable again?"

"I will," Cam assured her gravely. "I can be shocking at a moment's notice."

"I'm not surprised," Amelia said. "In fact, I'm fairly certain you would enjoy it."

Chapter Nine

The company at Westcliff's table had been relieved by the news that Beatrix had elected to spend the rest of the evening alone in quiet contemplation. No doubt they feared another interruption by yet some other pocket-sized pet, but Amelia had assured them there would be no more unexpected visitors at the table.

Only Lady Westcliff had seemed genuinely perturbed by Beatrix's absence. The countess excused herself sometime between the fourth and fifth courses and reappeared after a quarter hour. Amelia later learned that Lady Westcliff had sent for a supper tray to be brought to Beatrix in the library, and had visited her there.

"Lady Westcliff told me a few stories of when she was a girl, and how she and her younger sister used to misbehave," Beatrix recounted the next day. "She said bringing a lizard to supper was nothing compared to the things they had done—in fact, she said they were both diabolical and rotten to the core. Isn't that wonderful?"

"Wonderful," Amelia said sincerely, reflecting on how much she liked the American woman, who seemed relaxed and fun-loving. Westcliff was another matter. The earl was more than a little intimidating. And after Leo's callous dismissal of Westcliff's concerns over the Ramsay tenants, it was doubtful the earl would be kindly disposed toward the Hathaways.

Thankfully Leo had managed to steer clear of further controversies during supper, mostly because he had been drawn into flirtation with the attractive woman beside him. Although women had always been beguiled by Leo, with his height and good looks and intelligence, he had never been as ardently pursued as he was now.

"I think it says something odd about women's tastes," Win told Amelia privately as they stood in the Ramsay House kitchen, "that Leo wasn't chased by nearly as many women when he was nice. It seems the more odious he is, the more they like him."

"They're welcome to have him," Amelia replied grumpily. "I fail to see the appeal of a man who goes through each day looking as if he's either just gotten out of bed or is preparing to get back in it." She wrapped her hair in a protective cloth and tucked the ends under turban-style.

They were preparing for another day of cleaning, and the ancient house dust had a tendency to cling obstinately to the skin and hair. Unfortunately the hired help was not wont to arrive in a timely manner, if at all. Since Leo was still abed after a night of heavy drinking, and probably wouldn't arise until noon, Amelia was feeling particularly cross with him. It was Leo's house and estate—the least he could do was help restore it. Or hire proper servants.

"His eyes have changed," Win murmured. "Not merely the expression. The actual color. Have you noticed?"

Amelia went still. She took a long time to reply. "I thought it was my imagination."

"No. They were always dark blue like yours. Now they're mostly light gray. Like a pond after the sky has turned in winter."

"I'm certain the color of some people's eyes change as they mature."

"You know it's because of Laura."

A dark heaviness pressed against Amelia from all sides as she thought about the friend she had lost and the brother she seemed to have lost along with her. But she couldn't dwell on any of that now, there was too much to be done.

"I don't think such a thing is possible. I've never heard of—" She broke off as she saw Win wrapping her long braids in a cloth identical to hers. "What are you doing?"

"I'm going to help today," Win said. Although her tone was placid, her delicate jaw was set like a mule's. "I'm feeling *quite* well and—"

"Oh, no you're not! You'll work yourself into a collapse, and then you'll take days to recover. Find some place to sit, while the rest of us—"

"I'm tired of sitting. I'm tired of watching everyone else work. I can set my own limits, Amelia. Let me do as I wish."

"No." Incredulously Amelia watched as Win picked up a broom from the corner. "Win, put that down and stop being silly!" Annoyance whipped through her. "You're not going to help anyone by expending all your reserves on menial tasks."

"I can do it." Win gripped the broom handle with both hands as if she sensed Amelia was on the verge of wrenching it away from her. "I won't overtax myself."

"Put down the broom."

"Leave me alone," Win cried. "Go dust something!"

"Win, if you don't—" Amelia's attention was diverted as she saw her sister's gaze fly to the kitchen threshold.

Merripen stood there, his broad shoulders filling the doorway. Although it was early morning, he was already dusty and perspiring, his shirt clinging to the powerful contours of his chest and waist. He wore an expression they knew well—the implacable one that meant you could move a mountain with a teaspoon sooner than change his mind about something. Approaching Win, he extended a broad hand in a wordless demand.

They were both motionless. But even in their stubborn opposition, Amelia saw a singular connection, as if they were locked in an eternal stalemate from which neither wanted to break free.

Win gave in with a helpless scowl. "I have nothing to do." It was rare for her to sound so peevish. "I'm sick of sitting and reading and staring out the window. I want to be useful. I want . . ." Her voice trailed away as she saw Merripen's stern face. "Fine, then. Take it!" She tossed the broom at him, and he caught it reflexively. "I'll just find a corner somewhere and quietly go mad. I'll—"

"Come with me," Merripen interrupted calmly. Setting the broom aside, he left the room.

Win exchanged a perplexed glance with Amelia, her vehemence fading. "What is he doing?"

"I have no idea."

The sisters followed him down a hallway to the dining room, which was spattered with rectangles of light from the tall multipaned windows that lined one wall. A scarred table ran down the center of the room, every available inch covered with dusty piles of china . . . towers of cups and saucers, plates of assorted sizes sandwiched together, bowls wrapped in tattered scraps of gray linen. There were at least three different patterns all jumbled together.

"It needs to be sorted," Merripen said, gently nudging Win toward the table. "Many pieces are chipped. They must be separated from the rest."

It was the perfect task for Win, enough to keep her busy but not so strenuous that it would exhaust her. Filled with gratitude, Amelia watched as her sister picked up a teacup and held it upside down. The husk of a tiny dead spider dropped to the floor.

"What a mess," Win said, beaming. "I'll have to wash it, too, I suppose."

"If you'd like Poppy to help—" Amelia began.

"Don't you dare send for Poppy," Win said. "This is my project, and I won't share it." Sitting at a chair that had been placed beside the table, she began to unwrap pieces of china.

Merripen looked down at Win's turbaned head, his fingers twitching as if he were sorely tempted to touch a blond tendril that had slipped from beneath the cloth. His face was hard with the patience of a man who knew he would never have what he truly wanted. Using a single fingertip, he pushed a saucer away from the edge of the table. The china rattled subtly across the battered wood.

Amelia followed Merripen back to the kitchen. "Thank you," she said when they were out of her sister's hearing. "In my worry over making certain Win didn't tire herself, it hadn't occurred to me that she might go mad from boredom."

Merripen picked up a heavy, clattering box of discarded odds and ends, and hoisted it to his shoulder with ease. A smile crossed his face. "She's getting better." He strode to the door and shouldered his way outside.

It was hardly an informed medical opinion, but Amelia was certain he was right. Looking about the dilapidated kitchen, she felt a surge of happiness. It had been the right thing to come here. A new place offering new possibilities. Perhaps the Hathaways' bad luck had finally changed.

Armed with a broom, mop, dustpan, and a stack of rags, Amelia went upstairs to one of the rooms that hadn't yet been explored. She used her full weight to open the first door, which gave way with a cracking sound and a shriek of unoiled hinges. It appeared to be a private receiving room, with built-in wood bookcases.

There were two volumes on one shelf. Examining the dust-coated books, their aged leather covers shot with spidery cracks, Amelia read the first title: *Fine Angling, A Symposium on the Fisherman's Art With Much on Roach and Pike.* No wonder the book had been abandoned by its previous owner, she thought. The second title was far more promising: *Amorous Exploits of the Court of England in the Reign of King Charles the Second.* Hopefully it would contain some ribald revelations she and Win could giggle over later.

Replacing the books, Amelia went to open the shrouded windows. The draperies' original color had faded to gray, their velvet nap ragged and moth-eaten.

As Amelia labored to pull one fabric panel to the side, the entire brass rod came loose from the ceiling and clattered heavily to the floor. A cloud of dust enveloped her. She sneezed and coughed in the clotted air. She heard an inquiring shout from downstairs, probably from Merripen.

"I'm all right," she called back. Picking up a clean rag,

she wiped her face and unlatched the filthy window. The casing stuck. She pushed hard against the frame to loosen it. Another push, harder, and then a determined shove with all her weight behind it. The window gave way with astonishing suddenness, unsettling her balance. She pitched forward and caught the edge of the window in an attempt to find purchase, but it swung outward.

In the flash of forward-falling panic, she heard a muffled sound behind her.

Before another heartbeat had passed, she was snatched, pulled back with such force that her bones protested the abrupt reversal of momentum. She staggered, fetching hard against something solid and yet supple. Helplessly she tumbled to the floor in a tangle of limbs, some of them not her own.

Sprawled over a sturdy masculine chest, she saw a dark face below her, and she muttered in confusion, "Merri—"

But these were not Merripen's sable eyes, they were light, glowing amber. A shot of pleasure went through her stomach.

"You know, if I have to keep rescuing you like this," Cam Rohan remarked casually, "we really should discuss some kind of reward."

He reached up to tug off her hair covering, which was askew, and her braids tumbled down. Mortification swept away every other feeling. Amelia knew how she must look, disheveled and dust-stippled. Why did he never miss an opportunity to catch her at a disadvantage?

Gasping out an apology, she struggled to get off him, but the weight of her skirts and the stiffness of her corset made it difficult.

"No . . . wait . . ." Rohan inhaled sharply as she squirmed against him, and he rolled them both to their sides.

"Who let you into the house?" Amelia managed to ask.

Rohan gave her an innocent glance. "No one. The door was unlocked and the entrance hall was empty." He kicked his legs free of her clinging skirts and pulled her to a sitting position. She had never known anyone who possessed such ease of movement.

"Have you had this place inspected?" he asked. "The house is ready to fall off its timbers. I couldn't risk coming in here without offering a quick prayer to Butyakengo."

"Who?"

"A Gypsy protective spirit." He smiled at her. "But now that I'm here, I'll take my chances. Let me help you up."

He tugged Amelia to her feet, not letting go until her balance was secured. The grip of his hands sent thrills through her arms, and she gasped a little.

"Why are you here?" she asked.

Rohan shrugged. "Just paying a call. There isn't much to do at Stony Cross Park. It's the first day of fox hunting season."

"You didn't want to take part?"

He shook his head. "I only hunt for food, not sport. And I tend to sympathize with the fox, having been in his position once or twice."

He must have been referring to a Gypsy hunt, Amelia thought with concern and curiosity. She wanted to ask about it—but this conversation could not continue.

"Mr. Rohan," she said awkwardly, "I wish I could be a proper hostess and show you to the parlor and offer refreshments. But I don't have refreshments. I really don't even have a parlor. Please excuse me for sounding rude, but this isn't a good time to call—"

"I can help you." He leaned a shoulder against the wall, smiling. "I'm good with my hands."

There was no innuendo in his tone, but her color deepened nonetheless. "No, thank you. I'm sure Butayenko would disapprove."

"Butyakengo."

Anxious to demonstrate her competence, Amelia strode to the other window and began jerking at the closed draperies. "Thank you, Mr. Rohan, but as you can see, I have the situation well in hand."

"I think I'll stay. Having stopped you from falling through one window, I'd hate for you to go out the other."

"I won't. I'll be fine. I have everything under—" She tugged harder, and the rod clattered to the floor, just as the other had done. But unlike the other curtain, which had been lined with aged velvet, this one was lined with some kind of shimmering rippling fabric, some kind of—

Amelia froze in horror. The underside of the curtain was covered with bees. *Bees.* Hundreds, no, thousands of them, their iridescent wings beating in an angry relentless hum. They lifted in a mass from the crumpled velvet, while more flew from a crevice in the wall, where an enormous hive simmered. They must have found their way into a hollow space from a decayed spot in the outer wall. The insects swarmed like tongues of flame around Amelia's paralyzed form.

She felt the blood drain from her face. "Oh, God—"

"Don't move." Rohan's voice was astonishingly calm. "Don't swat at them."

She had never known such primal fear, welling up from

beneath her skin, leaking through every pore. No part of her body seemed to be under her control. The air was boiling with them, bees and more bees.

It was not going to be a pleasant way to die. Closing her eyes tightly, Amelia willed herself to be still, when every muscle strained and screamed for action. Insects moved in sinuous patterns around her, tiny bodies touching her sleeves, hands, shoulders.

"They're more afraid of you than you are of them," she heard Rohan say.

Amelia highly doubted that. "These are not f-frightened bees." Her voice didn't sound like her own. "These are *f-furious* bees."

"They do seem a bit annoyed," Rohan conceded, approaching her slowly. "It could be the dress you're wearing—they tend not to like dark colors." A short pause. "Or it could be the fact that you just ripped down half their hive."

"If you h-have the nerve to be *amused* by this—" She broke off and covered her face with her hands, trembling all over.

His soothing voice undercut the buzzing around them. "Be still. Everything's fine. I'm right here with you."

"Take me away," she whispered desperately. Her heart was pounding too hard, making her bones shake, driving every coherent thought from her head. She felt him brush a few inquisitive insects from her hair and back. His arms went around her, his shoulder sturdy beneath her cheek.

"I will, sweetheart. Put your arms around my neck."

She groped for him blindly, feeling sick and weak and disoriented. The flat muscles at the back of his neck shifted as he bent toward her, gathering her up as easily as if she were a child. "There," he murmured. "I've got you." Her feet left the floor, and she was floating and cradled at the same time. None of it seemed real: the swirling, droning bees that poured through the air, the hard chest and arms that enclosed her in a safe, secure grip. The thought came to her that she might have died if he hadn't been there. But he was so steady and deliberate, so utterly lacking in fear. The clamp of terror eased from around her throat. Turning her face into his shoulder, she relaxed as he carried her.

His breath fell in a warm, even rhythm on the curve of her cheek. "Some people think of the bee as a sacred insect," he said. "It's a symbol of reincarnation."

"I don't believe in reincarnation," she muttered.

There was a smile in his voice. "What a surprise. At the very least, the bees' presence in your home is a sign of good things to come."

Her voice was buried in the fine wool of his coat. "Wh-what does it mean if there are *thousands* of bees in one's home?"

He shifted her higher in his arms, his lips curving gently against the cold rim of her ear. "Probably that we'll have plenty of honey for teatime. We're going through the doorway now. In a moment I'm going to set you on your feet."

Amelia kept her face against him, her fingertips digging into the layers of his clothes. "Are they following?"

"No. They want to stay near the hive. Their main concern is to protect the queen from predators."

"She has nothing to fear from *me*!"

Laughter rustled in his throat. With extreme care, he lowered Amelia's feet to the floor. Keeping one arm around her, he reached with the other to close the door. "There.

We're out of the room. You're safe." His hand passed over her hair. "You can open your eyes now."

Clutching the lapels of his coat, Amelia stood and waited for a feeling of relief that didn't come. Her heart was racing too hard, too fast. Her chest ached from the strain of her breathing. Her lashes lifted, but all she could see was a shower of sparks.

"Amelia . . . easy. You're all right." His hands chased the shivers that ran up and down her back. "Slow down, sweetheart."

She couldn't. Her lungs were about to burst. No matter how hard she worked, she couldn't get enough air. *Bees . . .* the sound of buzzing was still in her ears. She heard his voice as if from a great distance, and she felt his arms go around her again as she sank into layers of gray softness.

After what could have been a minute or an hour, pleasant sensations filtered through the haze. A tender pressure moved over her forehead. The gentle brushes touched her eyelids, slid to her cheeks. Strong arms held her against a comfortingly hard surface, while a clean, salt-edged scent filled her nostrils. Her lashes fluttered, and she turned into the warmth with confused pleasure.

"There you are," came a low murmur.

Opening her eyes, Amelia saw Cam Rohan's face above her. They were on the hallway floor—he was holding her in his lap. As if the situation weren't mortifying enough, the front of her bodice was gaping, and her corset was unhooked. Only her crumpled chemise was left to cover her chest.

Amelia stiffened. Until that moment she had never known there was a feeling beyond embarrassment, that made one wish one could crumble into a pile of ashes. "My . . . my dress . . ."

"You weren't breathing well. I thought it best to loosen your corset."

"I've never fainted before," she said groggily, struggling to sit up.

"You were frightened." His hand came to the center of her chest, gently pressing her back down. "Rest another minute." His gaze moved over her wan features. "I think we can conclude you're not fond of bees."

"I've hated them ever since I was seven."

"Why?"

"I was playing out-of-doors with Win and Leo, and I stumbled too close to a rosebush. A bee flew at my face and stung right here." She touched a spot just below her right eye, high on the crest of her cheek. "The side of my face swelled until my eye closed . . . I couldn't see from it for almost two weeks—"

His fingertips smoothed over her cheek as if to soothe the long-ago injury.

"—and my brother and sister called me Cyclops." She watched him struggle not to smile. "They still do, whenever a bee flies too near."

He regarded her with friendly sympathy. "Everyone's afraid of something."

"What are you afraid of?"

"Ceilings and walls, mostly."

She stared at him in puzzlement, her thoughts still coursing too slowly. "You mean . . . you would rather live outside like a wild creature?"

"Yes, that's what I mean. Have you ever slept outside before?"

"On the ground?"

Her bewildered tone made him grin. "On a pallet beside a fire."

Amelia tried to imagine it, lying undefended on the hard ground, at the mercy of every creature that crawled, crept, or flew. "I don't think I could fall asleep that way."

She felt his hand playing slowly in the loose locks of her hair. "You could." His voice was soft. "I would help you."

She had no idea what he meant by that. All she knew was that as his fingertips reached her scalp, she felt a sensual shiver run down her spine. Clumsily she reached for her bodice, trying to pull the reinforced fabric together.

"Allow me. You're still unsteady." His hands brushed hers aside and he began to hook her corset deftly. Clearly he was familiar with the intricacies of a woman's undergarments. Amelia didn't doubt there had been more than a few ladies willing to let him practice.

Flustered, she asked, "Was I stung anywhere?"

"No." Mischief flickered in his eyes. "I checked thoroughly."

Amelia suppressed a little moan of distress. She was tempted to push his hands away from her, except that he was restoring her clothing far more efficiently than she would have. She closed her eyes, trying to pretend she wasn't sprawled in a man's lap while he fastened her corset.

"You'll need a local beekeeper to remove the hive," Rohan said.

Thinking of the enormous colony in the wall, Amelia asked, "How will he kill them all?"

"He may not have to. If possible, he'll sedate them with smoke and transfer the queen to a movable frame hive. The rest will follow. But if he can't manage that, he'll have to kill the colony with soap water. The larger problem is how to remove the comb and the honey. If you don't take it all out, it will ferment and attract all kinds of vermin."

Her eyes opened, and she looked up at him in worry. "Will the entire wall have to be removed?"

Before Rohan could reply, a new voice entered the conversation. "What's this?"

It was Leo, who had just arisen from bed and pulled on his clothes. He came barefoot from the direction of his bedroom. His bleary gaze moved over the pair of them. "Why are you on the floor with your buttons undone?"

Amelia considered the question. "I decided to have a spontaneous tryst in the middle of the hallway with a man I hardly know."

"Well, try to be quiet about it next time. A fellow needs his sleep."

Amelia stared at him quizzically. "For heaven's sake, Leo, aren't you worried that I may have been compromised?"

"Were you?"

"I . . ." Her face turned hot as she glanced into Rohan's vivid topaz eyes. "I don't think so."

"If you're not sure about it," Leo said, "you probably weren't." He came to Amelia, sank to his haunches, and stared at her steadily. His voice gentled. "What happened, sis?"

She pointed an unsteady finger at the closed door. "There are *bees* in there, Leo."

"Bees. Good God." Her brother gave her an affectionately mocking smile. "What a coward you are, Cyclops."

Amelia scowled, levering herself upward from Rohan's

lap. He braced her automatically, his arm firm behind her back. "Go see for yourself."

Leo sauntered lazily to the room, opened it, and stepped inside.

In two seconds, he had sped out, slammed the door, and lodged his shoulders against it. "Christ!" His eyes were wide and glazed. "There must be thousands of them!"

"I'd estimate at least two hundred thousand," Rohan said. Finishing the last of Amelia's buttons, he helped her to her feet. "Slowly," he murmured. "You might be a bit light-headed."

She let him support her while she assessed her uncertain balance. "I'm steady now. Thank you." Her hand was still clasped in his. Rohan's fingers were long and graceful, the thumb band gleaming against honey-colored skin.

Uneasily Amelia drew her hand away and told her brother, "Mr. Rohan saved my life twice today. First I nearly fell out the window, and then I found the bees."

"This house," Leo muttered, "should be torn down and used for matchsticks."

"You should order a full structural inspection," Rohan said. "The house has settled badly. Some of the chimneys are leaning, and the entrance hall ceiling is sagging. You've got damaged joinery and beams."

"I know what the problems are." The calm appraisal had annoyed Leo. He'd retained enough of his past architectural training to assess the house's condition accurately.

"It may not be safe for the family to stay here."

"But that's my concern," Leo said, adding with a sneer, "isn't it?"

Sensitive to the brittle disquiet in the atmosphere,

Amelia made a hasty attempt at diplomacy. "Mr. Rohan, Lord Ramsay is convinced the house poses no immediate danger to the family."

"I wouldn't be so easily convinced," Rohan replied. "Not with four sisters in my charge."

"Care to take them off my hands?" Leo asked. "You can have the lot of them." He smiled without amusement at Rohan's silence. "No? Then pray don't offer unwanted advice."

Despondent worry swept over Amelia as she saw the bleakness of her brother's face. He was becoming a stranger, this man who harbored despair and fury so deep inside that it had begun to eat at his foundations. Until, like the house, he would eventually collapse as the weakest parts of the structure gave way.

Unruffled, Rohan turned to Amelia. "In lieu of advice, let me offer some information. Two days hence, there'll be a Mop Fair held at the village."

"What is that?"

"It's a hiring fair, attended by all the local residents in need of work. They wear tokens to signify their trade—a servant girl will carry a mop, a thatcher carries a tuft of straw, and so forth. Give the ones you want a shilling to seal the contract, and you'll have them for a year's employment."

Amelia darted a cautious glance at her brother. "We do need proper servants, Leo."

"Go, then, and hire whomever you please. I don't give a damn."

Amelia gave a troubled nod and raised her hands to her upper arms, rubbing them over her sleeves.

It was cold, she thought, even for autumn. Icy drafts

crept around her stockinged ankles, beneath the edges of her cuffs, across the sweat-dampened back of her neck. Her muscles tensed against the strange, raw chill.

Both men had fallen silent. Leo's face was blank, his gaze focused inward.

It felt as if the space around them were folding in on itself, thickening until the air was as heavy as water. Colder, tighter, closer . . . instinctively Amelia stepped back, away from her brother, until she felt Rohan's chest against her shoulders. His hand came up to her arm, gently cupping her elbow. Shivering, she leaned harder against the warm, vital strength of his body.

Leo had not moved. He waited, his gaze unfocused, as if he were intent on absorbing the chill. As if he welcomed it, wanted it. His averted face was harsh and shadow-crossed.

Something divided the space between them, her and Leo. She felt the resonance of movement, softer than a breeze, more delicate than eiderdown . . .

"Leo?" Amelia murmured uncertainly.

The sound of her voice seemed to bring him back to himself. He blinked and stared at her with near-colorless eyes. "Show Rohan out," he said curtly. "That is, if you've been sufficiently compromised for one day." He walked away rapidly. Reaching his room, he closed the door with a clumsy swipe of his arm.

Amelia was slow to move, bewildered by her brother's behavior, and even more so by the splintering coldness in the hallway. She turned to face Rohan, who was staring after Leo with a level gaze.

He glanced down at her, keeping his expression carefully impassive. "I hate to leave you." There was a gently mocking edge to his tone. "You need someone to follow you around and keep you safe from mishaps. On the other hand, you also need someone to find a beekeeper."

Realizing he was not going to talk about Leo, Amelia followed his lead. "Will you do that for us? I would consider it a great favor."

"Of course. Although . . ." His eyes held a wicked glitter. "As I mentioned before, I can't keep doing favors for you with no reward. A man needs incentive."

"If . . . if you want money, I'll be glad to—"

"God, no." Rohan was laughing now. "I don't want money." Reaching out, he smoothed back her hair, letting the heel of his hand graze the edge of her cheekbone. The brush of his skin was light and erotic, causing her to swallow hard. "Goodbye, Miss Hathaway. I'll see myself out." He flashed a smile at her and advised, "Stay away from the windows."

On the way down the stairs, Rohan passed Merripen, who was ascending at a measured pace.

Merripen's face darkened at the sight of the visitor. "What are you doing here?"

"It seems I'm helping with pest eradication."

"Then you can begin by leaving," Merripen growled.

Rohan only grinned nonchalantly, and continued on his way.

After informing the rest of the family about the perils of the upstairs parlor, which was promptly dubbed "the bee room," Amelia investigated the rest of the upstairs with extreme caution. There were no more hazards to be found, only dust and decay and silence.

But it was not an unwelcoming house. When the windows were opened and light spilled across floors that had been untouched for years, it seemed the place was eager to open and breathe and be restored. Ramsay House was a charming place, really, with eccentricities, secret corners, and unique features that only needed some polish and attention. Not unlike the Hathaway family itself.

In the afternoon Amelia collapsed in a chair downstairs, while Poppy made tea in the kitchen. "Where is Win?"

"Napping in her room," Poppy replied. "She was exhausted after the busy morning. She wouldn't admit it, of course, but you can always tell when she gets all pale and drawn."

"Was she content?"

"She certainly seemed to be." Pouring hot water into a chipped pot filled with tea leaves, Poppy chattered about some of her discoveries. She had found a lovely rug in one of the bedrooms, and after she had beaten it for an hour, it had turned out to be richly colored and in good condition.

"I think most of the dust was transferred from the carpet to you," Amelia said. Since Poppy had covered the lower half of her face with a handkerchief during the carpet-beating, the dust had settled on her forehead, eyes, and the bridge of her nose. When the handkerchief was removed, it had left Poppy's face oddly two-toned, the top half gray, the lower half white.

"I enjoyed it immensely," Poppy replied with a grin. "There's nothing like whacking a carpet with a rug-beater to vent one's frustrations."

Amelia was about to ask what Poppy's frustrations were, when Beatrix entered the kitchen.

The girl, usually so lively, was quiet and downcast.

"Tea will be ready soon," Poppy said, busy slicing bread at the kitchen table. "Will you have some toast, too, Bea?"

"No, thank you. Not hungry." Beatrix sat in a chair beside Amelia's, staring at the floor.

"You're always hungry," Amelia said. "What's the matter, dear? Aren't you feeling well? Are you tired?"

Silence. A violent shake of her head. Beatrix was definitely upset about something.

Amelia settled a gentle hand on her youngest sister's narrow back, and leaned over her. "Beatrix, what is it? Tell me. Are you missing your friends? Or Spot? Are you—"

"No, it's nothing like that." Beatrix ducked her head until only the reddened arc of her cheek was visible.

"Then what?"

"Something's wrong with me." Her voice roughened with misery. "It's happened again, Amelia. I couldn't help myself. I barely remember doing it. I—"

"Oh, no," came Poppy's whisper.

Amelia kept her hand on Beatrix's back. "Is it the same problem as before?"

Beatrix nodded. "I'm going to kill myself," she said vehemently. "I'm going to lock myself in the bee room. I'm going to—"

"Hush. You'll do no such thing." Amelia rubbed her rigid back. "Quiet, dear, and let me think for a moment." Her worried gaze met Poppy's over Beatrix's downbent head.

"The problem" had occurred on and off for the past four years, ever since the Hathaways' mother had died. Every now and then Beatrix suffered an irresistible impulse to steal something, either from a shop or someone's home. Usually the objects were insignificant . . . a tiny pair of sewing scissors, hairpins, a pen nib, a cube of sealing wax. But every so often she took something of value, like a snuff box or an earring. As far as Amelia could tell, Beatrix never planned these small crimes—in fact, the girl often wasn't even aware of what she had done until later. And then she suffered an agony of remorse, and no small amount of fear. It was alarming to discover one wasn't always in control of one's actions.

The Hathaways kept Beatrix's problem a secret, of course, all of them conspiring to return the stolen objects discreetly and protect her from the consequences. Since it hadn't happened for nearly a year, they had all assumed Beatrix was cured of her inexplicable compulsion.

"I assume you took something from Stony Cross Manor," Amelia said with forced calm. "That's the only place you've visited."

Beatrix nodded miserably. "It was after I let Spot go. I went to the library, and looked in a few rooms on the way, and . . . I didn't mean to, Amelia! I didn't want to!"

"I know." Amelia wrapped her arms around her in a consoling hug. She was filled with a maternal instinct to protect, soothe, ease. "We'll fix it, Bea. We'll put everything back and no one will know. Just tell me what you took, and try to remember which rooms the things came from."

"Here . . . this is everything." Reaching into the pockets of her pinafore, Beatrix dumped a small collection of objects in her lap.

Amelia held up the first item. It was a carved wooden horse, no bigger than her fist, with a silk mane and a delicately painted face. The object was worn from much handling, and there were teeth marks along the horse's body. "The Westcliffs have a daughter, still quite small," she murmured. "This must belong to her."

"I took a toy from a baby," Beatrix moaned. "It's the lowest thing I've ever done. I should be in prison."

Amelia picked up another object, a card with two similar images printed side by side. She guessed it was meant to be inserted into a stereoscope, a device that would merge the two images into a dimensional picture.

The next stolen item was a household key, and the last . . . oh, dear. It was a sterling silver seal, with an engraved family crest on one end. One would use it to stamp a blob of melted wax and close an envelope. The object was heavy and quite costly, the kind of thing that was passed down from generation to generation.

"From Lord Westcliff's private study," Beatrix muttered. "It was on his desk. He probably uses it for his official correspondence. I'll go hang myself now."

"We must return this immediately," Amelia said, passing a hand over her dampening brow. "When they realize it's missing, a servant may be blamed."

The three women were silent with horror at the thought.

"We'll pay a morning call to Lady Westcliff," Poppy said, sounding a bit breathless from anxiety. "Is tomorrow one of her receiving days?"

"It doesn't matter," Amelia said, striving to sound calm. "There's no time to wait. You and I are calling tomorrow, whether or not it's a proper day."

"Shall I go too?" Beatrix asked.

"No," Amelia and Poppy answered simultaneously. They were both thinking the same thing—that Beatrix might not be able to control herself during another visit.

"Thank you." Beatrix seemed relieved. "Although I'm sorry you have to undo my wrongs. I should be punished somehow. Perhaps I should confess and apologize—"

"We'll resort to that if we're caught," Amelia said. "First let's try covering it up."

"Do we have to tell Leo or Win or Merripen?" Beatrix asked sheepishly.

"No," Amelia murmured, gathering her close and pressing her lips to her sister's unruly dark curls. "We'll keep this between the three of us. Poppy and I will take care of everything, dear."

"All right. Thank you." Beatrix relaxed and nestled against her with a sigh. "I only hope you can do it without getting caught."

"Of course we can," Poppy said brightly. "Don't you worry for one moment."

"Problem solved," Amelia added.

And above Beatrix's head, Amelia and Poppy looked at each other in shared panic.

Chapter Ten

"I don't know why Beatrix does these things," Poppy said the next morning, as Amelia held the ribbons of the barouche. They were on their way to Stony Cross Manor, with the stolen objects secreted in the pockets of their best day gowns.

"I'm certain she doesn't mean to," Amelia replied, her forehead furrowed with worry. "If it was intentional, Beatrix would steal things she truly wanted, like hair ribbons or gloves or candy, and she wouldn't confess afterward." She sighed. "It seems to happen when there's been a significant change in her life. When Mother and Father died, and when Leo and Win fell ill . . . and now, when we've uprooted ourselves and moved to Hampshire. We'll just smooth this over as best we can, and try to ensure that Beatrix is in a calm and serene atmosphere."

"There is no such thing as 'calm and serene' in our household," Poppy said glumly. "Oh, Amelia, why must our family be so odd?"

"We're not odd."

Poppy batted her hands in a dismissive gesture. "Odd people never think they're odd."

"I'm perfectly ordinary," Amelia protested.

"Ha."

Amelia glanced at her in surprise. "Why in heaven's name would you say 'ha' to that?"

"You try to manage everything and everyone. And you don't trust anyone outside the family. You're like a porcupine. No one can get past the quills."

"Well, I like that," Amelia said indignantly. "Being compared to a large prickly rodent, when I've decided to spend the rest of my entire life looking after the family—"

"No one's asked that of you."

"Someone has to do it. And I'm the oldest Hathaway."

"Leo's the oldest."

"I'm the oldest *sober* Hathaway."

"That still doesn't mean you have to martyr yourself."

"I'm not a martyr, I'm merely being responsible. And you're ungrateful!"

"Would you prefer gratitude or a husband? Personally, I'd take the husband."

"I don't want a husband."

They bickered all the way to Stony Cross Manor. By the time they arrived, they were both cross and surly. However, as a footman came to assist them out, they pasted false smiles on their faces and linked tense arms as they walked to the front door.

They waited in the entrance hall as the butler went to announce their arrival. To Amelia's vast relief, he showed them to the parlor and informed them that Lady Westcliff would be with them directly.

Venturing farther into the airy parlor, with its vases of fresh flowers, and satinwood furniture and light blue silk upholstery, and the cheerful blaze in the white marble fireplace, Poppy exclaimed, "Oh, it's so pretty in here, and it smells so lovely, and look how the windows sparkle!"

Amelia was silent, but she couldn't help agreeing. Seeing this immaculate parlor, so far removed from the dust and squalor of Ramsay House, made her feel guilty and sullen.

"Don't take off your bonnet," she said as Poppy untied her ribbons. "You're supposed to leave it on during a formal call."

"Only in town," Poppy argued. "In the country, etiquette is more relaxed. And I hardly think Lady Westcliff would mind."

A woman's voice came from the doorway. "Mind what?" It was Lady Westcliff, her slender form clad in a pink gown, her dark hair gathered at the back of her head in shining curls. Her smile was wrought of mischief and easy charm. She held hands with a dark-haired toddler in a blue dress, a miniature version of herself with big round eyes the color of gingerbread.

"My lady . . ." Amelia and Poppy both bowed. Deciding to be frank, Amelia said, "Lady Westcliff, we were just debating whether or not we should remove our bonnets."

"Good God, don't bother with formality," Lady Westcliff exclaimed, coming in with the child. "Off with the bonnets, by all means. And do call me Lillian. This is my daughter, Merritt. She and I are having a bit of playtime before her morning nap."

"I hope we're not interrupting—" Poppy began apologetically.

"Not at all. If you can tolerate our romping during your visit, we're more than happy to have you. I've sent for tea."

Before long they were all chatting easily. Merritt quickly lost all vestige of shyness and showed them her favorite doll named Annie, and a collection of pebbles and leaves from her pocket. Lady Westcliff—Lillian—was an openly affectionate and playful mother, showing no compunction about kneeling on the floor to look for fallen pebbles beneath the table.

Lillian's interactions with the child were quite unusual for an aristocratic household. Children were hardly ever brought out to see visitors unless it was a brief presentation, accompanied by a pat on the head and a quick departure. Most women of the countess's exalted position wouldn't see their own offspring more than once or twice a day, leaving the majority of child-rearing to the nanny and nursery maids.

"I can't help wanting to see her," Lillian explained candidly. "So the nursery servants have learned to tolerate my interference."

When the tea tray arrived, Annie the doll was propped up on the settee between Poppy and Merritt. The little girl pressed the edge of her teacup against the doll's painted mouth. "Annie wants more sugar, Mama," Merritt said.

Lillian grinned, knowing who was going to drink the highly sweetened tea. "Tell Annie we never have more than two lumps in a cup, darling. It will make her ill."

"But she has a sweet tooth," the child protested. She added ominously, "A sweet tooth *and* a temper."

Lillian shook her head with a *tsk-tsk*. "Such a headstrong doll. Be firm with her, Merritt."

Poppy, who had been watching the exchange with a grin,

adopted a perplexed look and wriggled slightly on the settee. "Dear me, I do believe I'm sitting on something . . ." She reached behind her and produced the little wooden horse, pretending she had found it lodged between the settee cushions.

"That's my horsie," Merritt exclaimed, her small fingers closing around the object. "I thought he'd run away!"

"Thank goodness," Lillian said. "Horsie is one of Merritt's favorite toys. The entire household has been searching for it."

Amelia's smile wavered as she met Poppy's gaze, both of them wondering if it had been discovered that other things were missing. The stolen objects, especially the silver seal, must be returned as soon as possible. She cleared her throat. "My lady . . . that is, Lillian . . . if you wouldn't mind . . . I should like to know where the convenience is . . ."

"Oh, certainly. Shall I have a housemaid show you the way, or—"

"No, thank you," Amelia said hastily.

After receiving Lillian's matter-of-fact instructions, Amelia excused herself from the parlor, leaving the three of them to continue their tea.

The first room she had to find was the library, where the stereoscope card and the key belonged. Recalling Beatrix's description of the main floor plan, Amelia hurried along the quiet hallway. She slowed her pace as she saw a maid sweeping the carpet, and tried to look as if she knew where she was going. The maid stopped sweeping and stood aside respectfully as she passed.

Rounding a corner, Amelia found an open door revealing a large library with upper and lower galleries. Better yet, it was empty. She rushed inside and saw a stereoscope on the massive library table. There was a wooden box nearby, stuffed with cards just like the one in her pocket. Tucking the card in with the others, she hurried out of the library, pausing only to insert the key into the empty lock case of the door.

Only one task left—she had to find Lord Westcliff's private study and return the silver seal. The weight of it bounced uncomfortably against her leg as she walked. *Please don't let Lord Westcliff be there,* she thought desperately. *Please let it be empty. Please don't let me be caught.*

Beatrix had said the study was close to the library, but the first door Amelia tried turned out to be the music room. Spying another door across the hallway, she discovered a supplies closet filled with pails, brooms, rags, and pots of wax and polish.

"Blast, blast, *blast,*" she muttered, rushing to another open doorway.

It was a billiards room. And it was occupied by a half-dozen gentlemen involved in a game. Worse, one of them was Christopher Frost. His handsome face was devoid of expression as his gaze met hers.

Amelia stopped, color flaring in her face. "Do excuse me," she murmured, and fled.

To her dismay, Christopher Frost moved as if to follow her. She was so intent on making her escape that she didn't see someone cut in front of Frost, neatly blocking him.

"Miss Hathaway."

At the sound of a man's voice, Amelia whirled around. She expected to see Christopher Frost, but was startled to find that Cam Rohan had followed her. "Sir."

Cam Rohan was in his shirtsleeves, and his collar was a

bit loose, as if he'd been tugging on it. His jet-black hair was casually disordered, as if he'd recently dragged his fingers through the shining layers. Her heart quickened. She waited stiffly as he approached her in fluid strides.

Lingering in the doorway, Christopher Frost gave them a last frowning glance before retreating into the room.

Rohan reached Amelia and stopped with a nod of greeting. "Is there something I can help you with?" he asked politely. "Have you lost your way?"

Abandoning caution in favor of expediency, Amelia seized a fold of his rolled-up sleeve. "Mr. Rohan, do you know where Lord Westcliff's study is?"

"Yes, of course."

"Show me."

Rohan looked at her with a quizzical smile. "Why?"

"There's no time to explain. Just take me there now. Please, let's hurry!"

Obligingly he led her across the hallway, two doors down, into a small rosewood-paneled room. A gentleman's study. The only ornamentation was a row of rectangular stained-glass windows along one wall. Here was where Marcus, Lord Westcliff, conducted most of his estate business.

Rohan closed the door behind them.

Fumbling in her pocket, Amelia retrieved the heavy silver seal. "Where does this go?"

"On the right side of his desk, near the inkwell," Rohan said. "How did you come by it?"

"I'll explain later. I beg you, don't tell anyone." She went to place the silver seal on the desk. "I only hope he didn't notice it was missing."

"Why would you want it in the first place?" Rohan asked idly. "Resorting to forgery, are we?"

"Forgery!" Amelia turned pale. A letter in Westcliff's name, sealed with his family emblem, would be a powerful instrument, indeed. What other interpretation could be drawn from the borrowing of the sterling seal? "Oh, no, I wouldn't have—that is, I didn't want—"

She was interrupted by the heart-stopping sound of the doorknob turning. In that one instant she was pierced with simultaneous anguish and resignation. It was over. She had been so close, and now she'd been caught, and God knew what the repercussions would be. There was no way to explain her presence in Westcliff's office other than to divulge Beatrix's problem, which would bring shame on the family and ruin the girl's future in polite society. A pet lizard was one thing, but thievery was another matter entirely.

All these thoughts flashed through Amelia's mind in one searing mass. But as she stiffened and waited for the ax to fall, Rohan came to her in two long strides. And before Amelia could move, or think, or even breathe, he had jerked her full length against him, and pulled her head to his.

Rohan kissed her with an indecent frankness that sent her reeling. His arms were firm around her, keeping her steady while his mouth caught hers at just the right angle. Her hands moved in tentative objection, her palms encountering the tough muscles of his chest, the catch of his shirt buttons. He was the only solid thing in a kaleidoscopic world. She stopped pushing as her body absorbed the arousing details of him, the hard masculine contours, the fresh outdoors scent, the sensuous probing of his mouth. She had relived his kiss a thousand times in her dreams. She just hadn't realized it until now.

Graceful fingers cupped around her neck and jaw, turning her face upward. The tips of his fingers found the fine skin behind her ears, where it met the silken edge of her hairline. And all the while he continued to fill her with concentrated fire, until the inside of her mouth prickled sweetly and her legs shook beneath her. He used his tongue delicately, exploring without haste, entering her repeatedly while she clung to him in bewildered pleasure.

His mouth lifted, his breath a hot caress against her lips. He turned his head as he spoke to whoever had entered the room.

"I beg your pardon, my lord. We wanted a moment of privacy."

Amelia turned crimson as she followed his gaze to the doorway, where Lord Westcliff stood with an unfathomable expression.

An electric moment passed while Westcliff appeared to marshal his thoughts. His gaze moved to Amelia's face, then back to Rohan's. A smile flickered in his dark eyes. "I intend to return in approximately a half hour. It would probably be best if my study were vacated by then." Giving a courteous nod, he took his leave.

As soon as the door closed behind him, Amelia dropped her forehead to Rohan's shoulder with a groan. She would have pulled away, but she didn't trust her knees to hold. "Why did you do that?"

He didn't look at all repentant. "I had to come up with a reason for both of us to be in here. It seemed the best option."

Amelia shook her head slowly, still resting her forehead

against him. The dry sweetness of his scent reminded her of a sun-warmed meadow. "Do you think he'll tell anyone?"

"No," he said immediately, reassuring her. "Westcliff isn't given to gossip. He won't say a word to anyone, except . . ."

"Except?"

"Lady Westcliff. He'll probably tell her."

Amelia considered that, thinking perhaps it wasn't so terrible. Lady Westcliff didn't seem like the kind of person who would condemn her for this. The countess seemed quite tolerant of scandalous behavior.

"Of course," Rohan continued, "if Lady Westcliff knows, there's a high probability she'll tell Lady St. Vincent, who's due to arrive with Lord St. Vincent by the end of the week. And since Lady St. Vincent tells her husband everything, he'll know about it, too. Other than that, no one will find out. Unless . . ."

Her head jerked upward like a string puppet's. "Unless what?"

"Unless Lord St. Vincent mentions it to Mr. Hunt, who would undoubtedly tell Mrs. Hunt, and then . . . everyone would find out."

"Oh, no. I can't bear it."

He gave her an alert glance. "Why? Because you were caught kissing a Gypsy?"

"No, because I'm not the kind of woman who is caught kissing *anyone*. I don't have rendezvous! When everyone finds out, I'll have no dignity left. No reputation. No— What are you smiling at?"

"You. I wouldn't have expected such melodrama."

That annoyed Amelia, who was not the kind of woman who indulged in theatrics. She wedged her arms more firmly between them. "My reaction is perfectly reasonable considering—"

"You're not bad at it."

She blinked in confusion. "Melodrama?"

"No, kissing. With a little practice, you'd be exceptional. But you need to relax."

"I don't want to relax. I don't want to . . . oh, dear Lord." He had bent his head to her throat, searching for the visible thrum of her pulse. A light, hot shock went through her. "Don't do that," she said weakly, but he was insistent, his mouth wickedly soft, and her breath hitched as she felt the brush of his tongue.

Her hands shot to his muscle-banked shoulders. "Mr. Rohan, you mustn't—"

"This is how to kiss, Amelia." He cradled her head in his palms, deftly tilting it to the side. "Noses go here." Another disorienting brush of his mouth, a wash of sensual heat. "You taste like sugar and tea."

"I already know how to kiss!"

"Do you?" His thumb passed over her kiss-heated lips, urging them to part. "Then show me," he whispered. "Let me in, Amelia."

Never in her life had she thought a man would say something so outrageous to her. And if the words were improper, the gleam in his eyes was positively immolating.

"I . . . I'm a spinster." She offered the word as if it were a talisman. Everyone knew that rakish gentlemen were supposed to leave spinsters alone. But it appeared no one had told Cam Rohan.

A covert smile deepened the corners of his mouth. "That's not going to keep you safe from me." She tried to turn away from him, but his hands guided her face back to his. "I can't seem to leave you alone. In fact, I'm reconsidering my entire policy on spinsters."

Before she could ask what his policy was, his mouth possessed hers again, while his fingers caressed the taut edge of her jaw, coaxing her to relax. Even in her most ardent moments with Christopher Frost, he had never kissed her like this, as if he were consuming her slowly. His lips rubbed over hers until they caught and sealed warmly, and his tongue found hers. He played with her, stroking and reaching, while his hands gathered her closer. He caressed her back and shoulders, while his lips broke from hers to explore the soft slope of her neck. He found a place that made her writhe, teasing gently until a helpless moan slipped from her throat.

Rohan's head lifted. His eyes glowed as if brimstone were contained within the dark-rimmed irises. He spoke slowly, as if he were collecting words like fallen leaves. "This is probably a bad idea."

Amelia nodded shakily. "Yes, Mr. Rohan."

His fingertips teased a fresh surge of color to the surface of her cheeks. "My name is Cam."

"I can't call you that."

"Why not?"

"You know why," came her unsteady reproach. A long breath was neatly rifted as she felt his mouth descend to her cheek, exploring the rosy skin. "What does it mean?"

"My name? It's the Romany word for 'sun.' "

Amelia could scarcely think. "As in . . . the offspring of a father, or in the sky?"

"Sky." He moved to the arch of her eyebrow, kissing the outward tip. "Did you know a Gypsy has three names?"

She shook her head slowly, while his mouth slid across

her forehead. He pressed a warm veil of words against her skin. "The first is a secret name a mother whispers into her child's ear at birth. The second is a tribal name used only by other Gypsies. The third is the name we use with non-Roma."

His scent was all around her, spare and fresh and delicious. "What is your tribal name?"

He smiled slightly, the shape of his mouth a burning motif against her cheek. "I can't tell you. I don't know you well enough yet."

Yet. The tantalizing promise embedded in that word shortened her breath. "Let me go," she whispered. "Please, we mustn't—" But the words were lost as he bent and took her mouth hungrily.

Suffused with pleasure, Amelia groped for his hair, finding acute satisfaction in the slide of heavy silk through her fingers. As he felt her touch him, he gave a low mutter of encouragement. The pattern of his breath changed, roughened, his kisses turning hard and languorous.

He took what she offered—more—sinking his tongue deeper, gathering sensation. And she responded until her soul was scorched at the edges, and her thoughts had vanished like sparks leaping from a bonfire.

Abruptly Rohan took his mouth from hers and held her tightly, too tightly, against his body. She felt herself straining in a subtle pendulum sway, needing friction, pressure, release. He kept her still, holding her close while she trembled and ached.

Rohan's grip eased. She was released by gradual degrees until he was finally able to push her away completely.

"Pardon," he eventually said. She saw the daze of heat

in his eyes. "I don't usually have such a difficult time stopping."

Amelia nodded blindly and wrapped her arms around herself. She wasn't aware of her foot's nervous tapping until Rohan came to her and slid one of his feet beneath her skirts to still her drumming toes.

"Hummingbird," he whispered. "You'd better go now. If you don't, I'll end up compromising you in ways you never knew were possible."

Amelia was never quite certain how she returned to the parlor without getting lost. She moved as if through the layers of a dream.

Reaching the settee where Poppy sat, Amelia accepted another cup of tea and smiled at little Merritt, who was fishing around in her own cup for a chunk of dropped sugar biscuit, and responded noncommittally to Lillian's suggestion that the entire Hathaway family join them on a picnic at week's end.

"I do wish we could have accepted her invitation," Poppy said wistfully on the way home. "But I suppose that would be asking for trouble, since Leo would probably be objectionable and Beatrix would steal something."

"And there's far too much for us to do at Ramsay House," Amelia added, feeling distracted and distant.

Only one thought was clear in her mind. Cam Rohan would return to London soon. For her own sake—and perhaps his as well—she would have to avoid Stony Cross Park until he was gone.

Perhaps it was because they were all weary of cleaning, repairing, and organizing, but the entire Hathaway family fell into a desultory mood that evening. Everyone but Leo gathered around the hearth in one of the downstairs rooms, lounging while Win read aloud from a Dickens novel. Merripen occupied a distant corner of the room, near the family but not quite part of it, listening intently. No doubt Win could have read names from an insurance register and he would have found it enthralling.

Poppy was busy with needlework, stitching a pair of men's slippers with bright wool threads, while Beatrix played solitaire on the floor near the hearth. Noticing the way her youngest sister was riffling through the cards, Amelia laughed. "Beatrix," she said after Win had finished a chapter, "why in heaven's name would you cheat at solitaire? You're playing against yourself."

"Then there's no one to object when I cheat."

"It's not whether you win but how you win that's important," Amelia said.

"I've heard that before, and I don't agree at all. It's much nicer to win."

Poppy shook her head over her embroidery. "Beatrix, you are positively shameless."

"*And* a winner," Beatrix said with satisfaction, laying down the exact card she wanted.

"Where did we go wrong?" Amelia asked of no one in particular.

Win smiled. "Her pleasures are few, dear. A creative game of solitaire isn't going to hurt anyone."

"I suppose not." Amelia was about to say more, but she was diverted by a cold waft of air that slipped around her ankles and turned her toes numb. She shivered and pulled her knitted blue shawl more snugly around herself. "My, it's chilly in here."

"You must be sitting in a draft," Poppy said in concern. "Come sit by me, Amelia—I'm much closer to the fire."

"Thank you, but I think I'll go to bed now." Still shivering, Amelia yawned. "Good night, everyone." She left as Beatrix asked Win to read one more chapter.

As Amelia walked along the hallway, she passed a small room that, as far as they had been able to tell, had been intended as a gentlemen's room. It featured an alcove that was just large enough for a billiards table, and a dingy painting of a hunting scene on one wall. A large overstuffed chair was positioned between the windows, its velvet nap eroded. Light from a standing lamp slid across the floor in a diluted wash.

Leo was drowsing in the chair, one arm hanging loosely over the side. An empty bottle stood on the floor near the chair, casting a spearlike shadow to the other side of the room.

Amelia would have continued on her way, but something about her brother's undefended posture caused her to stop. He slept with his head slumped over one shoulder, lips slightly parted, just as he had in childhood. With his face wiped clean of anger and grief, he looked young and vulnerable. She was reminded of the gallant boy he had once been, and her heart contracted with pity.

Venturing into the room, Amelia was shocked by the abrupt change of temperature, the biting air. It was far colder in here than it was outside. And it wasn't her imagination— she could see the white puffs of her breath. Shivering, she drew closer to her brother. The coldness was concentrated around him, turning so bitter that it made her lungs hurt to breathe. As she hovered over his prone form, she was swamped in a feeling of bleakness, a sorrow beyond tears.

"Leo?" His face was gray, his lips dry and blue, and when she touched his cheek, there was no trace of warmth. "Leo!"

No response.

Amelia shook him, pushed hard at his chest, took his stiff face in her hands. As she did so, she felt some invisible force pulling at her. She held on doggedly, knotting her fists in the loose folds of his shirt. "Leo, wake up!"

To her infinite relief, he stirred and gasped, and his lashes flickered upward. The irises of his eyes were as pale as ice. His palms came to her shoulders, and he muttered groggily, "I'm awake. I'm awake. Jesus. Don't scream. You're making enough noise to wake the dead."

"For a moment I thought that was exactly what I was doing." Amelia half collapsed onto the arm of the chair, her nerves thrilling unpleasantly. The chill was receding now. "Oh, Leo, you were so still and pale. I've seen livelier-looking corpses."

Her brother rubbed his eyes. "I'm only a bit tap-hackled. Not dead."

"You wouldn't wake up."

"I didn't want to. I . . ." He paused, looking troubled. His tone was soft and wondering. "I was dreaming. Such vivid dreams . . ."

"About what?"

He wouldn't answer.

"About Laura?" Amelia persisted.

His face closed, deep lines weathering the surface like fissures made by the expansion of ice inside rock. "I told you never to mention her name to me."

"Yes, because you didn't want to be reminded of her.

But it doesn't matter, Leo. You never stop thinking about her whether you hear her name or not."

"I'm not going to talk about her."

"Well, it's fairly obvious that avoidance isn't working." Her mind spun desperately with the question of what tack to take, how best to reach him. She tried determination. "I won't let you fall to pieces, Leo."

The look he gave her made it clear that determination had been a bad choice. "Someday," he said with cold pleasantness, "you may be forced to acknowledge there are some things beyond your control. If I want to go to pieces, I'll do it without asking your bloody permission."

She tried sympathy next. "Leo . . . I know what you've gone through since Laura died. But other people have recovered from loss, and they've gone on to find happiness again—"

"There's no more happiness," Leo said roughly. "There's no peace in any damn corner of my life. She took it all with her. For pity's sake, Amelia . . . go meddle in someone else's affairs, and leave me the hell alone."

Chapter Eleven

The morning after Amelia Hathaway's visit, Cam went to visit Lord Westcliff's private study, pausing at the open doorway. "My lord."

He suppressed a smile as he noticed a child's porcelain-head doll under the mahogany desk, propped in a sitting position against one of the legs, and the remains of what appeared to be a honey tart. Knowing of the earl's adoration for his daughter, Cam guessed he found it impossible to defend against Merritt's invasions.

Looking up from the desk, Westcliff gestured for Cam to enter. "Is it Brishen's tribe?" he asked without prelude.

Cam took the chair he indicated. "No—it's headed by a man named Danior. They saw the marks on the trees."

That morning, one of Westcliff's tenants had reported that a Romany camp had been set up by the river. Unlike other landowners in Hampshire, Westcliff tolerated the presence of Gypsies at his estate, as long as they made no mischief and didn't outstay their welcome.

On past occasions the earl had sent food and wine to

visiting Romas. In return, they had carved marks on trees by the river to indicate this was friendly territory. They usually stayed only a matter of days, and left without causing damage to the estate.

Upon learning of the Gypsy camp, Cam had volunteered to go talk to the newcomers and ask about their plans. Westcliff had agreed at once, welcoming the opportunity of sending an intermediary who spoke Romany.

It had been a good visit. The tribe was a small one, its leader an affable man who had assured Cam they would make no trouble.

"They intend to stay a week, no more," Cam told Westcliff.

"Good."

The earl's decisive reply caused Cam to smile. "You don't like being visited by the Rom."

"It's not something I would wish for," Westcliff admitted. "Their presence makes the villagers and my tenants nervous."

"But you allow them to stay. Why?"

"For one thing, proximity makes it easier to know what they're doing. For another . . ." Westcliff paused, seeming to choose his words with unusual care. "Many view the Romany people as bands of wanderers and itinerants, and at worst, beggars and thieves. But others recognize them as possessing their own authentic culture. If one subscribes to the latter view, one can't punish them for living as men of nature."

Cam raised his brows, impressed. It was rare for anyone, let alone an aristocrat, to deal with Gypsies in a fair manner. "And you subscribe to the latter view?"

"I am leaning toward it"—Westcliff smiled wryly as he added—"while at the same time acknowledging that men of nature can be, on occasion, a bit light-fingered."

Cam grinned. "The Rom believe no one owns the land or the life it sustains. Technically, one can't steal something that belongs to all people."

"My tenant farmers tend to disagree," Westcliff said dryly.

Cam leaned back, resting one hand on the arm of the chair. His gold rings glinted against the rich mahogany. Unlike the earl, who was precisely dressed in tailored clothes and a deftly knotted necktie, Cam wore boots and breeches and an open-necked shirt. It wouldn't have been appropriate to visit the tribe in the formal stiff-necked attire of a *gadjo*.

Westcliff watched him closely. "What was said between you? I would imagine they expressed some surprise upon meeting a Roma who lives with *gadje*."

"Surprise," Cam agreed, "along with pity."

"Pity?" The earl was not so enlightened as to comprehend that the Rom considered themselves vastly superior to the *gadje*.

"They pity any man who leads this kind of life." Cam gestured loosely at their refined surroundings. "Sleeping in a house. Burdened by possessions. Having a schedule. Carrying a pocket watch. All of it is unnatural."

He fell silent, thinking of the moment he had set foot in the camp, the sense of ease that had stolen over him. The sight of the wagons, *vardos,* with dogs lazing between the front wheels, the contented cob horses tethered nearby, the smells of woodsmoke and ashes . . . all of it had evoked warm childhood memories. And longing. He wanted that life, had never stopped wanting it. He had never found any-thing to replace it.

"To my mind there is nothing unnatural about wanting a roof over one's head when it rains," Westcliff said. "Or owning and tilling the land, or measuring the progress of the day with the use of a clock. It is man's nature to impose his will on his surroundings. Otherwise society would dis-integrate, and there would be nothing but chaos and war."

"And the English, with their clocks and farms and fences—they have no war?"

The earl frowned. "One can't view these matters so simplistically."

"The Rom do." Cam studied the tips of his boots, the worn leather coated with a dry film of river mud. "They asked me to go with them when they leave," he said almost absently.

"You refused, of course."

"I wanted to say yes. If not for my responsibilities in London, I would have."

Westcliff's face went blank. A speculative pause. "You surprise me."

"Why?"

"You're a man of unusual abilities and intelligence. You have wealth, and the prospect of acquiring much more. There's no logic in letting all that go to waste."

A smile touched Cam's lips. Although Westcliff was an open-minded man, he had strong opinions about how peo-ple should live. His values—among them honor, industry, and advancement—were not consistent with the Rom's. To the earl, nature was something to be managed and organized—flowers must be contained in garden beds, ani-mals must be trained or hunted, land must be cleared. And a young man must be steered into productive enterprises, and led to marry a proper woman with whom he would build a solid British family.

"Why would it be a waste?"

"A man must raise himself to his fullest potential," came the earl's unhesitating reply. "You could never do that living as a Roma. Your basic needs—food and shelter—would barely be met. You would face constant persecution. How in God's name could such a life appeal to you, when you have almost everything a man could possibly want?"

Cam shrugged. "It's freedom."

Westcliff shook his head. "If you want land, you have the means to purchase large amounts of it. If you want horses, you can buy a string of Thoroughbreds and hunters. If you want—"

"That's not freedom. How much of your time is spent directing estate affairs, investments, companies, having meetings with agents and brokers, traveling to Bristol and London?"

Westcliff looked affronted. "Are you telling me in earnest that you are considering giving up your employment, your ambitions, your future . . . in favor of traveling the earth in a *vardo*?"

"Yes. I'm considering it."

Westcliff's coffee-colored eyes narrowed. "And you think after years of living a productive life in London that you would adjust happily to an existence of aimless wandering?"

"It's the life I was meant for. In your world, I'm nothing but a novelty."

"A damned successful novelty. And you have the opportunity to be a representative for your people—"

"God help me." Cam had begun to laugh helplessly. "If it ever comes to that, I should be shot."

The earl picked up the silver letter seal from the corner of his desk, examining the engraved base of it with undue concentration. He used the edge of his thumbnail to remove a hardened droplet of sealing wax that had marred the polished surface. Cam was not deceived by Westcliff's sudden diffidence.

"One can't help but notice," the earl murmured, "that while you're considering a change in your entire way of life, you also seem to have taken a conspicuous interest in Miss Hathaway."

Cam's expression didn't change, the barrier of his smile firmly fixed. "She's a beautiful woman. I'd have to be blind not to notice her. But that's hardly going to change my future plans."

"Yet."

"Ever," Cam returned, pausing as he heard the unnecessary intensity of his own voice. He adjusted his tone at once. "I've decided to leave in two days, after St. Vincent and I confer on a few matters regarding the club. It's not likely I'll see Miss Hathaway again." Thank God, he added privately.

The handful of encounters he'd had with Amelia Hathaway were uniquely troubling. Cam couldn't recall when, if ever, he had been so affected by a woman. He was not one to involve himself in other peoples' affairs. He was loath to give advice, and he spent little time considering problems that didn't directly concern him. But he was irresistibly drawn to Amelia. She was so deliciously serious-minded, so busy trying to manage everyone in her sphere, it was an ungodly temptation to distract her. Make her laugh. Make her play. And he could, if he wished. Knowing that made it all the more difficult to stay away from her.

The tenacious connections she had formed with the others in her family, the extent she would go to take care of them . . . that appealed to him on an instinctual level. The Rom were like that. Tribal. And yet Amelia was his opposite in the most essential ways, a creature of domesticity who would insist on putting down roots. Ironic, that he should be so fascinated by someone who represented everything he needed to escape from.

It seemed the entire county turned out for the Mop Fair, which according to tradition had been held every October the twelfth for at least a hundred years. The village, with its tidy shops and white and black thatched cottages, was almost absurdly charming. Crowds milled about the distinctive oval village green or strolled along the main thoroughfare where a multitude of temporary stalls and booths had been erected. Vendors sold penny toys, foodstuffs, bags of salt from Lymington, glassware and fabrics, and pots of local honey.

The music of singers and fiddlers was punctuated by bursts of applause as entertainers performed tricks for passers-by. Most of the work-hiring had been done earlier in the day, with hopeful laborers and apprentices standing in lines on the village green, talking to potential employers. After an agreement was made, a fasten-penny was given to the newly hired servant, and the rest of the day was spent in merrymaking.

Merripen had gone in the morning to find two or three suitable servants for Ramsay House. With that business concluded, he returned to the village in late afternoon, accompanied by the entire Hathaway family. They were all delighted by the prospect of music, food, and entertainment. Leo promptly disappeared with a pair of village women, leaving his sisters in Merripen's charge.

Browsing among the stalls, the sisters feasted on hand-sized pork pies, leek pasties, apples and pears, and to the girls' delight, "gingerbread husbands." The gingerbread had been pressed into wooden man-shaped molds, baked and gilded. The baker at the stall assured them that every unmarried maiden must eat a gingerbread husband for luck, if she wanted to catch the real thing someday.

A laughing mock argument sprang up between Amelia and the baker as she flatly refused one for herself, saying she had no wish to marry.

"But of course you do!" the baker declared with a sly grin. "It's what every woman hopes for."

Amelia smiled and passed the gingerbread men to her sisters. "How much for three, sir?"

"A farthing each." He attempted to hand her a fourth. "And this for no charge. It would be a sad waste for a lovely blue-eyed lady to go without a husband."

"Oh, I couldn't," Amelia protested. "Thank you, but I don't—"

A new voice came from behind her. "She'll take it."

Discomfiture and pleasure seethed low in her body, and Amelia saw a dark masculine hand reaching out, dropping a silver piece into the baker's upturned palm. Hearing her sisters' giggling exclamations, Amelia turned and looked up into a pair of bright hazel eyes.

"You need the luck," Cam Rohan said, pushing the gingerbread husband into her reluctant hands. "Have some."

She obeyed, deliberately biting off the head, and he laughed. Her mouth was filled with the rich flavor of molasses and the melting chewiness of gingerbread on her tongue.

Glancing at Rohan, she thought he should have had at least one or two flaws, some irregularity of skin or structure . . . but his complexion was as smooth as dark honey, and the lines of his features were razor-perfect. As he bent his head toward her, the perishing sun struck brilliant spangles in the dark waves of his hair.

Managing to swallow the gingerbread, Amelia mumbled, "I don't believe in luck."

Rohan smiled. "Or husbands, apparently."

"Not for myself, no. But for others—"

"It doesn't matter. You'll marry anyway."

"Why do you say that?"

Before replying, Rohan cast a look askance at the Hathaway sisters, who were smiling benevolently upon them. Merripen, on the other hand, was scowling.

"May I steal your sister away?" Rohan asked the rest of the Hathaways. "I need to speak with her on some apiary matters."

"What does that mean?" Beatrix asked, taking the headless gingerbread husband from Amelia.

"I suspect Mr. Rohan is referring to our bee room," Win replied with a grin, gently urging her sisters to come away with her. "Come, let's see if we can find a stall with embroidery silks."

"Don't go far," Amelia called after them, more than a little amazed by the speed at which her family was abandoning her. "Bea, don't pay for something without bargaining first, and Win . . ." Her voice trailed away as they scattered among the stalls without listening. Only Merripen gave her a backward glance, glowering over his shoulder.

Seeming to enjoy the sight of Merripen's annoyance, Rohan offered Amelia his arm. "Walk with me."

She could have objected to the soft-voiced command, except this was probably the last time she would see him for a long while, if ever. And it was difficult to resist the beguiling gleam of his eyes.

"Why did you say I would marry?" she asked as they moved through the crowd at a relaxed pace. It did not escape her that many gazes strayed to the handsome Roma dressed like a gentleman.

"It's written on your hand."

"Palm-reading is a sham. And men don't read palms. Only women."

"Just because we don't," Rohan replied cheerfully, "doesn't mean we can't. And anyone could see your marriage line. It's as clear as day."

"Marriage line? Where is it?" Amelia took her hand from his arm and scrutinized her own palm.

Rohan drew her with him beneath the shade of a bulky beech tree on the edge of the green. Crowds milled across the cropped oval, while the last few swags of sunlight crumpled beneath the horizon. Torches and lamps were already being lit in anticipation of evening.

"This one," Rohan said, taking her left hand, turning it palm upward.

Amelia's fingers curled as a wave of embarrassment went through her. She should have been wearing gloves, but her best pair had been stained, and her second-best pair had a hole in one of the fingers, and she hadn't yet managed to buy new ones. To make matters worse, there was a scab on the side of her thumb where she'd gashed it on the edge of a metal pail, and her nails had been filed childishly short after she'd broken them. It was the hand of a housemaid, not a lady. For one wistful moment she wished she had hands like Win's, pale, long-fingered, and elegant.

Rohan stared for a moment. As Amelia tried to pull away, he closed his hand more firmly around hers. "Wait," she heard him murmur.

She had no choice but to let her fingers relax into the warm envelope of his hand. A blush raced over her as she felt his thumb nuzzle into her palm and stroke outward until all her fingers were lax and open.

His quiet voice seemed to collect at some hidden pleasure center at the base of her skull. "Here." His fingertip brushed over a horizontal line at the base of her little finger. "Only one marriage. It will be a long one. And these . . ." He traced a trio of small vertical notches that met the marriage line. "It means you'll have at least three children." He squinted in concentration. "Two girls and a boy. Elizabeth, Jane, and . . . Ignatius."

She couldn't help smiling. "Ignatius?"

"After his father," he said gravely. "A very distinguished bee farmer."

The spark of teasing in his eyes made her pulse jump. She took his hand and inspected the palm. "Let me see yours."

Rohan kept his hand relaxed, but she felt the power of it, bone and muscle flexing subtly beneath sun-glazed skin. His fingers were well tended, the nails scrupulously clean and pared nearly to the quick. Gypsies were fastidious, even ritualistic in their washing. The family had long been amused by Merripen's views on what constituted proper cleanliness, his preference to wash in flowing water rather than soak in a bath.

"You have an even deeper marriage line than I do," Amelia said.

He responded with a single nod, his gaze not moving from her face.

"And you'll have three children as well . . . or is it four?" She touched a nearly imperceptible line etched near the side of his hand.

"Only three. The one on the side means I'll have a very short betrothal."

"You'll likely be prodded to the altar by the end of some outraged father's rifle."

He grinned. "Only if I kidnap my fiancée from her bedroom."

She studied him. "I find it difficult to imagine you as a husband. You seem too solitary."

"Not at all. I'll take my wife everywhere with me." His fingers caught playfully at her thumb, as if he'd caught a wisp of dandelion thistle. "We'll travel in a *vardo* from one side of the world to the other. I'll put gold rings on her fingers and toes, and bracelets on her ankles. At night I'll wash her hair and comb it dry by the firelight. And I'll kiss her awake every morning."

Amelia averted her gaze from him, her cheeks turning blood-hot and sensitive. She moved away, needing to walk, anything to break the flushing intimacy of the moment. He fell into step beside her as they crossed the village green.

"Mr. Rohan . . . why did you leave your tribe?"

"I've never been quite certain."

She glanced at him in surprise.

"I was ten years old," he said. "For as long as I could remember, I traveled in my grandparents' *vardo*. I never knew my parents—my mother died in childbirth, and my father was an Irish *gadjo*. His family rejected his marriage and convinced him to abandon my mother. I don't think he ever knew she'd had a child."

"Did anyone try to tell him?"

"I don't know. They may have decided it wouldn't have changed anything. According to my grandparents, he was a young man"—he flashed a brief, mischievous smile in her direction—"and immature even for a *gadjo*. One day my grandmother dressed me in a new shirt she had made, and told me I had to leave the tribe. She said I was in danger and could no longer live with them."

"What kind of danger? From what source?"

"She wouldn't say. An older cousin of mine—his name was Noah—took me to London and helped me find a situation and a job. He promised to come back for me someday and tell me when it was safe to go home."

"And in the meantime you worked at the gaming club?"

"Yes, old Jenner hired me as a listmaker's runner." Rohan's expression softened with reminiscent fondness. "In many ways he was like a father to me. Of course, he was quick-tempered and a bit too ready with his fists. But he was a good man. He looked out for me."

"It couldn't have been easy for you," Amelia said, feeling compassion for the boy he had been, abandoned by his family and obliged to make his own way in the world. "I wonder that you didn't try to run back to your tribe."

"I had promised I wouldn't." Seeing a leaf fluttering down from an overhead tree branch, Rohan reached upward, the clever fingers plucking it from the air as if by sleight of hand. He brought the leaf to his nose, inhaling its sweetness, and gave it to her.

"I stayed at the club for years," he said in a matter-of-fact tone. "Waiting for Noah to come back for me."

Amelia chafed the crisply pliant skin of the leaf between the pads of her fingers. "But he never did."

Rohan shook his head. "Then Jenner died, and his daughter and son-in-law took possession of the club."

"You've been treated well in their employ?"

"Too well." A frown swept across his forehead. "They started my good-luck curse."

"Yes, I've heard about that." She smiled at him. "But since I don't believe in luck or curses, I'm skeptical."

"It's enough to ruin a Gypsy. No matter what I do, money comes to me."

"How dreadful. That must be very trying for you."

"It's damned embarrassing," he muttered with a sincerity she couldn't doubt.

Half amused, half envious, Amelia asked, "Had you ever experienced this problem before?"

Rohan shook his head. "But I should have seen it coming. It's fate." Stopping with her, he showed her his palm, where a cluster of star-shaped intersections glimmered at the base of his forefinger. "Financial prosperity," came his glum explanation. "And it won't end any time soon."

"You could give your money away. There are countless charities, and many people in need."

"I intend to. Soon." Taking her elbow, he guided her carefully around an uneven patch of ground. "The day after tomorrow, I'm returning to London to find a replacement factotum at the club."

"And then what will you do?"

"Live as a true Roma. I'll find some tribe to travel with. No more account books or salad forks or shoe polish. I'll be free."

He seemed convinced that he would be satisfied with a simple life—but Amelia had her doubts. The problem was, there was no middle ground. One could not be a wanderer and a domesticated gentleman at the same time. A choice had to be made. It made her thankful that no duality existed in her own nature. She knew exactly who and what she was.

Rohan brought her to a stall set up by the village wine shop, and bought two cups of plum wine. She drank the tart, slightly sweet vintage in thirsty gulps, making Rohan laugh quietly. "Not so fast," he cautioned. "This stuff is stronger than you realize. Any more and I'll have to haul you home over my shoulders like a felled deer."

"It's not that strong," Amelia protested, unable to taste any alcohol in the fruit-heavy wine. It was delicious, the dry plummy richness lingering on her tongue. She held out her cup to the wine-seller. "I'll take another."

Although proper women didn't ordinarily eat or drink in public, the rules were often cast aside at rural fairs and festivals, where gentry and commoners rubbed elbows and ignored the conventions.

Looking amused, Rohan finished his own wine, and waited patiently as she drank more. "I found a beekeeper for you," he said. "I described your problem to him. He said he would go to Ramsay House tomorrow, or perhaps the next day. One way or another, you'll be rid of the bees."

"Thank you," Amelia said fervently. "I am indebted to you, Mr. Rohan. Will it take long for him to remove the hive?"

"There's no way of knowing until he sees it. With the house having gone unoccupied for so long, the colony could be quite large. He said he'd once encountered a hive in an abandoned cottage that harbored half a million bees, by his estimate."

Her eyes turned enormous. "Half a million—"

"I doubt yours is that bad," Rohan said. "But it's almost certain part of the wall will have to be removed after the bees are gone."

More expense. More repairs. Amelia's shoulders slumped at the thought. She spoke without thinking. "Had I known Ramsay House was in such terrible condition, I wouldn't have moved the family to Hampshire. I shouldn't have taken the solicitor's word that the house was habitable. But I was in such a hurry to remove Leo from London—and I wanted so much for all of us to make a new start—"

"You're not responsible for everything. Your brother is an adult. So are Winnifred and Poppy. They agreed with your decision, didn't they?"

"Yes, but Leo wasn't in his right mind. He still isn't. And Win is frail, and—"

"You like to blame yourself, don't you? Come walk with me."

She set her empty wine cup at the corner of the stall, feeling light-headed. The second cup of wine had been a mistake. And going anywhere with Rohan, with night deepening and revelry all around them, would be yet another. But as she looked into his hazel eyes, she felt absurdly reckless. Just a few stolen minutes . . . she couldn't resist the lawless mischief of his smile. "My family will worry if I don't rejoin them soon."

"They know you're with me."

"That's why they'll worry," she said, making him laugh.

They paused at a table bearing a collection of magic lanterns, small embossed tin lamps with condensing lenses at the front. There was a slot for a hand-painted glass slide just behind the lens. When the lamp was lit, an image would be projected on a wall. Rohan insisted on buying one for Amelia, along with a packet of slides.

"But it's a child's toy," she protested, holding the lantern by its wire handle. "What am I to do with it?"

"Indulge in pointless entertainment. Play. You should try it sometime."

"Playing is for children, not adults."

"Oh, Miss Hathaway," he murmured, leading her away from the table. "The best kind of playing is for adults."

They hemmed the edge of the crowd, weaving in and out like an embroiderer's needle, until finally they drifted free of the torchlight and movement and music, and reached the dark, luminous quiet of a beech grove.

"Are you going to tell me why you had that silver seal from Westcliff's study?" he asked.

"I would rather not, if you don't mind."

"Because you're trying to protect Beatrix?"

Her startled glance cut through the shadows. "How did you . . . that is, why did you mention my sister?"

"The night of the supper party, Beatrix had the time and opportunity. The question is, why did she want it?"

"Beatrix is a good girl," Amelia said quickly. "A wonderful girl. She would never deliberately do anything wrong, and—you didn't tell anyone about the seal, did you?"

"Of course not." His hand touched the side of her face. "Easy, hummingbird. I wouldn't betray your secrets. I'm your friend. I think . . ." A brief, electrifying pause. "In another lifetime, we would be more than friends."

Her heart turned in a painful revolution behind her ribs. "There's no such thing as another lifetime. There can't be."

"Why not?"

"Occam's razor."

He was silent as if her answer had surprised him, and then a wondering laugh slipped from his throat. "The medieval scientific principle?"

"Yes. When formulating a theory, eliminate as few assumptions as possible. In other words, the simplest explanation is the most likely."

"And that's why you don't believe in magic or fate or reincarnation? Because they're too complicated, theoretically speaking?"

"Yes."

"How did you learn about Occam's razor?"

"My father was a medieval scholar." She shivered as she felt his hand glide along the side of her neck. "Sometimes we studied together."

Rohan pried the wire handle of the magic lantern from her shaky grip, and set it near their feet. "Did he also teach you that the complicated explanations are sometimes more accurate than the simple ones?"

Amelia shook her head, unable to speak as he took her shoulders, fitting her against himself with extreme care. Her pulse ran riot. She shouldn't allow him to hold her. Someone might see, even secreted in the shadows as they were. But as her muscles drew in the warm pressure of his body, the pleasure of it made her dizzy, and she stopped caring about anyone or anything outside his arms.

Rohan's fingertips drifted with stunning delicacy over her throat, behind her ear, pushing into the satiny warmth of her hair. "You are an interesting woman, Amelia."

Gooseflesh rose wherever his breath touched. "I can't f-fathom why you would think so."

His playful mouth traced the wing of her brow. "I find you thoroughly, deeply interesting. I want to open you like a book and read every page." A smile curled the corners of his lips as he added huskily, "Footnotes included." Feeling the stiffness of her neck muscles, he coaxed the tension out of them, kneading lightly. "I want you. I want to lie with you beneath constellations and clouds and shade trees."

Before she could answer, he covered her mouth with his. She felt a jolt of heat, her blood igniting, and she could no more withhold her response than stop her own heart from beating. She reached up to his hair, the beautiful ebony locks curling slightly over her fingers. Touching his ear, she found the faceted diamond stud in the lobe. She fingered it gently, then followed the taut satin skin down to the edge of his collar. His breath roughened as he deepened the kiss, his tongue penetrating in silken demand.

The white moon sent shards of light through the beech boughs, outlining the silhouette of Rohan's head, touching her own skin with an unearthly glow. Supporting her with one hand, he cradled her face with the other, his breath hot and scented with sweet wine as it fell against her mouth.

A curt voice shot through the humid darkness. "Amelia."

It was Christopher Frost, standing a few yards away, his posture rigid and combative. He gave Cam Rohan a long, hard stare. "Don't make a spectacle of her. She's a lady, and deserves to be treated as such."

Amelia felt the immediate tension in Rohan's body.

"I don't need advice from you on how to treat her," he said softly.

"You know what it will do to her reputation if she is seen with you."

It had immediately become apparent that the confrontation would turn ugly if Amelia didn't do something about it. She pulled away from Rohan. "This isn't seemly," she said. "I must go back to my family."

"I'll escort you," Frost said at once.

Rohan's eyes flashed dangerously. "Like hell you will."

"Please." Amelia reached up to touch her cool fingers to Rohan's parted lips. "I think . . . it's better that we part here. I want to go with him. There are things that must be said between us. And you . . ." She managed to smile at him. "You have many roads to travel." Clumsily she bent and retrieved the magic lantern at her feet. "Goodbye, Mr. Rohan. I hope you find everything you're looking for. I hope—" She broke off with a crooked smile, and felt a peculiar stinging pain in her throat and swallowed the bittersweet taste of longing. "Goodbye, Cam," she whispered.

He didn't move or speak. She felt him watching her as she went to Christopher Frost . . . she felt his gaze penetrating her clothes, lingering against her skin. And as she walked away, a sense of loss rushed through her.

They wandered slowly, she and Christopher, falling into a familiar harmony. They had walked often during their courtship, or gone on discreetly chaperoned drives. It had been a proper courtship, with earnest conversations and tenderly composed letters, and sweet stolen kisses. It had

seemed magical, unbelievable, that someone so handsome
and perfect would want her. In fact, Amelia had put him
off at the beginning for that very reason, telling him with a
laugh that she was sure he meant to trifle with her. But
Christopher had countered by saying he was hardly going
to trifle with his best friend's sister, and he was certainly
not some London rake who would play her false.

"For one thing, I don't dress nearly well enough to be a
rake," Christopher had pointed out with a grin, indicating
his well-tailored but sober attire.

"You're right," Amelia had agreed, looking him over
with mock solemnity. "In fact, you don't dress well enough
to be an architect, either."

"And," he had continued, "I have an exceedingly respectable history with women. Hearts and reputations all
left intact. No rake would make such a claim."

"You're very convincing," Amelia had observed, a bit
breathless as he had moved closer.

"Miss Hathaway," Christopher had whispered, engulf-
ing her cool hand with both of his warm ones, "take pity.
At least let me write to you. Promise you'll read my letter.
And if you still don't want me after that, I'll never bother
you again."

Intrigued, Amelia had consented. And what a letter it
had been . . . charming and eloquent and fairly blistering
in parts. They had begun a correspondence, and Christopher had visited Primrose Place whenever he could.

Amelia had never enjoyed any man's company so
much. They shared similar opinions on a variety of issues,
which was pleasant. But when they disagreed, it was even
more enjoyable. Christopher seldom became heated on
a subject—his approach was analytical, scholarly, rather

like her father. And if Amelia became annoyed with him, he laughed and kissed her until she forgot what had started the argument.

Christopher had never tried to seduce Amelia—he respected her too much for that. Even at the times when she had felt so stirred that she had encouraged him to go beyond mere kisses, he had refused. "I want you, little love," he had whispered, his breath unsteady, his eyes bright with passion. "But not until it's right. Not until you're my wife."

That was as close to a proposal as he had ever come. There had been no official betrothal, although Christopher had led her to expect one. There had only been a mysterious silence for almost a month, and then Leo had gone to find him on Amelia's behalf. Her brother had come back from London looking angry and troubled.

"There are rumors," Leo had told Amelia gruffly, taking her against his shirtfront, drying her tears with his handkerchief. "He's been seen with Rowland Temple's daughter. They say he's courting her."

And then another letter had come from Christopher, so devastating that Amelia wondered how mere scratches of ink on paper could rip someone's soul to shreds. She had wondered how she could feel so much pain and still survive. She had gone to bed for a week, not venturing from her darkened room, crying until she was ill, and then crying some more.

Ironically, the thing that had saved her was the scarlet fever that had struck Win and Leo. They had needed her, and caring for them had pulled her out of the depths of melancholy. She had not shed a tear for Christopher Frost after that.

But the absence of tears wasn't the same as an absence of feeling. Amelia was surprised now to discover that underneath the bitterness and caution, all the things she had once found appealing about him were still there.

"I'm the last person who should remark on how you conduct your personal affairs," Christopher said quietly. He offered an arm as they walked. She hesitated before taking it. "However, you know what people will say if you're seen with him."

"I appreciate your concern for my reputation." Amelia's tone was lightly salted with sarcasm. "But I'm hardly the only person to indulge in a few caprices at the village fair."

"If you're with a gentleman, a few caprices may be overlooked. But he's a Gypsy, Amelia."

"I noticed," she said dryly. "I would have thought you above such prejudice."

"It's not my prejudice," Christopher countered swiftly, "it's society's. Defy it if you wish, but there's always a price to pay."

"The argument is moot, at any rate," she said. "Mr. Rohan is leaving for London soon, and then for parts unknown. I doubt I'll ever see him again. And I can't fathom why you would care one way or another."

"Of course I care," Christopher said gently. "Amelia . . . I regret having hurt you. More than you could ever know. I certainly don't wish to see you endure further harm from yet another ill-advised love affair."

"I'm not in love with Mr. Rohan," she said. "I would never be so foolish."

"I'm glad to hear it."

His excessively soothing tone was grating. It made her

want to do something wild and irresponsible just to spite him. "Why aren't you married?" she asked abruptly.

The question was met with a long sigh. "She accepted my proposal to please her father, rather than out of any sincere attachment to me. As it happened, she was in love with someone else, a man her father didn't approve of. Eventually they eloped to Gretna Green."

"There's some justice in that," Amelia said. "You abandoned someone who loved you. And she abandoned you for someone she loved."

"Would it please you to know that I never loved her? I liked and admired her, but . . . it was nothing compared to what I felt for you."

"No, that doesn't please me in the least. It's even worse that you put ambition before all else."

"I'm a man who's trying to support himself—and someday a family—with an uncertain career. I don't expect you to understand."

"Your career was never that uncertain," Amelia shot back. "You had every promise of advancement, even without marrying Rowland Temple's daughter. Leo told me your talent would have taken you far."

"Would that talent were enough. But it's naïve to think so."

"Well, naïveté seems to be a common failing of the Hathaways."

"Amelia," he murmured. "It's not like you to be cynical."

She bent her head. "You don't know what I'm like now."

"I want the chance to find out."

That drew a glance of startled disbelief from her. "There's nothing to be gained by a renewed acquaintance with me, Christopher. I'm no wealthier, nor am I more advantageously connected. Nothing has changed since we last met."

"Perhaps I have. Perhaps I've come to realize what I lost."

"Threw away," she corrected, her heart thumping painfully.

"Threw away," he acknowledged in a soft tone. "I was a fool and a cad, Amelia. I would never ask that you overlook what I did. But at least give me the opportunity to make amends. I want to be of service to your family, if at all possible. And to help your brother."

"You can't," Amelia said. "You see what's become of him."

"He is a man of remarkable talents. It would be criminal to waste them. Perhaps, if I could befriend him again . . ."

"I don't think he would be very receptive to that."

"I want to help him. I have influence with Rowland Temple now. His daughter's elopement left him with a sense of obligation toward me."

"How convenient for you."

"I might be able to interest Leo in working for him again. It would benefit them both."

"But how would it benefit you?" she asked. "Why would you go to such trouble on Leo's behalf?"

"I'm not a complete villain, Amelia. I have a conscience, albeit a somewhat underused one. It's not easy to live with the memories of the people I hurt in the past. Including you and your brother."

"Christopher," she murmured, throwing him a distracted glance. "I don't know what to say. I need some time to consider things—"

"Take all the time you wish," he said gently. "If I can't be what I once was to you . . . I will have to be satisfied as a friend-in-waiting." He smiled slightly, his eyes filled with a tender glow. "And if you should ever want more . . . a single word is all it will take."

Chapter Twelve

Ordinarily Cam would have been pleased by the arrival of Lord and Lady St. Vincent at Stony Cross Park. However, Cam wasn't looking forward to the prospect of telling St. Vincent about his decision to quit the club. St. Vincent wouldn't like it. Not only would it be inconvenient to have to find a replacement manager, but the viscount wouldn't understand Cam's desire to live as a Roma. St. Vincent was nothing if not an enthusiastic advocate of fine living.

Many people feared St. Vincent, who possessed a lethal way with words and a calculating nature, but Cam was not one of them. In fact, he had challenged the viscount on more than one occasion, both of them arguing with a vicious articulateness that would have sliced anyone else to ribbons.

The St. Vincents arrived with their daughter Phoebe, a red-haired infant with an alarmingly changeable temperament. One moment the child was placid and adorable. The next, she was a squalling devil-spawn who could only be soothed by the sound of her father's voice. "There, darling," St. Vincent had been known to coo into the infant's ear. "Has someone displeased you? Ignored you? Oh, the insolence. My poor princess shall have anything she wants . . ." And, appeased by her father's outrageous spoiling, Phoebe would settle into hiccuping smiles.

The baby was duly admired and passed around in the parlor. Evie and Lillian chattered without stopping, frequently hugging and linking arms in the way of old friends.

After a while Cam, St. Vincent, and Lord Westcliff withdrew to the back terrace, where an afternoon breeze diffused the scents of the river and reed sweetgrass and marsh marigold. The raucous honks of greylag geese punctuated the peace of the Hampshire autumn, along with the lowing of cattle being driven along a well-worn path to a dry meadow.

The men sat at an outside table. Cam, who disliked the taste of tobacco, waved his hand in dismissal as St. Vincent offered him a cigar.

Under Westcliff's interested regard, Cam and St. Vincent discussed the progress of the club's renovations. Then, seeing no reason to tiptoe around the issue, Cam told St. Vincent of his decision to quit the club as soon as the work was completed.

"You're leaving me?" St. Vincent asked, looking perturbed. "For how long?"

"For good, actually."

As St. Vincent absorbed the information, his pale blue eyes narrowed. "What will you do for money?"

Relaxed in the face of his employer's displeasure, Cam shrugged. "I already have more money than anyone could spend in a lifetime."

The viscount glanced heavenward. "Anyone who says such a thing obviously doesn't know the right places to shop." He sighed shortly. "So. If I'm to understand correctly, you intend to eschew civilization altogether and live as a savage?"

"No, I intend to live as a Roma. There's a difference."

"Rohan, you're a wealthy young bachelor with all the advantages of modern life. If you've got ennui, do what every other man of means does."

Cam's brows lifted. "And that would be . . ."

"Gamble! Drink! Buy a horse! Take a mistress! For God's sake, have a little imagination. Can you think of no better option than to throw it all away and live like a primitive, thereby inconveniencing me in the process? How the devil am I to replace you?"

"No one's irreplaceable."

"You are. No other man in London can do what you do. You're a walking account book, you've got eyes in the back of your head, you've got the tact of a diplomat, the mind of a banker, the fists of a boxer, and you can put down a fight in a matter of seconds. I'd need to hire at least a half-dozen men for your job."

"I don't have the mind of a banker," Cam said indignantly.

"After all your investment coups, you can't deny—"

"That wasn't on purpose!" A scowl spread across Cam's face. "It was my good-luck curse."

Looking satisfied to have unsettled Cam's composure, St. Vincent drew on his cigar. He exhaled a smooth, elegant stream of smoke and glanced at Westcliff. "Say something," he told his old friend. "You can't approve of this any more than I."

"It's not for either of us to approve."

"Thank you," Cam muttered.

"However," Westcliff continued, "I urge you, Rohan, to reflect adequately on the fact that while half of you is a freedom-loving Gypsy, the other half is Irish—a race renowned for its fierce love of land. Which leads me to doubt that you will be as happy in your wandering as you seem to expect."

The point rattled Cam. He had always tried to ignore the *gadjo* half of his nature, lugging it around like some oversized piece of baggage he would have liked to set aside but for which he could never find a convenient place.

"If your point is that I'm damned whatever I do," Cam said tersely, "I'd rather err on the side of being free."

"All men of intelligence must eventually give up their freedom," St. Vincent replied. "The problem with bachelorhood is that it's far too easy, which makes it tedious. The only real challenge left is marriage."

Marriage. Respectability. Cam regarded his companions with a skeptical smile, thinking they resembled a pair of birds trying to convince themselves of how comfortable their cage was. No woman was worth having his wings clipped.

"I'm leaving for London tomorrow," he said. "I'll stay at the club until it reopens. After that I'll be gone for good."

St. Vincent's clever mind circumvented the problem, analyzing it from various angles. "Rohan . . . you've led a more or less civilized existence for years, and yet suddenly it has become intolerable. Why?"

Cam remained silent. The truth was not something he was readily able to admit to himself, let alone say aloud.

"There has to be some reason you want to leave," St. Vincent persisted.

"Perhaps I'm off the mark," Westcliff said, "but I suspect it may have something to do with Miss Hathaway."

Cam sent him a damning glare.

St. Vincent looked alertly from Cam's stony face to Westcliff's. "You didn't tell me there was a woman."

Cam stood so quickly the chair nearly toppled backward. "She has nothing to do with it."

"Who is she?" St. Vincent always hated being left out of gossip.

"One of Lord Ramsay's sisters," came Westcliff's reply. "They reside at the estate next door."

"Well, well," St. Vincent said. "She must be quite something to provoke such a reaction in you, Rohan. Tell me about her. Is she fair? Dark? Well formed?"

To remain silent, or to deny the attraction, would have been to admit the full extent of his weakness. Cam lowered back into his chair and strove for an offhand tone. "Dark-haired. Pretty. And she has . . . quirks."

"Quirks." St. Vincent's eyes glinted with enjoyment. "How charming. Go on."

"She's read obscure medieval philosophy. She's afraid of bees. Her foot taps when she's nervous." And other, more personal things he couldn't reveal . . . like the beautiful paleness of her throat and chest, the weight of her hair in his hands, the way strength and vulnerability were pleated inside her like two pieces of fabric folded together. Not to mention a body that had been designed for mortal sin.

Cam didn't want to think about Amelia. Every time he did, he was swamped with a feeling he'd never known before, something as acute as pain, as pervasive as hunger. The feeling seemed to have no purpose other than to rob him of sleep at night. There wasn't one millimeter of Amelia Hathaway that didn't attract him profoundly, and that was a problem so far outside his experience, he didn't begin to know how to address it.

If only he could take her, ease this endless ache . . . but having lain with her once, he might want her even more afterward. In mathematics, one could take a finite figure and divide its content infinitely, with the result that even though the content was unchanged, the magnitude of its bounds went on forever. Potential infinity. It was the first time Cam had ever comprehended the concept in the form of a woman.

Aware that Westcliff and St. Vincent had exchanged a significant glance, Cam said sourly, "If you're assuming that my plans to leave are nothing more than a reaction to Miss Hathaway . . . I've been considering this for a long time. I'm not an idiot. Nor am I inexperienced with women."

"To say the least," St. Vincent commented dryly. "But in your pursuit of women—or perhaps I should say their pursuit of you—you seem to have regarded them all as interchangeable. Until now. If you are taken with this Hathaway creature, don't you think it bears investigating?"

"God, no. There's only one thing it could lead to."

"Marriage," the viscount said rather than asked.

"Yes. And that's impossible."

"Why?"

The fact that they were discussing Amelia Hathaway and the subject of marriage was enough to make Cam blanch in discomfort. "I'm not the marrying kind—"

St. Vincent snorted. "No man is. Marriage is a female invention."

"—but even if I were so inclined," Cam continued, "I'm a Roma. I wouldn't do that to her."

There was no need to elucidate. Decent *gadjis* didn't marry Gypsies. His blood was mixed, and even though Amelia herself might harbor no prejudices, the routine discriminations Cam encountered would certainly extend to his wife and children. And if that wasn't bad enough, his own people would be even more disapproving of the match. *Gadje Gadjensa, Rom Romensa . . .* Gadje with Gadje, Roma with Roma.

"What if your heritage made no difference to her?" Westcliff asked quietly.

"That's not the point. It's how others would view her." Seeing that the older man was about to argue, Cam murmured, "Tell me, would either of you wish your daughter to marry a Gypsy?" In the face of their discomforted silence, he smiled without amusement.

After a moment, Westcliff stubbed out his cigar in a deliberate, methodical fashion. "Obviously you've made up your mind. Further debate would be pointless."

St. Vincent followed his lead with a resigned shrug and a facile smile. "I suppose now I'm obliged to wish you happiness in your new life. Although happiness in the absence of indoor plumbing is a debatable concept."

Cam was undeceived by the show of resignation. He had never known Westcliff or St. Vincent to lose an argument easily. Each, in his own way, would hold his ground long after the average man would have collapsed to his knees. Which made Cam fairly certain he hadn't heard the last word from either of them yet.

"I'm leaving at dawn," was all he said.

Nothing could change his mind.

Chapter Thirteen

Beatrix, whose imagination had been captured by the magic lantern, could hardly wait for evening to come so she could view the selection of glass slides again. Many of the images were quite amusing, featuring animals wearing human clothes as they played piano or sat at writing desks or stirred soup in a pot.

Other slides were more sentimental; a train passing through a village square, winter scenes, children at play. There were even a few scenes of exotic animals in the jungle. One of them, a tiger half-hidden in leaves, was particularly striking. Beatrix had experimented with the lantern, moving it closer to the wall then farther away, trying to make the tiger's image as distinct as possible.

Now Beatrix had taken to the idea of writing a story, recruiting Poppy to paint some accompanying slides. It was decided they would put on a show someday, with Beatrix narrating while Poppy operated the magic lantern.

As her younger sisters lounged by the hearth and discussed their ideas, Amelia sat with Win on the settee. She watched Win's slender, graceful hands as she embroidered

a delicate floral pattern, the needle flashing as it dove
through the cloth.

At the moment, her brother was lolling on the carpet
near the girls, slouched and half-drunk, his long legs
crossed native-fashion. Once he had been a kind and caring older brother, sympathetically bandaging one of the
children's hurt fingers, or helping to look for a lost doll.
Now he treated his younger sisters with the polite indifference of a stranger.

Absently Amelia reached up to rub the pinched muscles at the back of her neck. She glanced at Merripen as he
sat in the corner of the room, every line of his body lax
with the exhaustion of heavy labor. His gaze was distant as
if he, too, were consumed with private thoughts. It troubled her to look at him. The rich hue of his skin, the shiny
appleseed-darkness of his hair, reminded her too much of
Cam Rohan.

She couldn't seem to stop thinking about him this evening, and also Christopher Frost, the images forming a jarring contrast in her mind. Cam offered no commitment, no
future, only the pleasures of the moment. He was not a
gentleman, but he possessed a ruthless honesty that she
appreciated far more than smooth manners.

And then there was fair-haired, civilized, reasonable,
handsome Christopher. He had professed a desire to renew
their relationship. She had no idea if he was sincere, or
how she would respond if it turned out he was. How many
women would have been grateful for a second chance with
their first love? If she chose to overlook his past mistake
and forgive him, encourage him, it might not be too late
for the two of them. But she wasn't certain she wanted to
resume all those abandoned dreams. And she wondered if

it was possible to be happy with a man one loved but didn't trust.

Beatrix pulled a glass slide from the front of the lamp casing, laid it aside carefully, and reached for another. "This one's my favorite . . ." she was saying to Poppy, as she slid the next image in place.

Having lost interest in the succession of pictures on the wall, Amelia did not look up. Her attention remained on Win's embroidering. But Win made an uncharacteristic slip, the needle jabbing into the soft flesh of her forefinger. A scarlet drop of blood welled.

"Oh, Win—" Amelia murmured.

Win, however, didn't react to the pinprick. She didn't even seem to have noticed it. Frowning, Amelia glanced at her sister's still face and followed her gaze to the opposite wall.

The image cast by the magic lantern was a winter scene, with a snow-blurred sky and the dark cache of forest beneath. It would have been an unremarkable scene, except for the delicate outline of a woman's face that seemed to emerge from the shadows.

A familiar face.

As Amelia stared, transfixed, the spectral features seemed to gain dimension and substance until it seemed almost as if she could reach out and shape her fingers against the waxing contours.

"Laura," she heard Win breathe.

It was the girl Leo had loved. The face was unmistakable. Amelia's first coherent thought was that Beatrix and Poppy must be playing some horrid joke. But as she looked at the pair on the floor, chatting together innocently, she perceived at once that they didn't even see the dead girl's image. Nor did Merripen, who was watching Win with a questioning frown.

By the time Amelia's gaze shot once more to the projection, the face had disappeared.

Beatrix pulled the slide from the magic lantern. She fell back with a little cry as Leo charged toward her and made a grab for the slide.

"Give it to me," Leo said, more an animal growl than a human voice. His face was blanched and contorted, his body knotted with panic. He hunched over the little piece of painted glass and stared through it as if it were a tiny window into hell. Fumbling with the magic lantern, Leo nearly overset it as he tried to jam the slide back in.

"Don't, you'll break it!" Beatrix cried in bewilderment. "Leo, what are you doing?"

"Leo," Amelia managed to say, "you'll cause a fire. Careful."

"What is it?" Poppy demanded, looking bewildered. "What's happening?"

The glass fell into place, and the winter scene flickered on the wall once more.

Snow, sky, forest.

Nothing else.

"Come back," Leo muttered feverishly, rattling the lantern. "Come back. Come back."

"You're frightening me, Leo," Beatrix accused, hopping up and speeding to Amelia. "What's the matter with him?"

"Leo's foxed, that's all." Amelia said distractedly. "You know how he is when he's had too much to drink."

"He's never been like this before."

"It's time for bed," Win remarked. Worry seeped through her voice like a watermark on fine paper. "Let's go upstairs,

Beatrix . . . Poppy . . ." She glanced at Merripen, who stood at once.

"But Leo's going to break my lantern," Beatrix exclaimed. "Leo, do stop, you're bending the sides!"

Since their brother was apparently beyond hearing or comprehension, Win and Merripen efficiently whisked the younger girls from the room. A questioning murmur from Merripen, and Win replied softly that she would explain in a moment.

When everyone had gone and the sounds of voices had faded from the hallway, Amelia spoke carefully.

"I saw her, too, Leo. So did Win."

Her brother didn't look at her, but his hands stilled on the lantern. After a moment he removed the slide and put it back in again. His hands were shaking. The sight of such raw misery was difficult to bear. Amelia stood and approached him. "Leo, please talk to me. Please—"

"Leave me alone." He half shielded his face from her regard, palm turned outward.

"Someone has to stay with you." The room was getting colder. A tremor began at the top of Amelia's spine and worked downward.

"I'm fine." A few stunted breaths. With a titanic effort Leo lowered his hand and stared at her with strange light eyes. "I'm fine, Amelia. I just need . . . I want . . . a little time alone."

"But I want to talk about what we saw right in front of us."

"It was nothing." He was sounding calmer by the second. "It was an illusion."

"It was Laura's face. You and Win and I all saw it!"

"We all saw the same shadow." The barest hint of wry

amusement edged his lips. "Come, sis, you're too rational to believe in ghosts."

"Yes, but . . ." She was reassured by the familiar mockery in his tone. And yet she didn't like the way he kept one hand on the lamp.

"Go on," he urged gently. "As you said, it's late. You need to rest. I'll be all right."

Amelia hesitated, her arms chilled and stinging beneath the sleeves of her gown. "If you really want—"

"Yes. Go on."

She did, reluctantly. A draft from somewhere seemed to rush past her as she left the room. She hadn't intended to close the door fully, but it snapped shut like the jaws of a hungry animal.

It was difficult to make herself walk away. She wanted to protect her brother from something.

She just didn't know what it was.

After reaching her room, Amelia changed into her favorite nightgown. The white flannel was thick and shrunken from many washings, the high collar and long sleeves textured with white-work embroidery that Win had done. The chill she had taken downstairs was slow to fade, even after she had crawled beneath the bedclothes and curled tightly into a ball. She should have thought to light a fire at the hearth. She should do it now, to make the room warmer, but the idea of climbing out of bed was not appealing in the least.

Instead she occupied her mind with thoughts of hot things; a cup of tea, a woolen shawl, a steaming bath, a flannel-wrapped brick from the hearth. Gradually warmth accumulated around her, and she relaxed enough to sleep.

But it was a troubled rest. She had the impression of

arguing with people in her dreams, back-and-forth conversations that made no sense. Shifting, rolling to her stomach, her side, her back, she tried to ignore the bothersome dreams.

Now there were voices . . . Poppy's voice, actually . . . and no matter how she tried to ignore it, the sound persisted.

"Amelia. Amelia!"

She heaved herself up on her elbows, blind and confused from the sudden awakening. Poppy was by her bed.

"What is it?" Amelia mumbled, scraping back a tangled curtain of hair from her face.

At first Poppy's face was disembodied in the darkness, but as Amelia's eyes adjusted, the rest of her became dimly visible.

"I smell smoke," Poppy said.

Such words were never used lightly, nor could they ever be dismissed without investigation. Fire was an ever-present concern no matter where one lived. It could start in any number of ways, from overturned candles, lamps, sparks that leaped from the hearth or embers from coal-burning ovens. And fire in a house this old would be nothing less than disaster.

Struggling from the bed, Amelia hunted for the slipper box near the end of the bed. She stubbed her toe, and hopped and cursed.

"Here, I'll fetch them." Poppy lifted the tin lid of the slipper box and took the shoes out, while Amelia found a shawl.

They linked arms and made their way through the dark room with the caution of elderly cats.

Reaching the top of the stairs, Amelia sniffed hard but could detect nothing other than the familiar accumulation of cleaning soap, wax, dust, and lamp oil. "I don't smell any smoke."

"Your nose isn't awake. Try again."

This time there was a definite taint of something burning. Alarm speared through her. She thought of Leo, alone with the lantern, the flame and oil . . . and she knew instantly what had happened.

"Merripen!" The whip-crack force of her voice caused Poppy to jump. Amelia gripped her sister's arm to steady her. "Get Merripen. Wake everyone up. Make as much noise as you can."

Poppy obeyed at once, scampering toward her siblings' bedrooms while Amelia made her way downstairs. A sullen glow came from the direction of the parlor, an ominous flickering light bleeding beneath the door.

"Leo!" She flung the door open and recoiled at a furnace blast that struck her entire body. One wall was covered in flame, rippling and curling upward in hot tentacles. Through a bitter haze of smoke, her brother's bulky form was visible on the floor. She ran to him, grasped the folds of his shirt, and tugged so hard that the cloth began to give and the seams crackled. "Leo, get up, get up now!" But Leo was insensible.

Shrieking at him to wake up and gather his wits, Amelia tugged and dragged without success. Frustrated tears sprang to her smoke-stung eyes. But then Merripen was there, pushing her aside none too gently. Bending, he picked Leo up and hoisted him over a broad shoulder with a grunt. "Follow me," he said brusquely to Amelia. "The girls are already outside."

"I'll come out in just a moment. I have to run upstairs and fetch some things—"

He gave her a dangerous glance. "No."

"But we have no clothes—it's all going to go up—"

"Out!"

Since Merripen had never raised his voice to her in all the years they had known each other, Amelia was startled into obeying. Her eyes continued to smart and water from the smoke even after they had gone through the front door and out to the waiting darkness of the graveled drive. Win and Poppy were there, both huddled around Leo and trying to coax him into waking and sitting up. Like Amelia, the girls were dressed only in nightgowns, shawls, and slippers.

"Where's Beatrix?" Amelia asked. At the same moment, the estate bell began to peal, its high, clear tone traveling in every direction.

"I told her to ring it," Win said. The sound would bring neighbors and villagers to help, although by the time people reached them, Ramsay House would probably be consumed in flames.

Merripen went to lead the horse from the stable, in case that went up, too.

"What's happening?" Amelia heard Leo ask hoarsely. Before anyone could reply, he was seized by a spasm of coughing. Win and Poppy remained beside their brother, murmuring gently to him. Amelia, however, stood a few yards apart from them, knotting her shawl more tightly around her shoulders.

She was filled with bitterness and fury and fear. There was no doubt in her mind Leo had started the fire, that he had cost them the house and had nearly succeeded in killing them all. It would be a long time before she could trust herself to speak to him, this sibling she had once loved so dearly and who now seemed to have transformed into someone else entirely.

At this point there was little left of Leo to love. At best he was an object to be pitied, at worst a danger to himself and his family. They would all be better off without him, Amelia thought. Except that if he died, the title would pass to some distant relative or expire, and they would be left with no income whatsoever.

Watching Merripen, illuminated in the cloud-blunted moonlight as he worked to pull first the horse and then the barouche from the stables, Amelia felt a surge of gratitude. What would they ever have done without him? When her father had taken in the homeless boy so long ago, it had always been regarded by the residents of Primrose Place as an act of charity. But the Hathaways had been infinitely repaid by Merripen's quiet, steady presence in their lives. She had never been certain why he had elected to stay with the Hathaways—it seemed all to their advantage rather than his.

People had already begun to arrive on horseback, some from the village, some from the direction of Stony Cross Manor. The villagers had brought a handpump cart pulled by a sturdy draft horse. The wheeled cart was sided by troughs, which would be laboriously filled with river water, people carrying buckets back and forth. Cranking a wooden lever would push the water through a leather hose and expel it through a metal nozzle. By the time the process was under way, the fire would be raging out of control. However, it was possible the handpump would help to save at least a portion of the house.

Amelia ran to the approaching villagers to describe the shortest route to the nearby river. Immediately a group of men, accompanied by Merripen, set off at a run toward the water, buckets swinging from the yokes on their shoulders.

As she turned to go back to her sisters, Amelia bumped into a tall form behind her. Gasping, she felt a familiar pair of hands close over her shoulders.

"Christopher." Relief flooded her at his presence, despite the fact that he could do nothing to save her home. She twisted to look up at him, his handsome features bathed in erratic light.

He pulled her close as if he couldn't help himself, pressing her head to his shoulder. "Thank God you're not hurt. How did the fire start?"

"I don't know." Amelia went still against him, thinking dazedly that she had never expected to be held by him again. She remembered this, the way she fit against him, the security of his embrace. But remembering that he had betrayed her, she wriggled free and pushed her hair from her eyes.

Christopher released her reluctantly. "Stay away from the house. I'm going to help with the handpump."

Another voice came from the darkness. "You'll be of more use over there."

Amelia and Christopher both turned with a start, for the voice seemed to have come from nowhere. With his dark clothes and black hair, Cam Rohan seemed to emerge like a shadow from the night.

"Bloody hell," Christopher muttered. "One can barely see you, dark as you are."

Although Rohan could have taken umbrage at the remark, he did not respond. His gaze ran over Amelia in swift assessment. "Have you been hurt?"

"No, but the house—" Her throat clenched on a sob.

Cam shrugged off his coat and settled it around her, pulling the edges together at the front. The wool was permeated with warmth and a comforting masculine scent. "We'll see what we can do." He gestured for Christopher Frost to come with him. "Two canisters are being unloaded near the stairs. You can help me carry them inside."

Amelia's eyes turned round at the sight of the two large metallic vessels. "What are they?"

"An invention of Captain Swansea's. They're filled with pearl ash solution. We're going to use it to keep the fire from spreading until they've primed the water pump." Rohan slid a glance toward Christopher Frost. "Since Swansea is too old to carry the containers, I'll take one and you'll take the other."

Amelia knew Christopher well enough to sense his dislike of taking orders, especially from a man he considered his inferior. But he surprised her by acceding without protest, and followed Cam Rohan to the burning house.

Chapter Fourteen

Amelia watched as Cam Rohan and Christopher Frost lifted the ungainly copper containers, which had been fitted with leather hosing, and hauled them past the front door. Captain Swansea remained on the steps, shouting instructions after them.

The windows were shot with lurid flashes as fire began to digest the interior of the house. Soon, Amelia thought bleakly, nothing would be left but a blackened skeleton.

Making her way back to her sisters, Amelia stood beside Win, who was cradling Leo's head in her lap. "How is he?"

"He's ill from the smoke." Win ran a gentle hand over her brother's disheveled head. "But I think he'll be all right."

Glancing down at Leo, Amelia muttered, "The next time you try to kill yourself, I'd appreciate it if you wouldn't take the rest of us with you."

He gave no indication of having heard, but Win, Beatrix, and Poppy glanced at her in surprise.

"Not now, dear," Win said in gentle reproof.

Amelia stifled the hot words that rose to her lips and stared stonily at the house.

More people were arriving, some forming a line to pass water buckets back and forth from the river to the hand-pump. There was no sign of activity from within the building. She wondered what Rohan and Frost were doing.

Win seemed to read her mind. "It seems Captain Swansea finally has an opportunity to test his invention," she said.

"What invention?" Amelia asked. "And how do you know about it?"

"I sat next to him at supper, at Stony Cross Manor," Win replied. "He told me that during his experiments with rocketry design, he had the idea for a device that would extinguish fires by spraying them with pearl ash solution. When the copper canister is upended, a vial of acid mixes with the solution, and it creates enough pressure to force the liquid from the canister."

"Would that work?" Amelia asked doubtfully.

"I certainly hope so."

They both flinched at the sound of breaking windows. The handpump crew was making an opening large enough to direct a stream of water inside the burning room.

Becoming more worried by the moment, Amelia watched intently for any sign of Rohan or Frost. She was highly skeptical about the notion of running into a burning house with an untested device that could explode in one's face. Confronted by the chemicals, the smoke, and the heat, the men might be disoriented or overwhelmed. The idea of some harm befalling either of them was unbearable. Her muscles knotted with anxiety until streaks of pain fired through every limb.

Just as she began to consider the idea of venturing to the front threshold, Rohan and Frost emerged from the house with the emptied canisters and were immediately approached by Captain Swansea.

Amelia hurried forward with a cry of gladness, fully intending to stop once she reached them. Which was why it was a surprise when her legs insisted on carrying her forward.

Rohan dropped the canister and caught her tightly. "Easy, hummingbird."

She had lost his coat and her shawl somewhere amid the impetuous dash. The cold night air pierced the thin layer of her gown, causing her to shiver hard. He gripped her more closely, easing her into the pungent fragrance of smoke and sweat. His heartbeat was steady beneath her ear, his hand tracing warm circles on her back.

"The extinguishers were even more effective than I'd anticipated," she heard Captain Swansea say to Christopher Frost. "Two or three more canisters, and I do believe we could have put it down by ourselves."

Collecting herself, Amelia looked out from the circle of Rohan's arms. Frost stared at her with patent disapproval and something that might have been jealousy. She knew she was making a spectacle of herself with Cam Rohan. Again. But she couldn't make herself leave the comforting shelter of his arms just yet.

Captain Swansea was smiling, pleased with the results of his efforts. "The fire's under control now," he told Amelia. "I should think they'll have it out quite soon."

"Captain, I'll never be able to thank you enough," she managed to say.

"I've been waiting for an opportunity like this," he declared. "Though of course I wouldn't have wished for your home to serve as the testing site." He turned to view the progress with the handpump, which was now operating at full capacity. "I'm afraid," he said ruefully, "the water damage will be just as bad as that from the smoke."

"Perhaps some of the upstairs rooms are still habitable," Amelia said. "In a few minutes I should like to go up and see—"

"No," Rohan interrupted calmly. "You and the rest of the Hathaways are going to Stony Cross Manor. They have more than enough guest rooms to accommodate you."

Before Amelia could say a word, Christopher Frost answered for her. "I'm staying with the Shelsher family at the village tavern. Miss Hathaway and her siblings will go there with me."

Amelia felt the change in Rohan's hold. His hand came to her arm, and his thumb found the inside curve of her elbow, where her pulse thrummed hard beneath fragile skin. He touched her with the possessive intimacy of a lover.

"Westcliff's residence is closer," Rohan said. "Miss Hathaway and her sisters are standing outside in the cold, dressed in little more than their nightgowns. Their brother needs to be seen by a doctor, and if I'm not mistaken, Merripen does, too. They're going to the manor."

Amelia frowned as his words sank in. "Why does Merripen need a doctor? Where is he?"

Rohan turned her in his arms to face the opposite direction. "Over there, beside your sisters."

She gasped at the sight of Merripen huddled on the ground. Win was with him, attempting to pull the thin fabric of his shirt away from his back. "Oh, no." Amelia pulled away from Rohan and sped toward her family. She heard Christopher Frost calling out her name, but she ignored the sound.

"What happened?" she asked, dropping to the damp ground beside Win. "Has Merripen been burned?"

"Yes, on his back." Win ripped a makeshift bandage from the hem of her own gown. "Beatrix, would you take this, please, and soak it in water?"

Without a word, Beatrix scampered to the trough at the handpump.

Win stroked Merripen's thick black hair as he rested his head on his forearms. His breath hissed unevenly through his teeth.

"Does it hurt, or is it numb?" Amelia asked.

"Hurts like the devil," he choked out.

"That's a good sign. A burn is much more serious if it's numb."

He turned his head to give her a speaking glance.

Win kept her hand on the nape of Merripen's neck as she spoke to Amelia. "He went too close to the eaves of the house. The heat from the fire caused the flashing on the shingles to melt and drip down. Some molten lead fell on his back." She glanced up as Beatrix returned with a dripping cloth. "Thank you, dear." Lifting Merripen's shirt, she laid the wet cloth over the burn, and he let out a pained growl. Losing all sense of pride or decorum, he let Win pillow his head on her lap while he shook uncontrollably.

Glancing at Leo, who was faring little better, Amelia realized Cam Rohan was right—she needed to take her family to the manor immediately, and send for a doctor.

She made no protest as Rohan and Captain Swansea came to load the assembled Hathaways into the carriage. Leo had to be lifted bodily into the vehicle, and Merripen, who was unsteady and disoriented, required help as well.

Captain Swansea handled the ribbons deftly as he drove the family to Stony Cross Manor.

Upon their arrival, the Hathaways were greeted with considerable excitement and sympathy, servants running in all directions, houseguests volunteering extra clothes and personal items. Lady Westcliff and Lady St.Vincent took charge of the younger girls, while Amelia was dragged away by a pair of determined housemaids. It became clear they would not relent until she was bathed and fed and dressed.

An eternity had passed by the time the housemaids put Amelia into a fresh nightgown and a blue velvet robe. Another quarter hour crawled by as they painstakingly braided her damp hair into a neat plait behind each ear. When at last they were finished with her, Amelia thanked the maids and fled the guest room. She went to check on her siblings, starting with her brother.

A servant in the hallway directed her to Leo's room. The doctor, an elderly man with a neatly trimmed gray beard, was just leaving. He paused, bag in hand, as she asked about her brother's condition.

"All in all, Lord Ramsay is doing quite well," the doctor replied. "There is minor swelling of the throat—due to the smoke inhalation, of course—but it is mere tissue irritation rather than serious damage. His color is good, the heart is strong, and all signs are that he'll be good as new."

"Thank God. What about Merripen?"

"The Gypsy? His condition is a bit more worrisome. It's a nasty burn. But I've treated it and applied a honey dressing, which should keep the bandage from sticking as it heals. I will return tomorrow to check on his progress."

"Thank you. Sir, I don't wish to trouble you—I know the

hour is late—but could you spare a moment to visit one of my sisters? She has weak lungs, and even though she wasn't exposed to the smoke, she was out in the night air—"

"You're referring to Miss Winnifred."

"Yes."

"She was in the Gypsy's room. Apparently he shared your concern over your sister's health. Both of them were arguing quite strenuously over which one of them I should see first."

"Oh." A faint smile came to her lips. "Who won? Merripen, I suppose."

He smiled back at her. "No, Miss Hathaway. Your sister may have weak lungs, but she has no end of resolve." He bowed to her. "I wish you good evening. My sympathies on your misfortune."

Amelia nodded in thanks and went into Leo's room, where a lamp had been turned down low. He was lying on his side, eyes open, but he didn't spare her a glance as she approached. Sitting on the side of the mattress with care, she reached out and smoothed his matted hair.

His voice was a soft croak. "Have you come to finish me off?"

She smiled wryly. "You seem to be doing an excellent job of that all by yourself." Her hand shaped tenderly over his skull. "How did the fire start, dear?"

He looked at her then, his eyes so bloodshot they resembled two tiny coaching road maps. "I don't remember. I fell asleep. I didn't cause the fire on purpose. I hope you believe that."

"Yes." She leaned over and kissed his head as if he were a young boy. "Rest, Leo. Everything will be better in the morning."

"You always say that," he mumbled, closing his eyes. "Maybe someday it'll be true." And he fell asleep with startling quickness.

Hearing a noise at the door, Amelia looked up to see the housekeeper carrying a tray laden with brown glass bottles and bundles of dried herbs. The elderly woman was accompanied by Cam Rohan, who carried a small open kettle filled with steaming water.

Rohan had not yet washed the smoke from his clothes and hair and skin. Although he must have been tired from the night's exertions, he showed no signs of it. He took Amelia in with an all-encompassing glance, his eyes glowing like brimstone in his smudged, sweat-streaked face.

"The steam will help Lord Ramsay breathe more comfortably during the night," the housekeeper explained. She proceeded to light the candles beneath a bedside holder, onto which the kettle was placed.

As steam dispersed through the air, a strong, not unpleasant fragrance drifted to Amelia's nostrils. "What is it?" she asked in a hushed voice.

"Chamomile, thyme, and licorice," Rohan said, "along with slippery elm and horsetail leaves for the swelling in his throat."

"We've also brought morphine to help him sleep," the housekeeper said. "I'll leave it by the bedside, and if he awakens later—"

"No," Amelia said quickly. The last thing Leo needed was unsupervised access to a large bottle of morphine. "That won't be necessary."

"Yes, miss." The housekeeper departed with a quiet murmur for her to ring if anything was needed.

Cam remained in the room, casually leaning a shoulder

against one towering bedpost. He watched as Amelia went to investigate the contents of the steam kettle. She averted her gaze from his vibrant dark presence, the searching eyes, the quizzical cast of his mouth.

"You must be exhausted," she said, picking up a sprig of dried leaves. She brought the crackly fragrant herbs to her nose and sniffed experimentally. "It's very late."

"I've spent most of my life in a gaming club—by now I'm more or less nocturnal." A brief pause. "You should go to bed."

Amelia shook her head. Somewhere beneath the clamor of her pulse and the raffle of worries in her mind, there was a great ache of weariness. But any attempt to sleep would be useless—she would simply lie there and stare at the ceiling. "My head is spinning like a carousel. The thought of sleep . . ." She shook her head.

"Would it help," he asked gently, "to have a shoulder to cry on?"

She fought to conceal how much the question unnerved her. "Thank you, but no." Carefully she dropped the herbs into the kettle. "Crying is a waste of time."

" 'To weep is to make less the depth of grief.' "

"Is that a Romany saying?"

"Shakespeare." He studied her, seeing too much, reading what simmered beneath the forced calm. "You have friends to help you through this, Amelia. And I'm one of them."

Amelia was terrified that he might see her as an object of pity. She would avoid that at all cost. She couldn't lean on him, or anyone. If she did, she might never be able to stand on her own again. She moved away from him, around him, her hands fluttering as if to bat away any attempt to reach her. "You mustn't trouble yourself about the Hathaways. We'll manage. We always have."

"Not this time." Rohan watched her steadily. "Your brother is beyond helping anyone, including himself. Your sisters are too young, except for Winnifred. And now even Merripen is bedridden."

"I'll take care of them. I don't need help." She reached for a length of toweling draped at the foot of the bed, and folded it neatly. "You're leaving for London in the morning, aren't you? You should probably take your own advice and go to bed."

The light eyes turned flinty. "Damn it, why do you have to be so stubborn?"

"I'm not being stubborn. It's just that I don't want anything from you. And you deserve to find the freedom you've been deprived of for so long."

"Are you concerned about my freedom, or are you terrified of admitting you need someone?"

He was right—but she would rather have died than admit it. "I don't need anyone, least of all you."

His voice was no less blistering for being soft. "You don't know how easy it would be to prove you wrong." He began to reach for her, checked the movement, and looked at her as if he wanted to throttle her, kiss her, or both.

"Maybe next lifetime," she whispered, somehow managing a crooked smile. "Please go. Please, Cam."

She waited until he had left the room, and her shoulders sagged with relief.

Needing to escape the smothering confines of the house, Cam went outside. The night threaded weak moonlight through a weft of infinite darkness. He wandered to the ironstone wall that edged a bluff overlooking the river. Hoisting himself easily to the top of the wall, he sat with his feet dangling over the edge, and listened to the water and the night sounds. Smoke hung in the air, mingling with the scents of earth and forest.

Cam tried to sort through a tangle of emotions.

He had never known jealousy before, but when he had seen Amelia and Christopher Frost embracing earlier, Cam had experienced a violent urge to strangle the bastard. Every instinct raged that Amelia was *his,* his alone to protect and comfort. But he had no rights to her.

If Frost decided to pursue her, it was best that Cam not interfere. Amelia would be better off with her own kind, rather than a half-bred Roma. Cam would be better off, too. Good God, was he actually contemplating spending the rest of his life as a *gadjo,* bound in domesticity?

He should leave Hampshire, he thought. Amelia would make her own decision about Frost, and Cam would follow his destiny. No compromises or sacrifices on either side. He would never be anything more to Amelia than a brief, vaguely remembered episode in her life.

Lowering his head, he scrubbed his hands through his unruly hair. His chest ached in the way it always had when he yearned for freedom. But for the first time, he wondered if he was right about what he wanted. Because it didn't seem as if the pain would be cured when he left. In fact, it threatened to become a good deal worse.

The future spread before him in a great lifeless void. Thousands of nights without Amelia. He would hold and make love to other women, but none of them would ever be the one he truly wanted.

He thought of Amelia living as a spinster. Or worse, reconciling with Frost, perhaps marrying him, but always living with the knowledge that Frost had betrayed her once and might again. She deserved so much more than that. She deserved passionate, heart-scalding, overwhelming, consuming love. She deserved . . .

Oh, *hell.* He was thinking too much. Just like a *gadjo.*

He forced himself to face the truth. The fact was, Amelia was his, whether he stayed or left, whether they walked the same path or not. They could live on opposite sides of the world, and she would still be his.

The Roma half of him had seen that from the beginning.

And it was that side of himself he would listen to.

Amelia's bed was soft and luxurious, but it might as well have been made of bare wood planks. She rolled, turned, sprawled, but she could find no comfortable position for her aching body, and no peace for her tortured brain.

The room was still and stuffy, the air turning thicker by the minute. Craving a breath of clear, cold air, she slipped from the bed, went to the window, and pushed it open. A gasp of relief escaped her as a light breeze swept over her. She closed her sore eyes, used her knuckles to rub her wet lashes.

It was strange, but with all the problems she faced, the thing that kept her from sleeping was the question of whether or not Christopher Frost had ever really loved her. She had wanted to think so, even after he had abandoned her. She had told herself that love was a luxury for most people, that Christopher's career was a difficult one, and he had been faced with an impossible choice. He had done what he'd thought best at the time. Perhaps it had been wrong of her to expect him to choose her and damn the consequences.

To be desired above all else, to be wanted, needed, coveted . . . that would never happen to her.

The door opened in a well-oiled arc. She saw the shadows change, felt a presence in the room. Turning with a start, she saw Cam Rohan standing just inside the door. Her heart began to drum with furious force. He looked like something from a dream, a dark enigmatic ghost.

He approached her slowly. The closer he came, the more it seemed everything around her was unraveling, falling away, leaving her exposed and vulnerable.

Cam's breathing wasn't quite steady. Neither was hers. After a long pause, he finally spoke. "The Rom believe you should take the road that calls to you, and never turn back. Because you never know what adventures await." He reached for her slowly, giving her every opportunity to object. Through the cottony gauze of her nightgown, he touched the curve of her hips. He brought her close, into his hard weight.

"So we're going to take this road," he murmured, "and see where it leads."

He waited for a signal, some syllable of objection or encouragement, but she could only stare at him, transfixed and helpless.

He smoothed her hair, whispering for her not to fear him, he would take care of her, please her. His fingers found the sensitive curve of her scalp, cradling her head as he kissed her. He dragged his mouth across hers, again and again, and when her lips were open and damp, he sealed them with his.

Excitement flooded her, and she gave in to the dark pleasure, opening to the penetrating strokes of his tongue, struggling to capture the silkiness. His hands gently urged her backward until her balance collapsed. She lay on the tumbled bed as if on some pagan altar. Bending over her, Cam kissed her throat. There was a series of quick tugs at the front of her gown, and the edges of the garment parted.

She felt his urgency, the heat radiating from his body, but every movement was careful, lingering, as he reached beneath the fragile cotton and caressed her breast. Her knees drew up, her entire body arching to contain the pleasure of his touch. With a wordless sound Cam coaxed her to relax, his hand gliding from her chest to her knees. His parted lips brushed the naked tip of her breast, toying with the hardening bud, his tongue skimming wetly. She brought her hands to his hair, tangling her fingers in the ebony locks, trying to hold him to her. His mouth closed over her nipple, tugging lightly until she quivered and tried to roll away, unnerved by the feeling that she was being driven to the brink of some new sensation altogether.

Cam pulled her back to him and bent over her once more. His mouth covered hers, while his teasing fingers pulled the hem of her gown higher and found the tender backs of her thighs.

Amelia reached for his shirt with trembling hands. It was loose-cut and collarless, the kind that lifted over the head instead of buttoning. Cam moved to help her, pulling the garment off and tossing it aside. Moonlight gilded the supple, muscular lines of his body, his chest taut and smooth.

Flattening her palms against the hard flesh, she drew them gently downward to his sides and around his back. He shivered at her touch and lowered to the place beside her, one leg sliding between hers. The gown fell open to expose her chest completely, the hem bunching high on her thighs.

His lips descended to her breast again, while he cupped and kneaded the firm flesh. Arching up to him, she struggled to press closer, to bring his weight more fully over her. He resisted, his hands traveling over her in caresses meant to calm her. She quivered at his gentleness, her hands gripping his back. She couldn't think clearly, couldn't find words. Twisting against him, she felt the desire sharpen to unbearable intensity. "Cam . . . Cam . . ." She pressed her face to his shoulder.

Feeling the dampness of her lashes, he eased her head back and touched his tongue to an errant teardrop. "Patience, hummingbird. It's too soon."

She looked up into his shadowed features. "For you?"

There was a moment's pause, as if Cam were struggling to hold back a sudden laugh. "No, for you."

"I'm twenty-six years old," she protested. "How could it possibly be too soon for me?"

Cam couldn't suppress his laughter then, burying the low, rich sounds in her mouth.

The kisses turned harder, longer, and in between, Cam spoke in a mixture of Romany and English, and it was unclear if he even knew what language he used. Grasping her hand in his, he brought it down his body to the urgent thrust of his erection. Shocked and fascinated, Amelia eased her hand along the length of him, her fingers molding hesitantly over the hardness. Cam groaned as if in pain, and she snatched her hand back at once.

"I'm terribly sorry," she said, flushing. "I didn't mean to hurt you."

"You didn't hurt me." There was a flick of tender amusement in his voice. He caught her hand and brought it back down.

Amelia explored him shyly, her curiosity stirred by the heat and suggestion of movement beneath the taut fabric of his breeches. He seemed to revel in her touch, nearly purring as he moved over her to nuzzle and lick at her throat.

Both his legs were between hers now, widening the space between them, the nightgown crumpled around her waist. Exposed, mortified, excited, she felt one of his hands roaming low on her stomach. Soon there would be pain and possession, all mysteries solved. She thought perhaps now would be an opportune time to mention something.

"Cam?"

His head lifted. "Yes?"

"I've heard there are ways—that is, since this can lead to—oh, I don't know how to say it—"

"You don't want me to give you a baby." His fingertips played gently through her intimate dark curls.

"Yes. That is . . . no." Her breath tangled around a moan.

"I won't. Although there's always a chance." He found a place so alive with sensation that she jerked and drew her knees up. His fingers were light and gentle as he parted the soft cleft. "The question, love, is whether you want me enough to take the risk."

Her senses swam in shame and pleasure at the way he touched her. Her entire existence had dwindled to the sly teasing of one fingertip. And Cam knew. He waited for her answer, stroking, shaping the tenderness with his fingertips, paying careful attention to every shiver and twitch of her body.

"Yes," she said unsteadily. "I want you."

The pad of his thumb stroked downward, gliding through a patch of inexplicable wetness. Before she could say a word, he had pressed into the moisture with his thumb, invading her slightly.

His lashes lowered over devil-bright eyes. "Do you want this?" he whispered.

She nodded and tried to say yes, but all that came out was a low whimper.

Deeper, a gently inquiring stroke, until she felt the hard ridge of his thumb ring press against the entrance of her body. He made slow circles inside her, the smooth ring teasing and rubbing until she felt faint and hot. *Oh, dear heaven, yes, no, please* . . . another swirl, another, each one coiling the pleasure tighter until her heart was thundering and her hips nudged rhythmically against the heel of his hand. But then the exquisite invasion was withdrawn, and her body clasped desperately around the emptiness. She reached for him, clawing him in her frantic need, and Cam had the effrontery to laugh softly.

"Easy, sweetheart. We're still at the beginning. There's no need to hurry through it."

"The beginning?" Stunned and throbbing, she could hardly speak. If there was one thing she was certain of, it was that she couldn't bear much more of his refined torture. "I would have thought you'd have already finished by now."

She felt him smile as he kissed the inside of her elbow, working his way down to her wrist. "The point is to make it last as long as possible."

"Why?"

"It's better that way. For both of us." He pried her clenched fingers apart and kissed the palm of her hand. After pulling her nightgown back into place, he buttoned the front with meticulous care.

"What are you doing?"

"Taking you for a ride." As she sputtered with questions, he touched a gentle forefinger to her lips. "Trust me," he whispered.

Amelia complied in a daze as he pulled her from the bed, wrapped the velvet robe around her, and tucked her feet into soft slippers.

Clasping her hand firmly in his, Cam led her from the room. The house was still and soundless, the walls hung with portraits of aristocrats with disapproving faces.

They went out the back of the house to the great stone terrace, its wide curving steps leading down to the gardens. The moonlight was crossed with shredded clouds that glowed against a sky the color of black plums. Puzzled but willing, Amelia went with Cam to the bottom of the steps.

He stopped and gave a short whistle.

"What—" Amelia gasped as she heard the pounding of heavy hooves and saw a huge black form rushing toward them like something from a nightmare. Alarm darted through her, and she burrowed against Cam, her face hidden against his chest. His arm went around her, tucking her close.

When the thundering stopped, Amelia risked a glance at the apparition. It was a horse. A huge black horse, with puffing breaths that rose like wraiths in the raw air.

"Is this really happening?" she asked.

Cam reached in his pocket and fed the horse a sugar lump, and ran his hand over the sleek midnight neck. "Have you ever had a dream like this?"

"Never."

"Then it must be happening."

"You actually have a horse who comes when you whistle?"

"Yes, I trained him."

"What is his name?"

His smile gleamed white in the darkness. "Can't you guess?"

Amelia thought for a moment. "Pooka?" The horse turned his head to look at her as if he understood. "Pooka," she repeated with a faint smile. "Do you have wings, by any chance?"

At Cam's subtle gesture, the horse shook his head in an emphatic no, and Amelia laughed shakily.

Walking to Pooka's side, Cam swung up onto the pack-saddle in a graceful movement. He sidled close to the step on which Amelia was standing and reached down to her. She took his hand, managing to gain a foothold on the stirrup. She was lifted easily onto the saddle in front of him. Momentum carried her a little too far, but Cam's arm locked around her, keeping her in place.

Amelia leaned back into the hard cradle of his chest and arm. Her nostrils were filled with the scents of autumn, damp earth, horse and man and midnight.

"You knew I'd come with you, didn't you?" she asked.

Cam leaned over her, kissing her temple. "I only hoped." His thighs tightened, setting the horse to a gallop, and then a smooth canter. And when Amelia closed her eyes, she could have sworn they were flying.

Chapter Fifteen

Cam rode to the abandoned river encampment where the Gypsy tribe had stayed. The remains of the camp were still there; the ruts left by the wheels of the *vardos,* circles of grass eaten where the cobs had been tethered, the shallow fire pit filled with ash. And everywhere there was the sound of the sloshing, rushing river, pushing at the banks, soaking the yielding earth.

He dismounted and helped Amelia to the ground. At his direction, she sat on a fallen birch log while he set up a makeshift camp. She waited with her hands folded neatly in her lap, watching his every movement as he pulled a bundle of blankets from the packsaddle. In a few minutes he had made a fire in the stone-circled pit and laid out a pallet beside it.

Amelia hurried to the pile of blankets and burrowed beneath the layers of wool and quilted cotton. "Is it safe out here?" she asked, her voice muffled.

"You're safe from everything but me." Smiling, Cam lowered himself beside her. After removing his boots, he joined her beneath the blankets and pulled her against

him. Reminding himself of the rewards to be gained by
patience, he cuddled her close and waited.

As one second melted into the next, Amelia's body nestled more tightly against his. It felt so extraordinary just to
hold her that he did nothing for a long time. He listened to
the flow of her breathing, and felt the cold night air move
over them, while the warmth of their bodies collected beneath the blankets. They descended into the heart of a still,
quiet pleasure Cam had never known before. His pulse began a hard, rolling drum, the heat thickening between every
beat. He felt her hips pressing tentatively against his,
cradling the rigid shape of his arousal, bundling closer.
But still he didn't move, only let her cuddle and brush
against him until he was tense and fiercely aroused.

The fire flicked and snapped its yellow ribbons, lapping at
broken birch and oak. Hot . . . he had never been so hot in
his life. As he considered removing his shirt, he felt Amelia's
hands creeping under the loose hem. The small, cool fingers
roamed over his steaming skin. Wherever she touched, the
muscles rippled and tightened, and it felt so good that Cam
let out a faint groan against her hair. She grasped loose handfuls of his shirt and tugged upward. Without hesitation he sat
up, stripped the garment off and tossed it aside.

She crawled into his lap, her long hair streaming over his
naked chest and shoulders in a silken net. Entranced, Cam
held still as she pressed her mouth to his chest, his shoulders, the base of his throat, in a delicate frolic of kisses.

"Amelia . . ." His hands came to her head, stilling her.
The warm ripples of her hair slid over his arms, raising
gooseflesh.

"Monisha," he whispered, "I won't do anything you
don't want. I only want to give you pleasure."

Her face was glowing in the firelight, her lips the color of red currants. "What does that word mean?"

"*Monisha?* An endearment." He could hardly think straight. "A Roma says it to a woman he's intimate with."

Her hands came to his, fingers slipping into the spaces between his fingers. They held each other, their lips forming soundless words, mouths grazing and catching with damp heat.

Cam lowered her to the blankets, in the pool of dancing firelight. And he whispered in the old language, telling her that he wanted to chase her as the sun chased the moon across the sky, he wanted to fill her until they were *corthu,* one being, joined. He was only half aware of what he was saying, drunk on the scent of her and the heat rising from her body.

He opened her robe and gown, dreamily pulling the soft fabric away from the deep curves of her breasts and waist. She was so beautifully made, lush and firm, the pale skin burnished with light. Voluptuous shadows dipped into places he yearned to touch and taste. He followed her spreading blush with his mouth, pursuing the wash of color. She shivered beneath him, her hands gripping the bulging muscles of his upper arms.

He cupped her breasts and teased the peaks with his breath and tongue until they were hard and silken. Softly he drew one between his teeth, held it there until she whimpered and lifted upward.

Cam tugged at the tangled layer of her gown between them. The cove of her navel rose and fell with her breathing. Easing his mouth over it, he sank the tip of his tongue into the tight circle, filling the hollow.

"Cam . . . oh, wait . . ." She was squirming now, pushing

at him in earnest. He caught her hands and gripped them close against her body, and breathed hard against her stomach.

Fighting for self-control, Cam laid his cheek against her skin with all the gentleness he was capable of. "I won't hurt you," he whispered. "I'm only going to kiss you . . . taste you . . ."

Her voice was plaintive. "Not there."

Cam couldn't suppress a smile. This was new, this mixture of amusement and arousal. "Especially there." He let his fingers drift over her hip and thigh, into the soft curls. "I want to know every part of you, *monisha* . . . Hold still for me and . . . yes, love, *yes* . . ." He moved downward, shaking with hunger. The scents of intimate salt and female skin had kindled an unbearable craving. His mouth brushed intimately closed lips. He licked them open, delving into the heat, the taste of her pleasure.

Amelia was silent except for her broken gasps, her legs clamping hard against his sides. Helplessly she followed the sinuous pattern of his tongue, her entire body arching and yearning. He soothed her, provoked her, his mouth as playful as a swallow in flight. His breath fell rapidly on her wet flesh, her erotic incense. He slid a finger into the silkiness.

She made a sound of distress as she lost all self-control, and he gloried in it, his mouth punishing in its gentleness. He drew out the torment until the soft female moans broke into sobs. She tightened and twisted, her fingers closing in his hair, hips pulsing in helpless movements as he licked away every twitch and throb.

After a while he moved to gather her against him. She reached down to the fastenings of his breeches and worked at them until the garment was loose around his hips. The rigid length of him sprang free. Her hand curled around the burgeoning shape, stroking until Cam jerked back with a gasp.

Her face was flushed, eyes half-closed. She touched him again, urged him forward, instinctively making an open cradle of her hips and legs. He resisted, keeping his weight suspended above her, shielding her from the gaze of moonlight as he spread his fingers and trailed them over the front of her body. She shivered as the tip of his smallest finger brushed the tip of her breast. He traced a circle around it, watching the bud tighten.

"If you want me, love," he whispered, "tell me in Romany. Please."

Blindly Amelia turned her head and kissed the curve of his biceps. "What should I say?"

He murmured soft lyrical words, waiting patiently as she repeated them, helping her when she faltered. All the while he positioned himself against her, lower, tighter, and just as the last syllable left her lips, he thrust strongly inside her.

Amelia flinched and cried out in pain, and Cam was torn between acute regret at having hurt her, and the devastating pleasure of being inside her. Her innocent flesh cinched around the unfamiliar invasion, her hips lifting as if to throw him off, but every movement only drew him deeper. He tried to soothe away the hurt, stroking her, kissing her throat and breasts. Taking a rosy crest into his mouth, he sucked lightly, ran his tongue over it, until she relaxed beneath him and began to moan.

Cam couldn't stop from moving then, forgetting everything but the need to push deeper into the gently gripping flesh, the warm limbs curving around him, the sweet panting mouth beneath his. He whispered compulsively against her lips . . . one word, over and over, the ecstasy crowning higher every time. *"Mandis . . . mandis . . ."*

Mine.

Feeling the violent spill of release about to begin, Cam withdrew and thrust against the quivering velvet of her stomach. Heat jetted and slid between them. Cam buried his head in the crook of her neck and shoulder, groaning. No feeling had ever come close to this, he thought dizzily. Nothing could.

The pleasure lasted even after his heartbeat had returned to normal and he had regained his ability to think clearly, more or less. Amelia had gone lax beneath him, drowsing and sighing. He had to force himself to withdraw, when all he wanted was to revel in the feel of her.

He used a handkerchief to clean the blood and moisture from her body, dressed her in her nightgown, and went to replenish the fire. When he returned to settle beneath the blankets, Amelia snuggled in the crook of his arm.

Watching the crackling fire, relishing the trusting weight of her head on his shoulder, Cam stroked her hair as it streamed over his arm. She slept heavily, while the fire pitched shadows from her long lashes across her cheeks. Cam looked over her with a lover's vigilance, absorbing every detail, the feathery edge of her hairline, the neat slope of her nose, the small ears. He wanted to nibble at her ears, play with her, but he would do nothing to disturb her sleep.

He pulled a quilt higher over her snowy shoulder, stroked back a curl that had looped over her ear. Everything had changed, he thought. And there was no turning back.

Chapter Sixteen

Daybreak.

A perfect word for the way the morning had entered the bedroom in pieces, a shard of light falling across her bed, another on the floor between the window and the small hearth.

Amelia blinked and lay for a while in a torpor. There was a fire in the hearth—she must have slept right through the maid lighting the grate.

Fire . . . Ramsay House . . . the memory fell on her with an unpleasant thud, and she closed her eyes. They flew open again, however, as she thought of darkness and blue moonlight and warm male flesh. Goose bumps rose all over her.

What had she done?

She was in her bed, with only a murky recollection of riding back when it was still dark, Cam carrying her, tucking the mass of the bedclothes around her as if she were a child. *Close your eyes,* he had murmured, his hand a comforting pressure on her skull. And she had slept and slept. Now as she squinted at the cheerfully ticking mantel clock, she saw that it was nearly noon.

Panic thrashed inside her, until she reminded herself that it was impractical to panic. Nevertheless, her heart pumped something that seemed too hot and light to be blood, and her breath turned choppy.

She would have liked to persuade herself that it had all been a dream, but her body was still imprinted with the invisible map he had drawn with his lips, tongue, teeth, hands.

Raising her fingertips to her lips, Amelia felt that they were puffier, smoother than usual . . . they had been licked and abraded by his mouth. Every inch of her body felt sensitive, tender places still harboring an ache of pleasure.

A decent woman should certainly have felt shame over her actions. Amelia felt none. The night had been so extraordinary, so rich and dark and sweet, she would hoard the memory forever. It had been an experience not to be missed, with a man unlike anyone she had ever known or would ever meet again.

But oh, how she hoped he was gone by now.

With any luck, Cam would have already left to take care of his business in London. Amelia wasn't at all certain she could face him after last night. And she certainly didn't need the distraction he presented, when there was so much to be decided.

As for the memories of the night with Cam, all of it so gently refracted as if he were a prism her feelings had traveled through . . . now was not the time to think about any of that. There would be time later. Days, months, years.

Don't think about it, she told herself sternly, climbing out of bed. She rang for a maid, and fumbled to fasten her robe. In less than a minute, a sturdy light-haired maid with apple cheeks appeared.

"May I have some hot water?" Amelia asked.

"Aye, miss. I can bring some up, or if tha likes, I can draw a bath in the bathing room." The maid spoke in a broad, warm Yorkshire accent, the *r*'s slightly rolled, the consonants adhering to the back of her throat.

Amelia nodded at the second suggestion, remembering the modern bath from the previous night. She followed the maid, who identified herself as Betty, out of the room and along the hallway. "How are my sisters and brothers? And Mr. Merripen?"

"Miss Winnifred, Miss Poppy, and Miss Beatrix have all gone downstairs for breakfast," the maid reported. "The two gentlemen are still abed."

"Are they ill? Does Mr. Merripen have a fever?"

"Mrs. Briarly, the housekeeper, is of the mind they're both fine, miss. Only resting."

"Thank goodness." Amelia resolved to check on Merripen as soon as she was presentable. Burn wounds were dangerous and unpredictable—she was still quite worried for his sake.

They entered a room with walls covered in pale blue tiling. There was a chaise longue in one corner and a large porcelain tub in another. A richly colored Oriental curtain hung from the ceiling to provide a secluded dressing area. The bathing room was warm, thanks to the fireplace, and a large open wardrobe displayed neatly folded stacks of bath linens, Turkish towels, and various soaps and toiletries. The bath water was heated in the room by some kind of gas apparatus, with taps for cold, hot, or tepid water, and pipes leading outside.

Betty opened the taps and adjusted the water temperature. She laid out bath linens across the chaise longue in a precise row. "Shall I attend while tha bathes, miss?"

"No, thank you," Amelia said at once. "I'll manage by myself. If you wouldn't mind bringing my clothes to the adjoining dressing room . . ."

"Which dress, miss?"

That stopped Amelia cold. She realized she had come to Stony Cross Manor with no clothes whatsoever. "Oh, dear. I wonder if someone could be sent to Ramsay House to fetch my things . . ."

"They're likely all clarty and full of smoke, miss. But Lady St. Vincent had some of her own dresses put in your room—she and thee are more of a size than Lady West- cliff, who's taller, so she—"

"Oh, I can't wear Lady St. Vincent's clothes," Amelia said uncomfortably.

"Afraid there's no help for it, miss. There's a lovely red woolen—I'll fetch it for thee."

Since there appeared to be no possibility of retrieving any of her own gowns, Amelia nodded and murmured her thanks. She went behind the dressing screen and removed her robe, while the housemaid shut off the taps and left the bathing room.

As Amelia stripped away the nightgown and let it drop to the floor, she saw a flash of gold on her left forefinger. Startled, she lifted her hand and examined it. A small gold signet ring with an elaborate engraved initial. It was the one Cam always wore on his smallest finger. He must have put it on her last night, while she was sleeping. Had he meant it as a parting gift? Or did it have some other sig- nificance to him?

She tried to pull it off, and discovered it was firmly stuck. "Drat," she muttered, tugging at the thing in vain. She took a cake of soap from the wardrobe and brought it into the bath with her. The hot water soothed a myriad of small aches and stings, easing the soreness between her thighs.

Sighing deeply, Amelia soaped her hand and went to work on the ring. But no matter how she tried, it wouldn't budge. Soon the surface of the bathwater was covered with soap froth, and Amelia was cursing with frustration.

She couldn't let anyone see her wearing one of Cam's rings. How in God's name was she supposed to explain how and why she'd gotten it?

After pulling and twisting until her knuckle was swollen, Amelia gave up and finished her bath. She dried herself with a Turkish towel, its pile loose and soft against her skin. Entering the adjoining dressing room, she found Betty waiting for her with an armload of soft wine-colored wool.

"Here is the dress, miss. The dress will look right pretty on thee, with tha dark hair."

"Lady St. Vincent is too generous." The piles of crisp frothy undergarments looked so pristine, it was likely they had never been worn. There was even a corset, its white laces as neat as surgical sutures.

"Oh, she has many, many dresses," Betty confided, handing Amelia a pair of folded drawers and a chemise. "Lord St. Vincent sees to it that his wife is dressed like a queen. I'll tell thee summat: if she wanted the moon for her looking glass, he'd find a way to pull it down for her."

"How do you know so much about them?" Amelia asked, hooking the front of the corset while Betty moved behind her to pull the laces.

"I'm Lady St. Vincent's maid. I travel with her wherever she goes. She bid me to attend thee and the other

Miss Hathaways—'they need special care,' she said, 'after what they've endured.' "

Amelia held in her breath as the laces were tugged firmly. When they were finally tied, she expelled a quick breath. "That was very kind of her. And you. I hope my family hasn't been troublesome."

For some reason that produced a chuckle. "Tha art a shandy lot, if you don't mind my saying so, miss." Before Amelia could ask what that meant, the maid exclaimed, "What a small waist tha has! I expect Lady St. Vincent's dress will fit thee like a glove. But before we try it, tha'd better put thy hosen on."

Amelia took a handful of translucent black fabric from her. "Hosen?"

"Silk stockings, miss."

Amelia nearly dropped them. Silk stockings cost a fortune. And these were embroidered with tiny flowers, which made them even more expensive. If she wore them, she would be in terror of snagging them. However, there seemed to be no other choice, short of going without.

"Do put them on," Betty urged.

With a mixture of temptation and guilt, Amelia dressed in the most luxurious clothes she had ever worn in her life. The dress, lined with silk, was entirely ladylike, but it draped and molded over her figure in a way her own clothes never had. Straight, close-fitting sleeves went to her elbow, where they flared in spills of black lace. The same black lace trimmed the deep bias hem of the skirt, which was layered to suggest a multitude of underskirts. A black satin sash emphasized the neat curve of her waist, the ends crossed and pinned at the side with a sparkling jet brooch.

Sitting at the dressing table, Amelia watched as Betty dexterously braided black ribbons in her hair and pinned it up. Since the maid seemed friendly and talkative, Amelia ventured, "Betty . . . how long has Lady St. Vincent been acquainted with Mr. Rohan?"

"Since childhood, miss." Betty grinned. "That Mr. Rohan, he's a fine doorful of man, aye? You should see the carryings-on when he visits the master's house—every last one of us fighting for a turn at the keyhole, just to gawp at him."

"I wonder . . ." Amelia strove for a casual tone. "Do you think the relationship between Mr. Rohan and Lady St. Vincent was ever . . ."

"Oh, nay, miss. They was raised like brother and sister. There's even rumors that Mr. Rohan is her half brother. Wouldn't be the only bastard child sired by Ivo Jenner, for certain."

Amelia blinked. "Do you think the rumors are true?"

Betty shook her head. "Lady St. Vincent says nay, there's no blood 'twixt 'em. And she and Mr. Rohan bear no likeness. But she's fair fond of him." With a wry smile, Betty added, "She has warned me and the other maids to keep ourse'en far away from him. She says no good could come of it, and we'd find ourselves tupped and left. He's a wicked one, that Mr. Rohan. Charming enow to steal the sugar from your punch." Finishing Amelia's hair, Betty viewed her with satisfaction, and went to collect the used linens that had been heaped by a chair, including the discarded nightgown.

The maid paused for the measure of two, three seconds, with the nightgown in hand. "Shall I make a pad of clean rags, miss?" she asked carefully. "For thy monthly courses?"

Still pondering the unpalatable phrase "tupped and left," Amelia shook her head. "No, thank you. It's not time for—" She stopped with a little shock as she saw what the maid had noticed—a few rusty spots of blood on the nightgown. She blanched.

"Yes, miss." Folding the gown tightly into the bundle of bedlinens, Betty gave her a neutral smile. "Tha has only to ring, and I'll come." She went to the door and let herself out carefully.

Amelia propped her elbows on the dressing table, and rested her forehead on her fists. Heaven help her, there would be talk belowstairs. And until now she had never done anything worthy of gossip.

"Please, please let him be gone," she whispered.

Heading downstairs, Amelia mused that she believed in luck after all. It seemed as good a word as any to describe a consistent pattern of things. A dependable, predictable outcome for nearly every situation.

And hers happened to be bad luck.

As she reached the entrance hall, she saw Lady St. Vincent coming in from the back terrace, her cheeks wind-brightened, the hem of her gown littered with bits of leaves and grass. She looked like an untidy angel, with her lovely calm face and rippling red hair, and the playful spray of light gold freckles across her nose.

"How are you feeling?" Lady St. Vincent came to her at once and took her arm. "You look lovely. Your sisters are walking outside, except for Winnifred, who's having tea on the terrace. Have you eaten yet?"

Amelia shook her head.

"Come to the back terrace, we'll have a tray brought out."

"If I'm interrupting you—"

"Not at all," Lady St. Vincent said gently. "Come."

Amelia went with her, touched and yet disconcerted by Lady St. Vincent's solicitous manner.

"My lady," she said, "thank you for allowing me to wear one of your dresses. I will return it as soon as possible—"

"Call me Evie," came the warm reply. "And you must keep the dress. It is very becoming on you, and not at all on me. That particular shade of red clashes with my hair."

"You are too kind," Amelia said, wishing she didn't sound so stiff, wishing she could accept the gift without feeling the weight of obligation.

But Evie didn't seem to notice her awkwardness, just reached for her hand and drew it through her arm as they walked, as if Amelia needed to be led like a young girl. "Your sisters will be relieved to see you up and about. They said it was the first time they could ever remember you staying abed so long."

"I'm afraid I didn't sleep well. I was . . . preoccupied." Color climbed up the pale slopes of Amelia's cheeks as she thought of lying next to Cam's body, their clothes disheveled to reveal places of bareness and heat, lips and hands delicately investigating.

"Yes, I'm sure you—" A quick hesitation, then Evie continued in a bemused tone. "I'm sure you had much to consider."

Following her gaze, Amelia realized that Evie had glanced down at the hand that rested on her sleeve.

She had seen the ring.

Amelia's fingers curled. She looked up into the countess's curious blue eyes, and her mind went blank.

"It's all right," Evie said, catching Amelia's hand when she would have withdrawn it, pressing it back to her arm. She smiled. "We must talk, Amelia. I thought he wasn't quite himself today. Now I understand why."

There was no need to clarify who "he" was.

"My lady . . . Evie . . . there is nothing between Mr. Rohan and myself. Nothing." Her cheeks burned with agitated color. "I don't know what you must think of me."

They paused before the French doors that opened onto the back terrace, and Amelia withdrew her hand from Evie's arm. Tugging at the ring, which remained stubbornly clamped on her finger, she glanced at Evie in despair. To her astonishment, Evie did not seem at all shocked or critical, but rather understanding. There was something in her face, a sort of tender gravity, that made Amelia think, *No wonder Lord St. Vincent is besotted with her.*

"I think you're a capable young woman," Evie said, "who loves her siblings and bears a great deal of responsibility for them. I think that's a heavy burden for a woman to carry alone. I also think you have a gift for accepting people as they are. And Cam knows how rare that is."

Amelia felt anxious, as if she'd lost something and needed to retrieve it quickly. "I . . . is he still here? He should have left for London by now."

"He's still here, talking with my husband and Lord Westcliff. They rode to Ramsay House early this morning to see what was left of it, and make some early assessments."

Amelia didn't like the thought of them visiting the property without consulting her or Leo. The situation was being handled as if the Hathaways were nothing more than a group of helpless children. She squared her shoulders.

"That was very kind of them, but I can manage the situation now. I expect part of Ramsay House is still habitable, which means we won't need to prevail on Lord and Lady Westcliff's hospitality any longer."

"Oh, you must stay," Evie said quickly. "Lillian has already said you are welcome to remain until Ramsay House is fully restored. This is such a large house, you would never intrude on anyone's privacy. And Lillian and Lord Westcliff will be away for at least a fortnight. They're leaving for Bristol tomorrow—along with Lord St. Vincent and myself—to visit Lillian's younger sister Daisy, who is expecting a child. So you'll have the manor to yourselves, more or less."

"We'd reduce the place to a heap of rubble by the time they returned."

Evie smiled. "I suspect your family isn't as dangerous as all that."

"You don't know the Hathaways." Feeling the need to assert control over the situation, Amelia said, "I'll ride to Ramsay House myself after I have some breakfast. If the upstairs rooms are in suitable condition, my family will be back home by nightfall."

"Do you think that's best for Winnifred?" Evie asked gently. "Or Mr. Merripen, or Lord Ramsay?"

Amelia flushed, knowing she was being unreasonable. But the feeling of impotence, being stripped of all authority, was rising in a choking mass.

"Perhaps you should speak to Cam," Evie said, "before any decisions are made."

"He has nothing to do with my decisions."

Evie gave her a thoughtful look. "Forgive me. I shouldn't make assumptions. It's just that the ring on your finger . . . Cam's worn it since he was twelve years old."

Amelia tugged violently at the ring. "I don't know why he gave it to me. I'm sure it's of no significance."

"I think it has very great significance," Evie said softly. "Cam has been an outsider for his entire life. Even when he lived with the Rom. I think he's always secretly hoped he could someday find a place where he would belong. But until he met you, it didn't occur to him that it might not be a place he was looking for, but a person."

"I'm not that person," Amelia whispered. "Truly, I'm not."

Evie regarded her with kind sympathy. "It's your decision, of course. But as someone who has known Cam for a very long time, I must tell you . . . he's a good man, and entirely trustworthy." She pushed the French doors open for Amelia. "Your sisters are outside," she said. "I'll send for your dinner tray."

It was a damp, brisk day, the air saturated with the scents of mulch and roses and late-flowering grasses. The back terrace overlooked acres of meticulously tended gardens, all connected by graveled pathways. Tables and chairs had been set upon the flagstoned floor. Since most of Lord Westcliff's guests had departed at the conclusion of the latest hunting party, the terrace was largely unoccupied.

Seeing Win, Poppy, and Beatrix at a table, Amelia strode to them eagerly. "How are you?" she asked Win. "Did you sleep well? Did you cough?"

"I'm quite well. We were worried about you—I've never known you to sleep so long unless you were ill."

"Oh, no, not ill, couldn't be better." Amelia gave her an overbright smile. She glanced at her other sisters, who were both wearing new gowns, Poppy in yellow and Beatrix in green. "Beatrix . . . you look lovely. Like a young lady."

Smiling, Beatrix stood and executed a slow turn for her. The pale green dress, with its intricately pleated bodice and dark green corded trim, fit almost perfectly, the skirts falling down to the floor. "Lady Westcliff gave it to me," she said. "It belonged to her younger sister, who can't wear it anymore because she's in confinement."

"Oh, Bea . . ." Seeing her sister's pleasure in the grown-up dress, Amelia felt a pang of sorrowful pride. Beatrix should attend a finishing school, where she would learn French and flower arranging, and all the social graces the rest of the Hathaways lacked. But there was no money for that—and at this rate, there never would be.

She felt Win's hand slip into hers and give it a small squeeze. Glancing down into Win's understanding blue eyes, she sighed. They were still for a moment, hands clinging in mutual support.

"Amelia," Win murmured, "do sit by me. I want to ask you something."

Amelia lowered herself in the chair, which gave her a perfect vantage point of the gardens. There was a sharp pang of recognition in her chest as she saw a trio of men walking slowly along a yew hedge, Cam's dark and graceful form among them. Like his companions, Cam wore riding breeches and tall leather boots. But instead of the traditional riding coat and waistcoat, he wore a white shirt topped with a jerkin, an open collarless vest made of thin leather. A breeze played in the black layers of his hair, lifting the glossy locks and letting them settle.

As the three men walked, Cam interacted with his surroundings in a way the other two didn't, picking a stray leaf from the hedge, running his palm across the coppery tails of maidengrass. And yet Amelia was certain he didn't miss a word of the conversation.

Although nothing could possibly have alerted him to Amelia's presence, he paused and looked over his shoulder in her direction. Even across the distance of twenty yards, meeting his gaze gave her a small shock. Every hair on her body lifted.

"Amelia," Win asked, "have you come to some kind of arrangement with Mr. Rohan?"

Amelia's mouth went dry. She buried her left hand, the one with the ring, in the folds of her skirt. "Of course not. Where would you get such an idea?"

"He and Lord Westcliff and Lord St. Vincent have been talking ever since they returned from Ramsay House this morning. I couldn't help overhearing some of their conversation when they were on the terrace. And the things that were said—the way Mr. Rohan phrased himself—it sounded as if he were speaking for us."

"What do you mean, speaking for us?" Amelia asked indignantly. "No one speaks for the Hathaways except me. Or Leo."

"He seems to be making decisions about what needs to be done, and when." Win added in an abashed whisper, "As if he were the head of the family."

Amelia was flooded with indignation. "But he has no right . . . I don't know why he would think . . . oh, *Lord.*"

This had to be stopped right away.

"Are you all right, dear?" Win asked in concern. "You look pale. Here, have some of my tea."

Aware that all three of her sisters were staring at her

with round eyes, Amelia took the china cup and drained it in a few gulps.

"How long are we going to stay here, Amelia?" Beatrix asked. "I like it much better than our house."

Before Amelia could answer, Poppy joined in with, "Where did you get that pretty ring? May I see it?"

Amelia stood abruptly. "Excuse me—I need to speak with someone." She strode across the terrace and hurried down the curving steps to the garden walk.

As she approached the three men, who had paused beside a stone urn filled with dahlias, Amelia overheard a few snatches of conversation, such as ". . . extend the existing foundation . . ." and ". . . the remainder of quarried stone from Jenner's and have it carted here . . ."

Surely they couldn't be talking about Ramsay House, she thought with increasing alarm. They must not be aware of how paltry the Hathaways' yearly annuities were. Her family couldn't afford the materials and labor to rebuild.

Becoming aware of her presence, the three men turned. Lord Westcliff wore a kind, concerned expression, whereas Lord St. Vincent looked pleasant but aloof. Cam's face was unreadable, his gaze traveling over her in a quick, thorough sweep.

Amelia nodded in greeting. "Good day, gentlemen." She steeled herself not to flinch as she stared up into Cam's dark face. "Mr. Rohan, I had thought you would have been gone by now."

"I'll be leaving for London soon."

Good, she thought. That was for the best. But her heart thumped in an extra painful beat.

"And I'll return within a week," Cam stunned her by

adding calmly. "Along with an engineer and master builder to appraise the condition of Ramsay House."

Amelia was shaking her head even before he had finished. "Mr. Rohan, I don't wish to sound ungrateful, but that won't be necessary. My brother and I will decide how best to proceed."

"Your brother is in no condition to decide anything."

Lord Westcliff broke in. "Miss Hathaway, you are welcome to stay at Stony Cross Manor indefinitely."

"You are very generous, my lord. But since Ramsay House is still standing, we will live there."

"It was barely adequate before the fire," Cam said. "As things stand now, I wouldn't let a stray dog go in there. Most of the place will have to be razed to the foundation."

Amelia scowled. "Then we will move into the gatehouse on the approach road."

"That place is too small for the lot of you. And it's in bad condition."

"That's none of your concern, Mr. Rohan."

Cam gave her a long, intent stare. There was something new in his gaze, she realized. Something that made her insides tighten with apprehension and confusion.

"We need to speak privately," he said.

"No we don't." All her nerves shrilled in warning as she saw the glances the three men exchanged.

"With your permission," Lord Westcliff murmured, "we will withdraw."

"No," Amelia said swiftly, "you don't have to go, really, there's no need . . ." Her voice faded as it became apparent that her permission was not required.

Following Westcliff, Lord St. Vincent paused just long enough to murmur to Amelia, "Although most advice should be distrusted, particularly when it comes from myself . . . keep an open mind, Miss Hathaway. One should never look a rich husband in the mouth." He winked at her and left, striding to the back terrace along with Westcliff.

Thunderstruck, Amelia could only manage one word. *"Husband?"*

"I told them we were betrothed." Cam took her arm in a gentle but adamant grip and guided her around to the other side of the yew, where they could not be observed from the house.

"Why?"

"Because we are."

"What?"

They stopped in the concealment of the hedge. Aghast, Amelia looked up into his warm hazel eyes. "Are you mad?"

Taking her hand, Cam lifted it until the ring gleamed in the daylight. "You're wearing my ring. You slept with me. You made promises. Many in the Rom would say that constitutes full-blown marriage. But just to make certain it's legal, we'll do it the way of the *gadjos* as well."

"We'll do no such thing!" Amelia snatched her hand from his and backed away. "I'm only wearing this ring because I can't get the blasted thing off. And what do you mean, I made promises? Were those Romany words you asked me to repeat some kind of vow? You tricked me! I didn't mean what I said."

"But you did sleep with me."

She flushed in shame and outrage, and dragged a sleeve across her sweating brow. Whirling away from him, she strode rapidly along a graveled path that led deeper into the garden. "That didn't mean anything, either," she said over her shoulder.

He kept pace with her easily. "It meant something to me. The sexual act is sacred to a Roma."

She made a scornful sound. "What about all the ladies you seduced in London? Was it sacred when you slept with them, too?"

"For a while I fell into the impure ways of the *gadjo*," he said innocently. "Now I've reformed."

Amelia sent him a sideways glare. "You don't want this. You don't want me. One night can't change the entire course of someone's life."

"Of course it can." He reached for her, and Amelia skittered away, passing a mermaid fountain surrounded by stone benches. Cam caught her from behind and jerked her back against him. "Stop running from me and listen. I do want you. I want you even knowing if I marry you, I've got an instant family, complete with a suicidal brother-in-law and a Gypsy houseboy with the temperament of a poked bear."

"Merripen is not a houseboy."

"Call him what you like. He comes with the Hathaways. I accept that."

"They won't accept you," she said desperately. "There's no place for you in our family."

"Yes there is. Right by your side."

Breathing hard, Amelia felt his hand drift over the front of her body. Even though her breasts were contained in a padded corset, the pressure of his hand over her bodice caused her to shiver.

"It would be disastrous." Heat climbed in her breasts and throat and face. "You would resent me for taking away your freedom . . . and I would resent you for taking mine.

I can't promise to obey you, to accept your decisions and never again be entitled to my own opinions—"

"It doesn't have to be that way."

"Oh? Would you swear never to command me to do anything against my will?"

Cam turned her to face him, his fingers gentle on the burning surface of her cheek. He considered the question carefully. "No," he eventually said. "I couldn't swear that. Not if I thought something was for your own good."

As far as Amelia was concerned, that ended the debate. "I've always been the one to decide what is for my own good. I won't yield that right to you, nor to anyone."

Cam fingered her earlobe lightly, traced the side of her throat. "Before you make your final decision, there are some things you should consider. There's more than just the two of us at stake." As Amelia tried to step away from him, he gripped her hips and forced her to stay. "Your family's in trouble, sweetheart."

"That's nothing new to us. We're *always* in trouble."

Cam conceded the point. "Still, it's gotten bad enough that you'd be better off—even as the wife of a Roma— than if you tried to manage it all on your own."

Amelia wanted to make him understand that her objections had nothing to do with his Gypsy heritage.

But he was speaking again, his face close to hers. "Marry me, and I'll restore Ramsay House. I'll turn it into a palace. We'll consider it part of your bride-price."

"My what?"

"A Romany tradition. The groom pays a sum to the bride's family before the wedding. Which means I'll also settle Leo's accounts in London—"

"He still owes you money?"

"Not to me. Other creditors."

"Oh, no," Amelia said, her stomach dropping.

"I'll take care of you and your household," Cam continued with relentless patience. "Clothes, jewelry, horses, books . . . school for Beatrix . . . a season in London for Poppy. The best doctors for Winnifred. She can go to any clinic in the world." A calculated pause. "Wouldn't you like to see her well again?"

"That's not fair," she whispered.

"In return, all you have to do is give me what I want." His hand came up to her wrist, sliding along the line of her arm. A ticklish pleasure ran beneath the layers of silk and wool.

Amelia fought to steady her voice. "I would feel as if I'd made a bargain with the devil."

"No, Amelia." His voice was dark velvet. "Just with me."

"I'm not even certain what it is you want."

Cam's head lowered over hers. "After last night, I find that hard to believe."

"You could get *that* from countless other women. F-far more cheaply, I might add, and with much less trouble."

"I want it from you. Only you." A brief, somewhat uncomfortable pause. His mouth twisted. "The other women I've been with . . . I was a novelty to them. Someone different from their husbands. They wanted my company at night, but not during the day. I was never an equal. And I was never satisfied after being with them. With you, it's different."

Amelia closed her eyes as she felt the hot caress of his mouth against her forehead. "It was very wicked of you to sleep with married women," she said with difficulty. "Perhaps if you had tried to court a respectable one—"

"I live in a gambling club." Subtle amusement tempered his voice. "I've met very few respectable women. And—present company excluded—I've never gotten on well with them."

"Why not?"

His mouth wandered gently along the side of her face. "I seem to make them nervous."

She jumped at the touch of his tongue on her earlobe. "I c-can't imagine why."

He toyed with her ear, catching the rim delicately between his teeth. "I'll admit it wouldn't be easy, being married to a Romany male. We're possessive. Jealous. We prefer our wives never to touch another man. Nor would you have the right to refuse me your bed." His lips covered hers in a molten kiss, his tongue exploring deeply. "But then," he said, lifting his mouth, "you wouldn't want to." Another long, lazy kiss, and then Cam said against her mouth, "You'll wear the look of a well-loved woman, *monisha*."

Amelia was forced to hold on to him for balance. "You would leave me, eventually."

"I swear to you, I wouldn't. I've finally found my *atchen tan*."

"Your what?"

"Stopping place."

"I didn't know Romas had stopping places."

"Not all. Apparently I'm one of the few who do." Shaking his head, Cam added in a disgruntled tone, "My back is sore after sleeping on the ground all night. My *gadjo* half has finally gotten the better of me."

Amelia ducked her head and pressed a shaky smile against the cool smoothness of his jerkin. "This is lunacy," she muttered.

Cam held her closer. "Marry me, Amelia. You're what I want. You're my fate." One hand slid to the back of her head, gripping the braids and ribbons to keep her mouth upturned. "Say yes." He nibbled at her lips, licked at them, opened them. He kissed her until she writhed in his arms, her pulse racing. "Say it, Amelia, and save me from ever having to spend a night with another woman. I'll sleep indoors. I'll get a haircut. God help me, I think I'd even carry a pocket watch if it pleased you."

Amelia felt dizzy, unable to think. She leaned helplessly into the hard support of his body. Everything was him, every breath, beat, blink, quiver. He said her name, and his voice seemed to come from a great distance.

"Amelia . . ." Cam shook her a little, asking something, repeating the words until she gathered that he wanted to know when she had eaten last.

"Yesterday," she managed to reply.

Cam didn't look sympathetic as much as annoyed. "No wonder you're ready to faint. You've had no food and hardly any sleep. How are you to be of use to anyone when you can't manage to take care of your own basic needs?"

She would have protested, but he gave her no opportunity to explain anything. Fitting a hard arm around her back, he propelled her back to the house, offering caustic advice the entire way. It seemed to take all her strength to ascend the back staircase.

By the time they reached the top, Lillian, Lady Westcliff, was there, her dark gaze chasing over Amelia with concern. "You look as if you're about to cast up your crumpets," she said without preamble. "What's the matter?"

"I proposed to her," Cam said shortly.

Lillian's eyebrows lifted.

"I'm fine," Amelia told her. "I'm just a bit hungry."

Lillian accompanied them as Cam took Amelia to her sisters' table. "Did she accept?" she asked Cam.

"Not yet."

"Well, I'm not surprised. A woman can't possibly consider a marriage proposal on an empty stomach." Lillian watched Amelia with concern. "You're very pale, dear. Shall I take you inside to lie down somewhere?"

Amelia shook her head. "Thank you, no. I'm sorry to make a scene."

"Oh, you're not making a scene," Lillian said. "Believe me, this is nothing compared to the usual goings-on here." She smiled reassuringly. "If there is anything you need, Amelia, you have only to ask."

Cam led Amelia to her sisters. She sank gratefully into a chair, in front of a plate heaped with sliced ham, chicken, various salads, and a plate of bread. To her astonishment, Cam took the chair beside hers, cut a bite of something on the plate, and speared it with a fork.

He held the morsel up to her lips. "Start with this."

She scowled. "I'm perfectly capable of feeding mys—"

The fork was pushed into her mouth. Amelia continued to glare at him as she chewed. When she swallowed, she could only manage a few words—"Give me that"—before he shoved another bite in.

"If you're going to do such a poor job taking care of yourself," Cam informed her, "someone else will do it for you."

Amelia picked up a piece of bread and bit deeply into it. Although she longed to tell him that it was his fault she'd gotten so little sleep and missed breakfast in the bargain, she couldn't say a word with her sisters present. As she ate, she felt the color returning to her cheeks.

She was aware of conversation taking place around her, the younger Hathaway sisters asking Cam about the condition of Ramsay House, and what was left of it. A chorus of groans greeted the revelation that the bee room had been left intact, and the hive was still busy and thriving.

"I suppose we'll never be rid of those dratted bees," Beatrix exclaimed.

"Yes we will," Cam said. His hand lowered to Amelia's arm, which was resting on the table. His thumb found the delicate blue veins on the underside of her wrist and stroked the agitated throb of her pulse. "I'll see that every last one of them is removed."

Amelia didn't look at him. She picked up a cup of tea with her free hand and took a careful sip.

"Mr. Rohan," she heard Beatrix ask, "are you going to marry my sister?"

Amelia choked on her tea and set the cup down. She sputtered and coughed into her napkin.

"Hush, Beatrix," Win murmured.

"But she's wearing his ring—"

Poppy clamped her hand over Beatrix's mouth. *"Hush!"*

"I might," Cam replied. His eyes sparkled with mischief as he continued. "I find your sister a bit lacking in humor. And she doesn't seem particularly obedient. On the other hand—"

One set of French doors flew open, accompanied by the sound of breaking glass. Everyone on the back terrace looked up in startlement, the men rising from their chairs.

"No," came Win's soft cry.

Merripen stood there, having dragged himself from his sickbed. He was bandaged and disheveled, but he looked far from helpless. He looked like a maddened bull, his dark head lowered, his hands clenched into massive fists. And his stare, promising death, was firmly fixed on Cam.

There was no mistaking the bloodlust of a Roma whose kinswoman had been dishonored.

"Oh, God," Amelia muttered.

Cam, who stood beside her chair, glanced down at her questioningly. "Did you say something to him?"

Amelia turned red as she recalled her blood-spotted nightgown and the maid's expression. "It must have been servants' talk."

Cam stared at the enraged giant with resignation. "You may be in luck," he said to Amelia. "It looks as if our betrothal is going to end prematurely."

She made to stand beside him, but he pressed her back into the chair. "Stay out of this. I don't want you hurt in the fray."

"He won't hurt me," Amelia said curtly. "It's *you* he wants to slaughter."

Holding Merripen's gaze, Cam moved slowly away from the table. "Is there something you'd like to discuss, *chal*?" he asked with admirable self-possession.

Merripen replied in Romany. Although no one save Cam understood what he said, it was clearly not encouraging.

"I'm going to marry her," Cam said, as if to pacify him.

"That's even worse!" Merripen moved forward, murder in his eyes.

Lord St. Vincent swiftly interceded, stepping between the pair. Like Cam, he'd had his share of putting down fights at the gambling club. He lifted his hands in a staying gesture and spoke smoothly. "Easy, large fellow. I'm sure you can find a way to resolve your differences in a reasonable fashion."

"Get out of my way," Merripen growled, putting an end to the notion of civilized discourse.

St. Vincent's pleasant expression didn't change. "You have a point. There's nothing so tiresome as being reasonable. I myself avoid it whenever possible. Still, I'm afraid you can't brawl when there are ladies present. It might give them ideas."

Merripen's scorching black stare flickered to the Hathaway sisters, lingering an extra second on Win's pale, delicate face. She gave him an infinitesimal shake of her head, silently willing him to relent. To reconsider.

"Merripen—" Amelia began scratchily. The scene was mortifying. But at the same time it moved her that Merripen was so protective of her honor.

Cam silenced her with a touch on the shoulder. He leveled a cool stare at Merripen and said, "Not in front of the *gadjos*." Jerking his head in the direction of the back gardens, he headed to the stone staircase.

After a brooding hesitation, Merripen followed.

Chapter Seventeen

When the pair was out of sight, Lord Westcliff spoke to St. Vincent. "Perhaps we should follow at a distance to prevent them from killing each other."

St. Vincent shook his head, relaxing in his chair. He reached for his Evie's hand and began to play with her fingers. "Believe me, Rohan has the situation well in hand. His opponent may be a bit larger, but Rohan has the considerable advantage of having grown up in London, where he's interacted with criminals and remarkably violent brutes." Smiling at his wife, he added, "And those are just our employees."

Amelia had no fears for Cam's sake. A fight between the two men would be like wielding a cudgel against a rapier . . . the rapier, with its superior grace and adroitness, would win. But that outcome brought its own perils. With the possible exception of Leo, the Hathaways were intensely fond of Merripen. The girls wouldn't find it easy to forgive someone who had harmed him. Especially Win.

Glancing at her sister, Amelia began to say something

consoling, when she realized that Win's expression was not one of fear or helplessness.

Win was annoyed.

"Merripen has been injured," Win said. "He should be resting, not chasing about after Mr. Rohan."

"It's not my fault he got out of his sickbed!" Amelia protested in an indignant whisper.

Win's blue eyes narrowed. "You've done *something* to stir everyone up. And it's fairly obvious that whatever you did, Mr. Rohan was involved."

Poppy, who was listening avidly, couldn't resist adding, "*Intimately* involved."

The two older sisters glanced at her and said in unison, "Shut up, Poppy."

Poppy frowned. "I've been waiting my entire life for Amelia to stray from the straight and narrow. Now that it's happened, I'm going to enjoy it."

"I'd enjoy it, too," Beatrix said plaintively, "if I only knew what we're talking about."

Cam led the way along the yew hedge, going away from the manor until they reached a sunken lane stretching toward the wood. They stopped beside a thicket of Saint-John's-wort, its golden flowers in full bloom, and sedge spiked with bottlebrush stems in leaf. Deceptively relaxed, Cam folded his arms loosely across his chest. He was puzzled by the large, irate *chal,* a Roma with the air of a loner. The mysterious Merripen had no affiliation with a Gypsy tribe, but had instead chosen to make himself the watchdog of a *gadje* family. Why? What did he owe to them?

Perhaps Merripen was *mahrime,* designated by the Rom as one unworthy of trust. An outcast. If so, Cam wondered what Merripen had done to deserve such status.

"You took advantage of Amelia," Merripen said.

"Not that it matters," Cam said in Romany, "but how did you find out?"

Merripen's huge hands flexed as if longing to rip him apart. Lucifer himself could not have had blacker, more burning eyes. "Speak in English," he said harshly. "I don't like the old language."

Frowning in curiosity, Cam readily complied.

"The maids were talking about it," Merripen replied. "I heard them standing outside my door. You dishonored one of my family."

"Yes, I know," Cam said quietly.

"You're not good enough for her."

"I know that, too." Watching him intently, Cam asked, "Do you want her for yourself, *chal*?"

Merripen looked mortally offended. "She's a sister to me."

"That's good. Because I want her for my wife. And as far as I can see"—Cam gestured wide with his hands—"there aren't exactly queues forming to help the Hathaways. So I may be able to help the family."

"They don't need your money. Ramsay has an annuity."

"Ramsay will be dead soon. We both know it. And after he turns up his toes, the title will go to the next poor bastard in line, and there'll be four unmarried Hathaway sisters with few practical skills to speak of. What do you think will become of them? What about the invalid? She'll need medical care—"

"She's not an invalid!" Merripen made his face expressionless, but not before Cam had seen a flash of extraordinary emotion, something ferocious and tormented.

Apparently, Cam thought, not all of the Hathaways were like sisters to Merripen. Perhaps this was the key to him. Perhaps Merripen harbored a secret passion for a woman who was too innocent to realize it, and too frail ever to marry.

"Merripen," Cam said slowly, "you're going to have to find a way to tolerate me. Because there are things I can do for Amelia, and the rest of them, that you can't." He continued in a level tone despite the look on Merripen's face, which would have terrified a lesser man. "And I don't have the patience to battle you every step of the way. If you want what's best for them, either leave, or accept this. I'm not going anywhere."

As the huge *chal* glared at him, Cam could almost see the progression of his thoughts, the weighing of options, the violent desire to mow down his enemy, all of it overshadowed by the urge to do what was right for his family.

"Besides," Cam said, "if Amelia doesn't marry me, the *gadjo* will be after her again. And you know she'll be better off with me."

Merripen's eyes narrowed. "Frost broke her heart. You took her innocence. Why does that make you any better?"

"Because I'm not going to leave her. Unlike the *gadjos,* the Rom are faithful to our women." Cam paused and measured out five seconds before adding deliberately, "You probably know that better than I."

Merripen fixed his furious gaze at a point in the distance. "If you hurt her in any way . . ." he finally said, "I'm going to kill you."

"Fair enough."

"I may kill you anyway."

Cam smiled slightly. "You'd be surprised how many people have said that to me before."

"No," Merripen said, "I wouldn't."

Amelia paused nervously at the door of Cam's room. There were sounds of movement within, drawers opening and closing, objects being moved. She realized he must be preparing to leave for London.

The residents and guests of Stony Cross Manor had discreetly left the back terrace before Cam and Merripen had returned. Amelia had just caught sight of Merripen returning to his room, his ferocious scowl deepening as he had glanced at her. She had opened her mouth to ask something, apologize, she wasn't certain what, but he had cut her off. "Your choice," he muttered. "And it affects all of us. Don't forget that." He had closed the door before she could say a word.

Glancing up and down the hallway, Amelia made certain she was unobserved before she gave a feather-light rap at the door and let herself into the room.

Cam pushed a stack of neatly folded garments into a small gentleman's trunk at the foot of the bed. He looked up at her, a spill of black silk falling down to his eyes. He was so vibrant, so dark and beautiful, his skin like polished rosewood.

Amelia's voice came unevenly from her constricted throat. "I was afraid Merripen would bring you back in pieces."

Stepping away from the bed, toward her, Cam smiled. "All still here."

As Amelia glanced at the lean, fascinating contours of his body, she felt her temperature rise. She turned to the side and spoke rapidly.

"I've considered everything you said earlier. I've made a decision. But first I'd like to explain that it has nothing to do with your personal endowments, which are quite considerable. It's just that—"

"My personal endowments?"

"Yes. Your intelligence. Your attractiveness."

"Oh."

Wondering why his voice sounded odd, Amelia darted a questioning glance at him. The amber eyes were bright with laughter. What had she said to amuse him? "Are you paying attention?"

"Believe me, when my personal endowments are being discussed, I always pay attention. Go on."

She frowned. "Mr. Rohan, although I consider your offer a great compliment, and present circumstances being what they—"

"Let's get to the point, Amelia." His hands closed over her shoulders. "Are you going to marry me?"

"I *can't*," she said weakly. "I just can't. We don't suit. It's obvious we're not at all alike. You're impetuous. You make life-altering decisions in the blink of an eye. Whereas I choose one course and I don't stray from it."

"You strayed last night. And look how well it turned out." He grinned at her expression. "I'm not impetuous, love. It's just that I know when something is too important to be decided according to logic."

"And *marriage* is one of those things?"

"Of course." Cam settled a hand high on her chest, over

the wild pounding of her heart. "You have to decide it in here."

Amelia's chest felt tight beneath the warmth of his hand. "I've only known you for a matter of days. We're still strangers. I can't entrust the future of my entire family to a man I don't even know."

"A couple can be married fifty years and never know each other. Besides, you know the important things about me already."

Amelia heard an annoying drumming sound, and she thought at first it was the wild percussion of her heart. But as Cam's leg intruded gently among the folds of her borrowed dress and touched hers, she realized she was doing her blasted foot-tapping again. With an effort, she went still.

Sliding one arm around her, Cam picked up her left hand, bringing it to his mouth. His lips brushed over the chafed red patch on her knuckle, where she had tried to pull the ring off.

"It's stuck," she grumbled. "It's too small."

"It's not too small. Just relax your hand and it will come off."

"My hand *is* relaxed."

"*Gadjis,*" he said. "You're all as stiff as amaranth wood. It must be your corsets." His head bent, his mouth finding hers. He explored slowly, enticing her to open for him, hunting for the shy tip of her tongue. She stirred in dismay as she realized he was unfastening the back of her gown. The bodice loosened in front, sagging away from her neatly confined breasts.

"Cam . . . no . . ."

"Shhh . . ." The hot, exciting waft of his breath filled

her mouth. "I'm helping you remove the ring. That's what you want, isn't it?"

"Removing this ring has nothing to do with pulling my corset str—oh, no—" The web of stays had split open to expose a lush display of flesh. "This isn't helping." She tried to pull up her disassembled clothing with the clumsiness of someone moving underwater.

"It's helping me quite a lot." Cam's hand slipped into the back of her drawers. She wriggled in violated modesty, her clothes dropping ever more rapidly toward the floor.

"I have to see you in daylight." His mouth chased lightly, hungrily over her throat and shoulder. "*Monisha,* you are the most beautiful woman, the most . . ." His hands moved with increasing impatience, pulling hard at her clothes until a few stitches popped.

"Don't, this dress doesn't belong to me," Amelia said anxiously, fumbling to unfasten the borrowed garments herself rather than have them torn. She froze at the sound of footsteps coming along the hallway, passing the closed door without stopping. Most likely it was a servant. But what if someone had seen her entering Cam's room? . . . What if someone were searching for her at this very moment? "Cam, please, not now."

"I'll be gentle." He lifted her from the circle of discarded clothes. "I know it's soon after your first time."

She shook her head as he laid her on the bed. Clenching the fabric of her chemise with both hands to keep it in place, she whispered, "No, it's not that. Someone will find out. Someone will hear. Someone will—"

"Let go, hummingbird, so I can take this off you." There was a flick of devil's fire in his eyes as he said mildly, "Let go, or I'll rip it."

"Cam, don't—"

She was interrupted by the sound of rending linen. He had torn it completely down the front, the fragile material drooping on either side of her.

"You've ruined it," she said in disbelief. "How am I to explain this to the maid? And how am I to put my corset back on?"

Cam didn't look at all apologetic as he pulled the remnants of the chemise away from her body. "Take off your drawers. Or I'll have to rip those, too."

"Oh, God." Seeing no way to stop him, Amelia pulled the drawers down over her hips. "Lock the door," she whispered with a scarlet face. "Please, *please* lock it."

A quick smile passed over Cam's mouth. He left the bed and went to the door, stripping off his jerkin and shirt along the way. After turning the key in the lock, he took his time about returning to the bed, seeming to enjoy the sight of her burrowing beneath the bed linens.

He stood before her half-naked, the breeches riding low on his hips. Amelia dragged her gaze away from the sleek, tightly muscled surface of his torso, and shivered between the cold layers of the bedclothes. "You're putting me in a terrible position."

Cam finished undressing and joined her beneath the covers. "I know other positions you'll like much better."

She was pulled against him full-length, his body large and startlingly warm. He ran his hands over her, discovering she was still wearing garters and silk stockings. With a smoothness that left her gasping, Cam disappeared beneath the covers, his broad shoulders tenting the layers of linen, wool and velvet.

Amelia tried to struggle to a sitting position but fell

back with a whimper as she felt his mouth against the soft skin inside her thigh. He untied the garter, letting it fall away, and began to roll the stocking down her leg with torturous slowness, his lips following the path of furling silk. His tongue ventured into the hollow behind her knee . . . glided over the clenched muscle of her calf . . . the delicate side of her ankle. The silk was gently tugged away from her clenched toes. It took fierce concentration not to cry out as she felt his hot, wet mouth closing over her toes, one at a time, sucking and stroking while her ticklish foot jerked in response.

By the time the second stocking was removed, Amelia was steaming. She fought to push the covers back, away from her overheated skin. The tips of her breasts contracted tightly as they were exposed to the cool air. Cam pushed her thighs wide, her legs crooked over the hard bulwark of his shoulders. His fingers sifted through the springy curls, and he kissed her tenderly, licking into the heat and tension, circling and drawing lightly. Too much . . . not enough . . . Amelia strained beneath the soft-flicking torture.

He settled a hand over her stomach, rubbing in soothing circles. "Lie easy, sweetheart."

"I c-can't. Oh, do hurry!"

Cam laughed softly, his parted lips dragging across her sensitive flesh. He traced her with his tongue, made her wet, and blew against the dampened curls. "It's better for you if I don't hurry."

"No it's not."

"Much you know about it. This is only your second time."

She gave a little sob as he used his tongue again. "I can't bear much more of this."

He licked over her, fiendishly sweet, and inside her, lewd and deep, until she was breathing in moans and his hot breath was shivering against her. He moved upward, his body settling into the taut slip of her thighs, and he entered her in a thick slide. She gasped at the shock of him filling her, pushing until she gasped, and dug her fingertips into his shoulder.

Cam paused, staring down at her with dilated eyes, the irises bright gold rims around circles of fathomless midnight. "Amelia, love . . ." His kiss tasted of salt and intimacy. "Can you take a little more of me?"

She fought to think above the confusion of pleasure, and shook her head jerkily.

The corners of his lips deepened with a smile. He whispered, "I think you can."

His hands played over her, solicitous fingertips sliding to the place they were joined. He pressed inside her, a low rhythmic movement, and his fingers were astonishingly gentle, almost delicate, as they stroked in time to the patient thrusts. Gasping, she arched to take him deeper, and deeper still.

Every time he pushed, his body rubbed hers in exactly the right way. She began to lift eagerly, anticipating each invasion, panting for it, sensation building on sensation until it culminated in a blinding swell of delight . . . and another . . . another . . . she felt him begin to withdraw and she moaned and twined her legs around his hips.

"Amelia," he gasped, "no, let me . . . I've got to . . ." Shuddering, he spent helplessly inside her, while her body gripped and stroked the hard length of him.

Still locked together, Cam rolled Amelia to her side. He muttered something in Romany. Although she didn't understand a word, it sounded highly complimentary. Limp with pleasure and exhaustion, Amelia rested her head on the solid curve of his biceps, her breath catching as she felt the occasional twitch and pulse of him in the depths of her body.

Cam reached for her left hand. Taking the signet ring between his fingers, he drew it off easily and gave it to her. "Here. Although I'd rather you left it on."

Amelia's mouth fell open. She examined her hand, then the ring, and hesitantly pushed it back on the same finger. It slid over her knuckle and back again with ease. "How did you do that?"

"I helped you to relax." He ran a coaxing hand along her spine. "Put it back on, Amelia."

"I can't. That would mean I've accepted your proposal, and I haven't."

Stretching like a cat, Cam rolled her flat again, his weight partially supported on his elbows. Amelia drew in a quick breath as she felt him still firm within her. "You can't lie with me twice and then refuse to marry me." Cam lowered his head to kiss her ear. "I'll be ruined." He worked his way to the soft place behind her earlobe. "And I'll feel so cheap."

Despite the seriousness of the matter, Amelia had to bite back a smile. "I'm doing you a great favor by refusing you. You'll thank me for it someday."

"I'll thank you right now if you'll put the damned ring back on."

She shook her head.

Cam pushed a bit farther inside her, making her gasp. "What about my personal endowments? Who's going to take care of them?"

"You can take care of them"—she squirmed to the side to set the ring on the bedside table—"all by yourself."

Cam moved with her obligingly. "It's much more satisfying when you're involved."

As he reached to retrieve the ring, his body shifted higher in hers. She tensed in surprise. He felt harder inside her, thicker, his desire gaining new momentum. "Cam," she protested, glancing at the closed door. She grabbed for his wrist, trying to keep his hand away from the ring. He grappled with her playfully, turning until they had completed a full revolution across the mattress and she was under him again.

He was rampantly aroused now, teasing her with slow lunges. Twisting beneath him, Amelia pushed at his dark head as he began to kiss her breasts. "But . . . we just finished . . ."

Cam lifted his head. "Roma," he said, as if by way of explanation, and settled back over her. If there was a hint of apology in his tone, there was none in the insistent rhythm of his thrusts, deep caresses that invaded and soothed, and before long her protests had melted into purring moans.

Amelia wrapped her arms around him, her legs, trying to contain all that hard male flesh, while the steady, rocking pace of his thrusts brought her to the edge of release. But he withdrew before she could reach it, and turned her over, and for an agonizing moment she thought he had decided to stop. Covering her with his body, Cam used his knees to push hers wide. He muttered in a mixture of English and Romany, enough for her to understand that he wouldn't hurt her, this would be easier for her, and she whispered *yes, yes,* and then he was sliding impossibly deep, his hands steadying her hips as she backed up instinctively.

Her head dropped, her gasps muffled against the linen-covered mattress. His hand slid to her sex, fingers spreading the furrowed silk. Pleasure shimmered through her in waves, each one stronger, higher, until she was shuddering, drowning, sighing. Cam's sudden withdrawal was a shock of unwelcome emptiness as he made his last thrust against the sheets and groaned. Stunned and disoriented, Amelia remained with her hips propped high, her flesh pulsing and smarting with the need to have him back inside. His hand came to her buttocks, rubbing in a warm circle before he pushed her back down.

"You'll have me," Cam whispered. "You'll have me, hummingbird. I'm your fate—even if you won't admit it yet."

Chapter Eighteen

After Cam had gone, Amelia found herself wandering despondently through the large manor.

It was quiet in the house, everyone having retired to their rooms for afternoon naps. Preparations were being made for the earl and countess, and Lord and Lady St. Vincent, to leave for Bristol in the morning. They would stay at the home of Lillian's sister and brother-in-law, Daisy and Matthew Swift, for the last fortnight of Daisy's confinement.

Lillian was anxious to see her younger sister, with whom she was extremely close. "She's been in splendid health through the whole thing," Lillian had told Amelia, with obvious pride. "Daisy's healthy as a horse. But she's very small. And her husband is quite large," she added darkly, "which means any babies of his will probably be oversized, as well."

"One can't fault him for being tall," Lord Westcliff, who was sitting beside his wife, had pointed out laconically.

"I didn't say it was his fault," Lillian protested.

"You were thinking it," the earl murmured, and she

raised a pillow as if to hurl it at him. The effect of marital strife was spoiled, however, as they grinned at each other affectionately.

Lillian turned her attention to Amelia. "Will you and the others be all right in our absence? I hate to leave with things so unsettled, and Mr. Merripen under the weather."

"I expect Merripen will heal very quickly," Amelia said with utter confidence. Other than the time he had first come to them, he had never been ill. "He has a robust constitution."

"I've requested the doctor to visit daily," Westcliff said. "And if you have any difficulties, send word to Bristol. It isn't that far, and I'll come at once."

Heaven knew how they had been fortunate enough to have Lillian and Westcliff as neighbors.

Now, as Amelia made her way through the art gallery, her gaze moving over paintings and sculptures, she became aware of a terrible hollowness inside. She couldn't think how to make it go away. It wasn't hunger, fear, or anger, it wasn't exhaustion or dread.

It was loneliness.

Nonsense, she scolded herself, striding to a long row of windows that overlooked a side garden. It had begun to rain, a cold soaking glitter that fell steadily over the grounds and rushed in muddy streams toward the bluff and the river. *You can't be lonely. He hasn't even been gone for half a day. And there's no reason for it when your entire family is here.*

It was the first time she had ever felt the kind of loneliness that couldn't be cured with just any available company.

Sighing, she pressed her nose against the cold surface of a windowpane, while thunder sent vibrations through the glass.

Her brother's voice came from the other side of the gallery. "Mother always said that would flatten your nose."

Pulling back, Amelia smiled as Leo approached her. "She only said that because she didn't want me to make smudges on the glass."

Her brother looked drawn and hollow-eyed, the pastiness of his complexion a striking contrast to Cam Rohan's clover-honey tan. Leo was dressed in borrowed clothes, these so fine and precisely tailored, they must have been donated by Lord St. Vincent. But instead of hanging gracefully as they did on St. Vincent's elegantly spare frame, the garments strained over Leo's bloated waist and puffy neck.

"One can only hope you feel better than you look," Amelia said.

"I'll feel better once I can find some decent refreshment. I've asked thrice for wine or spirits, and the servants all seem damnably absentminded."

She frowned. "Surely it's too early in the day even for you, Leo."

He extracted a pocket watch from his waistcoat and squinted at its face. "It's eight o'clock in Bombay. Being an internationally minded fellow, I'll have a drink as a diplomatic gesture."

Ordinarily Amelia would have been resigned or annoyed. However, as she stared at her brother, who seemed so lost and miserable beneath his brittle façade, she felt a rush of compassion. Walking forward, she put her arms around him and hugged him. And wondered how to save him.

Startled by the impulsive gesture, Leo remained still, not returning the embrace but not pulling away, either. His hands came to her shoulders, and he eased her away.

"I should have known you'd be maudlin today," he said.

"Yes, well . . . finding one's brother nearly roasted to death tends to make a woman rather emotional."

"I'm just a bit charred." He stared at her with those strange, light eyes, not at all the eyes of the brother she had known all her life. "And not so altered as you, it seems."

Amelia knew immediately what he was leading to. Warily she turned away from him and pretended to inspect a nearby landscape of hills and clouds and a silvery lake. "Altered? I've no idea what you mean."

"I'm referring to the game of hide-the-slipper you've been playing with Rohan."

"Who told you that? The servants?"

"Merripen."

"I can't believe he dared—"

"For once he and I agree on something. We're going back to London as soon as Merripen is well enough. We'll stay at the Rutledge Hotel until we can find a suitable house to lease—"

"The Rutledge costs a fortune," she exclaimed. "We can't afford that."

"Don't argue, Amelia. I'm the head of this family, and I've made the decision. With Merripen's full support, for what that's worth."

"The two of you can go to blazes! I don't take orders from you, Leo."

"You will in this instance. Your affair with Rohan is over."

Feeling bitter and outraged, Amelia turned away from him. She didn't trust herself to speak. In the past year, there had been so many times she had longed for Leo to assume his place as the head of the family, to have an opinion about anything, to show concern for someone other than himself. And yet *this* was the issue that had provoked him to take action?

"I'm so glad," she said with ominous quietness, "that you've taken such an interest in my personal affairs, Leo. Now perhaps you might expand your interest to other topics of importance, such as how and when Ramsay House will be rebuilt, and what we're going to do about Win's health, and Beatrix's education, and Poppy's—"

"You won't distract me that easily. Good God, sis, couldn't you find someone of your own class to dally with? Have your prospects really sunk so low that you've taken a Gypsy to your bed?"

Amelia's mouth dropped open. She spun to face him. "I can't believe you would say such a thing. Our brother is a Roma, and he—"

"Merripen isn't our brother. And he happens to agree with me. This is beneath you."

"Beneath me," Amelia repeated dazedly, backing away from him until her shoulders flattened against the wall. "How?"

"There's no need for me to explain, is there?"

"Yes," she said, "I think there is."

"Rohan's a *Gypsy,* Amelia. They're lazy, rootless wanderers."

"You can say all that when you never lift a finger?"

"I'm not supposed to work. I'm a peer now. I earn three thousand pounds a year just by existing."

Clearly there was no headway to be made in an argument when one's opponent was insane.

"Until this moment, I had no intention of marrying him," Amelia said. "But now I'm seriously considering the merits of having at least one rational man in the household."

"Marriage?"

Amelia almost enjoyed the look on his face. "I suppose Merripen forgot to mention that minor detail. Yes, Cam has proposed to me. And he's rich, Leo. *Rich* rich, which means even if you decide to go jump in the lake and drown yourself, the girls and I would be taken care of. Nice, isn't it, that someone's concerned about our future?"

"I forbid it."

She gave him a scornful glance. "Forgive me if I'm less than impressed by your authority, Leo. Perhaps you should practice on someone else."

And she left him in the gallery, while the thunder rumbled and rain cascaded down the windows.

Cam stopped the driver on the way to London, wanting another look at Ramsay House before he departed Hampshire. He was in something of a quandary as to what should be done with the place. Certainly it would have to be restored. As part of an aristocratic entailment, the estate had to be maintained in a decent condition. And Cam liked the place. There were possibilities in it. If the slopes of the surrounding grounds were altered and landscaped, and the building itself was properly redesigned and rebuilt, the Ramsay estate would be a jewel.

But it was doubtful that the Ramsay title, and its entailments, would remain in the Hathaways' possession much longer. Not if everything depended on Leo, whose health and future existence were very much in question.

Considering the problem of his soon-to-be brother-in-law, Cam bid the driver to wait, and went into the ramshackle house, heedless of the rain that dampened his hair and coat. It didn't especially matter to him if Leo lived or died, but Amelia's feelings mattered very much indeed. Cam would do whatever was necessary to spare her grief or worry. If that meant helping to preserve her brother's worthless life, so be it.

The interior of the house was smoke-filmed and sagging like a once-jaunty creature that had been beaten into submission. He wondered what a builder would make of the place, and how much of the structure could be preserved. Cam imagined what it might look like when it was fully restored and painted. Bright, charming, a touch eccentric. Like his Hathaways.

A smile tugged at the corners of his lips at the thought of Amelia's sisters. He could easily become fond of them. Strange, how the idea of settling on this land, becoming part of a family, had become attractive. He was feeling rather . . . clannish. Perhaps Westcliff had been right—he couldn't ignore his Irish half forever.

Cam stopped at the side of the entrance hall as he heard a noise from upstairs. A thump, a tapping, as if someone were hammering at wood. The nape of his neck crawled. Who the hell could be here? Superstition struggled with reason as he wondered if the intruder were mortal or spectral. He made his way up the stairs with extreme care, his feet swift and silent.

Pausing at the top of the stairs, he listened intently. The sound came again, from one of the bedrooms. He made his way to a half-open door and looked inside.

The presence in the room was most definitely human. Cam's eyes narrowed as he recognized Christopher Frost.

It appeared Frost was trying to pry a piece of paneling from the wall, using an iron pry bar. The wood defied his efforts, and after a few seconds of exertion, Frost dropped the pry bar and swore.

"Need some help?" Cam asked.

Frost nearly leaped out of his shoes. "What the devil—" He whirled around, his eyes huge. "Damnation! What are you doing there?"

"I was going to ask you the same question." Leaning against the doorjamb, Cam folded his arms and stared at the other man speculatively. "I decided to stop here on my way to London. What's behind the panel?"

"Nothing," the architect snapped.

"Then why are you trying to remove it?"

Collecting himself, Frost bent to retrieve the pry bar. He held it casually, but with the slightest change in his grip, the iron bar could easily be turned into a weapon. Cam kept his posture relaxed, not taking his eyes from Frost's face.

"How much do you know about construction and design?" Frost asked.

"Not much. I've done some woodworking now and then."

"Yes. Your people sometimes work as tinkers and bodgers. Perhaps even roofing. But never *building*. You would never stay long enough to complete the project, would you?"

Cam kept his tone immaculately polite. "Are you asking about me specifically, or the Rom in general?"

Frost approached him, the pry bar firmly in his grasp. "It doesn't matter. To answer your previous question—I am inspecting the house to make an estimate of the damage, and to develop ideas for the new design. On behalf of Miss Hathaway."

"Did she ask you to inspect the house?"

"As an old friend of the family—and particularly Miss Hathaway—I've taken it upon myself to help them."

The phrase "particularly Miss Hathaway" uttered with just a hint of ownership, nearly shattered Cam's self-control. He, who had always congratulated himself on his equanimity, was instantly overrun with hostility. "Perhaps," he said, "you should have asked first. As it turns out, your services aren't needed."

Frost's face darkened. "What gives you the right to speak for Miss Hathaway and her family?"

Cam saw no reason to be discreet. "I'm going to marry her."

Frost nearly dropped the iron bar. "Don't be absurd. Amelia would never marry you."

"Why not?"

"Good God," Frost exclaimed incredulously, "how can you ask that? You're not a gentleman of her class, and . . . hell and damnation, you're not even a real Gypsy. You're a mongrel."

"All the same, I'm going to marry her."

"I'll see you in hell first!" Frost cried, taking a step toward him.

"Either drop that bar," Cam said quietly, "or I'll dislocate your arm." He sincerely hoped Frost would take a swing at him. To his disappointment, Frost set the bar on the ground.

The architect glared at him. "After I talk to her, she'll want nothing more to do with you. I'll make certain she understands what people would say about a lady who beds down with a Gypsy. She'd be better off with a peasant. A dog. A—"

"Point taken," Cam said. He gave Frost a bland smile designed to infuriate. "But it's interesting, isn't it, that Miss Hathaway's previous experience with a gentleman of her own class has now disposed her to look favorably on a Roma? It hardly reflects well on you."

"You selfish bastard," Frost muttered. "You'll ruin her. You think nothing of bringing her down to your level. If you cared for her at all, you would disappear for good."

He brushed by Cam without another word. Soon his footsteps could be heard as he descended the stairs.

And Cam stayed in the empty doorway for a long time, seething with anger, concern for Amelia, and even worse, guilt. He couldn't change the fact of what he was, nor would he be able to shield Amelia from all the arrows that would be aimed at the wife of a Gypsy.

But he would be damned if he would let her make her way through a merciless world without him.

Supper was a somber affair, with the Westcliffs and St. Vincents having departed for Bristol, and Leo having gone to the village tavern for amusement. It was a miserable night. Amelia found it hard to imagine there would be much revelry in the cold and wet, but Leo was probably desperate for more sympathetic company than could be found at Stony Cross Manor.

Merripen had remained in his room, sleeping most of the day, which was so unlike him that the Hathaways were all worried.

"I suppose it's good for him to rest," Poppy ventured, brushing idly at a few crumbs on the tablecloth. A footman came hurriedly to remove the crumbs for her with a napkin and silver implement. "It will help him to heal faster, won't it?"

"Has anyone had a look at Merripen's shoulder?" Amelia asked, glancing at Win. "It's probably time for the dressing to be changed."

"I'll do it," Win said at once. "And I'll take up a supper tray."

"Beatrix will accompany you," Amelia advised.

"I can manage the tray," Win protested.

"It's not that . . . I meant it's not proper for you to be alone with Merripen in his room."

Win looked surprised, and made a face. "I don't need Beatrix to come. It's only Merripen, after all."

After Win left the dining hall, Poppy looked at Amelia. "Do you think that Win really doesn't know how he—"

"I have no idea. And I've never dared to broach the subject, because I don't want to put ideas into her head."

"I hope she doesn't know," Beatrix ventured. "It would be dreadfully sad if she did."

Amelia and Poppy both glanced at their younger sister quizzically. "Do you know what we're talking about, Bea?" Amelia asked.

"Yes, of course. Merripen's in love with her. I knew it a long time ago, from the way he washed her window."

"Washed her window?" both older sisters asked at the same time.

"Yes, when we lived in the cottage at Primrose Place. Win's room had a casement window that looked out onto the big maple tree—do you remember? After the scarlet fever, when Win couldn't get out of bed for the longest time and she was too weak to hold a book, she would just lie there and watch a birds' nest on one of the tree limbs. She saw the baby swallows hatch and learn to fly. One day she complained that the window was so dirty, she could barely see through it, and it made the sky look grayish. So from then on Merripen always kept the glass spotless. Sometimes he climbed a ladder to wash the outside, and you know how afraid of heights he is. You never saw him do that?"

"No," Amelia said with difficulty, her eyes stinging. "I didn't know he did that."

"Merripen said the sky should always be blue for her," Beatrix said. "And that was when I knew he . . . are you crying, Poppy?"

Poppy used a napkin to dab at the corners of her eyes. "No. I just inh-haled some pepper."

"So did I," Amelia said, blowing her nose.

Win carried a light bamboo tray laden with broth, bread, and tea to Merripen's room. It hadn't been easy to persuade the kitchen maids that she could take the tray herself. They had felt strongly that no guest of Lord and Lady Westcliff's should carry anything. However, Win knew Merripen's dislike of strangers, and in his vulnerable state, he would be contrary and obstinate.

Finally a compromise had been reached: a housemaid

would bring the tray to the top of the stairs, and Win could take it from there.

As she neared his room, Win heard the sounds of something hitting a wall with a thud, and a few threatening growls that could only have come from Merripen. She frowned, her pace quickening as she proceeded along the hallway. An indignant housemaid was departing from Merripen's room.

"Well, I never," the maid exclaimed, red and bristling. "I went to stir the coals and add wood to the fire—and that nasty Gypsy shouted and threw his cup at me!"

"Oh, dear. I'm so sorry. You weren't injured, were you? I'm sure he didn't intend—"

"No, his aim was off," the maid said with dark satisfaction. "The tonic's made him higher than a Cable Street constable." The reference was to a mile-long road in London known for harboring a quantity of opium dens. "I wouldn't go in there if I were you, miss. He'd snap you in two as soon as you got within arm's length of him. The beast."

Win frowned in concern. "Yes. Thank you. I'll be careful." Tonic . . . the doctor must have left something extremely potent to dull the agony of a burn wound. It was probably laced with opiate syrup and alcohol. Since Merripen never took medicine and rarely even drank a glass of wine, he would be highly susceptible to intoxicants.

Entering the room, Win used her back to close the door, and went to set the tray on the bedside table. She started a little at the sound of Merripen's voice.

"I told you to get out!" he barked. "Told you—" He broke off as she turned to face him.

Win had never seen him like this before, flushed and

disoriented, his dark eyes slightly unfocused. He lay on his side, his white shirt falling open to reveal the edge of a heavy bandage, and muscles gleaming like polished bronze. He was tense and radiating what her mother had gingerly referred to as "animal spirits."

"Kev," she said gently, using his first name.

They'd made a bargain once, after she'd gotten scarlet fever, when he'd wanted her to take some medicine. Win had refused until he offered to tell her his name. She'd promised never to tell anyone, and she hadn't. Perhaps he had even thought she had forgotten.

"Lie still," she urged gently. "There's no need to work yourself into a temper. You frightened the poor housemaid half to death."

Merripen watched her sluggishly, having trouble keeping his gaze focused. "They're poisoning me," he told her. "Pouring medicine down my throat. My head's muddled. Don't want any more."

Win assumed the role of implacable nurse, when all she wanted was to baby and coddle him. "You'd be much worse off without it." She sat on the edge of the mattress and reached for his wrist. His forearm was hard and heavy as it lay across her lap. Pressing her fingers to his wrist, she kept her face expressionless. "How much of that tonic have they given you?"

His head lolled. "Too much."

Win agreed silently, feeling how weak his pulse was. Releasing his wrist, she felt his forehead. He was very warm. Was it the beginnings of a fever? Her worry sharpened. "Let me see your back." She tried to ease away, but he had reached up to press her cool hand harder against his forehead. He wouldn't let go.

"Hot," he said, and closed his eyes.

Win sat very still, absorbing the feel of him, the heavy masculine body beside hers, the smooth burning skin beneath her hand.

"Stay out of my dreams," Merripen whispered in the humid stillness. "Can't sleep when you're here."

Win let herself caress him, the thick black hair, the handsome face devoid of its usual sullen sternness. She could smell his skin, his sweat, the sweet opiated breath, the pungent whiff of honey. Merripen was always clean shaven, but now his bristle was softly scratchy against her palm. She wanted to take him into her arms, against her chest, like a little boy.

"Kev . . . let me look at your back."

Merripen moved, swift and powerful even now, more aggressive in his drugged state than he normally would ever have permitted himself to be. He had always handled Win with a sort of exaggerated gentleness, as if she would blow away like dandelion floss. But at this moment his grip was hard and sure as he pushed her to the mattress.

Breathing heavily, he glared down at her with glassy belligerence. "I said get out of my dreams."

His face was like the mask of some ancient god of war, beautiful and harsh, the mouth contorted, lips parted enough to reveal the edges of animal-white teeth.

Win was amazed, excited, the tiniest bit frightened . . . but this was Merripen . . . and as she stared at him, the edge of fear melted and she drew his head down to hers, and he kissed her.

She had always imagined there would be roughness, urgency, impassioned pressure. But his lips were soft, grazing over hers with the heat of sunshine, the sweetness of summer rain. She opened to him in wonder, the solid weight of him in her arms, his body pressing into the crumpled layers of her skirts. Forgetting everything in the passionate tumult of discovery, Win reached around his shoulders, until he winced and she felt the bulk of his bandage against her palm.

"Kev," she said breathlessly, "I'm so sorry, I . . . no, don't move. Rest." She curled her arms loosely around his head, shivering as he kissed her throat. He nuzzled against the gentle rise of her breast, pressed his cheek against her bodice, and sighed.

After a long, motionless minute, while her chest rose and fell beneath his heavy head, Win spoke hesitantly. "Kev?"

A slight snore was her reply.

The first time she had ever kissed a man, she thought ruefully, and she had put him to sleep.

Struggling out from beneath him, Win turned back the covers and grasped the hem of his shirt. The linen clung to the powerful slope of his back. Pulling the hem all the way up, she tucked it into the collarless neck of the shirt. Carefully she lifted the edge of the bandage, the cotton gauze sticky and reeking of honey. She blinked at the sight of the burn wound, which was angry and inflamed. The doctor had said a scab would form, but the oozing crust of the wound didn't remotely resemble healing.

Seeing a black mark on the other side of his back, Win frowned curiously and pushed his shirt a little higher. What she discovered caused her breath to catch, her eyes turning wide.

For all Merripen's robust physicality, he had always been an exceptionally modest man. The family had teased him, in fact, for his refusal to bathe in front of anyone, or remove his shirt even during strenuous exertions.

Was this why? What significance did this strange mark have, and what might it reveal about his past?

"Kev," she murmured in wonder, her fingers tracing the pattern on his shoulder. "What secrets are you hiding?"

Chapter Nineteen

The next morning Amelia awakened to the unwelcome news, delivered by Poppy, that Leo had not slept in his bed the previous night and couldn't be found anywhere, and Merripen had taken a turn for the worse.

"Bother Leo," Amelia grumbled, climbing out of bed and reaching for her robe and slippers. "He started drinking yesterday afternoon and doubtless didn't stop. I couldn't care less where he is, or what's happened to him."

"What if he wandered out of the house and . . . oh, I don't know . . . stumbled over a tree branch or something? Shouldn't we ask some of the gardeners and groundsmen to look for him?"

"God. How mortifying." Amelia pulled the robe over her head and buttoned it hastily. "I suppose so. Yes, although make it clear they're not to go on an all-out search. I should hate for their work to be interrupted just because our brother has no self-control."

"He's grieving, Amelia," Poppy said quietly.

"I know. But God help me, I'm tired of his grieving. And it makes me feel horrid to say so."

Poppy stared at her compassionately, and reached out to hug her. "You shouldn't feel horrid. It always falls to you to pick up the pieces of his muck-ups, not to mention everyone else's. I'd be tired, too, if I were you."

Amelia returned the hug, and stepped back with a sigh. "We'll worry about Leo later. Right now I'm more concerned about Merripen. Have you seen him this morning?"

"No, but Win has. She says he's definitely feverish and the wound isn't healing. I think she stayed up with him most of the night."

"And now she'll probably faint from exhaustion," Amelia said in exasperation.

Poppy hesitated and frowned. "Amelia . . . I can't decide whether this is the best or worst time to tell you . . . but there's a minor to-do belowstairs. It seems some of the silver flatware has gone missing."

Amelia went to the window and stared beseechingly up at the cloud-heavy sky. "Dear Merciful Lord, please don't let it be Beatrix."

"Amen," Poppy said. "But it probably is."

Feeling overwhelmed, Amelia thought in despair, *I've failed. The house is gone, Leo is missing or dead, Merripen is injured, Win is ill, Beatrix is going to prison, and Poppy is doomed to spinsterhood.* But what she said was, "Merripen first," and strode briskly from the room with Poppy at her heels.

Win was at Merripen's bedside, so exhausted she could barely sit up straight. Her face was blanched, her eyes bloodshot, her entire body drooping. She had so few reserves, it took very little to deplete them. "He has fever," she said, wringing out a wet cloth and draping it over the back of his neck.

"I'll send for the doctor." Amelia came to stand beside her. "Go to bed."

Win shook her head. "Later. He needs me now."

"The last thing he needs is for you to make yourself ill over him," Amelia replied shortly. She softened her tone as she saw the anguish in her sister's gaze. "Please go to bed, Win. Poppy and I will take care of him while you sleep."

Slowly Win lowered her face until their foreheads were touching. "It's going all wrong, Amelia," she whispered. "His strength has gone too quickly. And the fever shouldn't have come this fast."

"We'll get him through this." Even to her own ears, Amelia's words rang false. She forced a reassuring smile to her lips. "Go and rest, dear."

Win obeyed reluctantly, while Amelia bent over the patient. Merripen's healthy bronze color had been leached into ashen paleness, the black slashes of his brows and the fans of his lashes standing out in sharp contrast. He slept with his mouth partially open, shallow breaths rushing over the chapped surface of his lips. It didn't seem possible that Merripen, always so rugged and sturdy, could have sunk so fast.

Touching the side of his face, Amelia was shocked by the heat coming from his skin. "Merripen," she murmured. "Wake up, dear. Poppy and I are going to clean your wound. You must hold still for us. All right?"

He swallowed and nodded, his eyes cracking open.

Murmuring in sympathy, the sisters worked in tandem, folding back the covers to his waist, lifting the hem of his shirt to his shoulders, and laying out clean rags, pots of salve and honey, and fresh bandages.

Amelia went to ring the servants' bell, while Poppy removed the old dressing. She wrinkled her nose at the mildly unpleasant scent of the exposed raw flesh. The sisters exchanged worried glances.

Working as gently and quickly as possible, Amelia cleaned the exudate from the oozing wound, applied fresh salve, and covered it. Merripen was quiet and rigid, although his back flinched beneath the treatment. He couldn't stifle an occasional hiss of pain. By the time she had finished, he was trembling.

Poppy wiped his sweating face with a dry cloth. "Poor Merripen." She brought a cup of water to his lips. When he tried to refuse, she slid an arm beneath his head and raised it insistently. "Yes, you must. I should have known you'd be a terrible patient. Drink, dear, or I'll be forced to sing something."

Amelia stifled a grin as Merripen complied. "Your singing isn't that terrible, Poppy. Father always said you sang like a bird."

"He meant a parrot," Merripen said hoarsely, leaning his head on Poppy's arm.

"Just for that," Poppy informed him, "I'm going to send Beatrix in here to look after you today. She'll probably put one of her pets in bed with you, and spread her jacks all over the floor. And if you're very lucky, she'll bring in her glue pots, and you can help make paper-doll clothes."

Merripen gave Amelia a glance rife with muted suffering, and she laughed.

"If that doesn't inspire you to get well quickly, dear, nothing will."

But as the next two days passed, Merripen worsened. The doctor seemed powerless to do anything except offer more of the same treatment. The wound was turning sour, he admitted. One could tell by the way it was bleeding white and the skin around it was blackening, an inevitable process that would eventually poison Merripen's entire body.

Merripen dropped weight faster than one would have thought humanly possible. It was often that way with burn injuries, the doctor said. The body consumed itself in its effort to heal the wounds. What troubled Amelia more than Merripen's appearance was the increasing listlessness that even Win couldn't seem to penetrate. "He can't stand being helpless," Win told Amelia, holding Merripen's hand as he slept.

"No one likes to be helpless," Amelia replied.

"It's not a question of liking or not liking. I think Merripen literally can't tolerate it. And so he withdraws." Win gently stroked the lax brown fingers, so powerful and callused from work.

Watching the tender absorption of her sister's expression, Amelia couldn't help asking softly, "Do you love him, Win?"

And her sister, unreadable as a sphinx, turned mysterious blue eyes to her. "Why, of course. We all love Merripen, don't we?"

Which wasn't at all an answer. But Amelia felt she didn't have the right to pursue the matter.

A matter of increasing worry was Leo's continued absence. He had taken a horse but had packed no belongings. Would he have gone on the long ride to London on horseback? Knowing her brother's dislike of travel, Amelia didn't think so. It was likely Leo had remained in Hampshire, although where he could have been staying was a mystery. He was not at the village tavern, nor was he at Ramsay House, nor anywhere on the Westcliff estate.

To Amelia's relief, Christopher Frost came to call one afternoon, dressed in somber attire. Handsome and scented of expensive cologne water, he brought a perfectly arranged bouquet of flowers wrapped in stylish parchment lace.

Amelia met him in the downstairs parlor. In her distress over Merripen's illness and Leo's disappearance, all the constraint she might have felt toward Christopher was gone. The past hurts had receded to the back of her mind, and at the moment she needed a sympathetic friend.

Taking both her hands in his, Christopher sat with her on a plush settee. "Amelia," he murmured in concern. "I can see the state of your spirits. Don't say Merripen's condition is worse?"

"A great deal worse," she said, grateful for the sustaining grip of his hands. "The doctor seems to have no other remedy, nor does he think any of the local folk cures would have any effect other than to cause Merripen further discomfort. I'm so afraid we'll lose him."

His thumbs rubbed gently over her knuckles. "I'm sorry. I know what he has meant to your family. Shall I send for a doctor from London?"

"I don't think there's time." She felt tears rising, and held them back with an effort.

"If there is any help I can give, you have only to ask."

"There is something . . ." She told him about Leo's absence, and that she felt certain he was somewhere in Hampshire. "Someone has to find him," she said. "I would look for him myself, but I'm needed here. And he tends to go to places where . . ."

"Where respectable people don't go," Christopher finished wryly. "Knowing your brother as I do, sweet, it's probably best to let him stay wherever he is until he's slept it off and the fog has lifted."

"But he could be hurt, or in danger. He . . ." She perceived from his expression that the last thing Christopher wanted to do was search for her scapegrace of a brother. "If you would ask some of the townspeople if they have seen him, I would be very grateful."

"I will. I promise." He surprised her by reaching out for her, his arms closing around her. She stiffened but allowed him to draw her near. "Poor sweet," he murmured. "You have so many burdens to carry."

There had been a time when Amelia had passionately longed for a moment such as this. Being held by Christopher, soothed by him. Once this would have been heaven.

But it didn't feel quite the same as before.

"Christoph—" she began, moving away from him, but his mouth caught hers, and she froze in astonishment as he kissed her. This, too, was different . . . and yet for a moment, she remembered what it had been like, how happy she had once been with him. It seemed so long ago, that time before the scarlet fever, when she had been innocent and hopeful and the future had seemed full of promise.

She turned her face from his. "No, Christopher."

"Of course." He pressed his lips to her hair. "Now isn't the proper time for this. I'm sorry."

"I'm so concerned about my brother, and Merripen, I can't think of anything else—"

"I know, sweet." He turned her face back to his. "I'm going to help you and your family. There's nothing I want more than your safety and happiness. And you need my protection. With your family in turmoil, you could easily be taken advantage of."

She frowned. "No one is taking advantage of me."

"What about the Gypsy?"

"You're referring to Mr. Rohan?"

Christopher nodded. "I chanced to meet him on his way to London, and he spoke of you in a way that . . . well, suffice it to say, he's no gentleman. I was offended for your sake."

"What did he say?"

"He went so far as to claim that you and he were going to marry." A scornful laugh escaped him. "As if you would ever lower yourself to that. A half-bred Gypsy with no manners or education."

Amelia felt a rush of defensive anger. She looked into the face of the man she had once loved so desperately. He was the embodiment of everything a young woman should want to marry. Not all that long ago, she might have compared him to Cam Rohan and found Christopher superior. But she was no longer the woman she had been . . . and Christopher wasn't the knight in shining armor she had believed him to be.

"I wouldn't consider it lowering myself," she said. "Mr. Rohan is a gentleman, and highly esteemed by his friends."

"They all find him entertaining enough for social occasions, but he will never be their equal. And *never* a gentleman. That's understood by everyone, my dear, even Rohan himself."

"It's neither understood nor accepted by me," she said. "There is more to being a gentleman than fine manners."

Christopher stared intently into her indignant face.

"Very well, we won't discuss him, if it makes you heated. But never forget that Gypsies are renowned for their charm and deceit. Their ruling principle is to seek their own enjoyment without regard for responsibilities or consequences. Your faith in him is misplaced, Amelia. I only hope you haven't entrusted any of your family's business or legal affairs to him."

"I appreciate your concern," she replied, wishing he would leave and try to find her missing brother. "But my family's affairs will remain in the hands of Lord Ramsay and myself."

"Then Rohan won't be returning from London? Your connection with him is severed?"

"He will return," she admitted reluctantly, "to bring some professional men who will advise what can be done with Ramsay House."

"Ah." There was just enough condescension in his tone to set her teeth on edge. Christopher shook his head and was silent for a long moment. "And is it only *his* counsel you will accept on the matter?" he finally asked. "Or may I be allowed to make recommendations on a subject of which I have a fair amount of expertise and he has none?"

"I would welcome your recommendations, of course."

"Then I may visit Ramsay House to make some professional assessments of my own?"

"If you like. That is very kind of you. Although . . ." She paused uncertainly. "I wouldn't wish for you to spend too much of your time there."

"Any time in your service is well spent." He leaned forward and brushed his lips against hers before she had the chance to pull back.

"Christopher, I'm far more concerned about my brother than the house—"

"Of course," he said reassuringly. "I'll ask after him, and if there is any news, I will relay it to you at once."

"Thank you."

But somehow she knew as Christopher left that his search for Leo would be halfhearted at best. Despair crept through her in a cold, heavy wave.

The next morning Amelia awakened from a nightmare with her arms and legs thrashing, her heart pounding. She had dreamed of finding Leo floating facedown in a pond, and as she had swum to him and tried to pull him to the edge, his body had begun to sink. She couldn't keep him afloat, and as he retreated farther into the black water, she was pulled down with him . . . choking on water, unable to see or breathe . . .

Trembling, she climbed out of bed and hunted for her slippers and robe. It was early yet, the house still dark and quiet. She headed for the door, and paused with her hand on the doorknob. Fear pumped through her veins. She didn't want to leave the room. She was afraid of finding out that Merripen had died during the night . . . afraid, too, that her brother had met with tragedy . . . and most of all afraid that she wouldn't be able to accept the worst, if the worst should come. She didn't feel as if she had the strength.

It was only the thought of her sisters that caused her to grip the knob and turn it. For their sakes, she could act with purpose and confidence. She would do whatever needed to be done.

Hurrying along the hallway, she pushed at the half-open door of Merripen's room and went to the bedside.

The muted light of dawn barely leavened the darkness, but it was enough for Amelia to see two people in the bed. Merripen was on his side, the formerly strong lines of his body collapsed and sprawling. And there was the slim, neat shape of Win sleeping beside him, fully clothed, her feet tucked beneath the skirts of her house dress. Though it was impossible for such a delicate creature to protect someone so much larger, Win's body was curved as if to shelter him.

Amelia stared at them in wonder, understanding more from the tableau than any words could have conveyed. Their position conveyed longing and restraint, even in sleep.

She realized her sister's eyes were open—there was the shine of her eyes. Win made no sound or movement, her expression grave as if she were absorbed in collecting each second with him.

Overwhelmed with compassion and shared sorrow, Amelia tore her gaze from her sister's. Retreating from the bedside, she left the room.

She nearly bumped into Poppy, who was also walking through the hallway, her robe a ghostly white.

"How is he?" Poppy asked.

Her throat hurt. It was difficult to speak. "Not well. Sleeping. Let's go to the kitchen and put a kettle on." They went toward the stairs.

"Amelia, I dreamed all night about Leo. Terrible dreams."

"So did I."

"Do you think he's . . . done himself harm?"

"I hope not, with all my heart. But I think it's possible."

"Yes," Poppy whispered. "I think so, too." She heaved a sigh. "Poor Beatrix."

"Why do you say that?"

"She's still so young, to have lost so many people . . . Father and Mother, and now perhaps Merripen and Leo."

"We haven't lost Merripen and Leo yet."

"At this point, it would be a miracle if we could keep either of them."

"You're always so cheerful in the morning." Amelia caught her hand and squeezed it. Trying to ignore the weight of hopelessness in her own chest, she said firmly, "Don't give up yet, Poppy. We'll hold out hope for as long as we can."

They reached the bottom of the stairs. "Amelia." Poppy sounded vaguely annoyed. "Don't you ever feel like throwing yourself to the floor and crying?"

Yes, Amelia thought. *Right now, as a matter of fact.* But she couldn't afford the luxury of tears. "No, of course not. Crying never solves anything."

"Don't you ever want to lean on someone's shoulder?"

"I don't need someone else's shoulder. I've got two perfectly good ones."

"That's silly. You can't lean on your own shoulder."

"Poppy, if you mean to start the day by bickering—" Amelia broke off as she became aware of some noise from outside, the thunder and jangle and gravel-crunching of a carriage and team of horses. "Good heavens, who would come at this hour?"

"The doctor," Poppy guessed.

"No, I haven't sent for him yet."

"Perhaps Lord Westcliff has returned."

"But there would be no reason for that, especially for him to have come so early—"

A footman knocked at the door, the sound echoing through the entrance hall.

The sisters looked at each other uneasily. "We can't answer it," Amelia said. "We're in our nightclothes."

A maid came into the entrance hall. Setting down a pail of coal, she wiped her hands on her apron and hastened to the door. Unlocking the massive portal, she tugged it open and bobbed a curtsy.

"Come away," Amelia muttered, urging Poppy back to the stairs with her. But as she glanced back over her shoulder to see who had come, the sight of a man's tall, dark form struck sparks inside her. She stopped with her foot on the first step, staring and staring, until a pair of amber eyes looked in her direction.

Cam.

He looked disheveled and disreputable, like an outlaw on the run. A smile came to his lips, while he stared at her intently. "It seems I can't stay away from you," he said.

She rushed to him without thinking, almost stumbling in her haste. "Cam—"

He caught her up with a low laugh. The scent of outdoors clung to him; wet earth, dampness, leaves. The mist on his coat sank through the thin layer of her robe. Feeling her tremor, Cam opened his coat with a wordless murmur and pulled her into the tough, warm haven of his body. Amelia couldn't contain her shivering. She was vaguely aware of servants moving through the entrance hall, of her sister's presence nearby. She was making a scene—she should pull away and try to compose herself. But she couldn't. Not yet.

"You must have traveled all night," she heard herself say.

"I had to come back early." She felt his lips brush her tumbled hair. "I left some things unfinished. But I had a feeling you might need me. Tell me what's happened, sweetheart."

Amelia opened her mouth to answer, but to her mortification, the only sound she could make was a sort of miserable croak. Her self-control shattered. She shook her head and choked on more sobs, and the more she tried to stop them, the worse they became.

Cam gripped her firmly, deeply, into his embrace. The appalling storm of tears didn't seem to bother him at all. He took one of Amelia's hands and flattened it against his heart, until she could feel the strong, steady beat. In a world that was disintegrating around her, he was solid and real. "It's all right," she heard him murmur. "I'm here."

Alarmed by her own lack of self-discipline, Amelia made a wobbly attempt to stand on her own, but he only hugged her more closely. "No, don't pull away. I've got you." He cuddled her shaking form against his chest. Noticing Poppy's awkward retreat, Cam sent her a reassuring smile. "Don't worry, little sister."

"Amelia hardly ever cries," Poppy said.

"She's fine." Cam ran his hand along Amelia's spine in soothing strokes. "She just needs . . ."

As he paused, Poppy said, "A shoulder to lean on."

"Yes." He drew Amelia to the stairs, and gestured for Poppy to sit beside them.

Cradling Amelia on his lap, Cam found a handkerchief in his pocket and wiped her eyes and nose. When it became apparent that no sense could be made from her jumbled words, he hushed her gently and held her against his large, warm body while she sobbed and hid her face. Overwhelmed with relief, she let him rock her as if she were a child.

As Amelia hiccupped and quieted in his arms, Cam asked a few questions of Poppy, who told him about Merripen's condition and Leo's disappearance, and even about the missing silverware.

Finally getting control of herself, Amelia cleared her aching throat. She lifted her head from Cam's shoulder and blinked.

"Better?" he asked, holding the handkerchief up to her nose.

Amelia nodded and blew obediently. "I'm sorry," she said in a muffled voice. "I shouldn't have turned into a watering pot. I'm finished now."

Cam seemed to look right inside her. His voice was very soft. "You don't have to be sorry. You don't have to be finished, either."

She realized that no matter what she did or said, no matter how long she wanted to cry, he would accept it. And he would comfort her. That made her eyes water again. Her hand crept to the open neck of his shirt, partially open to reveal a glimpse of sun-burnished skin. She let her fingers curl around the linen placket. "Do you think Leo might be dead?" she whispered.

He offered no false hope, no empty promises, only caressed her damp cheek with the backs of his fingers. "Whatever happens, we'll deal with it together."

"Cam . . . would you do something for me?"

"Anything."

"Could you find some of that plant Merripen gave to Win and Leo for the scarlet fever?"

He drew back and looked at her. "Deadly nightshade? That wouldn't work for this, sweetheart."

"But it's a fever."

"Caused by a septic wound. You have to treat the source of the fever." His hand went to the back of her neck, soothing the tautly strung muscles. He stared at a distant point on the floor, appearing to think something over. His tangled lashes made shadows over his hazel eyes. "Let's go have a look at him."

"Do you think you could help him?" Poppy asked, springing to her feet.

"Either that, or my efforts will finish him off quickly. Which, at this point, he may not mind." Lifting Amelia from his lap, Cam set her carefully on her feet, and they proceeded up the stairs. His hand remained at the small of her back, a light but steady support she desperately needed.

As they approached Merripen's room, it occurred to Amelia that Win might still be inside. "Wait," she said, hastening forward. "Let me go first."

Cam stayed beside the door.

Entering the room with caution, Amelia saw that Merripen was alone in the bed. She opened the door wider and gestured for Cam and Poppy to enter.

Becoming aware of intruders in the room, Merripen lurched to his side and squinted at them. As soon as he caught sight of Cam, his face contracted in a surly grimace.

"Bugger off," he croaked.

Cam smiled pleasantly. "Were you this charming with the doctor? I'll bet he was falling all over himself to help you."

"Get away from me."

"This may surprise you," Cam said, "but there's a long list of things I'd prefer to look at rather than your rotting carcass. For your family's sake, however, I'm willing. Turn over."

Merripen eased his front to the mattress and said something in Romany that sounded extremely foul.

"You, too," Cam said equably. He lifted the shirt from Merripen's back and pried the bandage from the injured shoulder. He viewed the hideous seeping wound without expression. "How often have you been cleaning it?" he asked Amelia.

"Twice a day."

"We'll try four times a day. Along with a poultice." Leaving the bedside, Cam motioned for Amelia to accompany him to the doorway. He lowered his mouth to her ear. "I have to go out to fetch a few things. While I'm gone, give him something to make him sleep. He won't be able to tolerate this otherwise."

"Tolerate what? What are you going to put in the poultice?"

"A mixture of things. Including *apis mellifica*."

"What is that?"

"Bee venom. Extract from crushed bees, to be precise. We'll soak them in a water-and-alcohol base."

Bewildered, Amelia shook her head. "But where are you going to get—" She broke off and stared at him with patent horror. "You're going to the hive at Ramsay house? H-how will you collect the bees?"

His mouth twitched with amusement. "Very carefully."

"Do you . . . do you want me to help?" she offered with difficulty.

Knowing her terror of the insects, Cam slid his hands around her head and pressed a hard kiss to her lips. "Not with the bees, sweetheart. Stay here and dose Merripen with morphine syrup. A lot of it."

"He won't. He hates morphine. He'll want to be stoic."

"Trust me, none of us will want him to be awake while I'm applying the poultice. Especially Merripen. The Rom call the treatment 'white lightning' for good reason. It's not something anyone can be stoic about. So do whatever's necessary to put him out, *monisha*. I'll be back soon."

"Do you think the white lightning will work?" she asked.

"I don't know." Cam cast an unfathomable glance back at the suffering figure on the bed. "But I don't think he'll last long without it."

While Cam was gone, Amelia conferred with her sisters in private. It was decided that Win would be the one most likely to succeed in making Merripen take the morphine. And it was Win herself who stated flatly they would have to deceive him, as he would refuse to take it voluntarily no matter how they beseeched him.

"I'll lie to him, if necessary," Win said, shocking the other three into speechlessness. "He trusts me. He'll believe whatever I say."

To their knowledge, Win had never told a lie in her life, not even as a child.

"Do you really think you could?" Beatrix asked, rather awed by the notion.

"To save his life, yes." Delicate tension appeared between Win's fine brows, and splotches of pale pink appeared high on her cheeks. "I think . . . I think a sin committed for such a purpose may be forgiven."

"I agree," Amelia said swiftly.

"He likes mint tea," Win said. "Let's make a strong batch and add a great deal of sugar. It will help hide the taste of the medicine."

No pot of tea had ever been prepared with such scrupulous care, the Hathaway sisters hovering over the brew like a coven of young witches. Finally a porcelain teapot was filled with the strained and sugared concoction, and placed on a tray beside a cup and saucer.

Win carried it to Merripen's room, pausing at the threshold as Amelia held the door open.

"Shall I go in with you?" Amelia whispered.

Win shook her head. "No, I'll manage. Please close the door. Make certain no one disturbs us." Her slender back was very straight as she entered the room.

Merripen's eyes opened at the sound of Win's footsteps. The pain of the festering wound was constant, inescapable. He could feel the toxins leaking into his blood, feeding poison into every capillary. It produced, at times, a perplexing dark euphoria, floating him away from his wasting body until he was at the periphery of the room. Until Win came, and then he gladly sank back into the pain just to feel her hands on him, her breath on his face.

Win shimmered like a mirage in front of him. Her skin looked cool and luminous, while his body raged with miasma and heat.

"I've brought something for you."

"Don't . . . don't want—"

"Yes," she insisted, joining him on the bed. "It will help you to get better . . . here, move up a bit, and I'll put my arm around you." There was a delicious slide of female limbs against him, beneath him, and Merripen gritted his teeth against a dull burst of agony as he moved to accommodate her. Darkness and light played beneath his closed eyelids, and he fought for consciousness.

When Merripen could open his eyes again, he found his head resting against the gentle pillow of Win's breasts, one of her arms cradling him while her free hand pressed a cup to his lips.

A delicate porcelain rim clicked against his teeth. He recoiled as an acrid taste burned his cracked lips. "No—"

"Yes. Drink." The cup advanced again. Her whisper fell tenderly against his ear. "For me."

He was too sick—he didn't think he could keep it down—but to please her, he drank a little. The crisp-sour taste made him recoil. "What is it?"

"Mint tea." Win's angel-blue eyes stared into his without blinking, her beautiful face neutral. "You must drink all of this, and then perhaps another cup. It will make you better."

He knew at once Win was lying. Nothing could make him better. And the bitter tang of morphine in the tea was impossible to conceal. But Merripen sensed an intent in her, a strange deliberateness, and the idea came to him that she was giving him an overdose on purpose. His exhausted mind weighed the possibility. It must be that Win wanted to spare him more suffering, knowing the hours and days to come were beyond his endurance. Killing him with morphine was the last act of kindness she could offer him.

Dying in her arms . . . cradled against her as he relinquished his scarred soul to the darkness . . . Win would be the last thing he would ever feel, see, hear. Had there been any tears in him, he would have wept in gratitude.

He drank slowly, forcing down every swallow. He drank part of the next cup until his throat would no longer work, and he turned his face against her chest and shuddered. His head was spinning, and sparks were drifting all around him like falling stars.

Win set the cup aside and stroked his hair, and pressed her wet cheek to his forehead.

And they both waited.

"Sing to me," Merripen whispered as the blinding darkness rolled over him. Win continued to stroke his head as she crooned a lullaby. His fingers touched her throat, seeking the precious vibration of her voice, and the sparks faded as he lost himself in her, his fate, at last.

Amelia lowered herself to the floor and sat beside the door, her fingers laced in a loose basket. She heard Win's tender murmurs . . . a few rasping words from Merripen . . . a long silence. And then Win's voice, singing gently, humming, the tones so true and lovely that Amelia felt a fragile peace steal over her. Eventually the angelic sound faded, and there was more quiet.

After an hour had passed, Amelia, whose nerves had been stretched to the limit, stood and stretched her cramped limbs. She opened the door with extreme care.

Win was easing from the bed, tugging the bedclothes over Merripen's prone form.

"Did he take it?" Amelia whispered, approaching her.

Win looked weary and strained. "Most of it."

"Did you have to lie to him?"

A tentative nod. "It was the easiest thing I've ever done. You see? . . . I'm not such a saint after all."

"Yes you are," Amelia returned, and hugged her fiercely. "You are."

Even Lord Westcliff's well-trained servants were inclined to complain when Cam returned with two jars of live bees and brought them to the kitchen. The scullery maids ran shrieking to the servants' hall, the housekeeper retreated to her room to compose an indignant letter to the earl and countess, and the butler told the head groomsman that if this was the kind of houseguest Lord Westcliff expected him to attend, he was thinking seriously of retiring.

As the only person in the household who dared go into the kitchen, Beatrix stayed with Cam, helped in the boiling, straining, and mixing, and later reported to her revolted sisters that it had been great fun crushing bees.

Eventually Cam brought what appeared to be a warlock's brew up to Merripen's room. Amelia waited for him there, having laid out clean knives, scissors, tweezers, fresh water, and a pile of clean white bandages.

Poppy and Beatrix were commanded to leave the room, much to their disgruntlement, while Win closed the door firmly behind them. She took an apron from Amelia, tied it around her narrow waist, and went to the bedside. Placing her fingers at the side of Merripen's throat, Win said tensely, "His pulse is weak and slow. It's the morphine."

"Bee venom stimulates the heart," Cam replied, rolling up his shirtsleeves. "Believe me, it will be racing in a minute or two."

"Shall I remove his bandage?" Amelia asked.

Cam nodded. "The shirt, too." He went to the washstand and soaped his hands.

Win and Amelia removed the linen shirt from Merripen's prostrate form. His back was still heavily muscled, but he had lost a great deal of weight. The sides of his ribs jutted in ledges beneath the swarthy skin.

As Win went to discard the crumpled shirt, Amelia untucked the end of the bandage and began to pry it loose. She paused as she noticed a curious mark on his other shoulder. Leaning over him, she stared more closely at the black ink design. A chill of astonishment ran through her.

"A tattoo," was all she could manage to say.

"Yes, I noticed it a few days ago," Win remarked, coming back to the bed. "It's odd that he never mentioned it, isn't it? No wonder he was always drawing pookas and making up stories about them when he was younger. It must have some significance to—"

"What did you say?" Cam's voice was quiet, but it reverberated with such intensity, he might as well have been shouting.

"Merripen has a tattoo of a pooka on his shoulder," Win replied, staring at him questioningly as he reached the bed in three strides. "We've never known about it until now. It's a very unique design—I've never seen anything quite like—" She stopped with a gasp as Cam held his forearm next to Merripen's shoulder.

The black winged horses with the yellow eyes were identical.

Amelia lifted her gaze from the astonishing sight to Cam's blank face. "What does it mean?"

Cam couldn't seem to take his gaze from Merripen's tattoo. "I don't know."

"Have you ever known anyone else who—"

"No." Cam stepped back. "Sweet Jesus." Slowly he

paced around the foot of the bed, staring at Merripen's motionless figure as it were a variety of exotic creature he had never seen before. He picked up a pair of scissors from the tray of supplies.

Instinctively Win moved closer to the sleeping man's side. Noticing her protectiveness, Cam murmured, "It's all right, little sister. I'm just going to cut away the dead skin."

He leaned over the wound and worked intently. After a minute of watching him clean and debride the wound, Win went to a nearby chair and sat abruptly as if her knees had been unbuckled.

Amelia stood beside him, feeling a sting of nausea in her throat. Cam, on the other hand, was as detached as if he were repairing the intricate mechanism of a clock rather than treating festering human flesh. At his direction, Amelia fetched the bowl of poultice liquid, which smelled astringent but curiously sweet.

"Don't let it splash into your eyes," Cam said, rinsing the wound with salt solution.

"It smells like fruit."

"That's the venom." Cam cut a square of cloth and pushed it into the bowl. Fishing it out gingerly, he laid the dripping cloth over the wound. Even in the depths of his sleep, Merripen jerked in reaction and groaned.

"Easy, *chal*." Cam laid a hand on his back, keeping him in place. When he was assured Merripen was still again, he bandaged the poultice firmly in place. "We'll replace it every time we clean the wound," he said. "Don't tip the bowl over. I'd hate to have to go back for more bees."

"How will we know if it's working?" Amelia asked.

"The fever should go down gradually, and by this time tomorrow we should see a nice leathery scab forming." He felt the side of Merripen's throat and told Win, "His pulse is stronger."

"What about the pain?" Win asked anxiously.

"That should improve quickly." Cam smiled at her as he quoted a Latin phrase, *"Pro medicina est dolor, dolorem qui necat."*

"The pain that kills pain acts as medicine," Win translated.

"That would make sense only to a Roma," Amelia said, and Cam grinned.

He took her shoulders in his hands. "You're in charge now, hummingbird. I'm leaving for a little while."

"Right now?" she asked in bewilderment. "But . . . where are you going?"

His expression changed. "To find your brother."

Amelia stared at him with mingled gratitude and concern. "Perhaps you should rest first. You traveled all night. It may take a long time to find him."

"No it won't." His eyes glinted with irony. "Your brother is hardly one to cover his tracks."

Chapter Twenty

Approximately six hours after his search for Leo had begun, Cam knocked at the front door of a prosperous manor farm. A piece of tavern gossip had led to someone who had seen Ramsay with someone else, and they had gone to another place, where their plans had been overheard, and so forth, until finally the trail had led to this place.

The large Tudor house, with the date 1620 inscribed over the door, was located almost ten miles from Stony Cross Park. From the information Cam had gathered, the farm had once belonged to a noble Hampshire family, but had been sold out of necessity to a London merchant. It served as a retreat for the merchant's dissipated sons and their playmates.

Hardly a surprise that Leo had been drawn to such company.

The door was opened, and a trout-faced butler appeared. His lips twisted disdainfully as he saw Cam.

"Your kind isn't welcome here."

"That's fortunate, since I don't intend to stay long. I've come to collect Lord Ramsay."

"There is no Ramsay here." The butler began to close the door, but Cam braced a hand on it.

"Tall. Light eyes. Ruddy-complexioned. Probably reeking of spirits—"

"I have seen no one of that description."

"Then let me speak to your master."

"He is not at home."

"Look," Cam said irritably, "I'm here on behalf of Lord Ramsay's family. They want him back. God knows why. Give him to me, and I'll leave you in peace."

"If they want him," the butler said frostily, "let them send a proper servant. Not a filthy Gypsy."

Cam rubbed the corners of his eyes with his free hand and sighed. "We can do this the easy way or the hard way. Frankly, I'd rather not go through unnecessary exertion. All I ask is that you allow me five minutes to find the bastard and take him off your hands."

"Begone with you!"

After another foiled attempt to close the door, the butler reached for a silver bell on the hall table. A few seconds later, two burly footmen appeared.

"Show this vermin out at once," the butler commanded.

Cam removed his coat and tossed it onto one of the built-in benches lining the entrance hall.

The first footman charged him. In a few practiced movements, Cam landed a right cross on his jaw, flipped him, and sent him to a groaning heap on the floor.

The second footman approached Cam with considerably more caution than the first.

"Which is your dominant arm?" Cam asked.

The footman looked startled. "Why do you want to know?"

"I'd prefer to break the one you don't use as often."

The footman's eyes bulged, and he retreated, giving the butler a pleading glance.

The butler glared at Cam. "You have five minutes. Retrieve your master and go."

"Ramsay isn't my master," Cam muttered. "He's a pain in my arse."

"They've been in the same room for days," the footman, whose name was George, told Cam as they ascended a flight of carpeted stairs. "Food sent in, whores coming and going, empty wine bottles everywhere . . . and the stench of opium smoke all through the entire upper floor. You'll want to cover your eyes when you enter the room, sir."

"Because of the smoke?"

"That, and . . . well, the goings-on would make the devil blush."

"I'm from London," Cam said. "I don't blush."

Even if George hadn't been willing to lead Cam to the room of iniquity, he could have easily found it from the smell.

The door was ajar. Cam nudged it open and stepped into the hazy atmosphere. There were four men and two women, all young, all in various stages of undress. Although only one opium pipe was in evidence, it could have been argued that the entire room served as a huge pipe, so thick was the sweet smoke.

Cam's arrival was greeted with remarkable unconcern, the men listlessly draped across upholstered furniture, one coiled on cushions in the corner. Their complexions were cadaverous, their eyes filmy with narcotic dullness. A side table was littered with spoons and pins and a dish filled with what looked like black treacle.

One of the women, who was entirely naked, paused in the act of lifting a pipe to a man's slack mouth.

"Look," she said to the other woman, "here's a new one."

A drowsy giggle. "Good, we need him. They're all at half-mast. The only stiff thing left is the pipe." She twisted to look at Cam. "Gor, what a pretty man."

"Oh, let me have him first," the other one said. She petted herself invitingly. "C'mere, love, I'll give you a—"

"No, thank you." Cam was beginning to feel slightly dizzy from the smoke. He went to the nearest window, opened it, and let a cold breeze into the room. A few curses and protests greeted his actions.

Identifying the one in the corner as Leo, Cam went to the quiescent figure, lifted the head by the hair, and stared into his future brother-in-law's puffy face. "Haven't you inhaled enough smoke lately?" he asked.

Leo scowled. "Sod off."

"You sound like Merripen," Cam said. "Who, in case you're interested, may be dead by the time we return to Stony Cross Manor."

"Good riddance to him."

"I'd agree with you, except that agreeing with you probably means I'm on the wrong side of the argument." Cam began to tug Leo upward, and the other man struggled. "Stand up, damn you." Cam hoisted him with a grunt of effort. "Or I'll drag you out by the heels."

Leo's bloated bulk swayed against him. "I'm trying to stand," he snapped. "The floor keeps tipping."

Cam fought to steady him. When Leo had finally gotten

his bearings, he lurched toward the doorway, where the footman waited.

"May I escort you downstairs, my lord?" George asked politely. Leo responded with a surly nod.

"Close the window," one of the women demanded, her naked body shivering as the autumn wind swept through the room.

Cam glanced at her dispassionately. He had seen too many of her kind to feel much pity. There were thousands of them in London—round-faced country wenches, just pretty enough to attract the attention of men who promised, took, and discarded without conscience. "You should try some fresh air," he advised, reaching for a discarded lap blanket beside the settee. "It promotes clear thinking."

"What do I need to do that for?" she asked sourly.

Cam grinned. "Good point." He draped the blanket over her shivering white body. "Still . . . you should take some deep breaths." He bent to pat her pale cheek gently. "And leave this place as soon as you're able. Don't waste yourself on these bastards."

The woman lifted her bloodshot eyes, staring in wonder at the black-haired man, who was as swarthy and dashing as a pirate prince with the glittering diamond at his ear.

Her plaintive voice followed him as he left. "Come back!"

It took the combined efforts of Cam and George to load the grumbling, protesting Leo into the carriage. "It's like hauling five sacks of potatoes all at once," the footman said breathlessly, pushing Leo's foot safely inside the vehicle.

"The potatoes would be quieter," Cam said. He tossed the footman a gold sovereign.

George caught it in midair and beamed at him. "Thank you, sir! And may I say you're a gentleman, sir. Even if you are a Gypsy."

Cam's smile turned wry, and he climbed into the carriage after Leo. They started back to Stony Cross Manor in silence.

"Do you need to stop?" Cam asked midway through the trip, seeing that Leo's face had turned from white to green.

Leo shook his head morosely. "I don't wish to talk."

"You owe me an answer or two. Because if I hadn't had to spend the day searching through half of Hampshire to find you, I could have been in bed—" *With your sister,* he thought, but instead said, "Sleeping."

Those curiously light eyes turned toward him, the color of icicles when blue twilight shone through them. Unusual eyes. Cam had seen someone with eyes like that before, but he couldn't remember who or when. A distant memory hovered just beyond reach.

"What do you want to know?" Leo asked.

"Why do you bear Merripen such ill will? Is it his charming disposition, or the fact that he's a Roma? Or is it because he was taken in by your parents and raised as one of you?"

"None of that. I despise Merripen because he refused the only thing I ever asked of him."

"Which was?"

"To let me die."

Cam pondered that. "You must mean when he nursed you through the scarlet fever."

"Yes."

"You blame him for saving your life?"

"Yes."

"If it makes you feel any better," Cam said dryly, settling back in his seat, "I'm sure he's had second thoughts about it."

They were silent after that, while Cam relaxed and let his mind wander. As darkness fell and Leo was cast in shadow, the unnerving eyes flickered silver-blue—

—and Cam remembered.

It was in childhood, when Cam had still been with the tribe. There had been a man with a haggard face and brilliant colorless eyes, his soul ravaged by grief over his daughter's death. Cam's grandmother had warned him to stay away from the man. "He's *muladi*," she had said.

"What does that mean, Mamì?" Cam had asked, clinging anxiously to her warm hand, which was comfortingly gnarled and tough like the buttressing roots of ancient trees.

"Haunted by a dead person. Don't go near him, he's upset the balance of *Romanija*. He loved his daughter too much."

Feeling pity for the man, and worry for his own sake, Cam had asked, "Will I be *muladi* when you die, Mamì?" He had been certain that he loved his grandmother too much, but he couldn't stop feeling that way.

A smile had appeared in his grandmother's wise black eyes. "No, Cam. A *muladi* traps his beloved's spirit in the in-between because he won't let her go. You wouldn't do that to me, would you, little fox?"

"No, Mamì."

The man had died not long after that, by his own hand. It had been a horror, and yet a relief for the entire tribe.

Now, as Cam looked back on it with the understanding

of an adult rather than a small boy, he felt a chill of apprehension, followed by searing pity. How impossible it would be to relinquish a woman you loved. How could you stop yourself from wanting her? The seams of your heart would rip open with grief. Of course you would want to keep her with you.

Or follow her.

As Cam entered the manor with the unrepentant prodigal at his side, Amelia and Beatrix hurried toward them, the former frowning, the latter smiling.

Amelia opened her mouth to say something to Leo, but Cam caught her gaze and shook his head, warning her to be silent. To his surprise, she actually obeyed and swallowed back the sharp words. She reached out for Leo's coat. "I'll take that," she said in a subdued tone.

"Thank you." Both avoided looking at each other.

"We've just finished supper," Amelia muttered. "The stew is still hot. Will you have some?"

Leo shook his head.

Beatrix, missing the seething undercurrents in the air, launched herself at Leo and wrapped her arms around his thick waist. "You were gone so long! So many things have happened—Merripen is ill, and I helped make a potion for him, and—" She stopped, making a face. "You smell bad. What—"

"Tell me how you made the potion," Leo said gruffly, making his way to the stairs. Beatrix chattered without stopping as she accompanied him.

Cam looked over Amelia carefully, not missing a detail.

She was disheveled, her hair cascading down her back, her eyes tired. She needed to rest.

"Thank you for finding him," she said. "Where was he?"

"At a private home with some friends."

She drew closer to him, sniffing gingerly. "That smell . . . it's on both of you . . ."

"Opium smoke. Your brother's taken up an expensive new habit."

"We couldn't afford the old ones." Amelia scowled, her foot beginning a restless staccato beneath her skirts. She was so small and fierce and adorable that Cam could barely restrain himself from snatching her up and kissing her senseless. "The only reason I didn't murder him just now," Amelia continued, "is because he looked too numb to feel it. But when he sobers I'm going to—"

"How is Merripen?" Cam interrupted, running a gentle hand from her shoulder to her elbow.

The tapping stopped. "Still feverish, but better. Win's with him. We changed his poultice . . . the wound looks a bit less disgusting than before. Is that a good sign?"

"It's a good sign."

Her concerned gaze chased over him. "Shall I get you something to eat?"

Smiling, Cam shook his head. "Not before I have a good, thorough wash." There were many things they needed to discuss, but it could all wait. "Go to bed, *monisha*—you look weary."

"So do you," Amelia said, standing on her toes. Cam held very still as she pressed her lips to his cheek. A long hesitation, and then she asked tentatively, "Will you come to me tonight?"

The shy invitation nearly undid him. Here was an opening—a sign of acceptance—but he cared too much about her to take advantage when she was obviously tired. "No." He took her into his arms. "You need to sleep more than you need my groping and fondling."

She flushed a little, and leaned harder against him. "I don't mind your groping and fondling."

Cam laughed. "What a testament to my lovemaking skills."

"Come to me," she whispered. "Hold me while we sleep."

"Hummingbird," he returned, his lips brushing her brow, "if I hold you, I don't trust myself not to make love to you. So we'll sleep in separate beds." He looked down at her with a smile. "Just for tonight."

It took three soapings and rinsings for Cam to remove the taint of opium from his skin and hair. After toweling his hair dry, he donned a black silk robe and walked through the darkened hallway to his room. It was storming outside, the rain and thunder sweeping in on an easterly, battering the windows and roof.

The hearth in his room had been replenished, the blaze shedding warmth and light. Cam's eyes narrowed in curiosity as he saw a small shape beneath the covers.

Amelia's head lifted from the pillow. "I'm cold," she said, as if that were a perfectly reasonable explanation for her presence.

"My bed is no warmer than yours." Cam approached her slowly, trying not to feel like a predator, trying to ignore the heat that had ignited in his blood. His body had gone hard beneath the black silk, all his muscles tightening in anticipation. He knew what she wanted from him . . . and he would be more than happy to provide it.

"It would be warmer if you were in it," she said.

Her hair fell over her shoulders in dark ripples down to her hips. Sitting close beside her, Cam touched one of the shining locks, following it over her chest, the tip of her breast, down to the end. Amelia drew in a quick breath. He wondered if the blush on her face had spread to the skin he couldn't see.

Restraining his urgent need, Cam held still as she reached out to him with hesitant fingers, stroking the black silk that covered his shoulders. She rose to her knees and impulsively kissed his ear, the one with the diamond stud, and touched the damp, slightly curling locks of his hair.

"You're not like any man I've ever known," she said. "You're not even someone I could have dreamed. You're like someone from a fairy story written in a language I don't even know."

"The prince, I hope."

"No, you're the dragon, a beautiful wicked dragon." Her voice turned wistful. "How could anyone have a normal everyday life with you?"

Cam took her in a safe, firm grip and lowered her to the mattress. "Maybe you'll be a civilizing influence on me." He bent over the slope of her breast, kissing it through the muslin veil of her gown. "Or maybe you'll get a taste for the dragon." He found the bud of her nipple, wet the cotton with his mouth, until the tender flesh pricked up against his tongue.

"I th-think I already have." She sounded so perturbed that he laughed.

"Then lie still," he whispered, "while I breathe fire on you."

The women he had slept with in the past had never worn this kind of prim white nightgown, which struck Cam as the most erotic garment he had ever seen. It had intricate little folds and tucks and lace trimmings, and it went from the neck to the ankles. The way it lay over her, like a layer of pale, crisp icing, made his heart pound with primal force. He followed her shape, searching for her scent, her heat, through the cotton, lingering whenever she arched or shivered. The front was held closed by a long row of covered buttons. He worked at them while her hands slid restlessly over his silk-covered back.

He kissed her, his tongue searching the sweetness of her mouth. The top of the gown slipped open, revealing the gleaming rise of her breasts, the tempting shadow between. He pulled the garment lower, lower, until her arms were delicately trapped and her chest was exposed. His head lowered and he took what he wanted, licking a taut nipple, prodding with his tongue, making it wet and deep pink. Amelia sighed deeply, her eyes half-closed, her body lifting helplessly as he bent to her other breast.

Cam's breathing turned ragged as he pulled the gown lower, freeing her arms, exposing the curves of her hips and stomach. He spread his hands over her body, his fingers and palms translating heat into sensation. He kissed her navel, the ticklish skin around it, the place where the crisp curly hair started.

Her legs tautened against him, caught beneath his weight. Moving upward, he straddled her body. He took the signet ring off, the one she had refused before, and held it out to her.

"You can have what you want," he said. "But first put this on."

Amelia focused on the ring. "I can't."

"I won't make love to you unless you're wearing it."

"You're being absurd."

"You're being stubborn." Cam leaned over her, bracing his forearms on either side of her, kissing her sulky mouth. "Just for tonight," he whispered. "Wear my ring, Amelia, and let me pleasure you." He kissed her throat, his hips shunting gently against her. She gasped at the feel of him, hard and swollen behind the black silk. His mouth traveled slowly up to her ear. "I'll enter you, fill you, and then I'll hold you still and quiet in my arms. I won't move. I won't let you move, either. I'll wait until I feel you throbbing around me . . . I'll follow that rhythm deep in your body, that sweet pulse . . . I won't stop until you weep and shiver and cry out for more. And I'll give it to you, as long and hard as you want. Take my ring, love." His mouth descended to hers in a smoldering kiss. "Take me."

Fitting himself against her soft cleft, he felt her heat seep through the robe, wetness and silk stretched tightly between them. Her small hand touched his, fingers unfolding . . . and she let him slide the ring back on.

Cam stripped her naked and laid her back into his discarded robe, her skin startling white in the glimmering pool of black. He kissed her everywhere, the crooks of her elbows, the backs of her knees, every curve and hollow of the smooth feminine territory. She wrapped herself around him, her mouth innocently inquiring as she kissed every part of him she could reach.

He kissed between her thighs, cupping her hips with his hands while the scent of her lit an explosion of fire inside him. He licked into the tenderness, teasing, sucking lightly, until she groaned with every breath and reached down to his head, urging him upward with imploring fingers.

Fighting for self-control, Cam entered her, sliding deep. She moved and arched and nearly drove him insane. "Sweetheart, wait," he said shakily, trying to calm her. "Don't move. Please. Don't . . ." A laugh rustled in his throat as she hitched up against him desperately. "Be still," he whispered, brushing kisses across her parted lips. "Hold me inside you. Feel the way your body tightens around me."

Breathing hard, Amelia tried to obey. Her flesh pulsed helplessly around the invading hardness. Cam made them both wait, their bodies perspiring and tense as they concentrated on that subtle, luscious clenching. Finally he began to move, using himself to pleasure her. He made love to her, all of her, and as he sank into the fathomless dark delight, he was flooded with a fulfillment he had never known before.

She enclosed him in softness and heat, letting him feast on kisses while he rode the swift hot pulse, stroking her inside and out. He looked down with pleasure-hazed eyes, at her face so tenderly confined in the bracket of his hands, and he whispered in Romany, *I am yours*. He watched her eyes close in the sweet temporary blindness of rapture, he felt it echoing in himself, the waves rushing stronger and stronger until the world caught fire.

Afterward they lay tumbled side by side like the survivors of a shipwreck, stunned in the wake of a storm. When Cam could gather the strength to move—which was not soon—he rolled to his side and nuzzled Amelia's throat, loving the fragrant damp warmth of her.

Amelia groped for the ring and began tugging and twisting it. "It's stuck again." She sounded disgruntled.

Cam pinned her wrist and bent his head, taking her finger into his mouth. She gasped as his tongue swirled around the base, leaving it wet. Gently, he used his teeth to draw the gold band off. Taking the ring from between his lips, he slid it back onto his own finger. Her hand, now bare, flexed as if bereft, and she looked at him uncertainly.

"You'll get used to wearing it." Cam smoothed his hand along the plane of her midriff and stomach. "We'll try it on you a few minutes at a time. Like breaking a horse to harness." He grinned at her expression.

Pulling the covers over them both, Cam continued to stroke her. Amelia sighed, nestling against his shoulder and biceps.

"By the way," he murmured, "the flatware's back in the silver cabinet."

"It is?" she asked drowsily. "How . . . what . . ."

"I had a talk with Beatrix while we were crushing bees. She explained her problem. We agreed to find some new hobbies to keep her busy. To start with, I'm going to teach her to ride. She said she barely knows how."

"There hasn't really been time, with all the other—" Amelia began defensively.

"Shhh . . . I know that, hummingbird. You've done more than enough, keeping all of them together and safe. Now it's time for you to have some help." He kissed her gently. "For someone to keep you safe."

"But I don't want you to—"

"Go to sleep," Cam whispered. "We'll start arguing again in the morning. For now, love . . . dream of something sweet."

• • •

Amelia slept deeply, dreaming of resting in a dragon's nest, tucked beneath his warm leathery wing while he breathed fire on anyone or anything that dared to approach. She was woozily aware of Cam leaving the bed in the middle of the night, pulling on his clothes. "Where are you going?" she mumbled.

"To see Merripen."

She knew she should go with him—she was concerned about Merripen—but as she tried to sit up, she was reeling with exhaustion, stupefied with it.

Cam coaxed her back down into the welcoming depth of the bedclothes. She fell asleep again, stirring only when he returned to stretch out beside her and gather her in his arms. "Is he better?" she whispered.

"Not yet. But he's no worse. That's good. Now close your eyes . . ." And he soothed her back to sleep.

Merripen awakened in a dark bedroom, the only glimmer of light coming from the quarter-inch space between the closed draperies. That one sliver was brilliant with the whiteness of midday.

His head ached viciously. His tongue seemed twice its normal size, dry and swollen in his mouth. His bones were sore, and so was his skin. Even his eyelashes hurt. In fact, he had undergone some strange reversal in which everything hurt except his wounded shoulder, which glowed with a near-pleasant warmth.

He tried to move. Instantly someone came to him.

Win. Cool, frail, sweet-smelling, a lovely spirit in the darkness. Without speaking, she sat beside him and lifted his head, and gave him tiny sips of water until his mouth was moist enough to allow speech.

So he hadn't died. And if he hadn't by now, he probably wasn't going to. He wasn't certain how he felt about that. His usual rough appetite for life had been replaced by shattering melancholy. Probably the aftereffects of the morphine.

Still cradling Merripen's head, Win stroked her fingers through his matted, unwashed hair. The light scratch of her fingernails on his scalp sent chills of pleasure through his aching body. But he was so mortified by his uncleanliness, not to mention his helplessness, that he shoved irritably at the gentle hand.

"I must be in hell," he muttered.

Win smiled down at him with a tenderness he found unbearable. "You wouldn't see me in hell, would you?"

"In my version . . . yes."

Her smile turned quizzical, faded, and she laid his head carefully back on the bed.

Win would be featured prominently in Merripen's hell. The most profound, gut-wrenching pain he had ever experienced was because of her—the agony of wanting and never having, of loving and never knowing love. And now it appeared he was going to endure more of it. Which would have made him hate her, if he didn't worship her so.

Bending over him, Win touched the bandage on his shoulder, beginning to untuck the end.

"No," Merripen said harshly, moving away from her.

He was naked beneath the covers, stinking of sweat and medicine. A huge, hulking beast. And even worse, dangerously vulnerable. If she continued touching him, tending him, his defenses would be smashed, and God knew what he would say or do. He needed her to go as far away from him as possible.

"Kev," she said, her too-careful tone maddening him further, "I want to see the wound. It's almost time to change the poultice. If you'll just lie flat and let me—"

"Not you."

Lie flat. As if that were even possible, with the roaring erection that had sprung to life as soon as she had touched him. He was nothing more than an animal, wanting her this way even when he was ill and filthy and still drugged from morphine . . . even knowing that to make love to her was like signing her death warrant. Had he been a prayerful man, he would have begged the pitiless heavens never to let Win know what he wanted or how he felt.

A long moment passed before Win asked in a perfectly normal tone, "Who do you want to change the poultice, then?"

"Anyone." Merripen kept his eyes closed. "Anyone but you."

He had no idea what Win's thoughts were, as the silence became heavy and prolonged. His ears pricked at the sound of her skirts swishing. The thought of fabric moving and swirling around her slender legs caused every hair on his body to rise.

"All right, then," she said in a matter-of-fact tone as she reached the door. "I'll send someone else as soon as possible."

Merripen moved his hand to the place on the mattress where she had sat, his fingers splayed wide. And he fought to close his heart, which contained too many secrets and therefore could never be shut all the way.

◆ ◆ ◆

Descending the grand staircase carefully, Win saw Cam Rohan coming up. She felt a spasm of nerves in her stomach. Win had always felt a bit twittery around unfamiliar men, and she wasn't quite certain what to make of this one. Rohan had assumed a position of influence over her family with astonishing speed. He had stolen her older sister's heart with such adroitness that she didn't even seem to know it yet.

Like Merripen, Rohan was a big, virile male. And like Merripen he was a Roma, but he was so much easier with it, infinitely more comfortable in his own skin. Rohan was smooth and prepossessing whereas Merripen was secretive and brooding. But for all Rohan's charm, there was a subtle edge of danger about him, a sense that he was acquainted with a side of life the sheltered Hathaways had never been exposed to.

He was a man who harbored secrets . . . like Merripen. Those identical tattoos had caused Win to wonder at the connection between the two men. And she thought she might know what it was, even if neither of them did.

She stopped with a timid smile as they met on the stairs. "Mr. Rohan."

"Miss Winnifred." Rohan's unnerving golden gaze moved across her white face. She was still upset from her encounter with Merripen. She could feel the color burning across the crests of her cheeks.

"He's awake, I take it," Rohan said, reading her expression far too accurately.

"He's cross with me for tricking him into drinking the tea with morphine."

"I suspect he would forgive you anything," Rohan replied.

Win rested her hand on the balcony railing and looked over the edge absently. She had the curious feeling of wanting, needing, to communicate to this friendly stranger, and yet having no idea what she wanted to say.

Rohan waited in companionable silence, in no apparent hurry to go anywhere. She liked his company. Having long been accustomed to Merripen's brusqueness, and Leo's self-destructiveness, she thought it was rather nice to be in the presence of such a levelheaded man.

"You saved Merripen's life," she ventured. "He's going to get well."

Rohan watched her intently. "You care for him."

"Oh, yes, we all do," Win said too quickly, and paused. Words gathered and flew inside her as if they had wings. The effort to hold them back was exhausting. She was suddenly glassy-eyed with frustration and desolation, thinking of the man upstairs and the untraversable distance that was always, always between them. "I want to get well, too," she burst out. "I want . . . I want . . ." She closed her mouth and thought, *Good Lord, how must I sound to him?* Feeling chagrin at her loss of self-control, she passed a hand over her face and rubbed her temples.

But Rohan seemed to understand. And mercifully, there was no pity in his gaze. The honesty in his voice comforted her immeasurably. "I think you will, little sister."

She shook her head as she confessed, "I want it so much, I'm afraid to hope."

"Never be afraid to hope," Rohan said gently. "It's the only way to begin."

Chapter
Twenty-one

Amelia was at a loss to understand how she could have slept until after luncheon. She could only attribute it to Cam, whose mere presence in the house caused her to relax. It was as if her mind automatically handed over worries and cares to him, allowing her to sleep like an infant.

She didn't like it.

She didn't want to depend on him, and yet she couldn't seem to stop it from happening.

Dressing smartly in a chocolate-colored gown with pink velvet trim, she went to visit Merripen, whose surliness didn't dampen her joy in his recovery.

Upon going downstairs, she was told by the housekeeper that a pair of gentlemen had just arrived from London, and Mr. Rohan was meeting with them in the library. Amelia guessed one of them was the builder whom Cam had sent for. Curious about the visitors, she went to the library and paused at the doorway.

The masculine voices stopped. There were men grouped around the library table, two seated, one leaning casually against it, and another—Leo—lurking in the corner. The men all rose, except for Leo, who merely shifted in his chair as if the courtesy were too much effort to be bothered with.

Cam was dressed with his usual disheveled elegance: well-tailored clothes but a conspicuous lack of a cravat. Approaching Amelia, he took one of her hands. He raised it to his lips and pressed a lingering kiss to the backs of her fingers in a territorial gesture not likely to be lost on anyone.

"Miss Hathaway." Cam's tone was polite, while a heathen glint danced in his eyes. "Your timing is perfect. Some gentlemen have arrived to discuss the restoration of the Ramsay estate. Allow me to introduce them."

Amelia exchanged bows with the men: a master builder named John Dashiell, who appeared to be in his late thirties, and his assistant, Mr. Francis Barksby. Dashiell had gained a sterling reputation as the builder of the Rutledge Hotel several years earlier, and subsequently carried out private and public projects all over England. He and his brother had established a prosperous firm with the relatively new concept of employing all his subcontractors internally, rather than hiring outside workers and craftsmen. By keeping all his employees under one roof, Dashiell maintained an unusually high degree of control over his projects.

Dashiell was a large-framed, ruggedly attractive man with a ready smile. One could easily imagine him in his early days as a carpenter's apprentice, hammer in hand. "A pleasure, Miss Hathaway. I was sorry to learn of the Ramsay House fire, but very glad everyone escaped alive. Many families are not so fortunate."

She nodded. "Thank you, sir. We are grateful to have

your judgment and insights, and to find out what can be made of our house now."

"I'll do my best," he promised.

"Mr. Dashiell, do you employ an architect at your firm?"

"As it happens, my brother is quite proficient at architectural design. But he is rather occupied with work in London. We're searching for a second architect to manage the surplus." He cast a quick glance at Leo, and turned back to Amelia. "I hope to persuade Lord Ramsay to accompany us to the estate. I would welcome his opinions."

"I've given up having opinions," Leo said. "Hardly anyone agrees with them, and if someone does, it's proof he has no judgment whatsoever."

But somehow, by some verbal equivalent of a sleight-of-hand trick, Cam managed to get Leo to accompany them to Ramsay House. Later in the day Cam described it to Amelia in private, the way Leo had mumbled and sulked for most of the visit while Mr. Dashiell had made notes and sketches. But there had been moments when Leo had seemed unable to resist commenting on his abhorrence of baroque trimmings and flourishes, and how the house should be designed with symmetry and proportion.

"Did you mention to Mr. Dashiell that Mr. Frost is currently staying in Hampshire?" Amelia asked.

They walked slowly along a path that led into the wood, the sky blushing with the advent of evening. A brisk wind sent leaves skipping and whispering over the ground. Cam adjusted his stride to match Amelia's shorter one. Drawing off one of her gloves, he deposited it in his pocket and kept her bare hand in his.

"No," he replied, "I didn't mention him. Why would I?"

"Well, Mr. Frost is a very accomplished architect, and as a friend of the family, he has offered to give us the benefit of his expertise—"

"He's not a friend of the family," Cam said shortly. "And we don't need his expertise. There's no way in hell he's going to have anything to do with Ramsay House."

"He wishes to make amends. He was very kind in offering his services, if we should need—"

"When?"

Disconcerted by his tone, the word fast and sharp as a rifle shot, Amelia blinked. "When what?"

Cam stopped and turned her to face him, his face hard. "When did he offer his bloody services?"

"He came to visit while you were gone." Having never seen a display of temper from him before, Amelia pushed uneasily at his hands, which were gripping her shoulders a shade too tightly. "All he wanted," she continued, "was to offer help."

"If you believe that was all he wanted, you're more naïve than I thought."

"I am *not* naïve," she said indignantly. "And there's no reason to be jealous. Nothing improper was said or done."

His eyes held dangerous heat. "Were you alone in the room with him?"

Amelia was amazed by his intensity. No man had ever regarded her with such possessive fury. She wasn't certain whether she was flattered, annoyed, or alarmed. Or perhaps all three. "Yes, we were alone," she said, "with the door open. All very conventional."

"For *gadjos,* perhaps. But not for Romas." He lifted her until her weight was balanced precariously on her toes.

"You are never to be alone with him, or any man, except your brother or Merripen. Unless I give my permission."

Amelia's mouth fell open. *"Permission?"*

"Never," he repeated grimly.

Her own temper flared, but she managed to keep her voice even. "You see, *this* is why I'm not going to marry you. I will not be dictated to. I will not—"

Cam lowered his head and silenced her with his mouth, clenching his hand in her hair as she tried to turn her face away. She felt him press her lips open, delving inside, and her will to resist was undermined by a shock of pleasure. Since she had no hope of freeing herself, she tried to remain cold and still beneath the passionate assault. Feeling her lack of response, he lifted his head and glared at her.

Amelia glared back at him. "It's not your house, and I'm not your—"

He kissed her again, taking her head in his hands, concentrating on her mouth until she was pulsing everywhere. She moaned and went weak against him. Muttering in Romany, he pulled her to the trunk of the largest beech, its smooth gray bark knobbed and time-scarred. The branches had been weighted by their own mass until they touched the earth and reached upward again, as if the tree were a lazy giant resting on ancient elbows.

Untying Amelia's bonnet ribbons, Cam tossed the garment to the ground. His mouth covered hers, his tongue stabbing inside her in rough, delicious strokes. He pushed her against the trunk where a huge branch diverged in a bulky joist, and dug his knee into her skirts to keep her there. Beechnut husks crackled beneath their feet with each shift of their weight. With every kiss, Cam found a new angle, a deeper taste, making love to her mouth with blatant sensuality.

The pale gold leaves blurred overhead. "Cam, no," Amelia whispered as his lips traveled down to her throat.

Ignoring her, he unfastened the front of her bodice and untied it with a roughness that made her gasp. He bent to a cool, tight nipple, heating it with his mouth, biting tenderly at the tip.

"Not here," she managed.

Cam kissed his way up the taut column of her neck. "Here," he said thickly. "Where we are no different than any wild creature in the wood." Taking her hand, he pulled it to the straining hardness of his sex. Her eyes half closed as she felt the hardness and heat of him even through the fabric of his trousers. And she realized she wanted him so badly that she was shaking. Her fingers worked helplessly against the heavy shaft while he dragged up her skirts in great handfuls.

He tugged at the tapes of her drawers, loosening them until the garment dropped to her knees. His hand slipped insistently between her thighs, pushing them apart. He touched inside her, seducing her with unbearably intimate caresses. Withdrawing, he used a fingertip to make slippery-soft circles around the sensitive bud. He kissed and whispered against her mouth, tightening his arm around her squirming body.

The wind caused the tree branches to whip and flail overhead, leaves falling in a dark flurry. Evening settled outside the wood, seeping inward through the trees. Cam turned Amelia away from him, guiding her down until her front was supported by the gigantic beech branch, and her hands, one gloved, one bare, were clutched on the paper-flat bark.

He shoved the mass of her skirts upward, heaped them at her waist, and drew his palms over her hips.

The head of his shaft brushed the wet entrance of her body. She couldn't help cocking her hips upward, inviting more. She strained back into the satiny pressure as he gripped his sex and used it to tease her, circling, crossing, entering briefly and sliding back, until the beech bark was wet beneath her bare palm, and all she could do was wait, trembling, with her head lowered. She didn't dare speak for fear she would cry out like one of the wild creatures he had spoken of. But a groan did leave her as he finally pushed forward in a long, aggressive slide, filling her exquisitely.

Cam's hand slid to her front, between her thighs, and he played with her as he thrust steadily, rooting out spasms of white-hot delight. She sensed the wild hunger in him, but he disciplined it for her, for her pleasure, and her body responded with violent throbbing convulsions. Pulling out with a groan, he urged his slick length against the smooth skin of her buttocks, letting the hot fluid spill.

Amelia wanted him inside her. She had wanted to pull him as deep as possible in that final moment. Instead she lay passively over the beech wood. Her legs were so weak, she doubted they would take her all the way back to the manor. Cam restored her clothing slowly, his strong hands lifting her from the beech. Crushing her close, he muttered something incomprehensible against her hair. Another spell to bind her, she thought hazily, her cheek pressed to his smooth, hard chest. "You're speaking in Romany," she mumbled.

Cam switched to English. "Amelia, I—" He stopped, as if the right words eluded him. "I can't stop myself from being jealous, any more than I can stop being half Roma. But I'll try not to be overbearing. Just say you'll be my wife."

"Please," Amelia whispered, her wits still scattered, "let me answer later. When I can think clearly."

"You do too much thinking." He kissed the top of her head. "I can't promise you a perfect life. But I can promise that no matter what happens, I'll give you everything I have. We'll be together. You inside me . . . me inside you." He held her close and sighed shortly. "All right. Give me an answer later. But remember . . . a dragon has only so much patience."

Mr. Dashiell and his assistant stayed in Hampshire one more day, visiting Ramsay House to make additional sketches of the structure and the surrounding land. The assistant, Mr. Barksby, would take initial survey measurements and gather information. At Dashiell's invitation, Amelia accompanied them, pleased by the opportunity to watch them work.

Cam, meanwhile, was forced to remain at the manor to meet with an estate manager, Mr. Gerald Pym. The manager worked for a Portsmouth firm that held a long-standing contract to supervise the Ramsay estate. Pym had been hastily dispatched after news of the fire to compile an initial report of the damage and take stock of the situation. Rents, repairs, and development of the estate land would be discussed, as well as the contracts with John Dashiell. Much would have to be decided in short order, to keep the few existing Ramsay tenants from fleeing. Hopefully in the future, with good management, more tenants might be attracted to the estate, providing badly needed income for the Hathaways.

All of that was conditional, of course, on how long Leo would remain alive.

Since meeting with Mr. Pym was the responsibility of the current Lord Ramsay, Cam bullied Leo into attending the meeting with him. Not because Leo would have anything sensible to contribute, but merely as a symbolic gesture.

"Besides," Cam had told Amelia grimly, "if I have to be bored witless talking about *gadjo* affairs, there's no reason Leo should be spared." He had swept a proprietary glance over her, taking in the green wool walking dress and fur-trimmed black cloak. "I shouldn't let you go with Dashiell and Barksby," he said. "You'll be the only woman there. I don't like it."

"Oh, it's all very circumspect. They're both gentlemen, and I'm—"

"Spoken for," he had said curtly. "By me."

Her heart beat a little faster. "Yes, I know," she admitted without looking at him.

The small concession seemed to please him. He pushed the door closed with his foot, and reached beneath her cloak with importunate hands. He kissed her as if he could breathe her in. Fierce kisses, hard ones, teasingly articulate ones, soft enticing ones, kisses to light bonfires and fill the sky and hold the stars aloft.

When Cam finally relented and eased her away from the door to open it, he said one word in her scarlet ear before she fled. The word went down to the marrow of her bones.

"Tonight."

• • •

Walking around the ragged exterior of Ramsay House, Amelia talked animatedly with John Dashiell, asking about his past projects, his ambitions, and whether there were difficulties in working with one's brother.

"We knock heads quite often, I'm afraid," Dashiell replied, squinting against the afternoon sun. A quick grin illuminated his face. "We both hate to compromise. I accuse him of being set in his ways, and he accuses me of arrogance. The pity of it is, we're both right."

Amelia laughed. "But the job gets done."

"Yes, we're inspired to reach a compromise by the necessity of paying the bills. Here, take my arm. The ground is uneven."

His arm was firm and steady beneath her gloved hand. She felt a rush of liking for him. "I'm very glad you came to Hampshire, Mr. Dashiell. I know Lord Ramsay appreciates your efforts on our behalf."

"Does he?"

"Oh, yes. I'm sure he would have said so, except that he's had a great deal hanging on his mind of late."

"I met him once, actually," Dashiell said. "Two years ago, when he was still articled to Rowland Temple. Though your brother doesn't seem to recollect the meeting. I was very much impressed with him at the time—he was a pleasant and prepossessing man, full of plans."

Amelia lowered her gaze. "I'm sure he is greatly altered from the time you saw him last."

"He seems a different man altogether."

"He hasn't yet recovered from his fiancée's death." Amelia's voice dropped to a near-whisper as she confided, "Sometimes I fear he never will."

Dashiell stopped and turned her to face him. Compassion flickered in his eyes. "Ah. That is the price of love, I'm afraid—the pain one suffers from its loss. I'm not convinced it's worth it. Perhaps if one must love, one should do so in moderation."

That sounded sensible. But as Amelia opened her mouth to agree, the words stuck in her throat. And what finally came out was an unsteady laugh. "Moderation in love," she mused aloud. "It's not something that would inspire a poet, is it?"

"A poet's view of the world would make for an uncomfortable life, wouldn't it? Everyone at the mercy of his or her passions, all of us tearing our hair out for the sake of love . . ."

"Or riding off at midnight," Amelia said. "Living out one's dreams and fantasies . . ."

"Exactly. It has all the makings of disaster."

"Or romance," she said, hoping he didn't notice the slight catch in her voice.

"Spoken like a woman."

Amelia laughed. "Yes, Mr. Dashiell, I'll confess that I am not immune to the idea of romance. I hope that doesn't lessen your opinion of me."

"Not in the slightest. In fact . . ." His voice gentled. "I hope that I will be able to visit you as the work on Ramsay House progresses. I would greatly enjoy the company of such a charming and lovely woman, with an obviously sensible disposition."

"Thank you," Amelia said, the color in her cheeks rising. But as she stared at the well-dressed gentleman before her, her mind summoned the image of a handsome face with wicked golden eyes and the mouth of a fallen angel, his head silhouetted against a sky flooded with midnight stars. Exotic, unpredictable, a man who would never be quite tame.

You inside me, me inside you . . .

"I would enjoy your company as well, sir," she heard herself say. She blushed as she added, "But you should know that I have an understanding with Mr. Rohan."

Thankfully, her companion was quick to grasp her meaning. He did not seem surprised. "I was afraid that might be the case. I couldn't help but notice Rohan's regard for you. He gives a decided impression of wanting you all to himself." Dashiell smiled ruefully. "One can hardly blame him."

Flattered, uncertain how to reply, Amelia returned her attention to the house. She was not accustomed to men making such comments about her. Her gaze traveled along the uneven roofline. The house looked so shipwrecked, so weary, the windows like wounds in the side of a fallen beast. The windows . . . she saw movement in one of them, a shimmer, something that looked like a tangle of moonbeams and shadows.

A face.

She must have made a sound, for Mr. Dashiell looked at her closely, and his gaze followed hers to the house. "What is it?" he asked at once.

"I thought . . ." She found herself clutching a fold of his sleeve like a frightened child. Her thoughts were in chaos. "I thought I saw someone at the window."

"Perhaps it was Barksby."

But Mr. Barksby was coming round the corner of the house, and the face had been at a second-floor window.

"Shall I go in to have a look?" Dashiell asked quietly, his eyes narrowed with concern.

"No," Amelia said at once, managing a shallow smile. She let go of his sleeve. "It must have been a curtain moving. I'm sure no one is there."

After Dashiell and Mr. Barksby had departed for London, Cam returned to the study with Mr. Pym to discuss a few last items of business. Having had enough of estate management, Leo abandoned all pretense of interest in Pym's concerns, and disappeared up to his room. Although Cam had sardonically assured Amelia that she was welcome to participate in the meeting with Mr. Pym, she declined hastily, suspecting that she would not be able to endure the tedious discussion with any more grace than her brother had.

Instead, she went to find Win.

Her sister was in a private family parlor upstairs, curled in the corner of a settee with a book in her lap. Win turned a page without seeming to read it, looking up with evident relief as Amelia came to her.

"I've wanted to talk with you all day." Win moved her feet to make room for Amelia. "You seemed so distracted after the visit to Ramsay House. Was it seeing the house? . . . Did it make you melancholy? Or was it Mr. Dashiell? Did he try to flirt with you?"

"Heavens," Amelia said with a disconcerted laugh, "what could have given you the idea that he would want to flirt with me?"

Win smiled and shrugged a little. "He seems rather charmed by you."

"Pshaw."

Win's smile broadened until she looked like her old mischievous self, as she had been in the days before the scarlet fever. "You only say 'Pshaw' because you have Mr. Rohan on the string."

Amelia's eyes widened, and she looked around as if fearing someone might have overheard them. "Hush, Win! I don't have anyone on the string. What a horrid expression. I can't believe—"

"Face the truth," Win said, enjoying her sister's discomfort. "You've become a femme fatale."

Amelia rolled her eyes. "Continue to make jest of me, and I won't tell you what happened during the visit to Ramsay House."

"What? Oh, do tell, Amelia. I've nearly withered away from boredom."

Amelia found it difficult to speak casually about the event. She swallowed hard. "I feel like a lunatic, saying it. But . . . when I was walking with Mr. Dashiell and looking at the house, I saw a face in one of the upstairs windows."

"Someone was inside?" Win asked in a thready whisper. She reached out and took Amelia's chilled fingers in hers.

"Not a person. It was . . . it was Laura."

"Oh." The word was a mere wisp of sound.

"I know it's difficult to believe—"

"No it isn't. Remember, I saw her face on the magic lantern slide, the night of the fire. And—" Win hesitated, her slim white fingers moving over the back of Amelia's hand. "Having been close to death once, I find it easy to believe such apparitions could be real."

The silence was cold and tense. Amelia struggled to be

rational, to make sense of impossible things. She spoke with difficulty. "Then you think Laura is haunting Leo?"

"If she is," Win whispered, "I think it's out of love."

"I think he's going mad from it." At Win's silence, the lack of disagreement, Amelia said desperately, "How can we stop it from happening?"

"We can't. Leo's the only one who can."

Annoyed, Amelia jerked her hand away. "Pardon me if I can't be fatalistic about it. Something has to be done."

"Then do something," Win said coolly, "if you're willing to risk pushing him over the edge."

Amelia leaped from the settee and glared at her. What in God's name did Win expect of her? . . . To stand aside passively while Leo destroyed himself?

Weariness cut through the vibrating anger. She was tired of everything, all of it, tired of thinking and worrying and fearing, and getting nothing for it but the singular ingratitude of her siblings.

"Damn this family," she said hoarsely, and left before even harsher words could be exchanged.

Forgoing supper, Amelia went to her room and lay on the bed fully clothed. She stared up at the ceiling until the room grew quite dark, the sun was extinguished, the air became still and cool. She closed her eyes, and when she opened them again, the room was filled with impenetrable blackness. There was movement around her, beside her, and she started and put her hand out. She encountered warm human flesh, an arm lightly covered with hair, a strong wrist. "Cam," she whispered. Relaxing, she felt the smooth gold band at the base of his thumb.

Cam didn't say a word. He undressed her slowly, one garment at a time, and she accepted his ministrations in a dreamlike silence. The troubled feeling in her chest eased as sensations rose and blossomed.

He found her mouth and licked it open, kissing her fully. She lifted her arms to the dark, gorgeous creature over her, the flowing strength of him covering her. With every breath he took, his chest slid against the stiff tips of her breasts, the light friction eliciting muted cries from her throat.

His mouth broke from hers, exploring her shoulders and chest with hot open kisses, as if he were intent on tasting every part of her. He caressed her stomach with the backs of his fingers, teased his thumb around the rim of her navel . . . his hands clever and sublimely gentle. He had not entered her yet, but she already felt him at the center of her, the pulse, the pleasure. *You inside me . . .* She reached for him blindly, her limbs folding around him.

He resisted with a silken laugh, playing, stretching her limbs out and spreading her wide beneath him. His mouth dragged over her, sucking and teasing, and between her thighs she went absolutely wet. He touched her with his tongue, delving with the tip until he found the sensitive place that throbbed so exquisitely. The muscles in his arms bulged as he slid them beneath her legs, making a cradle of her hips. She struggled a little, not in protest but supplication, shivering with each swirl and glide of his tongue.

Dazed and aching, she felt herself lifted in the darkness, his hands arranging her, closing on her legs. He made her kneel over him, pulling her hips down, pushing them back and forth in a gentle rhythm. His mouth was on her again, and she groaned helplessly as she was rubbed repeatedly across the heat and wetness and the tender flicking tongue. His teasing fingers slid inside her, and she began to pant with ecstasy, sensation wrapping around on itself—

A knock at the door shattered the voluptuous quiet.

"Oh, God," Amelia whispered, freezing.

The knock repeated, more urgent this time, along with Poppy's muffled voice.

Cam took his mouth from her, his fingers slowly withdrawing from her clenching flesh.

"Poppy," Amelia called out weakly, "can't it wait?"

"No."

Amelia clambered off Cam, her nerves throbbing viciously at the abrupt halt to their lovemaking. Cam rolled to his stomach and uttered a soft curse, his fingers digging into the bedclothes.

Lurching around the room as if she were on the deck of a tossing ship, Amelia managed to find her robe. She pulled it on and fastened a few random buttons down the front.

She went to the door and opened it a mere two inches. "What is it, Poppy? It's the middle of the night."

"I know," Poppy said anxiously, finding it difficult to meet her gaze. "I wouldn't have—it's just—I didn't know what to do. I had a bad dream. A terrible nightmare about Leo, and it seemed so real. I couldn't go back to sleep until I made certain he was all right. So I went to his room, and . . . he's gone."

Amelia shook her head in exasperation. "Bother Leo. We'll look for him in the morning. I don't think any of us should go chasing after him tonight in the dark and cold. He probably went to the village tavern, in which case—"

"I found this in his room." Poppy held out a slip of paper to her.

Frowning, Amelia read the note.

I'm sorry.
I don't expect you to understand.
You'll be better off this way.

There were another few words, scratched out.

I hope someday

And at the bottom, once again,

I'm sorry.

There was no signature. No need for one.

Amelia was surprised by how calm her own voice sounded. "Go to bed, Poppy."

"But his note—I think it means—"

"I know what it means. Go to bed, dear. Everything will be all right."

"Are you going to find him?"

"Yes, I'll find him."

Amelia's artificial composure vanished the moment the door closed. Cam was already yanking on his clothes, tugging his boots on, while Amelia lit the bedside lamp. She gave the note to him with trembling fingers. "It's not an empty gesture." She found it hard to breathe. "He means to do it. He may have already—"

"Where is he most likely to go?" Cam interrupted. "Somewhere on the estate?"

Amelia thought of Laura's spectral face in the window. "He's at Ramsay House," she said through chattering teeth. "Take me there. Please."

"Of course. But first you may want to put on some clothes." Cam gave her a reassuring smile, stroking the side of her face with his hand. "I'll help you."

"Any man," she muttered, "who wanted to marry into the Hathaway family after this should be shut away in an institution."

"Marriage is an institution," he said reasonably, retrieving her gown from the floor.

They rode to Ramsay House on Cam's horse, whose long-stretching canter covered ground at near-frightening speed. It all seemed part of another nightmare, the rushing darkness and gnawing cold, the feeling of hurtling forward beyond her control. But there was Cam's steadfast form at her back, one arm locking her securely in place. She feared what they would find at Ramsay House. If the worst had already happened, she would have to accept it. But she was not alone. She was with the man who seemed to understand the very warp and weft of her soul.

As they approached the house, they saw a horse grazing disconsolately over patches of grass and gorse. It was a welcome sight. Leo was here, and they wouldn't have to go scouring through Hampshire to find him.

Helping Amelia to the ground, Cam took her hand in his. She held back, however, as he tried to pull her toward the front door. "Perhaps," she said tentatively, "you should wait here while I—"

"Not a chance in hell."

"He may be more responsive if I approach him by my-self, just at first—"

"He's not in his right mind. You're not going to face him without me."

"He's my brother."

"And you're my *romni*."

"What is that?"

"I'll explain later." Cam stole a quick kiss and slid his arm around her, guiding her into the house. It was as still as a mausoleum, the chilled air scented of smoke and dust. Exploring the first floor silently, they found no sign of Leo. It was difficult to see in the darkness, but Cam made his way from room to room with the sureness of a cat.

There came a sound from overhead, the squeak of shifting floorboards. Amelia felt a quake of nervousness, and at the same time, relief. She hastened toward the stairs. Cam checked her, his hand tightening on her arm. Understanding that he wanted her to go slowly, she forced herself to relax.

They went to the staircase, Cam leading the way, testing each step before allowing Amelia to follow him. Accumulated grit scraped beneath their quiet feet. As they ascended, the air turned colder, and colder still, driving needles into her bones. It was an unholy chill, too bitter and ghastly to have come from a temporal source. A coldness that dried her lips and made her teeth ache. Her hand tightened inside Cam's, and she kept as close to him as possible without tripping him.

A feeble frosted glow came from a room near the end of an upstairs hallway. Amelia made a sound of distress as she realized where the lamplight was coming from.

"The bee room."

"Bees don't fly at night," Cam murmured, his hand coming to the back of her neck, sliding across her nape. "But if you'd rather wait here—"

"No." Summoning her courage, Amelia squared her shoulders and went with him down the hall. How like Leo, perverse wretch that he was, to hole up in a place that scared her witless.

They paused at the open doorway, Cam partially blocking Amelia from view.

Peering around his shoulder, she gasped.

It was not Leo, but Christopher Frost, his lean form gilded in lamplight as he stood before an open panel in the wall that contained the bee colony. The bees were subdued but far from quiet, millions of wings beating in a thick, ominous hum. The stench of exposed wood decay and fermented honey hung thick in the air. Shadows pooled on the floor like spilled ink, while the lamplight twisted and writhed at Christopher's feet.

At the swift intake of Amelia's breath, he swiveled and pulled something from his pocket. A pistol.

The three of them froze in a dark tableau, while a sting of shock ran over Amelia's skin.

"Christopher," she said in bewilderment. "What are you doing here?"

"Get back," Cam said harshly, trying to shove her behind him. But since she was no more eager to have Cam in front of the pistol than herself, she ducked beneath his arm and came up beside him.

"You've come for it, too, I see." Christopher sounded astonishingly calm, his gaze flicking to Cam's face and then Amelia's. The pistol was steady in his hand. He did not lower it.

"Come for what?" Bewildered, Amelia stared at the gaping hole in the wall, a rectangular space at least five feet tall. "Why have you made that opening in the wall?"

"It's a sliding panel," Cam said tersely, not taking his gaze from Christopher. "Made to conceal a hiding place."

Wondering why they both seemed to know something about Ramsay House that she didn't, Amelia asked blankly, "A hiding place for what?"

"It was designed long ago," Christopher replied, "as a place for persecuted Catholic priests to conceal themselves."

Her bewildered mind tried to make sense of things. She had read about such places. Long ago Roman Catholics had been hunted and executed by law in England. Some of them had escaped by hiding in the homes of Catholic sympathizers. She had never suspected, however, that such a place had been incorporated in Ramsay House.

"How did you know about . . ." Finding it difficult to speak, she gestured stiffly to the cavity in the wall.

"It was referenced in the private journals of the architect, William Bissel. The notes are now in the possession of Rowland Temple."

And now, Amelia thought, after two centuries, this hiding place had been revealed . . . with a colony of bees in residence. "Why did Mr. Temple tell you about it? What are you hoping to find?"

Christopher glanced at her with amused contempt. "Are you pretending ignorance, or do you really have no idea?"

"I can guess," Cam said. "It probably has something to do with a bit of local lore concerning hidden treasure at Ramsay House." He shrugged a little at their curious glances. "Westcliff mentioned it once in passing."

"Treasure? *Here?*" Amelia scowled in disgruntlement. "Why has no one mentioned it to me before?"

"It's nothing but unfounded rumor. And the origins of the supposed treasure aren't usually mentioned in polite company." Cam sent Christopher a cold glance. "Put the gun away. We've no intention of interfering."

"Yes we do!" Amelia said irritably. "If there is some kind of treasure at Ramsay House, it belongs to Leo. And why are the origins of it so unmentionable?"

Frost answered, the gun still trained on Cam. "Because it consists of tokens and jewels given by King James to his lover back in the sixteenth century. Someone in the Ramsay family."

"The king had an affair with Lady Ramsay?"

"With Lord Ramsay, actually."

Amelia's jaw slackened. "Oh." She frowned and rubbed her frozen arms through her sleeves in a futile effort to warm them. "So you think this treasure is here in one of Bissel's hiding places. And all this time you've been trying to find it. Your offer of friendship—your regret for having abandoned me—that was all a sham! For the sake of some wild-goose chase."

"It wasn't all a sham." Christopher gave her a scornful, vaguely pitying glance. "My interest in renewing our relationship was genuine, until I realized you had taken up with a Gypsy. I don't accept soiled goods."

Infuriated, Amelia started for him with her fingers curled into claws. "You aren't fit to lick his boots!" she cried, struggling as Cam hauled her backward.

"Don't," Cam muttered, his hands like iron clamps on her body. "It's not worth it. Calm yourself."

Amelia subsided, glaring at Christopher, while increasing cold chills rippled through the air. "Even if the treasure were here, you wouldn't be able to retrieve it," she snapped. "The wall is filled with a hive containing at least two hundred thousand bees."

"That's where your arrival turns fortuitous." The pistol was trained directly at her chest. He spoke to Cam. "You're going to get it for me . . . or I'll put a bullet in her."

"Don't you dare," Amelia said to Cam, gripping one of his arms in both of hers. "He's bluffing."

"Are you going to risk her life on the possibility, Rohan?" Christopher inquired almost diffidently.

Amelia struggled to hold on to Cam as he disengaged his arm from her grasp. "Don't do it!"

"Easy, *monisha*." Cam gripped her shoulders and gave her a little shake. "Hush. You're not helping." He looked at Christopher. "Let her leave," he said evenly. "I'll do whatever you ask."

Christopher shook his head. "Her presence provides an excellent incentive for you to cooperate." He gestured with the pistol. "Get over there and start looking."

"You've gone mad," Amelia said. "Hidden treasure and pistols and skulking about at midn—" She stopped as she saw a shimmer of movement, of silvery whiteness, in the air. A rush of biting cold swept through the room, while the shadows congealed around them.

Christopher seemed not to notice the abrupt drop in temperature, or the dance of translucent paleness between them. "*Now,* Rohan."

"Cam—"

"Hush." He touched the side of Amelia's face and gave her an unfathomable glance.

"But the bees—"

"It's all right." Cam went to pick up the lamp from the floor. Carrying it to the open panel, he held it inside the hollow space and leaned in. Bees began to settle and crawl over his arm, shoulders, and head. Staring at him fixedly, Amelia saw his arm twitch, and she realized he'd been stung. Panic tightened around her lungs, making her breathing quick and shallow.

Cam's voice was muffled. "There's nothing except bees and honeycomb."

"There has to be," Christopher snapped. "Go in there and find it."

"He can't," Amelia cried in outrage. "He'll be stung to death."

He aimed the pistol directly at her. "Go," Christopher commanded Cam.

Bees were showering onto Cam, crawling over his shining black hair and face and the back of his neck. Watching him, Amelia felt as if she were trapped in a waking nightmare.

"Nothing's here," Cam said, sounding astonishingly calm.

Now Christopher seemed to take a vicious satisfaction in the situation. "You've hardly looked. Go inside and don't come out without it."

Tears sprang to Amelia's eyes. "You're a monster," she said furiously. "There's nothing in there, and you know it."

"Look at you," he said, sneering, "weeping over your Gypsy lover. How low you've fallen."

Before she could respond, a blue-white burst of light filled the room in a noiseless strike. The lamp flame was extinguished in a freezing blast. Amelia blinked and rubbed the moisture from her eyes, and turned in a bewildered circle as she tried to find the source of the light. Something shimmered all around them, coldness and brilliance and raw energy. She stumbled toward Cam with her arms outstretched. The bees lifted in a mass and flew back to the hive, the blue light causing their wings to glitter like a rain of sparks.

Amelia reached Cam, and he caught her in a warm, hard grip. "Are you hurt?" she asked, her hands frantically searching him.

"No, just a sting or two. I—" He broke off with a sharp inhalation.

Twisting in his arms, Amelia followed his gaze. Two hazy forms, distorted in the broken light, struggled for possession of the gun. Who was it? Who else had come into the room? Not a heartbeat had passed before Cam had shoved her to the floor. "Stay down." Without pausing, he launched himself toward the combatants.

But they had already broken apart, one man tumbling to the floor with the pistol in his grip, the other running for the door. Cam went for the fallen man, while the air crackled as if the room were filled with burning Catherine wheels. The other man fled. And the door slammed shut behind him . . . although no one had touched it.

Dazed, Amelia sat up, while the fractured light dissolved into a faint blue radiance that clung to the outlines of the men nearby. "Cam?" she asked uncertainly.

His voice was low and shaken. "It's all right, hummingbird. Come here."

She reached them and gasped as she saw the intruder's face. "*Leo*. What are you—how did you—" Her voice faltered at the sight of the pistol in his hand. He held it loosely against his thigh. His face was calm, his mouth curved with a faint wry smile.

"I was going to ask you the same thing," Leo said mildly. "What the devil are you doing here?"

Amelia sank to the floor beside Cam, her gaze remaining on her brother. "Poppy found your note," she said breathlessly. "We came here because we thought you were going to . . . to do yourself in."

"That was the general idea," Leo said. "But I went to the tavern for a drink on the way. And when I finally got here, it was a bit crowded for my taste. Suicide is something a fellow likes a bit of privacy for."

Amelia was unnerved by his tranquil manner. Her gaze fell to the pistol in his hand, then returned to his face. Her hand crept to Cam's tense thigh. The ghost was with them, she thought. The air had turned her face numb, making it difficult to move her lips. "Mr. Frost was treasure-hunting," she told her brother.

Leo gave her a skeptical glance. "A treasure, in this rubbish pile?"

"Well, you see, Mr. Frost thought—"

"No, don't bother. I'm afraid I can't summon any interest in what Frost thought. The idiot." He looked down at the pistol, his thumb gently grazing the barrel.

Amelia wouldn't have expected a man contemplating suicide to appear so relaxed. A ruined man in a ruined house. Every line of his body spoke of weary resignation. He looked at Cam. "You need to take her out of here," he said quietly.

"Leo—" Amelia had begun to tremble, knowing that if they left him here, he would kill himself. She could think of nothing to say, at least nothing that wouldn't sound theatrical, unconvincing, absurd.

Her brother's mouth quirked as if he were too exhausted to smile. "I know," he said gently. "I know what you want, and what you don't want. I know you wish I could be better than this. But I'm not."

He blurred before her. Amelia felt tears sliding from her eyes, the wetness turning icy by the time they reached her chin. "I don't want to lose you."

Leo bent both his knees and braced an arm across them, his fingers remaining curled around the gun handle. "I'm not your brother, Amelia. Not anymore. I changed when Laura died."

"I still want you."

"No one gets what they want," Leo muttered. "Not now."

Cam watched her brother intently. A long silence unfolded in pained degrees, while a burning cold breeze fanned over the three of them. "I could try to persuade you to set the gun aside, and go home with us," he said eventually. "To hold off one more day. But even if I stopped you this time . . . one can't keep a man alive when he doesn't want to be."

"True," Leo said.

Amelia opened her mouth with a shuddering protest, but Cam stopped her, his fingers pressing gently over her lips. Cam continued to stare at Leo, not with concern but a sort of detached contemplation, as if he were focusing on some mathematical equation. "No one can be haunted," he said quietly, "without having willed it. You know that, don't you?"

The room grew even colder, if that were possible, the windows rattling, the lamplight flickering. Alarmed by the taut vibrations in the air, the unseen presence circling them, Amelia huddled against Cam's back.

"Of course I do," Leo said. "I should have died when she did. I never wanted to be left behind. You don't know what it's like. The thought of finally ending this is a bloody relief."

"But that's not what she wants."

Hostility flared in the light eyes. "How the hell would you know?"

"If your situations were reversed, would you choose this for her?" Cam gestured to the gun in his hand. "I wouldn't ask that sacrifice of someone I love."

"You have no bloody idea what you're talking about."

"I do," Cam said. "I understand. And I'm telling you to stop being selfish. You grieve too much, my *phral*. You've forced her to come back to comfort you. You have to let her go. Not for your sake, but hers."

"I can't." But emotion had begun to spread across Leo's face like cracks in an eggshell. Blue light danced through the room, while a frigid wind lifted a few locks of Leo's hair like invisible fingers.

"Let her be at peace," Cam said, more quietly now. "If you take your own life, you'll end up condemning her, as well as yourself, to an eternity of wandering. It's not fair to her."

Leo gave a wordless shake of his bent head, cradling his folded knees in a posture that reminded Amelia of the boy he'd once been. And she understood his grief with a thoroughness that had been impossible for her before.

What if Cam were taken from her without warning? She could never again know the feel of his hair in her hands or the caress of his lips against hers. No consummation of all she had begun to feel, the promises, smiles, tears, hopes, all ripped from her grasp. Forever. How much she would miss. How much could never be replaced by anyone else.

Aching with compassion, she watched as Cam moved to her brother. Leo hid his face and jerked a hand up, fingers spread, palm facing out in a broken, helpless gesture. "I can't let her go," he choked.

The lamp blew out, and a pane of glass shattered, while a freezing blast of air struck them. Energy crackled through the room, tiny snaps of light appearing around them.

"You can do it for her," Cam said, putting his arms around her brother in the way he might have comforted a lost child. "You can."

Leo began to cry harder, each breath a burst of angry despair. "Oh, God," he groaned. "Laura, don't leave me."

But as he wept, the atmosphere seemed to settle, glacier-cold and calm, and the blue light, like the afterglow of a distant dying star, began to fade. There was a quiet drone of wings—a few bees venturing from the hive, then flying back to settle for the night.

Cam was murmuring something now, holding Leo in a firm protective grasp. He spoke in Romany, the words drifting into the thinning air. A promise, a compact, offered to a fading, formless spirit.

Until all that was left were three people sitting among shattered glass in the darkness, a discarded weapon on the floor.

"She's gone," Cam said softly. "She's free."

Leo nodded, his face hidden. He was damaged but still alive. Broken, but not beyond the hope of repair.

And reconciled to life, at last.

Chapter
Twenty-two

After they had taken Leo back to Stony Cross Manor and put him to bed, Amelia stood outside his room with Cam. Her emotions were brimming so high and strong, it took all her strength to contain them. "I'm going to tell Poppy that he's all right," she whispered.

Cam nodded, silent and somewhat distracted. Their fingers tangled briefly.

They parted company, and Amelia went to find her sister.

Poppy was in bed, lying on her side, her eyes fully open. "You found Leo," she murmured as Amelia came to her.

"Yes, dear."

"Is he . . . ?"

"He's fine. I think . . ." Amelia sat on the edge of the mattress and smiled down at her. "I think he'll be better from now on."

"Like the old Leo?"

"I don't know."

Poppy yawned. "Amelia . . . will you be grumpy if I ask something?"

"I'm too tired to be grumpy. Ask away."

"Are you going to marry Mr. Rohan?"

The question filled Amelia with dizzying delight. "Should I?"

"Oh, yes. You've been compromised, you know. Besides, he's a good influence on you. You're not nearly so much of a porcupine when he's around."

"Delightful child," Amelia observed to the room in general, and grinned at her sister. "I'll tell you in the morning, dear. Go to sleep."

She walked through the somber stillness of the hallway, feeling as nervous as a bride as she went to find Cam. It was time to be open, honest, trusting, as she had never been before, not even in their most intimate moments. Her heartbeat resounded everywhere, even in the tips of her fingers and toes. She went to Cam's room, where lamplight seeped through the fissure of the partially opened door.

Cam was sitting on the bed, still clothed. His head was lowered, hands braced on his knees in the posture of a man who was deep in thought. He glanced up as she came into the room and closed the door.

"What's the matter, love?"

"I . . ." Amelia approached him hesitantly. "I'm afraid you won't let me have what I want."

His slow smile robbed her of breath. "I have yet to refuse you anything. I'm not likely to start now."

Amelia stopped before him, her skirts crowded between his parted knees. The clean, salty, evergreen scent of him drifted to her nostrils. "I have a proposition for you," she said, trying for a businesslike tone. "A very sensible one. You see—" She paused to clear her throat. "I've been thinking about your problem."

"What problem?" Cam played lightly with the folds of her skirts, watching her face alertly.

"Your good-luck curse. I know how to get rid of it. You should marry into a family with very, *very* bad luck. A family with expensive problems. And then you won't have to be embarrassed about having so much money, because it will flow out nearly as fast as it comes in."

"Very sensible." Cam took her shaking hand in his, pressed it between his warm palms. And touched his foot to her rapidly tapping one. "Hummingbird," he whispered, "you don't have to be nervous with me."

Gathering her courage, Amelia blurted out, "I want your ring. I want never to take it off again. I want to be your *romni* forever"—she paused with a quick, abashed smile— "whatever that is."

"My bride. My wife."

Amelia froze in a moment of throat-clenching delight as she felt him slide the gold ring onto her finger, easing it to the base. "When we were with Leo, tonight," she said scratchily, "I knew exactly how he felt about losing Laura. He told me once that I couldn't understand unless I had loved someone that way. He was right. And tonight, as I watched you with him . . . I knew what I would think at the very last moment of my life."

His thumb smoothed over the tender surface of her knuckle. "Yes, love?"

"I would think," she continued, " 'Oh, if I could have just one more day with Cam. I would fit a lifetime into those few hours.' "

"Not necessary," he assured her gently. "Statistically speaking, we'll have at least ten, fifteen thousand days to spend together."

"I don't want to be apart from you for even one of them."

Cam cupped her small, serious face in his hands, his thumbs skimming the trace of tears beneath her eyes. His gaze caressed her. "Are we to live in sin, love, or will you finally agree to marry me?"

"Yes. Yes. I'll marry you. Although . . . I still can't promise to obey you."

Cam laughed quietly. "We'll manage around that. If you'll at least promise to love me."

Amelia gripped his wrists, his pulse steady and strong beneath her fingertips. "Oh, I do love you, you're—"

"I love you, too."

"—my fate. You're everything I—" She would have said more, if he had not pulled her head to his, kissing her with hard, thrilling pressure.

They undressed with haste, tugging at each other's clothes with a clumsiness wrought of desire and fervor. When at last their skin was laid bare, Cam's urgency eased. His hands glided over her with deliberate slowness, every caress bringing tremors of pleasure to the surface. His features were austerely beautiful as he rolled her to her back. His mouth lowered to her breasts, his hands cupping the rounded flesh, tongue and teeth gently navigating the tips.

Amelia moaned his name, surrendering helplessly as he rose to kneel between her legs. His hand closed over her hips, lifting and bracing them on his spread thighs. Cam watched her, his eyes flashing demon-fire as he stroked her, toying with the soft cleft, the sensitive flesh within.

She reached for him, needing his weight on her, unable

to pull him down. All she could do was whimper and arch as he filled her with his fingers, his thumb making wicked swirls, his thighs solid beneath her straining hips. Her breath hissed between her teeth, while her hands tightened around handfuls of the bed linens.

His fingers slid away from her, leaving her shuddering as her body closed in vain around the emptiness. But then he was pushing into her, filling her completely. She lifted high to take him, and gasped as he eased over her with deliberate slowness.

Her hand crept blindly from his shoulder to his face, where she felt the shape of his smile. "Don't tease," she muttered, trembling with need. "I can't bear it."

"Sweetheart . . ." His silky whisper caressed her cheek. "I'm afraid you'll have to."

"Wh-why?" She caught her breath as he withdrew, giving her only the tip of his shaft.

"Because there's nothing I love more than teasing you." And he took an eternity to push inside her again, his hands caressing her, every movement so incremental and delicious and merciless that by the time he entered her completely, she had already climaxed. Twice.

"Stay inside me," she begged hoarsely, as he began a steady rhythm, the heat building again. "Stay, stay—" The words flattened into a long moan.

Cam bent over her, driving ruthlessly hard, his breath coming in hot strikes against her face and throat. He stared into her dazed eyes, taking fierce satisfaction in the sight of her pleasure. His hands slipped beneath her skull, cradling her head as he kissed her. He buried a vehement groan into the sweet depths of her mouth, and let his release spin out inside her.

Cuddling her afterward, Cam traced lazy patterns on her back and shoulders. Amelia rested on him, enjoying the steady lift and fall of his breathing.

"After the wedding," he murmured, "I may take you away with me for a little while."

"Where?" she asked readily, turning to press her lips against his chest.

"To look for my tribe."

"You've already found your tribe." She hitched a leg over his hips. "It's called the Hathaways."

A chuckle vibrated in his chest. "My Romany tribe, then. It's been too many years. I'd like to find out if my grandmother is still alive." He paused. "And I want to ask some questions."

"About what?"

Drawing her hand to his forearm, Cam pressed it to his tattoo. "This."

Thinking of Merripen's identical tattoo, and the strange, impossible coincidence of it, Amelia frowned in curiosity. "What kind of connection might there be between you and Merripen?"

"I have no idea." Cam smiled ruefully. "God help me, I'm half afraid to find out."

"Whatever it is," she said, "we'll trust in fate."

Cam's smile widened. "So you believe in fate now?"

"And luck," Amelia said, her hand tightening on his arm. "Because of you."

"That reminds me . . ." He raised himself on one elbow and looked down at her, dark lashes sweeping over glowing amber. "I have something to show you. Don't move—I'll bring it here."

"Can't it wait?" she protested.

"No. I'll be back in a few minutes. Don't fall asleep."

He left the bed and drew on his clothes, while Amelia took possessive pleasure in the sight of him.

To keep from falling asleep while he was gone, she went to the washstand and used a cold cloth to freshen herself. Hurrying back to the bed, she sat and tucked the covers beneath her arms.

Cam returned, noiseless as a cat, carrying an object that was approximately the shape and size of a slipper box. Amelia regarded it quizzically as he set it beside her. The heavy box was made of wood and heavily tarnished and pitted silver, the whole of it giving off an acid-sweet reek. As Amelia ran her fingers experimentally over the surface, she discovered the surface was slightly tacky.

"Fortunately it was wrapped in oilcloth," Cam said. "Otherwise it would have been soaked in fermented honey."

Amelia blinked in astonishment. "Don't say this is the treasure that Christopher Frost was looking for?"

"I found it when I was getting the crushed bees for Merripen's poultice. I brought it back for you." He looked vaguely apologetic. "I meant to tell you about it earlier, but it slipped my mind."

Amelia stifled a laugh. The average man would hardly forget something like a cache box possibly containing treasure . . . but to Cam, it probably had little more significance than a box of hazelnuts. "Only you," she said, "could go looking for bee venom and find hidden treasure." Lifting the box, she shook it gently, feeling the movement of weighty objects within. "Blast, it's locked." She reached in the wild disarray of her coiffure. Finding a hairpin, she handed it to him.

"Why do you assume I can pick a lock?" he asked, a sly flicker in his eyes.

"I have complete faith in your criminal abilities," she said. "Open it, please."

Obligingly he bent the pin and inserted it into the ancient lock.

"Why didn't you tell Mr. Frost that you'd already found the treasure?" Amelia asked as he worked to find the catch. "Then you might have been spared being swarmed by all those bees."

"I wanted to save this for your family. Frost had no right to it." Before another minute had passed, the lock had clicked and the box was open.

Amelia's heart pounded with excitement as she lifted the lid. She found a sheaf of letters, perhaps a half-dozen, tied with a thin braided lock of hair. Gingerly she picked up the bundle, pulled the top letter out, and unfolded the ancient yellowed parchment.

It was indeed a love letter from a king, signed, simply, "James." Scandalous, ardent, and sweetly written, it seemed far too intimate for her to read. It had never been meant for her eyes. Feeling like an interloper, she closed the brittle folds and set it aside.

Cam, meanwhile, had begun to pull objects from the box and lay them in her lap; a loose ruby at least an inch in diameter, pairs of diamond bracelets, ropes of massive black pearls, a brooch made of an oval-shaped sapphire easily the size of a sovereign, with a teardrop diamond hanging beneath, and an assortment of jeweled rings.

"I don't believe it," Amelia said, jostling the glittering heap. "This must be enough to rebuild Ramsay House twice over."

"Not quite," Cam said, casting an experienced glance over the lot, "but close."

She frowned as she sorted through the trove of priceless jewels. "Cam . . . ?" she asked after a long moment.

"Hmmn?" He seemed to have lost interest in the treasure, absorbed in playing with a loose lock of her hair.

"Would you mind if we kept this from Leo until he's . . . well, a bit more rational? Otherwise I'm afraid he'll go out and do something irresponsible."

"I'd say that's a valid concern." He picked up the jewelry in careless handfuls, dumping it into the box and closing it. "Yes, we'll wait until he's ready."

"Do you think," Amelia asked hesitantly, "that Leo will change from the way he is now? Will he get better?"

Hearing the worry in her tone, Cam reached out and nestled her against him. "As the Rom say, 'No wagon keeps the same wheels forever.' "

The covers slipped between them. Amelia shivered as the cool air wafted over her naked back and shoulders. "Come back to bed," she whispered. "I need you to warm me."

Cam stripped away his shirt, and laughed quietly as he felt her hands plucking at the buttons of his trousers. "What happened to my prudish *gadji*?"

"I'm afraid"—she reached into his open falls and stroked his aroused flesh—"that continued association with you has made me shameless."

"Good, I was hoping for that." His lashes lowered, and his voice turned slightly breathless at her touch. "Amelia, if we have children . . . will you mind that they're part Roma?"

"Not if you don't mind that they're part Hathaway."

He made a sound of amusement and finished undressing. "And I thought life on the road would be a challenge. You know, it would terrify a lesser man, trying to manage your family."

"You're right. I can't imagine why you're willing to take us on."

He gave her naked body a frankly lascivious glance as he joined her beneath the covers. "Believe me, the compensations are well worth it."

"What about your freedom?" Amelia asked, snuggling close as he lay beside her. "Are you sorry to have lost it?"

"No, love." Cam reached to turn down the lamp, enfolding them in velvet darkness. "I've finally found it. Right here, with you."

And he lowered himself into the clasp of her waiting arms.

Read on for an excerpt from

Sugar Daddy

by Lisa Kleypas

NOW AVAILABLE FROM ST. MARTIN'S PAPERBACKS

When I was four, my father died in an oil-rig accident. Daddy didn't even work for the drilling outfit. He was a company man who wore a suit and tie when he went to inspect the production and drilling platforms. But one day he stumbled on an opening in the rig floor before setup was completed. He fell sixty feet to the platform below and died instantly, his neck broken.

It took me a long time to understand Daddy was never coming back. I waited for him for months, sitting at the front window of our house in Katy, just west of Houston. Some days I stood at the end of the driveway to watch every car that passed. No matter how often Mama told me to quit looking for him, I couldn't give up. I guess I thought the strength of my wanting would be enough to make him appear.

I have only a handful of memories of my father, more like impressions. He must have carried me on his shoulders a time or two—I remember the hard plane of his chest beneath my calves, the sensation of swaying high in the air, anchored by the strong pressure of his fingers around my ankles. And the coarse drifts of his hair in my hands, shiny black hair cut in layers. I can almost hear his voice singing "Arriba del Cielo," a Mexican lullaby that always gave me sweet dreams.

There is a framed photograph of Daddy on my dresser, the only one I have. He's wearing a Western dress shirt and jeans with creases pressed down the front, and a tooled leather belt with a silver and turquoise buckle the size of a breakfast plate. A little smile lingers in one corner of his mouth, and a dimple punctuates the smoothness of his swarthy cheek. By all accounts he was a smart man, a romantic, a hard worker with high-carat ambitions. I believe he would have accomplished great things in his life if he'd been given the gift of more years. I know so little about my father, but I'm certain he loved me. I can feel it even in those little wisps of memory.

Mama never found another man to replace Daddy. Or maybe it's more accurate to say she found a lot of men to replace him. But hardly any of them stayed around for long. She was a beautiful woman, if not a happy one, and attracting a man was never a problem. Keeping one, however, was a different matter. By the time I was thirteen, Mama had gone through more boyfriends than I could keep track of. It was sort of a relief when she found one she decided she could stick with for a while.

They agreed they would move in together, in the east Texas town of Welcome, not far from where he'd grown up. As it turned out, Welcome was where I lost everything, and gained everything. Welcome was the place where my life was guided from one track to another, sending me to places I'd never thought of going.

On my first day at the trailer park, I wandered along a

dead-end road that cut between rows of trailers lined up like piano keys. The park was a dusty grid of dead-end streets, with a newly built loop that circled around the left side. Each home sat on its own concrete pad, dressed in a skirt made of aluminum or wooden latticework. A few trailers were fronted by patches of yard, some featuring crape myrtle with blossoms crisped a pale brown and the bark shredded from the heat.

The late afternoon sun was as round and white as a paper plate tacked to the sky. Heat seemed to come equally from below as above, uncurling in visible waves from the cracked ground. Time moved at a crawl in Welcome, where people considered anything needing to be done in a hurry wasn't worth doing. Dogs and cats spent most of the day sleeping in the hot shade, rousing only to lap a few tepid drops from the water hookups. Even the flies were slow.

An envelope containing a check crackled in the pocket of my denim cutoffs. Mama had told me to take it to the manager of Bluebonnet Ranch, Mr. Louis Sadlek, who lived at the redbrick house near the entrance of the trailer park.

My feet felt like they'd been steamed inside my shoes as I shuffled along the broken edges of asphalt. I saw a pair of older boys standing with a teenage girl, their postures relaxed and loose-limbed. The girl had a long blond ponytail with a ball of hair-sprayed bangs in the front. Her deep tan was exposed by short shorts and a tiny purple bikini top, which explained why the boys were so absorbed in conversation with her.

One of the boys was dressed in shorts and a tank top, while the other, dark-haired one wore a weathered pair of Wranglers and dirt-caked Roper boots. He stood with his weight shifted to one leg, one thumb hooked in a denim pocket, his free hand gesturing as he talked. There was something striking about his slim, rawboned form, the hard edge of his profile. His vitality was almost jarring in those heat-drowsed surroundings.

Although Texans of all ages are naturally sociable and call out to strangers without hesitation, it was obvious I was going to walk by this trio unnoticed. That was just fine with me.

But as I walked quietly along the other side of the lane, I was startled by an explosion of noise and movement. Rearing back, I was set upon by what appeared to be a pair of rabid pit bulls. They barked and snarled and peeled their lips back to reveal jagged yellow teeth. I had never been scared of dogs, but these two were obviously out for the kill.

My instincts took over, and I spun to escape. The bald soles of my old sneakers slipped on a scattering of pebbles, my feet went out from under me, and I hit the ground on my hands and knees. I let out a scream and covered my head with my arms, fully expecting to be torn to pieces. But there was the sound of an angry voice over the blood rush in my ears, and instead of teeth closing over my flesh, I felt a pair of strong hands take hold of me.

I yelped as I was turned over to look up into the face of the dark-haired boy. He gave me a swift assessing glance and turned to yell some more at the pit bulls. The dogs had retreated a few yards, their barking fading to peevish snarls.

"Go on, damn it," the boy snapped at them. "Get your hindquarters back home and stop scaring people, you sorry pair of sh—" He checked himself and darted a quick glance at me.

The pit bulls quieted and slunk backward in a startling change of mood, pink tongues dangling like the half-curled ribbons of party balloons.

My rescuer viewed them with disgust and spoke to the boy in the tank top. "Pete, take the dogs back to Miss Marva's."

"They'll git home by theirselves," the boy protested, reluctant to part company with the blond girl in the bikini top.

"Take 'em back," came the authoritative reply, "and tell Marva to stop leaving the damn gate open."

While this conversation was taking place, I glanced down at my knees and saw they were oozing and peppered with gravel dust. My descent into the pit of soul-shriveling embarrassment was complete as the shock wore off and I started to cry. The harder I gulped against the tightness of my throat, the worse it became. Tears runneled from beneath my big plastic-framed glasses.

"For God's sake . . ." I heard the boy in the tank top mutter. Heaving a sigh, he went to the dogs and grabbed them by the collars. "Come on, troublemakers." They went with him willingly, trotting smartly on either side as if they were auditioning for the 4H state dog show.

The dark-haired boy's attention returned to me, and his voice gentled. "Here, now . . . you're okay. No need to cry, honey." He plucked a red handkerchief from his back pocket and began to mop at my face. Deftly he wiped my eyes and nose and told me to blow. The handkerchief held the sharp bite of male sweat as it clamped firmly over my nose. Back then men of every age had a red handkerchief tucked in the back pocket of their jeans. I'd seen kerchiefs used as a sieve, a coffee filter, a dust mask, and once as a makeshift baby diaper.

"Don't ever run from dogs like that." The boy tucked the kerchief in his back pocket. "No matter how scared you are. You just look to the side and walk away real slow, understand? And shout 'No' in a loud voice like you mean it."

I sniffled and nodded, staring into his shadowed face. His wide mouth held the curve of a smile that sent a quiver down to the pit of my stomach and knotted my toes inside my sneakers.

True handsomeness had escaped him by millimeters. His features were too blunt and bold, and his nose had a crook near the bridge from having been broken once. But he had a slow burn of a smile, and blue-on-blue eyes that seemed even brighter against the sun-glazed color of his skin, and a tumble of dark brown hair as shiny as mink fur.

"You got nothing to fear from those dogs," he said. "They're full of mischief, but as far as I know they've never bitten anyone. Here, take my hand."

As he pulled me up and set me on my feet, my knees felt like they'd been set on fire. I hardly noticed the pain, I was so occupied with the fury of my heartbeat. The grip of his hand was strong around mine, his fingers dry and warm.

"Where do you live?" the boy asked. "Are you moving into the new trailer on the loop?"

"Uh-huh." I wiped a stray tear off my chin.

"Hardy . . ." The blond girl's voice was sweetly cajoling. "She's all right now. Come walk me back. I got somethin' in my room to show you."

Hardy. So that was his name. He remained facing me, his vivid gaze shifting to the ground. It was probably just as well the girl couldn't see the wry smile secreted in the corners of his mouth. He seemed to have a pretty good idea of what she wanted to show him.

"Can't," he said cheerfully. "I have to take care of this little one."

The disgruntlement I felt at being referred to as if I were a toddler was promptly replaced by the triumph of being chosen over the blond girl. Although I couldn't figure out why in the world he wasn't leaping at the chance to go with her.

I wasn't a homely child, but neither was I the kind people made much of. From my Mexican father I had inherited dark hair, heavy eyebrows, and a mouth I thought was twice the size it needed to be. From Mama I had gotten a skinny build and light-colored eyes, but they weren't a clear sea-green like hers, they were hazel. I had often longed to have Mama's ivory skin and blond hair, but Daddy's darkness had won out.

It didn't help matters that I was shy and wore glasses. I was never one to stand out in the crowd. I liked to stay in corners. And I was happiest when I was alone reading. That and the good grades I got in school had doomed any chance of being popular with my peers. So it was a foregone conclusion that boys like Hardy were never going to take notice of me.

"Come on," he urged, leading the way to tan single-wide with concrete steps at the back. A hint of a strut livened Hardy's walk, giving him the jauntiness of a junkyard dog.

I followed cautiously, wondering how mad Mama would be if she found out I'd wandered off with a stranger. "Is this yours?" I asked, my feet sinking into the crackling beige grass as we went toward the trailer.

Hardy replied over his shoulder. "I live here with my mom, two brothers, and a sister."

"That's a lot of people for a single-wide," I commented.

"Yeah, it is. I've got to move soon—there's no room for me in there. Mom says I'm growing so fast I'm like to bust the walls of the trailer out."

The notion that this creature still had some growing to do was almost alarming. "How big are you going to get?" I asked.

He chuckled and went to a spigot attached to a dusty gray garden hose. Turning it with a few deft twists, he started the flow of water and went to find the end of the hose. "Don't know. I'm already taller than most of my kin. Sit on that bottom step and stretch your legs out."

I obeyed, looking down at my scrawny calves, the skin covered with childish dark fuzz. I had experimented a few times with shaving my legs, but it hadn't yet become an established routine. I couldn't help comparing them to the smooth tanned legs of the blond girl, and the heat of embarrassment rose inside me.

Approaching me with the hose, Hardy sank to his haunches and warned, "This'll probably sting a little, Liberty."

"That's all right, I—" I stopped, my eyes widening in amazement. "How did you know my name?"

A smile lurked in one corner of his mouth. "It's written on the back of your belt."

Name belts had been popular that year. I had begged Mama to order one for me. We'd chosen pale pink leather with my name tooled in red letters.

I inhaled sharply as Hardy rinsed my knees with a stream of tepid water, washing off the blood and grit. It hurt more than I expected, especially when he passed his thumb over a few stubborn particles of rock to loosen them from my swollen skin.

He made a soothing sound as I flinched, and talked to distract me. "How old are you? Twelve?"

"Fourteen and three quarters."

His blue eyes sparkled. "You're kind of little for fourteen and three quarters."

"Am not," I replied indignantly. "I'm a sophomore this year. How old are you?"

"Seventeen and two fifths."

I stiffened at the gentle mockery, but as I met his gaze, I saw a flicker of playfulness. I had never felt the allure of another human being this strongly, warmth and curiosity mixing to form an unspoken question in the air.

A couple of times in your life, it happens like that. You meet a stranger, and all you know is that you need to know everything about him.

"How many brothers and sisters do you have?" he asked.

"None. It's just me and Mama and her boyfriend."

"Tomorrow if I get a chance, I'll bring my sister, Hannah, to meet you. She can introduce you to some of the kids around here and point out the ones to stay clear of." Hardy took the water off my raw knees, which were now pink and clean.

"What about the one you were just talking to? Is she someone I should stay clear of?"

A flash of a smile. "That's Tamryn. Yeah, stay away from her. She doesn't like other girls much." He went to turn the water off and came back to stand over me as I sat on the doorstep, his dark brown hair spilling over his forehead. I wanted to push it back. I wanted to touch him, not with sensuality but in wonder.

"Are you going home now?" Hardy asked, reaching

down for me. Our palms locked. He pulled me to my feet and made certain I was steady before letting go.

"Not yet. I have an errand. A check for Mr. Sadlek." I felt for my back pocket to make sure it was still there.

The name caused a frown to tug between his straight dark brows. "I'll go with you."

"You don't have to," I said, although I felt a surge of shy delight at the offer.

"Yes I do. Your mama should know better than to send you to the front office by yourself."

"I don't understand."

"You will after you meet him." Hardy took my shoulders in his hands and said firmly, "If you ever need to visit Louis Sadlek for any reason, you come get me first."

The grip of his hands was electrifying. My voice sounded breathless as I said, "I wouldn't want to put you to trouble."

"No trouble." He looked down at me for a moment longer and fell back a half step.

"That's real nice of you," I said.

"Hell." He shook his head and replied with a smile, "I'm not nice. But between Miss Marva's pit bulls and Sadlek, someone's got to watch out for you."

We walked along the main drive, Hardy shortening his long stride to correspond with mine. When the pace of our feet matched perfectly, I felt a deep inner pang of satisfaction. I could have gone on walking like that forever, side by side with him. There had been few times in my life I had ever inhabited a moment so fully, with no loneliness lurking at the edges.

When I spoke, my voice sounded languid to my own

ears, as if we were lying in lush grass beneath a shade tree. "Why do you say you're not nice?"

A low, rueful-sounding chuckle. "Because I'm an unrepentant sinner."

"So am I." It wasn't true, of course, but if this boy was an unrepentant sinner, I wanted to be one too.

"No you're not," he said with lazy certainty.

"How can you say that when you don't know me?"

"I can tell by looking."

I darted a covert glance at him. I was tempted to ask what else he read from my appearance, but I was afraid I already knew. The unkempt tangle of my ponytail, the modest length of my cutoffs, the big glasses and unplucked brows . . . it didn't exactly add up to the picture of a boy's wildest fantasies. I decided to change the conversation. "Is Mr. Sadlek mean?" I asked. "Is that why I shouldn't visit him alone?"

"He inherited the trailer park from his parents about five years ago, and ever since then he's harassed every woman who crosses his path. He tried it with my mother a time or two until I told him if he did it again I'd make sure he was nothing but a smear on the ground from here to Sugar Land."

I didn't doubt the claim for a minute. Despite Hardy's youth, he was big enough to inflict quite a lot of damage on someone.

We reached the redbrick ranch house, which clung to the flat arid land like a deer tick. A large black-and-white sign proclaiming BLUEBONNET RANCH MOBILE HOME ESTATES had been planted on the side of the house closest to the main drive, with clusters of faded plastic bluebonnets tacked to the corners. Just beyond the sign a parade of pink yard flamingos riddled with bullet holes had been arranged precisely along the roadside.

I was to find out later it was the habit of some residents from the trailer park, including Mr. Sadlek, to visit a neighbor's field for target practice. They shot at a row of yard flamingos that bobbed and sprang back whenever they were shot. When a flamingo was too full of holes to be useful, it was strategically placed at the front entrance of the trailer park as an advertisement of the residents' shooting skills.

An OPEN sign hung in the little side window by the front door. Reassured by Hardy's solid presence beside me, I went to the front door, knocked tentatively and pushed it open.

A Latina cleaning lady was busy mopping the entranceway. In the corner, a cassette player spat out the cheerful polka rhythm of tejano music. Glancing upward, the girl spoke in rapid-fire Spanish. *"Cuidado, el piso es mojado."*

I only knew a few words of Spanish. Having no idea what she had meant, I shook my head apologetically. But Hardy replied without missing a beat, *"Gracias, tendremos cuidados."* He put a hand on the center of my back. "Careful. The floor's wet."

"You speak Spanish?" I asked him in mild surprise.

His dark brows lifted. "You don't?"

I shook my head, abashed. It had always been a source of vague embarrassment that despite my heritage I couldn't speak my father's language.

A tall, heavy figure appeared in the doorway of the front office. At first glance Louis Sadlek was a good-looking man. But it was a ruined handsomeness, his face and body showing the decay of habitual self-indulgence. His striped Western shirt had been left untucked in an effort to hide the billow of his waist. Although the fabric of his pants looked like cheap polyester, his boots were made of blue-dyed snakeskin. His even, regular features were marred by the florid bloat around his neck and cheeks.

Sadlek stared at me with casual interest, his lips pulling back in a dirty joke of a smile. He spoke to Hardy first. "Who's the little wetback?"

Out of the corner of my eye, I saw the cleaning lady stiffen and pause in her scrubbing. It seemed she had been exposed to the word often enough to know its meaning.

Seeing the instant tension in Hardy's jaw, and the clenching of the fist at his side, I broke in hastily. "Mr. Sadlek, I'm—"

"Don't call her that," Hardy said in a tone that made the hairs rise on the back of my neck.

They stared at each other with palpable animosity, their gazes level. A man well past his prime, and a boy who hadn't yet entered it. But there was no doubt in my mind how it would have ended if there had been a fight.

"I'm Liberty Jones," I said, trying to smooth the moment over. "My mother and I are moving into the new trailer." I dug the envelope from my back pocket and extended it to him. "She told me to give you this."

Sadlek took the envelope and tucked it into his shirt pocket, letting his gaze slide over me from head to toe. "Diana Jones is *your* mama?"

"Yes, sir."

"How'd a woman like that get a little dark-skinned girl like you? Your daddy musta been a Mexican."

"Yes, sir."

He gave a scornful snicker and shook his head. Another grin eased across his mouth. "You tell your mama to drop off the rent check herself next time. Tell her I got stuff I want to talk about."

"All right." Eager to be out of his presence, I tugged at Hardy's rigid arm. After a last warning glance at Louis Sadlek, Hardy followed me to the door.

"You'd best not run with white trash like the Cateses, little girl," Sadlek called out after us. "They're trouble. And Hardy's the worst of the lot."

After a scant minute in his presence, I felt as if I'd been wading through chest-high garbage. I turned to glance at Hardy in amazement.

"What a jerk," I said.

"You could say that."

"Does he have a wife and kids?"

Hardy shook his head. "Far as I know, he's been divorced twice. Some women in town seem to think he's a catch. You wouldn't know it to look at him, but he's got some money."

"From the trailer park?"

"That and a side business or two."

"What kind of side business?"

He let out a humorless laugh. "You don't want to know."

We walked to the loop intersection in contemplative silence. Now that evening was settling there were signs of life at the trailer park . . . cars turning in, voices and televisions filtering through the thin walls, smells of frying food. The white sun was resting on the horizon, bleeding out color until the sky was drenched in purple and orange and crimson.

"Is this it?" Hardy asked, stopping in front of my white trailer with its neat girdle of aluminum siding.

I nodded even before I saw the outline of my mother's profile in the window of the kitchenette. "Yes, it is," I exclaimed with relief. "Thank you."

As I stood there peering up at him through my brown-framed glasses, Hardy reached out to push back a piece of hair that had straggled loose from my ponytail. The callused tip of his finger was gently abrasive against my hairline, like the tickle of a cat's tongue. "You know what you remind me of?" he asked, studying me. "An elf owl."

"There's no such thing," I said.

"Yes there is. They mostly live to the south in the Rio Grande Valley and beyond. But every now and then an elf owl makes its way up here. I've seen one." He used his thumb and forefinger to indicate a distance of five inches. "They're only about this big. Cute little bird."

"I'm not little," I protested.

Hardy smiled. His shadow settled over me, blocking the light of sunset from my dazzled eyes. There was an unfamiliar stirring inside me. I wanted to step deeper into the shadow until I met his body, to feel his arms go around me. "Sadlek was right, you know," he said.

"About what?"

"I am trouble."

I knew that. My rioting heart knew it, and so did my weak knees, and so did my heat-prickling stomach. "I like trouble," I managed to say, and his laugh curled through the air.

He walked away in a graceful long-legged stride, a dark and solitary figure. I thought of the strength in his hands as he had picked me up from the ground. I watched him until he had disappeared from sight, and my throat felt thick and tingly like I'd just swallowed a spoonful of warm honey.

The sunset finished with a long crack of light rimming the horizon, as if the sky were a big door and God was taking one last peek. Good night, Welcome, I thought, and went into the trailer.